MAKER
MESSIAH

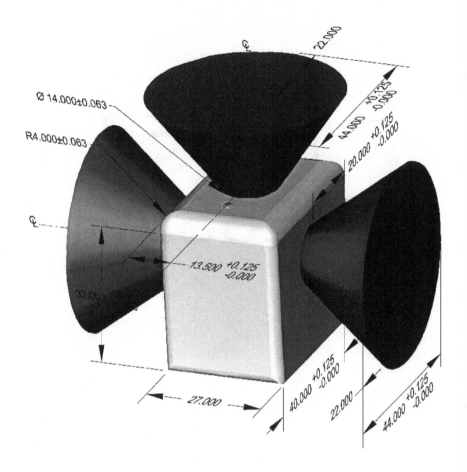

Ø 14.000±0.063

R4.000±0.063

22.000

44.000 +0.125 -0.000

20.000 +0.125 -0.000

13.500 +0.125 -0.000

32.000

27.000

40.000 +0.125 -0.000

22.000

44.000 +0.125 -0.000

MAKER MESSIAH

ED MIRACLE

A Russian Hill Press Book
United States • United Kingdom • Australia

R
H
P Russian Hill Press

The publisher is not responsible for websites or their content that are not owned by the publisher.

ISBN: 9780999516270
LCCN: 2019939949

Cover design by Eric Wilder

First Edition

For Brian and Steven

ACKNOWLEDGMENTS

The author would like to thank the following people for their help and support during the creation of *Maker Messiah*, especially those who invested hours of their lives without compensation.

Long-suffering Wife: Jean Miracle

Invaluable Critique Partners: Jordan Bernal, Marlene Dotterer, and Lani Longshore.

Patient Editors: Charlotte Cooke, Tom Flood, C.S. Lakin, Julie Tibbott, Elisabeth Tuck, and Donna Wierzbowski.

Eagle-eyed Copy Editor: Violet Carr Moore.

Hardworking Publisher: Paula Chinick.

Artful Cover Designer: Eric Wilder.

Talented Art Resources: Katie Caulk and Linda Stewart.

Generous Beta Readers: John Bluck, Jeff Carlson, Bruce Conrad, Willy Joslin, Sally Kimball, Don H. McNichols, Camille Minichino, Steve Petersen, Michael Picco, Elaine Schmitz, and Sharon Svitak.

Resource Contributors: Linda Lee Chernoff, Chinere Duru, Margie Lawson, Janie Panagopoulos, Ann Parker, and Viviane Parker.

PROLOGUE

PHILIP MACHEN SAT ON A ROCKY LEDGE of the great Nevada nowhere and turned up the collar of his peacoat. Since midnight, a bully wind had dashed fat clouds against the mountain, smacking the lightning out of a few but releasing no rain. Beyond the glow of his computer screen, the tempest howled, impatient and buffeting. A dazzle flashed and was swallowed by darkness, as time had swallowed his moments.

Just because your math is solid doesn't mean you can do this.

Philip nodded at the memory of his father reading his son's precious equations and not seeing what they really meant. Leonard Machen, part-time philosopher, full-time math teacher, should have helped him back then, but he died a week later. *Dad should be here too.*

Across the sandstone ledge raced a four-legged skitter.

"I have a secret," Philip called after it.

The skitter stopped, terrified by his voice or puffed with reptilian contempt. *My rock.*

"Okay," Philip said. "But we're in this together, Old Shoe, live or die."

The lizard responded with push-ups. *My rock.*

Philip tossed a pebble at it. "Take cover, pal."

Because it was time to poke the universe, to push the big red button and shatter his stuckness. The blast he was about to unleash might vaporize half of Nevada. Or collapse to a singularity that would burrow through Lander County and devour the earth from beneath his feet. What a vision that would be.

His equations predicted three mutually exclusive possibilities: one would kill everything for five miles around; one would swallow the Earth before plunging its remains into the Sun; and one would change the world forever. So his hopes for the evening—perhaps his last—lay in the third prospect. If that outcome prevailed, his moments would continue, and the lizard could keep its rock.

Should the attempt fail, however, if the blast produced noise and debris but no quantum effects, his future would die with the echo. Then he would erase his equations, expunge them from every medium, and dispose of himself. Without a way forward, there could be no advent, no Philip Machen worth keeping, and stuckness would prevail.

The sky flashed again, bright and close. He poised a finger over the icon on his screen. Tonight he would succeed for all time or fail forever. Thunder cracked and rolled away. His flinch sent the signal: Begin, begin.

Half a mile north, at the bottom of a deserted pit mine, a circuit closed and two cylinders the size of rail cars detonated. Shock waves imploded the carbon sphere stationed between them as flash channels pumped gamma rays into its collapsing heart. For a fraction of a second, pressures and temperatures exceeded those of the solar core. The genius part came next.

Seeded by a gumball of depleted uranium and charged by intense radiation, nuclear reactions multiplied the forces generating quantum fluctuations at their center and forming not one but two entities never observed in nature. Microscopic and invisible, separate yet coupled, these quantum effects should have flashed to pure energy in mutual annihilation or collapsed to a singularity that would destroy the Earth. Yet they could not. Conforming to fractal twists of space-time inherent to their ten-dimensional geometries, they embraced ferociously but could not merge. They whirled mightily, but could not escape. Hyper-geometrically each entity fell continuously through the other, while their frantic tango consumed just enough mass to make up for dimensional boundary losses, as Philip predicted. In twelve milliseconds, the imprisoned pair became the first quantum duplex.

The flash from its birth turned the desert wedding-cake white, brilliant even through closed eyes. His rocky ledge heaved Philip off balance, while stones and dust rained from above.

Holy shit. Not his favorite expression, but . . . *Damn.*

When he could see again, the ruckus had stolen his laptop, abducted it down some crevice, though there was no time for a search. If the duplex had formed as he hoped, they needed to stabilize it right away. He had plans for that, but the darned thing might wink out of existence before they reached it. Or explode. Quantum freaking dynamics.

He brushed his coat, buffed his scalp, and hurried to the tow truck. Tanner and Uncle Orin would drive their rig down from the west rim, while he would enter from the south. If either access was blocked, they hoped the other would remain passable, and that the duplex would not be too heavy or too radioactive.

An icy dawn was blotting shadows from the mine when they unearthed the product of their labors. Centered on the steel crash plate intended to support it, lay a crystalline lump of diamond the size of a tennis ball, a perfect jewel-cradle for the newborn duplex. Its radiations were low-level betas, no gammas or neutrons, so Philip laid a cable mesh beside it on the plate. Then his uncle and his best friend helped him lever the glassy black sphere onto the mesh. As they hoisted it clear, a strain gauge rendered a verdict: 717

pounds.

Philip stopped the winch and sank to his knees. Swaying at the end of a taut chain, the black diamond's unnatural mass affirmed every lonely moment he had endured to create it. From the exhausted grip of what must be, he had prised the first breath of what could be. Tonight was not an irrecoverable end. It was the beginning for which he yearned. His equations worked. Their possibilities had beaten their probabilities, and his duplex was no longer a mathematical curiosity. It was here. It was real. It was his.

One touch of its obsidian face and the anguish of his twenty-seven years sloughed away. He inspected the veins of his hands as he had the night his family was murdered. Flesh and bones are made of stardust, his father used to say, from thirteen-point-seven-billion-year-old protons and electrons, bequeathed to us through our parents' love.

No matter what lay ahead for him now—destruction or glory—he had confirmed his vows and bound himself to their consequences. There could be no turning back. He straightened and stood. If success were the best revenge, his would be perfect. Lizards, especially, would be amazed.

ONE

Seven years later, Tracy, California. Saturday, April 18
Maker Advent, Day One

ON THE NIGHT of Philip Machen's worldwide announcement, twenty-two-year-old Everett Aboud threaded his motorcycle between the ranks of taillights descending herd-like into California's Central Valley. The herd bunched and surged as Everett passed among them, numb to the cold, yet hyper-alert. One distracted driver might cancel his choreography, but splitting lanes on his way home from work was the best he'd felt all day. He was making thirty-miles-an-hour, versus twenty for the herd, eastbound over the sagging shoulders of Altamont Pass. Eight more miles in fourteen minutes brought him to a swath of tract houses, tile-roofed kudzu spreading outward from the old valley town of Tracy. Then finally home to a peeling white clapboard he and his father rented in a neighborhood of tall trees, wooden porches, and detached garages.

He parked beside the sentinel of their barren flowerbeds, a stone-quiet Powerpod. Waist-high and loaf-shaped, the white, ceramic monolith could have formed the base for a monument or a statue. Except for three saucer-sized disks bolted to its front, its back, and its top. Moisture dripped from the eaves overhead, emphasizing its silence.

Everett stretched and flexed, removed his helmet, and shook out his ebony hair. Johnny Mathis on a motorcycle, the boss' wife had called him this morning. A singer, not a biker, he learned, so he took it as a compliment. He might resemble someone who had actually made a difference.

He stomped through the back door into a stale potpourri of cigarette butts, gun oil, and powder solvent. Used cleaning patches littered the kitchen counter between two antique revolvers his father, Bobby, never fired but had lately been trying to sell. In the living room, Bobby was collecting dead Budweisers from the sofa. He wasn't drunk, but the smell was on him. The first time too many Budweisers had punched Everett in the mouth, ten years ago, was the start of him calling his father Bobby instead of Dad.

"There's a guy coming from Stockton tomorrow about those Colts," Bobby said. "And I made a hundred dollars lumping furniture for Dario."

"That'll help." Everett peeled off his riding leathers and hung them in the laundry. "General paid me in cash."

His father, clad in habitual denim, came into the light. "I should go over there and thank him personally."

This was Everett's first week at General Johnson's Shoes-for-You in Oakland, a forty-eight-mile commute from Tracy. The job was temporary, but with the rent due Tuesday, he and Bobby needed the money.

"Remember that hulking box of parts we got?" Bobby opened the refrigerator and removed two bottles. "The junk that Powerpods Company has been sending to people who didn't order it? They're making an announcement tonight on the internet. Supposed to be a big deal."

Why would anyone care? "Spaghetti all right with you, Pop?"

"Sure." Bobby decapped a beer and sipped. "You want to

watch the announcement?"

"I need to check my email." One of his long-shot resumes might snag another interview.

Bobby shrugged, held out the second bottle.

"No thanks," Everett said. "I'm flying tomorrow."

"Did you get a charter?"

"Just an hour with a student." For which he might clear thirty bucks. He moved past Bobby to the drawer where they kept their cash. He fished his wages from a pocket and stuffed all but a single twenty into the rent envelope. "We're two hundred short."

Bobby nodded, cleared his mess from the counter. His thick gray mane shifted against his collar as he dumped an ashtray. Smoker's wrinkles like Bobby's would never crease Everett's face, and he hoped to stay as trim and muscular when he reached fifty. But it was clear his father's fate could easily become his own, lurching from one shaky, no-benefits job to the next, reduced to odd jobs and day labor. It wasn't supposed to be this way.

Flying was supposed to be a career, not a supplement. Three years ago, Bobby sold his heating and air conditioning business in Oakland and moved inland for the lower rents, just to finance Everett's dream. But the investment wasn't paying off. More than a year had passed since Everett graduated from an expensive flying school in Florida where he flew every day and loved every minute. Except for seaplanes and jumbos, he could pilot anything with wings. Yet flying jobs were as scarce as others, so he took students and occasional charters from the service at Stockton. Between engagements, he launched resumes at every airline and charter outfit in North America and rode long distances to interviews that came to nothing. Probably because his name—*Aboud*—remained suspect, automatically an Arab, potentially a terrorist, even though he was third-generation Lebanese-American, not a Muslim. At least tomorrow the automatic Arab could fly.

Bobby set the table then switched on the wall screen. "Here we go."

Up on the screen, a sturdy blond teenager strolled through a rose garden wearing a sleeveless yellow blouse and a cheerleader's grin. She approached a familiar white boulder the size and shape of a steamer trunk: a Powerpod. Six years of upbeat marketing and they still looked like tombstones.

"We have exciting news for all Powerpod owners," she said.

Everett filled a saucepan with water and set it on the stove.

"A new paradigm that will change your life." Nothing to buy. Blah, blah, blah. "You must see Philip Machen, Saturday, April 18, at 9:00 p.m. for the most amazing demonstration of your life. Got power? Get Powerpods."

A countdown clock appeared at the corner of the screen, while *Mock-en* rattled through Everett's head. Philip Machen, the millionaire inventor of Powerpods, never gave interviews, never spoke publicly. When President Washburn hung that medal around his neck last year, the guy said, "Thank you," then returned to his cave, or wherever he lived, a place the paparazzi with all their cameras could not find.

The screen displayed PhilipMachen.com and played elevator music, which Bobby muted. "Ten minutes to go," he said.

Everett boiled water and fed noodles into the pot. *How could a stupid commercial change anything?* Into another pan, he stirred red sauce with a wooden spoon and tasted it—tomato, basil, oregano.

"So what do you think, Son?"

"Who cares?" More than fatigue weighted his voice.

"You know," Bobby said, "we can make it on day-labor and help from friends like General Johnson, but not if we had to pay for electricity. Having that Pod is saving our butts."

"You were afraid of them."

"Yeah, there's something weird about sucking electricity out of bits of tap water," Bobby said, "but nobody's getting zapped or polluted. If the rest of the world worked as good as Powerpods, we wouldn't be stuck in this damn recession, that's for sure."

Everett dumped boiling noodles into a colander and hoped

Bobby wasn't warming to a Dad-lecture. Bobby lived in a world of manifest duties and summary order, from which he imparted his judgments, no extra charge. Everett ladled sauce over a plate of noodles.

"Here you go, Bobby."

As usual, they ate in silence, until the screen came back to life and Bobby un-muted it. Everett expected another episode of the Powerpods commercial, featuring a guy cutting a Pod in half with a giant chop saw to prove it contained nothing hazardous. This time a smooth-faced white guy with skinny arms and wispy blond hair gazed at them, eager to begin. His flowing white shirt stood open at the collar, sleeves rolled—a pale academic trying to look manly. Except for his eyes, which seemed to draw the light out of the sky and reflect it back, brighter. Ghosts would have eyes that gray.

"Hello. My name is Philip Machen. What I am about to show you is going to change your life, and mine, forever."

"See," Bobby said. Everett stabbed the last of his noodles.

"In this introduction, I will show you a Maker and demonstrate it. In the next segment, I will show you how to convert your Powerpod into a Maker, to begin making things you need or enjoy."

Everett carried his plate to the sink.

"In later segments . . ." The ghost cleared his throat. "I will describe some of the changes we can expect Makers to bring, and why you should use your Maker to secure your family in a new and universal prosperity. My webpage and the free Cambiar internet phones I sent to every Powerpod owner contain complete documentation, including a Maker guidebook."

Infomercials sucked, but a movement caught Everett's attention.

A darker man with hairy arms rolled a Powerpod, still on its delivery cart, to Machen's side. The modifications were bizarre. From the Pod's two broadest sides and from its top, fluted metal cones protruded at right angles. About a meter in depth and diameter, each jet-black cone tapered to a saucer-sized flange, bolted to the Pod. Hinged metal doors covered the wide ends of the cones. Stadium speakers, it seemed, sprouting from a fat, white tombstone.

"This is our prototype, the world's first Maker. It makes perfect duplicates of anything that fits into its chambers." Machen smiled like a kid with a frog in his pocket.

Bobby blew across the top of his bottle, producing a soft hoot. "Big deal. It's a 3-D printer."

Everett waved for silence. This wasn't the usual Powerpods spiel. On-screen, the hairy arms passed a garden hose to Machen, who lifted a top-cone cover and directed a stream of water into it.

"Any material which fits in the upper chamber can be used, but water may be the handiest. Consider this water to be the raw material from which you will make your copies. Your raw material does not have to be water or even a liquid. It could be any sort of scrap, from lawn trimmings to sewage, to common dirt. The imperative restriction is that the mass of the raw material in the upper chamber must always be greater than the mass of any item you wish to copy."

"Mass?" Bobby peered down the neck of his bottle.

Everett snatched the remote and increased the volume.

The upper cone overflowed, splashing Machen, who ducked too late and threw the hose aside. He opened a side-cone door. The camera zoomed to reveal a wire shelf spanning the interior. Machen unclasped his wristwatch, held it to show a twitching second hand, and laid the watch on the shelf.

"Place your original item in one of the copy chambers. It doesn't matter which side, except the opposite chamber must always be empty." He shut the door and reached between the cones to the Powerpod.

"Then you press the green button."

Hairy Arms retrieved a second watch from the opposite chamber, while Machen removed his original. They held them to show identical straps and faces with perfectly synchronized minute, hour, and second hands.

Everett stared. *How could this not be a trick?*

"You may copy anything that fits in the chambers," Machen said, "so long as there is sufficient raw material in your upper cone."

Hairy Arms brought out an old-fashioned, boom-box stereo. One arm steadied the box on a table while the other pressed a running circular saw against it. With a whine and a screech, it lopped off a jagged corner, leaving the case splintered. Hairy placed this wounded artifact into one of the cones and shut the doors.

Again, Machen pressed his button. The emergent stereos were identical in every visible respect including their ripped edges.

"Wonder how they do that," Bobby said.

Everett shushed him. If anyone could do the impossible, it would be the guy who had already conjured electricity from artificial boulders.

Next, Machen and his assistant copied the circular saw, followed by a baguette of French bread, a plate of fish, and a wicker tray of fruits and vegetables. Holding up a tiny white speck, Machen waited for the camera to focus on it.

"From a single grain of wheat or rice, anyone with a Maker can feed a city. Copy one grain and you have two. Copy two grains and you have four. Within an hour, you could fill a truck."

Machen produced a toad in a red-wire cage and placed the cage in one of the cones. A close-up showed the amphibian panting and blinking.

"Never," he said, "never try to copy a living animal. This means *any* animal. Your Maker will kill it." He pressed the button. Two cages emerged, each containing a collapsed, motionless toad.

"At the molecular level these toads are identical, but they are both dead. Nothing with a nervous system can survive duplication. If your children try to copy a pet, the pet will die. This is very important. Children must never play with your Maker. In particular, they must never play hiding games in the cones. Maker cones should be locked shut when not in use. Please be careful with living things."

Everett's stomach churned.

"Duplicate toads," Bobby said through a belch. He held his bottle at arm's length, swirled it by the neck. "Didn't think I drank that much."

Machen strolled to a bigger Maker. This one's side-cones exceeded his height, and the towering top-cone, supported by steel struts, cast a shadow. Nestled between the cones, a central Powerpod was jacked waist high.

"As you can see, larger items may be copied by extending the size of the chambers. Among the first things you will want to copy is a friend's Powerpod, along with the cone segments he will need to turn it into a Maker. Copy as many Pods and cones as you wish, and share them with your friends. Ask them to do the same. In this way, you will help ensure that everyone who wants a Powerpod or a Maker will have one. It will cost you nothing but the effort to do it." He backed from the machine and faced the camera.

"Then together, you and I will eliminate poverty and scarcity for all time."

Everett froze. His limbic brain, beneath the conscious one, locked every motor impulse against a tectonic shift that it alone detected. Hairy Arms rolled a second Powerpod into view, and Everett held his breath. The narration faded. Hairy jacked his Powerpod chest-high and set a bridge into one of the big side cones. He aligned the rails and shoved a twelve-hundred-pound Powerpod into the chamber. Only when Machen leaned between the struts to press his green button did Everett breathe again. Thump, a boulder falling on moss. Then Machen and his assistant extracted two identical Powerpods.

Everett stood. "If that thing is real . . . ."

Machen continued, his ghost-eyes blazing.

"Just as a lens splits and rejoins patterns of light, Makers split and rejoin patterns of mass and energy. $E=mc2$. The mass-equivalent energy of the item being copied is drawn into folded dimensions within the machine where an equal mass-equivalent energy is drawn from the raw material in the top cone. The Maker splits these energies between the two-receptor chambers to form perfect duplicates—all in the wink of an eye.

"While a full description of this process requires some advanced mathematics, I assure you there is nothing mystical or supernatural about it. It only looks like magic."

His half-smile blossomed into a grin.

"Makers are not about making more stuff. They are about getting stuff out of our way. As Maker owners convert their goods into free commodities, they will free us to focus our compassion and humanity on improving the world. For the first time, Makers will allow us to—"

Everett wielded the remote to skip the baloney. "Where's the part about setting it up?"

"You going to build one?" Bobby set down his bottle.

Everett found a menu and clicked *Assemble Your Maker*. A training video commenced, and they viewed the first part, learned how to attach the cones. When the voice went on about extending the cones to build a larger Maker, Everett switched it off.

"Do we have—"

"Still in the crate, behind the garage." Bobby spoke with his fist against his mouth. "I was going to throw them away."

Everett strode toward the door, and Bobby rushed to catch up.

"Do you suppose this thing is for real?" Bobby said. "I mean, if we can copy the copy machine, how will that guy make any money?"

Everett stopped to glare at him.

"Bobby, nobody's going to make toads or wristwatches."

"Holy cow." Realization flowed into Bobby's rheumy eyes. "Everybody's got one, everybody's going to get one, and everybody's going to make . . . money."

They unpacked the parts and lugged them to their Powerpod. Working in the glow of a fluorescent drop light, they assembled and attached the small cones, then filled the top one with water. First, they tried Bobby's wallet.

When Everett pressed the green button, the machine thumped softly, and the house lights blinked. As the drop light flickered back to life, he extracted two identical wallets containing duplicate cards, identical driving licenses, and two wads of currency. They sat on the damp grass, comparing Federal Reserve Notes: three sets of fives, a pair of tens, and a pair of twenties.

After a moment Bobby couldn't decide. "Which are the real ones?"

Without a word, Everett got up and slipped into the house. He returned with Bobby's favorite pistol—a semi-automatic, still in its holster—and stuffed it in the machine.

"Stand back, Dad. It might cook off the ammo."

Bobby scrambled as Everett pressed the button. A louder thump. Again the lights blinked. Identical holsters and pistols emerged, right down to the worn bluing, the scratches, the serial numbers. Even the smell. Disbelieving, Everett hefted one in each hand.

"Son . . . of . . . a . . . bitch."

Then Everett Aboud, the automatic Arab, pointed his father's pistols at the lawn and pulled both triggers. The double blast woke every dog in the neighborhood.

TWO

"GIMME THOSE." Bobby grabbed the guns, leaving Everett to stare at his empty hands. "What did you do that for? Get inside. Quick." Bobby yanked the drop light and ran. Everett followed. Inside, they rushed from room to room, turning off the lights. When the dogs quieted down, and nobody came knocking, Bobby said, "Well, that was stupid."

Everett went to his room. Bobby always said playing with guns will get you seriously killed, and Everett agreed, but he wasn't playing out there in the yard. He pulled those triggers on purpose. Something didn't make sense. Something was wrong. Yet those ear-splitting reports, those blinding flashes, the sting that lingered in his hands, they were real. Those pistols weren't just lumps of steel, inert and heavy, devoid of consequence. They fired, serious as could be.

Everett lay on his bed and pressed his toes to the wall, tried to stop the buzz in his hands from migrating to his head, knowing it was too late. Already, an old lyric presented itself. "Things as they are, Are changed upon a blue guitar." Instant copies meant instant stuff. Just stuff. More of the junk we already have. Some freaky machine generates confusion and stuff. *Now that's stupid.* But it didn't quell the buzz tattooing his skull from the inside.

He drew a pillow over his head. Too much thinking made his head hurt. He breathed a hundred slow breaths until he sagged into an old familiar dream.

Once again, irresistible gravity pinned him to a dusty rug of the old house in Oakland. Once again, he was ten years old, flexing skinny fingers, unable to release the weight they held. No amount of wiggling would rid his hand of that ugly Colt .45 pistol. Involuntarily, he strained for its trigger. For the hundredth time he watched the hammer snap, a fireball erupt, and the top of the Colt flick back like a steel cobra. *Boom.* Once again, his mother rushed into the room, her muffled cries and frantic waves stirring the cordite stink. Once again, a softball-size gap appeared in his sister's bassinet, and the wall was spattered red.

"What did you do?" his mother screeched. "What did you do?"

Her wails sucked the air from the room and out of his lungs. His chest refused to rise. Flattened, he waited for the buzz to stifle his bounding pulse. High above, his mother leaned over the crib and wailed. "What did you do?"

Everett blinked awake, choked on a burlap tongue. It didn't happen that way. His guilt was real, but the nightmare was false. The bullet passed into the ceiling that day, never touching his baby sister. Yet the next morning, his mother stood on the porch of their old house and told him, "Choose me or choose your father." He didn't understand. He was ten years old and he didn't want to choose. When he said nothing, she took Melinda and departed for Canada. Remembering that day, fresh as a slap, made him gasp all over again. It was the same buzz.

Something beyond his control or understanding demanded a response. Only this time he was supposed to know what to do. But he didn't, so he drew the covers over his head and waited for the buzz to fade. *Why does the world have to change before I find my place in it?*

SUNDAY MORNING, Everett rose before Bobby and retrieved his Cambiar internet phone from the laundry. It came free in the mail a month ago, no fees or charges, from the same people who shipped those Maker cones.

He turned it on and scrolled through his email. Nothing from Montana Skies, where he interviewed three weeks ago. They might still respond. Midway Aero in Chicago liked his resume but had no openings. Don't call us, we'll call you. Buster's Dusters said they wouldn't consider him without experience-in-type, meaning 500 hours in a Turbo AgCat. So much for crop dusting out of Fresno. And the last note, sent by his student pilot, canceled their session this morning without asking to reschedule. *Damn.*

Bobby shuffled through the kitchen in his underwear.

"Too bad you're flying," he said. "Winter finals start today."

"Well, my eight o'clock just canceled, so how much is it worth to you?"

Bobby smirked. "You're not that good, kid."

"Oh yeah? I haven't shot trap since we left Oakland, but I can still knock clay pigeons better than anyone at your club."

"Yeah? Prove it."

Everett rubbed two fingers with a thumb.

Bobby feigned disgust. "Top score buys doughnuts," he said.

"No wonder you guys can't shoot. That's reverse incentive. You gotta reward the talent, Old Man. You gotta pay."

Bobby raised his hands, defeated. "Okay, I'll spring for doughnuts, but only if you break ninety-five."

"You really need the points, don't you. Did any of you guys shoot a ninety-five all season?"

"Like I said, we could use some help."

"I'm expecting a call from an Italian actress. We might go to her place."

Bobby laughed, indulged the fantasy. "Hey, if I can shoot with a hangover, you can shoot with lover's nuts."

Laughing felt so good, Everett made a counter-offer.

"You help me with my engine this afternoon, and I'll carry your cross-eyed team."

He was rebuilding a Honda four-cylinder to replace the one on his bike, partly to save money and partly for the experience. Motorcycle engines mimicked their aviation cousins, so if he found work with some fixed-base operator in Outer Podunk, knowing the tools and the skills would come in handy. Also, an ironclad rule of the Aboud household was no booze while handling weapons or tools, so here was a chance to wean Bobby off the alcohol for a while.

By the time they arrived at the gun club, the strangeness of the previous night had gone. No one under the overcast sky spoke about Makers, or copying money, or duplicating pistols. Bobby's team was happy to see him, as if nothing had happened. As if everyone had missed Philip Machen's announcement and had not yet done the impossible.

Bobby sold ten boxes of twelve-gauge reloads. Everett shot a ninety-six, earning his doughnut, and everyone grinned and slapped his back. Their team, The Hardly Ables, won the match.

As lunchtime came, Everett and Bobby returned to their backyard, still wary from the night before. Now they were the neighborhood weirdos, the troglodytes with machinery despoiling the lawn. They copied food and ate it, and Bobby fetched a six-pack. Bottles copied from the fridge emerged cold from the Maker, so he tasted one.

"Not bad for homemade," he said, smacking his lips.

Everett munched a cloned Oreo. "You can have your cookies and eat them too." He grinned like a fourth-grader, showing off his black-and-white teeth. Afterward, Bobby copied his antique pistols, twice.

"We can start a business," he said, "and never run out of

stock."

Everett's rebuilt engine was too big to fit into the small cones, so they spent two hours assembling extensions and erecting a full-sized Maker. By the time they wrestled identical motors out of the cast-aluminum caverns, the afternoon was fading, and Everett decided to postpone his engine swap. Tomorrow he might copy the whole bike. This idea pleased him so much he took one of Bobby's beers and slouched in a lawn chair beside him. They'd done enough for a Sunday afternoon.

Bobby opened his eyes. "What about the rent?"

Everett was sipping Budweiser, thinking about flying for Montana Skies.

"Well, I guess we should put our cash in the bank and write a check. Otherwise, the agency will figure we copied the money. If everybody does a few dollars, just to prove it works, nobody will be able to say for sure what's real or what's been duplicated. They can't match serial numbers against every other serial number, every time. It's going to be a mess."

Bobby got up. "If we combine our budget envelopes, we can deposit the rent today." He strode for the house. "You drive."

When he returned, Everett was warming his motorcycle.

The line at the teller machine was seven-deep, all men, each one guarding a stuffed envelope. Something was happening after all, and here it was. They were drawing stares from passing motorists.

"Machine on Eleventh Street stopped taking deposits," one guy said. "Sure hope we get a turn before this one fills up."

THREE

Livermore, California. April 19
Still Sunday

PHILIP MACHEN COMPLETED his walk-around inspection, tipped open the canopy of his red, two-seater sailplane, and stepped into its rear seat. He fastened his seatbelt and turned the key for the master switch. His instrument screen hummed and displayed a preflight checklist.

Tiedowns, *Off.* Voltage, *Green.* Control locks, *Off.*

Leaving good places and good people always crushed him. He glanced at the two gray pavilions of the ranch house they had rented. In the hangar behind them, he and Tanner had turned their quantum duplex into the first Powerpod, and then into the first Maker. For seven years they had lived here and worked here, even hired Karen Lavery here. His throat tightened at the thought of her, and he brushed an imaginary cobweb from his brow.

The night they announced Makers, he and Tanner had celebrated with poolside drinks and a tin of Hawaiian Poke. Raw, marinated tuna. They should have held a proper party, but a torrent of logistics swept away the brightest triumph of his thirty-four years. He had yet to absorb the reality of what they'd accomplished or to savor his feelings about it. There was simply no time.

The authorities would surely come for them, as they would come for Karen. Six years ago, when they first met, her mossy-green eyes had probed him like a jeweler searching for flaws. She was everything a marketing executive should be: smart, adept, and tenacious. Now 44, she'd sold 55 million Powerpods, world-wide, and still presented herself as a classic Mediterranean diva. She was everything he wanted in a woman but could not have.

How could he possibly protect her? Loiter in the East Bay and wait to get arrested with her? He shook his head.

Altimeter, *Set*. Display, *Ground Mode*. Engine Start Air, *2,000 psi*.

He needed her so desperately. Needed to know she would be safe. But since he'd made his announcement, she wasn't answering his calls or texts. Maybe her daughter would help. He keyed his Cambiar internet phone, hoping Tiffany Lavery would respond. Electronic tones played five times, then six. His thumb poised itself until the petulant face of his favorite teenager appeared in his hand.

"Tiffany, how are you?"

"What do you want, Philip?"

"I need to reach your mother."

"She's downstairs, auditioning martinis. She can't hear me yakking in the closet, sitting on a pile of shoes."

"Sorry."

"No, you're not. She got your notes, but she's not going to reply. Your big surprise chopped her off at the knees, you know. She pretty much hates you."

He nodded, more than aware. "I don't blame her, but we need to talk. Can you put her on your phone?"

"Then she'd hate me, too."

"I need to explain, Tiff. Help her see what she needs to do."

"She's counting on her new boyfriend, the hotshot attorney from San Francisco."

"Terry Quinn doesn't have the horsepower to shield her from what's coming. It won't be just subpoenas and lawsuits. She needs to disappear until Makers—"

"She won't go anywhere, not with you. And she won't hide, either. She's sending me to Grandma's."

"That's good, that's good. I think she doesn't appreciate the magnitude—"

"Philip, she's downstairs throwing a double-PMS hissy fit because of you. She's not going to listen to you or me anytime soon. So don't . . . . Oh, shit. She's coming upstairs."

"Call me," he said. "Tomorrow. Please."

The connection dropped, and he pounded his knee. He needed to apologize to her, to explain, to help her escape. Which was why he was lingering at the ranch, daring the world to show up with cameras and warrants and handcuffs, while Tanner trucked their gear south.

Behind Pleasanton ridge, a murky sunset was collecting its colors to leave. To his right, a column of baby thunderheads extended eastward over the hills. He would love to switch on his variometer and go thermal-hunting over there. Soar engine-off, like a natural-born hawk, on slender red wings, just for the joy of it. But one by one, twilight was stealing his options.

Clear the Area, *Check*. Throttle, *Set for start*. Engine Sequencer, *Ready*.

He pressed the START icon, and the baby turbofan behind his seat whooshed up to an urgent idle.

He must not pursue Karen Lavery, nor any woman. He must avoid attachments. Though he had already attached, hadn't he? Exposed himself to another unacceptable loss. He needed to store his feelings for her on that mental shelf he reserved for future projects. He could admire her up there as often as he wished, examine her in detail, and invite her into his dreams, but always from a safe distance.

Oil Pressure, *Green*. Lights and Beacons, *On*. Flaps, *10 degrees*.

If he couldn't control his feelings, "She pretty much hates you" might bring down the whole shebang. His attempts to help the woman he loved would only imperil the advent. Because Makers were just the beginning. If the advent failed, his deeper project would die stillborn. His father's legacy would not survive the terrible fire that had killed him, and the world would collapse into chaos for which he, Philip, would forever be blamed.

This is not a stunt, folks. Time to figure it out.

He released his brakes, turned his little red plane into the wind, and shoved the throttle full forward.

FOUR

Tracy, California. Monday, April 20
Day Three

JUST AFTER DAWN, Everett copied a fuel can and filled his motorcycle with free gas, which was pretty cool. But his westward commute was disgustingly normal. He rolled with the herd, up the treeless Altamont Pass and down through Livermore valley. Then up Dublin Grade on the west side, descending at last through a brushy gap that revealed San Francisco Bay.

Despite his weird weekend, nothing had changed. Suburbia sprawled as dormant and oblivious as ever. Beneath a vaporous sun, commuters still commuted, as if they always had and forever would. At Castro Valley, when the freeway angled north, he caught a twinkling glimpse of the bay.

Oakland Shoes-for-You didn't open until ten, so he kept to lane speed and did not split ahead. Arriving early, he maneuvered into his spot across from the store. He dismounted and stretched. Up and down Grand Avenue, from the hillside condos in the north to the old Grand Lake Theater down by the freeway, a hazy sheen of normalcy clung to everything and everyone.

Across the avenue, General Johnson was cranking his security curtain into its recess. Even from a distance, it was clear why people called him General, and why they were delighted to learn it was truly his name. Despite a silvery frost on the man's black hair, Everett could imagine him still in his Navy uniform, straight and vigorous. Military bearing, Bobby called it. Everett suspected General Johnson had possessed it as a child. The Abouds and the Johnsons were neighbors once, in a different part of town, in a different time, before his mother took off for Calgary.

"Looks to be a fine day," General said when Everett joined him inside. "How is Admiral Aboud?"

"He sends his thanks for the work."

General nodded. He unlocked the register and slid a change tray into its drawer.

In the back room, Everett stripped off his leathers and sweatshirt. He donned a Shoes-for-You T-shirt, hung up his riding gear, and joined his boss at the counter.

"Cops across the street," General said.

Everett peered.

Two officers holstered their pistols in front of the jewelry store next to the bar where Everett parked his motorcycle. A third officer stood at the store entrance, arguing with a fat man in a beige suit. The officers soon departed and traffic resumed on the avenue.

"Looks like Alonso is okay," General said. "He's never been robbed before, if you can imagine that, in Oakland."

Everett shrugged. "Maybe it's not a robbery."

The beige suit noticed them, waved as if he were dusting a shelf, and retreated into his shop. General snorted.

"I'll get it out of him later. Here's your chore for the morning." He laid a scanner on the counter. "I inventoried the storeroom, so I want you to do the sales floor."

"Display items too?"

"No, they're from the storeroom." General unfolded his

ancient laptop computer and turned his back.

Half an hour later, a woman in a culinary uniform herded three young boys into the store and made them sit. Shoes-for-You was self-serve, with most of its stock on the sales floor, but General was always friendly and helpful. The lady beamed as he approached her.

"Baseball," she said, indicating the oldest boy, "and cross trainers for these two."

General showed her the sports shoes and helped the kids fit proper sizes. When Everett looked up again, the lady was departing, and her boys were hop-dodging in new footgear.

As they left, the pudgy jeweler entered, carrying a leather case. He held the door for the woman then rushed to the counter.

General greeted him. "Alonso, what happened? We saw police."

Alonso searched the room, glowering as if someone had kicked his dog. He acknowledged Everett as an employee before replying.

"It's counterfeit, General. I came to warn you. Don't take any cash. The bastards got me, and the cops can't touch them."

"Alonso, sit down." General offered his stool.

Alonso flopped his case onto the counter. "Here," he said, "Look at this." He scooped a sheaf of currency and thrust it at his friend. "I should have known."

Everett drew closer as General fanned the bills playing-card style.

"Coffee stains?"

"That's how I noticed too. But those are just the pearls I sold. Here are the diamond earrings." He waved a clip of bills. "Even Connie's painting—I sell my wife's paintings." He waved a pair of fifties.

"It was such a good morning. Everybody paid cash. Then, when I figured it out, here comes a guy with a stack of hundreds, bold as a red bocce ball. I pressed my alarm, and the bum took off. It was all I could do to keep from punching him in the mouth, the son-of-a-bitch. It had to be more counterfeit. For all I know, every penny I took in today is counterfeit."

His expression soured.

"You can't spot the phonies until you see a duplicate serial number. And it's everywhere. The news said the cops can't handle all the calls. When they came for my alarm, they told me not to bother them, that I should notify the Secret Service in San Francisco. But their number is busy too. You don't even get voicemail, just that stupid buzzing. My insurance company—their line says go to their website."

General opened his register and found identical fifties and twenties. "Damn. She was just somebody's momma."

"You'd better close up, my friend. Go home like me, until they stop these bastards."

General shook his head. "We can't, Alonso. At least you have insurance. We have to make up our losses by selling more sneakers."

The jeweler lowered his voice. "It's going to get worse, my friend."

"Yeah?"

"Today a few are doing it. Tomorrow it will be thousands, then millions. Nobody can stop them because anyone can do it. I'm so stupid. Last night—saints forgive me—I copied some things, just to show my foolish head this is possible. I should have known."

"Sit down, Alonso. What are you talking about?"

Alonso didn't sit. From the case, he withdrew a sparkling waterfall of diamonds.

"Finest necklace I ever designed. Isn't it beautiful? The materials alone cost thirty-five thousand. But it's a copy. Perfect in every way. Real platinum, real stones. I could have sold it for fifty thousand, sixty maybe. I should have sold it to one of those damn counterfeiters because I got it from the machine behind my porch."

"Say what?"

"My Powerpod. Don't you have one?"

"Sure, but—"

"You put cones on your Powerpod, and then you copy things.

Anything at all. Do you know what this means, General? You and I are out of business. We are wiped out. People who sell things that other people make, we are ruined. Anybody can copy anything, so nobody has to buy. Everything is free. Costs you nothing. Just put something in your cone, push the button, and presto—there's your copy." Perspiration streaked his face.

"Alonso, you're upset. I'd buy you a cappuccino, but I can't leave the store. We'll just have to stop taking cash until they catch the crooks."

"They won't, General." Alonso shook his head as he put away his treasure. "They can't. In a few days, there won't be any customers either. Just vultures looking for fresh swag to copy. You and I are destroyed, don't you see? They are going to copy your shoes. They will copy them and give them away, or trade them, or sell them for half what you paid, and your business will die." He grabbed General's wrist.

"I came to warn you, old friend. It's too crazy for your head right now. You don't understand. But you will." Tears welled in his eyes.

"Alonso, you okay? Let me show you some Italian slip-ons, better than Gucci's."

"Thank you, General. I'm all right. You take care of yourself. Watch the news. They will tell us what's happening."

The fat man shut his case and trudged away. Across the avenue, his windows stood dark and empty. His security curtain was down and locked.

After he left, General found a marker and made a sign from a box lid. Everett nailed this high on the post behind the counter. "NO CASH—Cards or Checks Only."

Descending from the ladder, Everett confessed. "I should have said something earlier. I wasn't sure, but now I am. I think you should take your cash right away and put it in the bank, all of it before it's too late."

"You knew about this?" His father's best friend waved

counterfeit in his face. Everett met his eyes.

"I wasn't sure."

General Johnson knew baloney when he heard it, and his scowl said so. Everett took a breath and tried to explain.

"How do you tell people that something impossible just happened? Over the weekend something changed, and you're not sure what it means. You don't want to be Chicken Little, crying counterfeit is coming! Counterfeit is coming! Who would believe you?"

General returned to his stool and glared while Everett told him about testing his Maker. Like most people, the Johnsons had ignored Philip Machen's advertising and hadn't watched his infomercial. As Everett finished, General was shaking his head.

"You're right. I wouldn't have believed you before this." He shook the bills. "Or before Alonso. This had better not be some elaborate hoax you and your father cooked up with Alonso."

"And some woman with three kids," Everett said.

General frowned. He used his Cambiar to call upstairs. While they waited for Mrs. Johnson to join them, he said, "Did you ever wonder why this is the only store on the block with living quarters on the second floor? In the old days, before telephones, it was a funeral parlor, and the director lived upstairs, in case business showed up during the night, which I guess it did. Kind of like your Maker machines."

Mrs. Johnson had always been healthy and cheerful, but today she descended the stairs with a limp and a grimace.

"Daddy is asleep," she said, "so you check him every ten minutes, Gen. Good morning, Everett."

"Good morning, Charlene."

"Arthritis," she said, answering his look.

There was no time to explain why the daily deposit had to be run so early, so General didn't try. He simply gave her the zippered pouch and a peck on the cheek.

"Drive carefully," he said, and they watched her depart.

Even for a Monday, sales were slow. By noon they had sold only two more pairs—for credit—and General switched off the shopping music. He tuned his dusty receiver to a news channel, interrupting the bell tones of a news cut-over.

Counterfeit is sweeping the nation, the announcer said. Thieves using counterfeit emptied the vending machines at New York's Kennedy airport. From Seattle to Miami, coin dealers, pawnshops, and jewelry exchanges had stopped buying or making loans on collectibles, jewelry, tools, firearms, and other easily copied valuables. And everyone, the announcer said, was refusing cash. In Washington D.C., the Treasury Secretary called the situation an international crisis and urged all citizens to defer cash transactions until a solution could be found.

General switched it off. He sagged onto his stool.

"Maybe Chicken Little was right."

A slender young woman in clingy gray slacks and a plunging black blouse entered from the storeroom. She strode to the counter, pressing a Cambiar to her ear.

"Dammit, answer me. Pick up the phone." She stopped at the ladder and regarded Everett as if he were a blob of used chewing gum. "Who're you?"

General stood.

"Marcy, meet an old family friend. Everett Aboud, this is my niece, Marcy Johnson."

Everett's brain melted. He searched for a clever word, but when he dropped a shoulder and said, "W'sup," she laughed.

"Say, Home Boy."

He cringed and hoped she wouldn't notice. In the presence of a slinky brown goddess, he had revealed his inner jerk. Still in jerk mode, he offered his hand, just as her focus snapped to her phone.

"Hello? Hello? I don't have time for stupid voicemail. Pick up, will you please?" She strangled the instrument. Then she accepted Everett's hand and liquefied his brains with a thousand-volt smile.

"I'm sorry," she said, and the sparkle in her glance made it true.

"It's just that I have this interview in an hour, and I don't have a cameraman. My regular's gone to L.A. and no one else is answering."

Everett didn't know about interviews, but— "I do cameras."

"Commercial videos?"

"Sure." He shrugged the lie into submission.

"This is not your sister's birthday or your cousin's wedding. I need a pro here. That's pro, as in Steady-cams, dolly setups, and two-camera interview splits. You gotta handle the audio too."

Again he shrugged. "I can do that."

He looked to General, pleading, while Marcy jiggled her keys.

"Okay," she said. "You're temporary. Until somebody returns my calls. But you don't get scale unless your work is up to par, do you understand? Otherwise, you get a cheese sandwich, if you're lucky." She addressed her uncle. "Can I borrow this hotshot, or do you need him?"

"We need him."

"He can go," Mrs. Johnson overruled from the storeroom door. "If it's important to Marcy, we can manage without Everett for an afternoon. For an interview? With whom?"

A customer entered through the avenue door, setting off a chime. Marcy licked her perfect teeth.

"Can't say until we're done, Auntie, but you'll be proud when I go national tonight. If New Guy here doesn't screw up."

Mrs. Johnson nodded. General shrugged.

"You going to the City?" Charlene asked.

"No, to Pleasanton. And we gotta leave now. C'mon, Home Boy." Marcy strode away and called over her shoulder, "Thank you, Uncle. Thank you, Auntie."

"Yeah, thanks," Everett managed.

FIVE

FOLLOWING MARCY to her car made his day. Men have killed for much less than the sway of Marcy's hips. She made him sit in the back seat with the cameras while she drove.

"We start as soon as we get there," she said. "So get familiar with the tools and get ready."

He did what she said and asked no questions, which seemed to disturb her, but he was enjoying himself. Not just his sexy new companion and her gadgets, but suddenly everything about everything. He was having a peak moment in the back of a white Mitsubishi as it shredded the speed limit on a brightening day, headed for something he'd never done. And a wild, dark goddess was leading his way.

He probed a coffee mug that turned out to be a satellite uplink and fondled the cameras. He tested each one, checked their responses. Then he donned the battery harness and powered-up a Steadicam. He could do this.

Marcy passed him a news printout.

"Here's our subject. We met last year at Mills. That's a college. Our little piece went to an internet site, where the nationals picked it up, and that was my break into mainstream video journalism. It's been a year and a half, and she still remembers me. Can you believe it?"

On the page, a striking fortyish woman in a glittery gown was emerging from a limo on the arm of a tuxedo. The caption read "Karen Lavery, Powerpods Company CEO, and sponsor of last year's Black and White Ball, arrives at Davies Symphony Hall with activist attorney Terrance Quinn."

Marcy powered through the sparse traffic, retracing Everett's commute, shooting up and then down the East Bay hills to arrive at Stoneridge Mall in Pleasanton. But Ms. Lavery was not at the juice bar near the west entrance as expected. Marcy phoned and left a message, but they had missed her. Cradling his Steadicam and shifting in the clunky harness, Everett was drawing glances from the other patrons, as if his presence were sucking sugar out of their drinks. Marcy drummed her red-lacquered nails on the table.

"Maybe they grabbed her already."

Grabbed? He sipped a strawberry smoothie as Marcy made another call. She looked terrific through the viewfinder.

Behind them, a taut pair of Lycra shorts clacked across the tiles on cyclist's shoes and stopped at their booth. A sunny ponytail sprouted from the girl's bicycle helmet, and Everett hoped she would smile because she looked familiar.

"Ms. Johnson?"

Marcy squelched her Cambiar. "I'm Marcy Johnson."

"I'm Tiffany." No smile. "Come with me."

They followed her at a vigorous pace. Outside, Ms. Grim Face hesitated.

"Where's your car?"

Marcy pointed. "That row. Shall we follow you?"

"I'm riding with you."

"There's no room for your bike."

"Then I'll leave it." The girl shrugged. "I have another one—identical actually."

Tiffany sat in front with Marcy and directed them south from the mall into the sheltered community of Castlewood. Big trees and fancy houses, backed against a tortuous golf course. Lots of pools and security cameras. Old money. Tiffany told Marcy to skip the manned gate, to continue to a blind curve in a secluded canyon, where she told her to stop. Marcy parked, and they got out.

"This way."

Tiffany led them downhill, through stiff grass, along a deer trail that wended among acacia, madrone, and manzanita. When a thicket of rosemary appeared at the base of a redwood fence, she produced a Cambiar and removed her cycling helmet.

That's where Everett had seen her, in Philip Machen's video. Tiffany Lavery was the cheerleader in the perky yellow blouse who narrated the introduction. She tossed her helmet over the fence and spoke briefly to her phone. Then she faced Everett and indicated the fence.

"Give us a boost."

Her presumption annoyed him.

"Please?" For the first time, she met his eyes.

Much better. He planted his feet and squatted, elbows on his knees, fingers laced. When she stepped into his hands, he launched her, almost too high. At the top, she balanced on the fence, selected a spot on the other side, and hopped over.

"Now Ms. Johnson."

Marcy put her hand on his shoulder. "Don't drop me, Everett."

He beamed with the rush of their sudden proximity.

After Tiffany's graceful ascent, Marcy's was awkward, but she wobbled across and landed without injury. Everett considered heaving his equipment over first but chose to grunt his way across. He landed on a bed of shredded bark and lodged a splinter in his thumb. Tiffany let him recover before leading them across a perfect lawn to a white, Colonial-style house. Without hesitation, she trampled a copse of agapanthus beneath an open window.

Inside, a middle-aged woman—the auburn beauty from the gossip photo—helped them over the sill and onto their feet, amid a floral oasis. Bookcases faced the windows behind scores of flowers arranged in crystal vases.

"Marcy, thank you for coming," the woman said. "We don't have much time."

"This is Everett," Marcy said as she brushed herself. "My cameraman."

In a single glance, Ms. Lavery absorbed everything about him, and he was sure he would not forget her either. For the second time today, he restarted his brain. Then he set the satellite uplink on the window sill and switched it on. Her matriarchal gaze followed this with approval. When he brought the camera up to her face, she bestowed on him a smile that confirmed what he already knew: she owned him.

"You can see them on our security screens," she told Marcy. "We are surrounded."

Ms. Lavery led them under a staircase to a vaulted entry that soared three stories above a white terrazzo floor. She touched one of six images on a flat screen, expanding the view of her front porch, where a pale hand zoomed at them, many times larger than life. A door chime accompanied the visual intrusion. Ms. Lavery touched her screen.

"Who are you? What do you want?

A badge and photo ID filled the display.

"Ms. Lavery? I'm Les Parker, FBI. I believe we spoke earlier."

The badge withdrew and was replaced by a Hollywood-handsome face screwed into a business suit. Behind him wavered an orange-haired frizz who could not possibly be his wife.

Ms. Lavery plucked a Cambiar from her pocket and keyed the number scribbled on her palm.

The man on the porch put a cellphone to his ear. "Parker," he said. "I assure you, Ms. Lavery, Nedra and I have not come to arrest you. However, we would like to chat a bit regarding Mr. Machen, if you would kindly grant us a few minutes of your time."

Ms. Lavery chained the door. Behind her, Everett bounded up the stairway and charged to the second-floor landing. The women gaped as if he'd lost his mind. He ignored Marcy's frantic waves and wedged a pocket camera into the banister, angled it at the entry below as Ms. Lavery opened the door against its chain.

"Agent Parker," she said. "I've no idea where Mr. Machen might be, and frankly I don't care."

"Well, that's to be expected, isn't it, Ms. Lavery? Under the circumstances, I mean. You do know a few things that might help us though, don't you? Mr. Machen's habits, his acquaintances, where he vacations, etcetera? A few details that might be of service to your country? May we come in and speak more directly?" His cologne had already entered.

Everett rushed down from the stairs, then backed slowly with his Steadicam, framing Ms. Lavery at the door.

"What about that SWAT team around the corner?" she said.

"I'm afraid I cannot speak for those gentlemen." Parker shrugged his apology.

"Can you keep them away while we talk?"

Everett braced himself against the opposite wall. Behind Agent Parker, The Frizz shook her head and thrust a hand into her purse, not from the top but the rear, like a holster.

"I doubt we can prevail upon their generosity," Parker said.

"Yes or no, Parker?" Ms. Lavery threw her weight against the door and bolted it.

The face on the screen winced and withdrew. Then a blur smashed the door. Ms. Lavery staggered backward into Marcy, who pulled Tiffany between them.

A muffled count: two, three. Bang! The door splintered.

"Uplink," Marcy shouted. "Switch to the uplink, Everett."

"Already did," he yelled. He framed the women in his viewfinder.

"This is Marcy Johnson, and I am with Karen Lavery, owner of Powerpods Company, at her home in Pleasanton, California. Law enforcement officers have surrounded the house. No doubt they are seeking answers to the same questions we would like to ask. Ms. Lavery, what do you know about these Maker machines and when did you know it?"

The door erupted again, straining the bolt.

"Nothing," said Ms. Lavery. "I knew nothing. He tricked us too. Philip Machen used my company and my employees to deceive the world. He used us. He betrayed us."

The door slammed wide open. A blur flew in and exploded, dazzling everyone. Its concussion broke their eardrums. Through the shock and the smoke charged a phalanx of black-clad warriors, each brandishing a machine gun and shouting the same angry command.

"Down! Get down!"

The women raised their hands and huddled at the credenza where each of them was forced to kneel before having her face shoved to the floor.

"Press," Marcy called. "I'm a report—oof."

Everett braced himself, capturing the action until a rifle butt slammed his neck and his camera spiraled away. Sliding down the wall, he covered his face and curled into a ball. Metallic agony cinched one wrist, twisted it, and latched to the other. Then his assailant heaved him onto his face.

Radios crackled and laser dots zoomed. Everett rolled to his side to witness as much as possible. The women shrieked as rough hands pinned them and bound their wrists in steel. Two-man squads stomped through the house, shouting "Police!" and "Clear!"

The entry teams ignored his balcony camera until the women were dragged on their knees to separate rooms. When a raider spotted Everett's little Sony, he booted it from the landing and followed it down to the floor. Six feet from Everett's face, he stomped it to pieces.

SIX

Oakland, California. Still Monday, April 20
Day Three

THE FEDS HELD Everett in a windowless room in downtown Oakland and questioned him. Where is Philip Machen? How do you know him? What do you do for him? Who does he work for? Why is he doing this? Why are you protecting him? Tell us his habits, his friends, his politics, his religion, his sexual preferences. Same questions about Ms. Lavery. Everett repeated himself over and over while they insisted he was lying. For two hours, they pounced on every hesitation, every apparent inconsistency. Marcy's voice sounded once from the hall, but he saw only his captors. There was no time to think or feel anything but his impotence, his isolation, and his throbbing neck.

They examined his driving and pilot licenses, his judgment decree from San Francisco Superior Court, and a letter from the Western Regional Director, U.S. Homeland Security Department.

Agent Parker wrinkled his official nose. "You say?"

"Everything is there." Everett glanced to a vacant corner,

wishing he had brought that article from the *East Bay Times*. About the smart aleck pot-smoker getting busted at the airport BART Station with a plane ticket and a five-inch melon knife in his boot. Pot Boy thought it was cute to give a false name, but data from Homeland Security arrests were widely shared, and other jurisdictions soon obtained the original posting for Everett A. Aboud, arrested under the influence of drugs and in possession of a deadly weapon, at San Francisco International Airport.

"Stolen ID, huh?"

Apparently, Federal databases were up-to-date because Parker returned Everett's papers and did not rearrest him for his old "crimes." The bad news was, those databases now contained a new record, with new fingerprints, a new photo, and a fresh DNA swipe bearing his name. Once again, he was a Federal person of interest.

Parker and the orange-haired woman grilled him until they released him, abruptly, at 6:00 p.m. Downstairs in the lobby, his uniformed escort said he could make a phone call. He could summon Bobby or General Johnson to come for him, or he could hire a cab. But he didn't want a ride, and he was sick of explaining. He shook the tension from his arms and shoulders and headed out the enormous brass door.

Free at last on a chilly sidewalk, he pulled the neck of his Shoes-for-You T-shirt askew and hurried eastward. As a breeze invigorates a fire, the cold air enraged him. He needed to get away and run off his resentment, though running would draw suspicion, maybe another cop, so he walked fast. No crime in walking, last he heard.

But this time it was not his stolen identity or his Arab name. This was trouble of his own making, the full consequences of which might not arrive for weeks. Would he ever work in an airline cockpit? Maybe Bobby was right. Maybe he should indenture himself to the military, sell himself for six years for the privilege of flying heavy metal. If he didn't wash out, he could start over, build his career, and repay his father. If they let him.

People on the street were rushing past him, ant-like, chasing bits of personal business. *Don't they realize something is wrong? How do I know this while they don't?*

When he reached Broadway, the cold began to bite. Twenty minutes later, he arrived at Shoes-for-You, muscles knotted by twitches and shivers. Upstairs, a golden light glowed from the windows. Though his motorcycle beckoned from across the boulevard, he would freeze without his helmet and leathers.

General answered the delivery door with a baseball bat cocked over his shoulder. He recognized his employee and lowered the bat.

"You two are shit magnets, did you know that?"

"Is she here?"

"You look bad, son. How about some dinner?"

"Is she okay? I need to get my stuff."

General admitted him, bolted the door, and led him upstairs into a warm and aromatic kitchen.

"Look what the kitty left at the door."

Charlene and Marcy looked up from half-eaten bowls of stew, plates of dark bread. They were spoon-feeding an ancient man who wore a bath towel for a bib. This would be Daddy, General's father.

"We thought they kept you," Marcy said.

"Must be a limit for trout and Lebanese-Americans. They threw me back."

Charlene quizzed Marcy. "Don't you think he looks like Johnny Mathis?"

"Too young. Too white." Marcy's grin faded. "We were kneecapped, kiddo. The national media refused our clips and went with the pool footage—Ms. Lavery strolling peacefully to a nice government car, wearing those comfy handcuffs, just your routine, everyday perp-walk."

Everett rubbed his arms.

"Take a seat, Mr. Aboud." General pretended to announce a menu. "Tonight we offer a lovely two-dollar Merlot to compliment Charlene's priceless rainbow stew."

"Yes, thank you. Two gallons of each, please." He sat across from Marcy, who focused her pique on the flat-screen behind the table, a news webcast.

"Three sites bought our feed," she said, "but that didn't replace my equipment. The Feds are keeping it, for whatever reason. So I'm grounded, and nobody cares what happened today. Ms. Lavery went to jail without a statement, and the world is safe again, except for Philip Machen."

"What about the girl?" Everett said.

"Tiffany? I don't know. Why would they keep her?"

General set a tumbler before his guest and filled it with red wine.

"I was kidding," Everett said.

"We'd better get ourselves one of those Maker machines, Charlene. Everett's thirsty."

Marcy laughed but cut it short.

"We're waiting for a news conference," she said. She leaned on her elbows, which brought her face into the light. "You did some fine work this afternoon, Everett. That second camera kept us in the game, you know? And feeding it to the uplink from the beginning—that was pretty sharp. For a new guy."

"Sorry it didn't work out."

"Hey, I sold a few clips. So thanks, I'm glad you came along."

"Me, too."

She spied the bruise on his neck. "But not too glad, huh?"

He gazed into her velvet-brown eyes. *Be my nurse.*

General brought a bowl of stew and a spoon.

Everett yawned. "I'm just tired of being arrested all the time, that's all."

Three faces turned.

Oops. He explained between mouthfuls. By the time the news conference started, the stew and half the wine had disappeared, and Marcy turned up the volume.

"Live from Washington, D.C., here is Attorney General Nicholas T. Brayley."

A tumult of heads and shoulders bobbed at the foot of a tiny stage. Cameras snapped as the crowd jostled against a cordon of dark uniforms. The Attorney General, whose sour expression drew into a scowl, labored to the dais. His bald head and ruddy complexion glistened.

"I have just briefed President Washburn and Vice President Fletcher about the unprecedented and illegal conversion of Powerpods, now flooding the world with counterfeit.

"Although our investigations are just beginning I have reported to the president that Mr. Philip Machen, and three persons in his employ have deliberately launched an economic Trojan horse against the currency of the United States, as well as against other national currencies."

He cleared his throat.

"This financial terrorism is nothing short of a direct assault on our economic recovery. At this time we believe it is not, I repeat not, sponsored by any known terrorist group or foreign power. However, we will continue to investigate any links between Mr. Machen or his confederates and known criminals and extremists.

"This morning I ordered the Secret Service and the FBI to arrest Philip Machen, plus three others—Ms. Karen Lavery, who is now in custody, Mr. Orin G. Machen, and Mr. Tanner A. Newe. We are coordinating our search for these suspects with state and local agencies and with corresponding foreign services throughout the world. We will bring Philip Machen and all counterfeiters to justice. We will arrest and prosecute anyone who possesses or attempts to pass counterfeit currency or fake financial instruments, and we will confiscate any equipment suspected of producing counterfeit. To this end, President Washburn has ordered an emergency cabinet meeting tomorrow morning to coordinate our response."

A flurry of shouts pursued him as he departed. The scene lingered before cutting to a newsreader's calm visage. "That was Nicholas T. Brayley, Attorney General of the United States, live from—"

General switched it off. "So now what are they going to do?"

Marcy massaged her wrist. "Lock 'em up."

"Okay, and then what? Lock up the Maker machines? Half the country runs on Powerpods, you know. A lot of the old generator plants are shut down, torn up. We can't go back to coal or gas very soon, even if we wanted to. And why should we? Powerpods don't become counterfeiting machines until you put on those cones."

"Such a fuss," Charlene said, finishing with Daddy.

Everett wasn't listening. Marcy's temple had a pulse at the hairline. She caught him staring and pushed back from the table.

"Thank you, Aunt Charlene. Thank you, Uncle General. It's been a long day."

Everett stood as well, offered his thanks, and took his leave. He made it downstairs and retrieved his riding gear in time to intercept Marcy at the back door.

"She might give you a jailhouse interview," he suggested.

"I suppose." Marcy shoved the door open. "Good night, Mr. Aboud."

"You said something about a cheese sandwich, but I'll settle for a beer."

"When they card you in the bars, kiddo, do they make you leave?"

"Not anymore."

"All right. One beer."

They circled to the front and crossed Grand Avenue's four lanes. The door to Maurice's Club, behind his motorcycle, stood open like a cave. Inside, they settled on stools, and Marcy paid with a card. Even the dim light favored her face.

"So what do you want from me, Everett?"

He shrugged and tried to provoke a smile. "I'd rather annoy you than not see you again."

"Get used to it, kid. I'm not in the market. Not for you or anyone else."

"Man-eating career-woman of the world."

"Look Mr. Barely-a-Beer-Drinker, you're cute, but you don't need me, and I sure as hell don't need you. So if we see each other again, it's going to be as friendly co-workers, and that's all. Because if you make a pass at me, I'll bust you in the mouth."

"Exactly what I was going to say."

"Ha!" She teetered. "You did well, Aboud, and I paid you scale. You did me a favor, so I'm buying, and I thank you. Our books are clean."

"What you did this afternoon," he said, "jumping into that lady's train wreck just to tell the world about it, that was amazing. Maybe we didn't make a difference, but you were great."

"Look, Everett. You can't admire me into hooking up with you. You're young and sharp. You'll do fine." She slipped from her stool and headed for the door. "You just need to get out there and fly."

He cringed, then followed her to the door.

"I'm a pilot," he called.

She waved without looking back.

BOBBY WAS SNORING into the sofa cushions when Everett got home, but before he showered, he needed to check his emails. Montana Skies, where he interviewed last fall, had finally replied. "It is our pleasure to offer you a six-month probationary position as Second Officer on our Billings-to-Minneapolis circuit, beginning May 1."

Everett wiped the screen of his Cambiar and read it again. The hours would be long and the pay minimal, but this was the most beautiful text he had ever received. At last, all of his hard work and all of Bobby's sacrifices would be . . . hammered.

He laid his head on the cold tiles and pounded the counter. The Feds didn't have to arrest him, just put his fancy Arab name on the no-fly list, in case he was in cahoots with Philip Machen and might try to leave the country. *Tell us about your counterfeiting machine, Mr. Aboud, your secret meeting with Mr. Machen's business partner.* That's all it would take. He was certain they would do this—probably already had. He stuffed his phone and sought the shadows.

He should accept Montana Skies offer, fight the system once more, and save his career. It might work, eventually. *What do I tell Bobby if I don't try? That his faith and commitments to me are misplaced?*

He left the kitchen for the garage. Under a buzzing work light, he clamped a pine board in the old vise and took up a carpenter's plane. His first stroke jammed, so he adjusted the blade and rammed it again, this time slicing a clean, bright edge. Now the tool did not bind, and long curls fell as he stroked. Reducing a six-inch board to a one-inch stick absorbed him for three minutes. Switching arms, he set another board. He planed this one to half-size when the door smacked open.

"The hell are you doing?" Bobby looked like a butcher shop accident, all creases and folds under bloodshot eyes.

"Making tinder." He kicked the shavings.

"We don't have a fireplace."

Everett nodded. When the second board was too thin to continue, and his breathing came deep and steady, only the pine scent and the muscle burn remained. Bobby had gone, and Everett's mind was clear. Now he could clean up and get some sleep.

SEVEN

Tracy, California. Tuesday, April 21
Day Four

NEXT MORNING, the news on Everett's way to work was the financial markets crashing. Depressed as they were, the indices fell thirty percent more before trading was halted. As commodity prices plummeted, trading stopped. There were no buyers. Except for government bonds, trading ceased everywhere, halted by the rules of each exchange, rules meant to prevent exactly what was happening. When the regulated exchanges closed, traders moved to the internet where markets continued to evaporate, worldwide, heedless of regulations.

General Johnson did not greet him when he entered the store. For the first time since Everett had known him, his father's friend had nothing to say. General was perched on his stool, intent on his screen, watching the vast, intangible wealth of traders and money mongers devolve to the present value of a knock-knock joke.

Outside, a kid on a decrepit bicycle rode up and hopped off. When he rapped on the glass door, Everett checked the time and let him in. The boy rushed to a shelf where he yanked a box of sneakers, size nine, and placed them on the counter.

"Loan me these shoes, Mister General."

General looked up.

"This isn't a public library. We don't lend things here."

"Loan me these shoes, Mister General. They be coming back perfect, I swear. Never be worn. You keep my phone if I don't bring them back. All I need is twenty minutes." He slapped a battered cell phone on the counter. "Here."

General Johnson stood up to his full height.

"What do you say, Mister General? You can keep my bike too. But then I need thirty minutes."

Everett stationed himself at the door. Gang kids could run a till-tap and be out of the store before anyone noticed.

"These be the best, Mister General." The boy patted the box. "I never had no shoes like these. I just need one pair to copy. Then I promise two pairs coming back. Three pairs. All perfect, just like these. That's a fine deal, Mister General—three pairs for twenty minutes loan."

General raked the box aside, and the boy retreated.

"I got more guarantees. I be back."

"Hold on." General came around the counter. "You don't look old enough for a driving license. Do you have any ID? A school card, with your picture?"

The boy fished in his pockets.

"What are you doing out of class, anyway," General said, "on a Tuesday morning?"

The boy offered a plastic card.

General took it in one hand and keyed the boy's phone with the other. "Hello, Officer Nichols, please."

The kid's eyes widened. He glanced at Everett.

"Officer Nichols? This is General Johnson at Shoes-for-You on Grand Avenue. I have a young man name of Michael Mayes over here. Might be a gangster. Says he goes to Westlake Middle School.

His student number is 61231. Do you know anything about him? Yes, I'll wait." He covered the phone. "Are you a thief, Michael Mayes? Are you a gangster?"

"No, sir."

General listened to his phone. "He's a thief?"

"That's a lie, Mister General." The kid jumped. "I never took nothing from nobody. That's a lie."

"Thank you, Officer Nichols." General put the kid's phone in his pocket, along with his ID card. "He says you're not a thief, so you have nineteen minutes to get back here with four pairs of sneakers."

The kid grabbed the box and bolted, leaving his bicycle slumped against the window.

"That was probably a mistake," Everett said.

General nodded.

"It's a law of nature," he said. "Tuesdays go sideways. This one's headed off a cliff."

Everett motioned to General's screen, still whispering on the counter.

"You watching your retirement go south?"

General shook his head. "The store is our retirement. We never put anything in the markets. Figured Social Security for a supplement, and never thought that would pay much either. But now . . . who knows?"

He left Everett at the counter and went upstairs. When a retired lady came in and lingered among the walking shoes, Everett helped her. A few minutes later the door chimed again. A uniformed policeman strode in with a bulging trash bag in one hand and the bicycle kid in his other.

"You folks missing some shoes?" He dumped the sack on the counter but kept his grip on the boy.

General came downstairs while Everett peeled the sack. Four yellow shoe boxes emerged, all size nine.

"Last night it was drunks and rowdies," said the cop. "This

morning the gangs are doing smash-and-grabs." He surveyed the store. "Three places over on Telegraph, two more downtown. If you can't stop them at the door, your merchandise is gone."

"Thank you, officer, but this boy is not a thief." General opened and shut each box as he arranged them in a stack. "This young man was running an errand for me."

"You sure?" The cop tightened his hold of the kid's jacket.

General nodded. "Which direction was he headed when you stopped him? Toward the store, or away?"

"Okay, Mr. Johnson, if you say so." He released the boy and turned to leave. "Protecting them doesn't help, you know."

"These shoes are not stolen, Officer. Mr. Mayes here was helping me make up my mind about something, that's all."

"Okay, sir." The cop paused at the door. "You might want to escort your customers or move your stock behind a counter. That's what the liquor stores are doing."

General nodded. "Thank you, officer."

"By the way, did you hear?" The cop angled his chin at their No Cash sign. "President Washburn suspended habeas corpus for counterfeiters. That ought to stop them."

General waited.

The policeman touched the bill of his hat. "Later, sir."

As the door closed, the boy grinned with pride and wonder at his new patron.

"Thank you, Mr. General. We did a fine deal, didn't we?"

General gave him a Cheshire cat grin and spoke through gritted teeth.

"Get your butt back to school, Michael Mayes. And do your deals when your homework is finished, not before." He returned the kid's phone and ID card.

The boy ran for his bike in sparkling new sneakers. The retired lady followed him out. When they were gone, General whispered, "Were you watching her?"

Everett nodded. "I don't think she took anything." He

collected the boxes from the counter, put one on the shelf and the rest in the storeroom. General was on the phone when he returned.

"What's up, sweetheart?"

Everett stopped.

"Now? I suppose we could. Any word on your equipment? Okay, okay. I'll hurry. Thanks for the heads-up." He broke the connection.

"Marcy's all excited. Philip Machen is giving another webcast. She wants us to check it out."

Everett scanned the room. "No customers."

Charlene joined them at the counter as General projected a news site from his Cambiar.

"What irony," said a man in a gray suit, "that Powerpods so recently touted as an economic silver bullet, a bootstrap to lift the nation out of its protracted recession, have suddenly become instruments of financial destruction. And if today's market declines are not reversed, there may be further repercussions."

"Looks like the recession finally hit Wall Street," Charlene said.

The man in the suit cleared his throat. "The following does not represent the views of WebNews or any of its business partners. The opinions expressed are solely those of the speaker, Mr. Philip Machen."

EIGHT

GENERAL TURNED up the volume.

"Hello. I'm Philip Machen." He wore a white, long-sleeved shirt that framed his college boy face.

"Last weekend I announced the advent of three-dimensional copy machines I called Makers. Today, people everywhere are converting their Powerpods into Makers, creating new lives and new futures."

The camera drew closer.

"Makers are my gift to all who will share them. I am convinced that Makers should belong to ordinary people, such as you and your family. I believe only you know how best to use your Makers, only you know how best to provide for your well-being, and only you know how best to conduct your affairs. I hope Makers will enrich your lives and promote your fulfillment as humane, generous, responsible citizens."

Everett caught a whiff of agenda.

"From the beginning, I kept Makers secret, until millions of Powerpods were spread around the world. I did this to make it harder for agents of repression to deny you your economic liberty. I alone decided to present Makers this way. Before last weekend, no one at Powerpods Company had any knowledge of them. Please do not blame the honest women and men at Powerpods Company for what I have done."

Machen looked down, then up.

"Makers are tools, of course, and they will soon become the dominant means of production. Because we are so busy with our daily routines and small pleasures, we seldom notice that the means by which we produce our material necessities are fundamental to our ways of life. Makers are about to change our means and our cultures."

Everett glanced to General, tried to read his expression.

"No longer must we struggle to produce enough for everyone. No longer must we endure natural scarcities, nor those deliberately imposed by others. No longer must ordinary people bind themselves to meaningless drudgery solely because they lack the means to produce for themselves the goods their families require. Now, anyone can enjoy the abundance and the independence previously available only to the wealthy. Prosperity and liberty are at hand for all who will produce and trade and share.

"The danger will come, as it always does, from those who would use force and deceit against peaceful, honest people. Great change is upon us. Our lives are disrupted, and we feel uncertain. Power-holders and power-seekers will feel threatened by these changes, and you can expect them to try to destroy your Makers, or to take them from you by force."

Everett nodded but hoped otherwise.

"I believe there is no property worth a single human life. I believe no righteousness can make attacking or threatening any nonviolent human being a moral thing to do. Protect yourselves and your families. Protect your Makers. Help others to do likewise.

Beware the agents of sanctimonious force, and do not be drawn into their destructive games of us-versus-them. When the principal means of production is free, we must insist that everyone share that freedom. Wherever you are, *whoever* you are, there is no longer any *them*. There is only *us*, the free and responsible people of the world."

Everett shook his head. *Good luck with that.*

"I expect Makers will create a new and universal human right— to own and to use a personal means of production. And I strongly believe that in the coming days, everyone will need to acquire their own Maker.

"Makers are free. Makers are safe. They are yours to do with as you please. I ask only that you consider well and act responsibly. What does this mean? What should you do?"

Everett shifted his weight, flexed his toes.

"First, talk to your friends and neighbors. Form a neighborhood support group, a Maker enclave. Make sure you and your loved ones are safe, and that you have food and other necessities. Trade with friends and share what you have. Especially, share your Makers. It will cost you nothing but the effort to do it. When everyone has a Maker, sharing will no longer mean sacrifice. Where scarcity once divided us, sharing will connect us. People with Makers can help each other in a thousand ways.

"Second, help those who need help. It's always the right thing to do.

"Third, obey the laws against theft and fraud and violence. Many laws, based on the obsolete ethics of scarcity, no longer make sense. In time, we will change them. But remember, when you are truly free, you don't need to cheat anyone or steal anything. When you are truly free, you create and cooperate and trade."

Everett stuffed his restless fingers into his pockets.

"Finally, stay calm, stay home if you can, and think about what you truly want to do. Being free from your old economic shackles should soon feel normal and proper—because it is. Enjoy yourself. Hold a copy party. Invite your friends to exchange things they need or want, and pretend you just inherited a fortune. Because now you are empowered to be as free and as prosperous as any person on Earth. You have your own personal means of production. You have a Maker.

"Thank you for listening."

When Machen's ghost-gray eyes turned away, a full-blown buzz rolled over Everett's scalp. *Nice words, no plan.*

"That's it?" General switched it off. "Man sets the world on its ear, and all he says is you're free, have a good time, and be sure to behave yourselves? We are definitely in trouble."

"Been a while since I heard a sermon," Charlene allowed.

General considered this, then soured. "Trouble is coming, that's for sure. People are going to go nuts, and we had better get ready. We need to build Fort Apache, Oakland, California." He aimed a *saddle-up* look at Everett, who was still absorbing his buzz.

"You think looters will come?" Charlene asked. "The man said we can share. Nobody has to steal."

"Well, some folks never get the word, you know. It seems to me if you want to keep anything after this, you had better get it inside where you can protect it because people are going to be grabbing everything they can get their hands on. They are going to stock up on what they need and then stop buying. If everyone shares and nobody has to buy, the whole supply chain will collapse. Alonso was right."

"We have shoes," Charlene said. "If we build one of those Maker machines, we can have shoes forever."

"Story of my life."

"Maybe I should get some groceries, just in case." She eyed the door.

"Good idea. And more of Daddy's medicine. Everett, I want you to take the van over to Builder's Supply. Get enough plywood to protect the downstairs windows. Everett?"

Everett cast off his reverie and shrugged into action. He measured the windows and figured thirteen sheets would cover them.

When General totaled the cost, he scratched his head. "Are you thinking what I'm thinking?"

"Buy one and make copies."

General squinched.

"Why buy more," Everett said, "if one is all you need?" Which sounded strange, as if someone else had said it. "Save a tree," he added, even more unlike himself.

"Can we get a full sheet into one chamber?"

Everett checked the dimensions. "Flat against the base, if we set up the bigger cones."

General nodded and his eyes glazed. "I was just going to run a test," he said, "to see how it works. You know, play with it. But all of a sudden, we need a bigger Maker. How the hell did that happen?" He shook it off. "Get going, Everett. One sheet of five-eighths exterior ply and a box of bugle-head screws."

Everett took General's van and found his way to the lumber store. At the loading dock stood two big Makers. Workers were rolling a garden cart out of one and wrestling a bathtub into the other. By the time Everett wheeled his goods to the checkout, the line was five deep, and his Cambiar was vibrating.

"We need sixteen-penny nails," General told him, "and a two-by-four, and a four-by-four. Get eight-footers, not studs."

When Everett returned to Shoes-for-You, General's full-size cone sections lay exposed in their crate, blocking the driveway. In the storeroom, four shelves were pushed askew, their stock half-spilled, and General's Powerpod—now sprouting three black appendages—rose from the clutter like a stupendous aluminum weed.

"Had my eye on these for a long time," General said, when Everett found him at the register. "Now there's no excuse." General's tassel loafers were cast aside for a shiny pair of cowboy boots, black with silver toes. "You want some, Everett? Help yourself. Boots-on-the-house."

"No thanks. You wear those things, you wind up on a horse wondering what sane people do."

Charlene came huffing through the door, carrying an overstuffed grocery bag.

"What a mess you've made," she said. Then she saw the boots. "I might have guessed."

"Did you get what we need?" General asked.

"Everything on my list. But those people made me so nervous, Gen. All the way home I kept thinking, what am I forgetting? Everyone is rushing, stocking up, like you said."

"It's fun, Charlene." General scuffed his slippery new soles on the rough carpet. "You should try it. I copied a few other styles so we won't run out. But you know, I had this feeling when I pushed the button that I was taking something I hadn't earned, as if it were stealing."

"You paid for them," Everett said. "No matter what you do with the copies, it won't be stealing. No reason you shouldn't sell them either. They're not fakes."

General shook his head.

"I suppose it's not stealing, but I wonder—when everyone starts using these machines—what are we losing?"

"Scarcity?" Everett perched on the counter, still surprising himself.

General grunted. "If everyone has this free and easy way to make things," he said, "that should be a good thing, right? Food and medicine—plenty for everyone. But what are we getting ourselves into?"

Charlene tried to buoy him. "We'll figure it out, hon."

General parked himself on the counter beside Everett and dangled his new boots.

"Maybe we should be grateful," he said. "But in a few days there won't be a choice, will there? If we don't use our Makers, other folks will use theirs, and some of them will take advantage. Because nobody can stop them. So, just to keep up, we will have to use our

Makers, too, or folks will pass us by. They'll pass us by and try to take over."

Everett stared at General's boots. Happy-feet, they used to call it. Dancing, skipping, jumping.

He went to the storeroom to check his Cambiar. No emails from the FBI or the Federal Aviation Agency, although these were just a matter of time, weren't they? His immediate future could only bring more runarounds, more pleading with bureaucrats, more shuffling and waiting behind more gates. What if everything changed before he got to the end of all that permission-seeking? What if Makers turned everyone's plans kerflooey?

Once again he brought up his Montana Skies job offer, his long-sought ticket to a professional cockpit. Before he could change his mind, he took a breath and keyed a reply. "Thank you, but I am unable to accept your offer at this time." He exhaled, pressed Send, and his saliva turned to brine.

Against all delays and disappointments, his flying career had been the buffer, his light in the distance. He could do drudge work, endure long hours at low pay, wait for months knowing he would fly one day for an airline. But it wasn't working. One way or another, somebody always put him off or jerked away his dream. He was tired of pleading, tired of playing by rules that only held him back. He hit Send again and mashed it hard. His anger pierced every gauzy future he had imagined for himself. It slammed like a hammer into his sacred inner core, the place of no more crap. He was a pilot, dammit, capable and proven, while those gatekeepers were not. So screw them.

The shelves seemed to tilt and close ranks. The storeroom funk grew warm and thick. He swallowed the panic collecting beneath his tongue and lurched for the door.

Through the vacant showroom he bolted, into a narrow shaft of sunlight, bright and unexpected, that stopped him at the outer door. He had no plan, no place to go, only this wild urge to rid himself of his constant cosmic inertia. To stop waiting, to move forward, to do what he ought to be doing.

Traffic on the avenue swelled and then careened. Drivers and pedestrians were not pondering their futures or thinking about Philip Machen. They were not worried about Marcy or whether the sky would fall. Above all, they were not seeking permission. They were squinting into sunbursts, surfing personal waves of circumstance to destinations none of them could fathom, like the kid who copied sneakers. Later, if at all, they would figure it out and adjust their heads. *Ready. Fire. Aim.*

NINE

Victorville, California. Tuesday, April 21
Still Day Four

PHILIP TAPPED the retaining bolt until it seated, then secured it with a cotter pin. Now with wings attached, the fourth copy of his little red sailplane was nearly ready to fly. Above him loomed the much larger wing of an old MD-11 cargo jet and over that, spidery trusses held up the vast roof of Chuck Zarbaugh's maintenance hangar. Good old Chuck, an irascible skinhead twice Philip's age, who loved flying and kept his mouth shut about what they were doing.

At the rear of the hangar, a metal door screeched open, then slammed shut. Tanner Newe called across the cavern, "It's tense out there, like waiting for a hurricane. I didn't see any Makers around town. " He strode into view with a pink shoebox tucked under his arm like a holiday ham. "But a bunch of homeless people set up a Maker Maker outside the abandoned Air Force barracks. Do they count as an enclave?"

Philip wiped his hands on his coveralls. Homeless folks have no influence. Where are the middle class enthusiasts, the Maker entrepreneurs? "At least they're sharing," he said.

Tanner set his pink box on a tool cart and removed its lid. "Also, Gloria says Hi."

Chuck's wife, Gloria, did restorative tattoos for mastectomy patients, which was perfect for what Philip needed. After sixteen years, the burn scar on his left wrist had faded. He wanted it visible again, proud and purple, as it was in the beginning. He laid aside his hammer and rolled up his sleeve.

Tanner snapped on a pair of nitrile gloves, hefted Gloria's gizmo, and plugged it in. Apparently, a maniac had welded a dentist's handpiece to an extension cord and two testicular solenoids. After unwrapping the tool's sterile parts, Tanner swabbed Philip's wrist with alcohol, then anointed the scar with ink. The handpiece buzzed in electrical menace as he put it to work.

"Ow." Philip knew the sting would come but his mouth didn't.

Tanner stopped. "Gloria says burn scars are thicker than normal skin, so we need to go deeper." Then he resumed, a tad too cheerfully.

Philip flexed his fingers and pretended not to feel anything. He seldom thought about the fire anymore, of the incandescent shard that branded him that night. Of struggling in the snow with a Michigan policewoman, who kept him from charging into the flames. Of his best friend, Tanner, and Tanner's mom, braving the black ice with flashlights to bring him warm blankets. Still, a bitter image would ignite from memory now and then, and the ensuing heart-stab would remind him of his terrible impotence that night. He had watched his family burn to death, as he begged to join them.

Once again, bright orange flames from sixteen years ago demanded he tend to his vows: to persist among the living, to transmute matter and energy, and to memorialize his murdered family. For him, the past had never really vanished. It persisted as indelible, replayable Kabuki, flickering scenes authenticated by pain and projected onto the rice paper screen in his mind.

"Okay," Tanner said. He swabbed the blemish and covered it

with gauze. "Good to go."

Philip rolled down his sleeve and buttoned the cuff. He selected the least greasy of two armchairs, the only seats around, and dropped into it.

"Have you heard from Big O?"

Tanner laid Gloria's needle knocker to rest and shook his head. "Nope."

Yesterday, and again this morning, they'd watched Uncle Orin's video selfie taken Sunday in Hong Kong. He was wheelchairing through the airport terminal, flapping his flannel shirtsleeves and tipping his red ballcap, giving away the remaining Cambiar phones from his satchel. But Monday morning, his flight arrived in Los Angeles without him, and he didn't respond to calls, texts, or emails.

Philip pulled out his Cambiar, intending to alert Chuck to prepare the MD-11 for another long trip, but a blinking text caught his attention.

Mr. Orin Machen is detained by People's Armed Police, Mainland. Status unknown. With greatest apologies, Charlotte Lau Tours & Guides, Hong Kong.

He stood, read it again, and "mainland" felled him back into the chair. His gaze turned inward as his lungs filled with storms and wheezes.

"They took him," he said, "to a place we cannot go."

TEN

San Leandro, California. Wednesday, April 22
Day Five

THE NEXT MORNING, in a second-floor guest room of the San Leandro Best Western Hotel, FBI Special Agent Leslie David Parker was blending a perfect cappuccino. At a chipped sideboard, he steamed three ounces of milk with his beloved Gaggia machine, producing a creamy froth.

"We do make accommodations, Ms. Lavery," he said. He ladled foam into a delicate porcelain cup of espresso, added a sprinkle of cinnamon, and served it on a silver-rimmed Lenox saucer. "But there must be limits, you understand."

Karen Lavery, Philip Machen's 44-year-old business partner, accepted the coffee. "Your friends were not very accommodating yesterday."

Parker pulled another espresso for himself while she raised her cup and flipped the saucer to check its pedigree. He smiled to himself and settled on the sofa. Ms. Lavery was such a lovely change from his usual clientele—a classy corporate beauty up to her pearls in trouble. And it was his agreeable task to help her do her duty.

Between them on a tray lay two manila folders, one thick with papers, the other flat and new. Parker sipped espresso, pleased that his cappuccino was brightening Ms. Lavery. He tapped the bigger folder.

"This is Philip Machen. I met him before you did, seven years ago. Did he tell you about his experiments in Nevada, his explosions?"

She contained her mild surprise.

"Something to do with super-density, or so he claimed. Twice, a burst of neutrons triggered alarms on our treaty verification satellites. The inspectors couldn't find any residual radiation, so they let it go. Why we didn't shut him down immediately is beyond my unscientific comprehension, but it seems our clever young friend really was up to something, wasn't he? And it turned out to be a weapon of sorts, after all. So I want you to understand, Ms. Lavery, that you are in quite a bit more trouble than simple counterfeiting. You and Mr. Machen are the subjects of a National Security Inquiry."

He sipped his demitasse.

"Your file," he said, waving the thin folder. "For your sake, you and I need to fill this with every exculpatory tidbit you can provide."

She drained her cup, crossed her smooth white legs, and scowled.

"Release my daughter."

"Philip wanted you to marry him, did he not?"

"How did . . . ?" Her green eyes sharpened. "That's none of your business."

Parker waited for the obvious to strike her. It was Tiffany who had revealed her mother's secrets, including her love of cappuccino.

"Release her, you creep. She's just a girl. She doesn't know anything about Philip that you couldn't find on the internet. You've no right to hold her."

"I agree," he said, "that her heart is pure. She corrected many false impressions last night, in her efforts to protect you." He sat back, draped an arm across the cushions. "By the public data alone, Ms. Lavery, many people would conclude that you and Philip Machen are co-conspirators, if not lovers. Right now your credibility is less than zero. Shall we improve that?"

She shoved her cup and saucer to the table's edge.

"Parker, if you don't let me call my attorney right now, I shall have him inform the court of your delays when I do reach him."

He opened her file, extended to her a paper from the Federal District Court, authorizing her indefinite detention.

"Until released or charged with a crime," he recited, "a material witness for a national security investigation does not warrant any consultations or communications beyond the place of detention." He returned the page to her file.

"Ms. Lavery, the U.S. Attorney in San Francisco is most eager to make your acquaintance. Prosecuting you would make her day, maybe her career. But this . . ." he waved the file ". . . keeps you in our care. You must help us. Depending on what you provide, we may be able to dissuade her from charging you with a crime. As we have done for others."

"I don't know where Philip is," she said, "or what he's doing, and neither does Tiffany."

From his pocket, Parker withdrew a phone, keyed it, and handed it to her. Her scowl deepened as the screen displayed a surveillance-camera view of Tiffany Lavery, lounging, bored and alone, in a different guest room of this same hotel.

"All right," she said, handing it back. "Release her, and I will tell you what you want to know."

Parker flipped open his notebook, poised his pen. Ms. Lavery crossed her arms and composed herself.

"Philip and I were never lovers. We had dinner once, to get acquainted. That was six years ago, after I agreed to run Powerpods Company for him. We went to a matinee at the Curran, then dined at Fleur-de-Lis, in the City."

"Where he proposed marriage?"

She nodded.

"I told him what a fine fellow he was, and that I expected our relationship would remain cordial, but seeing as I was ten years older and had no romantic feelings for him, there could never be anything so . . . personal. He took it well. Didn't press. And we did become friends, through our work and through his teaching Tiffany to fly. But that's all. He was my business partner and a family friend. Until Sunday."

"Yet two weeks ago, you thought he might propose."

"Tiffany invited him to the house and served us a champagne dinner. She hoped Philip would divert me from marrying Terry Quinn, whom she hates. To save me, so to speak."

Parker scribbled.

"Philip is just one of those lonely men who develops a crush on the most convenient woman. He seemed to expect me to join him, just like that, because it fit so well into his plans. Everything being convenient and self-evident, I should feel honored and swoon in his arms. Men like Philip don't give up sometimes, but I'm sure Tiffany and I were just flowers along his path. He loved us in his conditional way, then yanked us up by the roots. When he called Monday, he expected us to come away with him."

She folded her hands. "Release Tiffany."

Parker finished his note, then keyed his phone. "Bring her now, please."

Ms. Lavery tensed. When the door opened, she rushed to the girl and embraced her. Official business or not, staging reunions for tactical purposes made Parker queasy. Joy, replete with hugs and strokes, would soon give way to resentment. He was not immune to what he was doing. For the moment, mother and daughter clung to each other, relieved and oblivious. Each assured the other she was okay, and then they stood apart, uneasy in his presence.

He collected the Lenox cups, gave the women a few minutes to trade captivity stories until Tiffany broke it off.

"They wouldn't stop, Mom. They tricked me into saying things that I had to explain because they took everything the wrong way. I should have kept my mouth shut."

"We are not criminals," Ms. Lavery said to her. "Nothing you told them can change that."

"So why won't they let us go?"

Ms. Lavery raised her voice. "Agent Parker says you can leave now."

Parker met her eyes. "We release minors only to adult guardians."

"Her grandmother lives in Pleasanton."

Tiffany backed toward the door. "No. You have to come too."

"Thank you, honey, but the sooner you are safe with Grandma, the sooner we can clear this up."

Tiffany backed farther.

"Don't tell him anything, Mom. Whatever you say, he will turn it against you. I thought telling the truth would help, but I was wrong. They don't care about truth. They want you and Philip in jail."

Ms. Lavery seemed to consider this. "Makers are hurting people," she said. "They need someone to blame. If I don't tell them what really happened, they are going to invent false stories and blame me."

"Don't you see, Mom? Philip didn't do anything wrong either. He's just trying to help. He's helping poor people out of their poverty and the rest of us out of our ruts. Makers are feeding people. Nobody pays a dime. They only have to share. He didn't attack us. He didn't steal anything. He's only given. Okay, so everybody's cash turned into confetti. But he didn't steal it or destroy it. He just made it obsolete." Tears welled in her eyes.

"We owe him everything," she said. "If Philip hadn't picked you to sell Powerpods, you wouldn't have been dancing all night at the Black and White Ball, that's for sure."

Ms. Lavery recoiled. "Maybe so, but he's ripped that to pieces, hasn't he? Philip used us, Tiffany. Then he dumped us. Sold us for . . . for less than money."

"You're just pissed because he ruined your stupid ball." Tiffany spun around and charged.

Parker sidestepped, let her reach the door and throw it open. In the hall, a matron and a U.S. Marshal engulfed her.

"Tiffany, come back." Ms. Lavery tried to follow, but the marshal slammed the door in her face. She rattled the knob, pounded the door, then turned to Parker.

"You son of a bitch. You told me she was safe. I begged you to release her, but you had her strip-searched. You held her in one of those dinky rooms and grilled her half the night, scared to pieces. She's just a girl, you creep. Why don't you leave us alone and go find Philip?"

She shoved him with both hands and stomped to a far corner. "Until I know Tiffany is safe with my mother, I have nothing more to say."

Parker strolled to the sideboard. He wiped each cup with a cloth and placed them in their box. He resealed the coffee pouch and laid it with his Gaggia machine. The pittance Ms. Lavery might surrender to threats or bullying would not suffice. He wanted everything she knew and everything she thought she knew. He finished packing and indicated the armchair.

"Give me something."

She stood immobile, fists on her hips.

He strolled to the sofa, sat deliberately, and opened his notebook.

"Ms. Lavery, I'm not your enemy."

She marched to the chair, sat, and crossed her arms, glaring.

"I know what scares him. How he thinks he might fail." She unfolded her arms. "Ryles's theory for social tipping points. We didn't sell enough Pods."

"Enough for what?" He took out his phone and laid it nearby.

She tracked the gesture, evaluated the cut of his suit, the color of his eyes.

"I have his diary," she said. "That's what he called it, anyway. Now let her go."

Parker pressed a key, put the phone to his ear.

"Drive the girl to her grandmother's and have her call me at this number when she arrives." He clicked off and laid it down.

Before Ms. Lavery could speak, the phone vibrated. He checked its screen and held up two fingers. "Excuse me, please." Then to the phone, "Parker."

"Get your butt over here. You have an STU-5 coming from Washington in ten minutes."

"Yes, and good morning, Derek, but I won't arrive that quickly, will I? Are you sure it's me they want? I'm quite involved at present."

"They want you and only you, asshole. And they are in a mood. I'll buy you some time, but I want you rolling, code-fucking-three, right now."

"Coming," he said to a dead connection. He leaned back. "Where is it?"

She snorted at some private irony. "My desk at home, middle drawer. A memory stick."

He wanted to console her, to sympathize his way into her confidence, to learn her story. But he dared not ignore a summons from headquarters, even with progress staring at him through those lovely green eyes.

Eleven

PARKER DROVE eight miles to downtown Oakland under red lights and siren—code three—feeling foolish. Surely his witnesses were more important than this interruption. Why the STU-5, for pity's sake? His duty phone was secure enough, although the STU-5 had Class-A encryption and a zero-emission fiber optic connection. Sequestered as it was in a soundproof cubicle in the Communications Center, he'd never used one for real. Mere mortals were seldom invited.

The SAC, his Special-Agent-in-Charge, Derek Majers, was nowhere to be seen when Parker arrived at the dispatcher's fifth-floor sanctuary. The C-shift voice of Oakland's FBI was uncommonly standing, not sitting, at her console. She pointed to the windowless chamber, as if he needed directions, and shrugged off his question. "Who is it, by the way?"

Latching the door triggered a green light on the machine. Parker paused to collect himself, dragged a comb across his head, and smoothed his jacket. When he touched the yellow button, a man's face appeared, harried and unkempt.

"Parker? Log your ID, please."

He plugged his card into the slot. "Who is calling, if I may ask?"

"Your ID is confirmed. Sit down, Parker. Your head is out of frame. Attorney General Brayley will join you in a moment."

Parker swallowed. Ten seconds later, the AG's bulldog face filled the screen and stared through him from behind gold-rimmed glasses.

"Agent Parker, this morning I briefed the president of the United States from that pusillanimous crap you sent us yesterday, and it didn't fly. Homeland Security giggled behind her hands. Probably wet her skivvies. I'm here to tell you this is never going to happen again.

"Your SAC says you have the confidence of Ms. Powerpods, but all you've sent us so far is a crock of suppositories." He waved a sheaf of papers. "I'm telling you that suppositions derived from polite chitchat are *not* better than nothing. They invite second-guessing, not to mention the giggles. We need leads, Parker, not surmises. President Washburn wants facts. Do you read me? This case is going to make you or break you. If you fail to produce, I will see that you and your SAC spend the rest of your days cleaning latrines in Dismal Seepage, Afghanistan. Do I make myself clear?"

"Perfectly, sir."

"You left gaps. Even Homeland noticed. Machen quit college without a degree, yet five years later he comes up with Powerpods. How? You don't know. Then his girlfriend peddles them all over the world for six years until he announces Makers. But what was he doing while she was selling his Trojan horses? He already had the Makers. That's how he made 55 million Powerpods. He wasn't sipping Mai Tais with a squadron of super-models, now was he?"

"Sir, we found a quarter mile of scorched grass behind the hangar at his ranch."

"But nothing in the hangar. So what was he working on?

Another gizmo? A weapon?"

"Not sure, sir."

"Well, get sure, Parker. Do you know how feeble that sounds? You will fill these gaps and tell me what that bastard is up to, or your career is finished. I will boot you out the door myself."

"Yes, sir, I understand." *Collecting evidence is Derek's domain. I do motives and probabilities.*

Brayley hunched as if to share a secret. "It's revenge, you say, for the murder of his family? What are we supposed to do with that? Declare the guy insane and hope somebody turns him in? He's just a nerd with a gadget, for Christ's sake."

Parker raised a hand.

"The Lansing State Journal called his father an atheist recruiter who had to move his family four times to escape the backlash. The guy who killed his family was—"

"Yes, yes," Brayley said. "Some religious bozo set fire to their house, so the kid wants revenge. But why attack the whole world? We caught the bastard who burned his family. The kid knows which jail we put him in. What more does he want? Revenge against the world gives us no leverage, Parker, even if you're right. How do we find this guy? How do we stop him?"

Parker sniffed.

"By all accounts, he is sane, averse to confrontation, and highly motivated. People say he's thoughtful and—"

"Vengeance drives the man, you said. He plots destruction behind a show of benevolence. If we wind up with mass unemployment and street riots, then a lot of people are going to suffer, so his generosity is double-talk."

"One of his teachers called him cerebral, even spiritual."

"I saw that, too, Parker, and it's crap. There are no spiritual atheists. Even if there were, what's it got to do with stopping this one? I give you until eight o'clock tomorrow morning, Eastern Standard Time, to dump your psychobabble and come up with some solid leads. I want Philip Machen, and I want him now. Bend that Lavery bitch over a sawbuck and beat it out of her."

The screen went blank. *Surely the AG didn't mean that, not literally.*

Parker was right not to have mentioned Ms. Lavery's daughter. Tiffany knew Philip far better than her mother did, and just as clearly, he must protect them both from the likes of Nick Brayley. Secrets of the flowers are best coaxed by a friendly bee, he was thinking, a bee with the culprit's diary in hand. Brayley's urge to jackboot the garden was most disturbing.

TWELVE

Washington, D.C. Thursday, April 23
Day Six

ATTORNEY GENERAL NICOLAS T. BRAYLEY surveyed the supercilious faces gathered around the Cabinet Room table, and he wanted to spit. Obviously, they didn't understand. They'd wasted most of the morning plowing the counterfeiting furrow, wondering whether cash might truly be dead, and debating strategies for moving everyone to electronic money. With those irrelevancies settled, only minutes remained to address the real problem.

"If we don't eliminate the sources," he said, "counterfeit will be nothing but a sideshow."

"Back to terrorism, are we, Nick?" The vice president's jibe delighted half the room.

"We were not grandstanding yesterday," Nick replied. "There is no such thing as a friendly Trojan horse. We are under attack. That idiot is trying to torpedo America, not just our currency, and so far he's succeeding."

"We take your point, Nick." Vice President Harlan Fletcher

peered over his wire-rimmed spectacles at his rival for the Republican nomination. "However, we must treat this Machen fellow as we would a common fugitive. We must not inflate his importance by dwelling on his crimes or speculating about his motives. We must deprive this screwball and his cause—whatever it is—of every public soapbox while we undo what he's done. As far as we are concerned, these machines fell out of the sky. Does everyone understand that? Our agenda must stand before the public, not his. The media are with us, are they not, Lon?"

Lon Kissler, the president's hawk-nosed Chief of Staff, nodded.

Nick nodded, too, but for a contrary reason. Public relations, it seemed to him, was the practice of sewing your rectum shut while swearing it never produced that smell. This was no time for business-as-usual, even if it soothed public anxieties.

"We will stop these Makers," Fletcher said. "But seizing private property from law-abiding citizens requires the appearance of due process, especially with elections coming. The public is taking a hit from this counterfeiting—everyone has lost some money—so they are blaming him, not us. Let's keep it that way. Remind them who started this, and assure them we will end it."

Nick huffed.

"You can't stop malaria," he said, "by swatting mosquitoes and ignoring their larvae. If we confiscate every Maker but leave the components to build them, folks are simply going to take an extra Powerpod or two, and hide them somewhere, along with a few of those cones. It's human nature. Free goods are too juicy to resist. But if we ban Powerpods, also—and link them to the chaos that Makers are causing—we have a chance to abort this thing before it metastasizes. As of Monday, fewer than one in six American households owned a Powerpod. At a minimum, we must keep that number from growing."

He downshifted to a growl.

"Only an immediate, comprehensive ban can work. If we ban

Makers while ignoring Powerpods, the public will understand we don't mean business, that we don't have the guts to do what's right, and that they are truly on their own. Precisely what Machen wants them to believe. We should appeal to their patriotism. These machines are no damned good. They are destroying the country. But if our actions don't match our words, all is lost. I say hit 'em hard and hit 'em now. Outlaw Powerpods as well as Makers, and do it today."

Secretary of Homeland Security, Geraldine Fullwood, who was also Fletcher's Election Committee chair, could not conceal her alarm.

"There aren't any convenient abstractions to hide behind, Nick. This is not some airy-fairy civil right that everyone argues over but no one can see or touch. You are asking us to invade people's homes and seize their personal power sources, to shut them down to candlelight, with no refrigeration or air conditioning. Seizures on the scale of one-in-six households will generate enormous resentment. Even if we control the media and offer compensation, many will resist. Violent images are bound to surface, as they have overseas, and those images will generate more resistance. The Democrats will pounce, and we can kiss our hopes for the election goodbye."

"When somebody punches you in the face," he said, "you don't respond by tying one hand behind your back. If you won't defend yourself with everything you have, you are going to get clobbered. We can't risk the economy just to win the election."

Half the room frowned, the other half smirked, and Geraldine spoke to the ceiling.

"Holding the line against this recession is our proudest achievement, Nick. We can't afford to give the economy back to the Democrats. It would be giving whiskey to alcoholics."

"It's not the economy," he shot back, "It's our country." *And my nomination.*

General Clinton Holmes, Chairman of the Joint Chiefs, said,

"I don't see where this Machen fellow has any traction with the public. He's pissed off everyone with this counterfeiting, and the markets are spooked. If the markets stay down, it will cost jobs and threaten pensions. Seems to me he's handed us all the moral authority we need to roll up his little insurgency."

Geraldine hoisted an eyebrow. "What insurgency? There's been no call to arms."

"You make my point, ma'am." Holmes looked askance as heads swiveled.

"Like hell I do," she said. "Have you seen the bloodshed in Guatemala? France? Indonesia? To seize a few thousand machines? Consider that most Powerpods were sold right here, to millions of law-abiding Americans. Forget Philip Machen—in six months we face the voters. If we seize their property and turn off their lights, they will remember how this Republican administration treated them. Better to let things simmer while we build a mandate. Nobody can predict where this Maker thing will go, so until we see job losses, I counsel restraint. We cannot march into November looking like thugs."

From his place at the center of the table, President Washburn tipped back in his leather chair, once again looking too young to be sitting there. The president cleared his throat.

"Nick said it earlier. We are the government. We are supposed to ban things. So let's signal our intentions. Get Congress in bed with us. We have to stop the Makers, but circumstances warrant a staged approach. We need to demonstrate control, even if setting it up takes a day or two. Meanwhile, financial jitters work in our favor." He sat up straight.

"We go high-profile, ban Makers outright and demand that Congress ratify the ban. Then we push them to outlaw Powerpods. That spreads the heat to Congressional backsides. Either they join us, or come November, they will face the voters with empty hands. That should work, shouldn't it, Lon?"

Chief of Staff Lon Kissler nodded from his chair behind the

president, eager to protect his boss's legacy.

"The markets will go for anything with muscle," said Kissler, "and we can count on our base. The mainstream media will not oppose, so the votes should be there. Soon as our polls indicate Joe Sixpack is nervous about his paycheck, we hit the patriotism button, and demand that he surrender his Powerpods. Any opposition, we smear as weak-kneed socialism and un-American. Should be a cakewalk."

"Good." The president looked to his right. "Nick, do you agree no one is paying attention to Machen? His credibility is nil?"

All eyes turned to him.

"So far, yes, sir."

The president scanned their faces.

"Well, I think the public is with us on this. For once the stakes are personal and visible. I want you to draft the order, Nick, to ban Makers only. Have your people send it over this afternoon."

"Yes, sir."

"Lon, assemble a legal team to review Nick's stuff, then get me a meeting with the House Speaker and the Senate Majority Leader, pronto."

"Yes, sir," Kissler said.

The president shifted in his chair.

"If we can push a bill through Congress in a week or so, there won't be time for hairsplitting over Pods versus Makers. There won't be any public resistance because there won't be any violence to ignite it. We will ban Makers but encourage voluntary compliance. Enforcement comes only to scofflaws who refuse to cooperate. Do you have that, Nick? We begin with citations then move to confiscation, at our discretion. We get the media to say this is prudent. Same for Powerpods when Congress gives them the boot. That's how we fix this thing. Now make it happen."

The president stood, and Kissler followed him out.

Geraldine was too smart to gloat, but her glance told Nick he should be grateful for the compromise, for getting half-a-loaf. She was only doing her job, as he was doing his. Which was total crap. Jack Washburn's ill-advised incrementalism was going to cost a lot more than the next election. *And it's my election, damn it.*

Thirteen

Oakland, California. Still Thursday, April 23
Day Six

THAT EVENING, SUNSET YELLOWS filtered over West Oakland, casting shadows down the streets. Pedestrians strolled past shuttered buildings and bolted storefronts. Groups convened on wooden stoops of old houses or mixed with idlers at the corners. Elsewhere the traffic was commuters, but here it was slack-faced young men and their male companions, cruising without a destination, their speakers thudding like fists. Some drank openly from brown bottles.

Everett Aboud guided the Shoes-for-You van among them, still wondering about Montana Skies and if he had made a giant mistake. General Johnson rode stony-faced at his side. Last night there had been wilding and gunfire in this neighborhood. A liquor store was looted. General decided Marcy should move into the shoe store for a while until things settled down.

At the next corner, under a limp sales banner, a clutch of onlookers cheered two drunks smashing windshields in a used car lot. General directed Everett to turn, and they continued to a three-story building the color of railroad grit, where he parked.

"Keep the motor running."

Across the street, a score of people queued on a barren knoll, looking like the returns line at a department store. Each bore a box or a sack, which they took pains to conceal, lest anyone trouble them. In the shadows of their building stood a full-size Maker.

The supplicants waited turns to use the machine then rushed away afterward, guarding their fresh copies. A skinny woman in shower shoes shined a flashlight into their bundles, occasionally accepting an item from those who had finished, and passing this tribute to a girl who took it inside. A boy straddled a fire hose roped to a cone strut where he cycled a valve to refill the upper cone after each copy.

The van door rumbled open. General stuffed a blue duffel and a green suitcase under the middle seat. Then Marcy climbed in behind Everett, and they traded glances.

"Say, Home Boy."

"Sister Newshound. You been getting into trouble?"

"No, but I came close this morning, up in Berkeley."

General got in and shut the door.

"Take us home, Everett."

Everett chose a parallel street to avoid the windshield smashers.

"So what happened in Berkeley?" Her face eluded him in the mirror.

"I got some clips and sold them," she said. "Enough to pay for a new camera. But I should have taken someone with me. Seems everybody who wasn't in the frame wanted to help. Spent half my time shooing away helpers."

Everett could imagine.

"Anyway," she said, "somebody set up one of those big Makers in the park, at the edge of the university. And they hung a sign, People's Maker. By nine o'clock it was a party, with drums and flutes and folks copying stuff. One guy had a bugle and was giving away copies, so things were getting loud. Of course, the cops came. To keep people from making dope or guns. But the crowd was already lit, so it was this honking, thumping street celebration, with incense and ganja and drinks from paper bags, until a blue convertible pulled up to the stoplight.

"Some dude calls out a name, and five guys jump this motorist, yank him out of his Caddie, and commence pounding him. He whips out a pistol, which goes off in the scuffle. Scares the fun right out of everybody. But instead of running away, the crowd piles on. They got the gun away from him, so nobody got shot. By this time, the cops have their guns drawn, and they're shouting for everybody to get down and don't move. Then they drag this driver out from under the dog pile and arrest him."

Everett squirmed against his seatbelt, trying see her face.

"Turns out Mr. Motorist sells dope, and the crowd wanted retribution for him getting rich off poor junkies, selling poison and such. The cops let me interview him before they hauled him away.

"Picture this guy. He's Samoan or something—enormous man. And he's bawling like a baby, saying he can't make his game no more on account of his cash is trash. And he can't take no checks or cards on account of they're traceable. His clients are making their own junk, so they don't buy no more from him. Says he owes five thousand dollars to his supplier, and he can't pay, all his funds being tied up in drugs or worthless cash. He was happy to be arrested, so his supplier can't kill him."

Everett guided the van onto Broadway and headed east.

"Anyway,"Marcy said, "I recorded this sidewalk sociology and sold it to WebNews."

"Good way to get shot," General said.

"I have to go where things are happening, Uncle General. There's no news if I play it safe, sitting on my rotunda."

General shook his head.

Everett recalled her rotunda. He longed to know what her

scent might be, should they ever get that close. She was tracking Maker events and Maker people, following the Big Story. If he ever found a steady job in a cockpit, he would be flying over a changed world, one he needed to understand. Which was why, more than ever, he needed Marcy. If she knew Ms. Lavery, she must be close to figuring it out.

"Call me," he said, leaning on the sincerity. "Next time."

In the rear-view mirror, her face was all shadows, though her silence seemed to hover one notch short of "no." A positive sign.

When they arrived at Shoes-for-You, Marcy disappeared upstairs with her luggage while General chained the driveway and Everett mounted plywood covers over the first-floor windows. When he finished and had locked the security screen over the door, there was no reason to hang around. So he said good night and departed on his motorcycle.

Just before the freeway, the streetlights flickered out. To his left, the Grand Lake Theater marquee hissed into darkness. He turned around, in case the Johnson's needed help.

Farther up the avenue, islands of illumination appeared in the hills. People with Powerpods, including Shoes-for-You, still had electricity. So he returned to the freeway and merged into the flow, feeling better about things.

He hadn't expected to see Marcy again, though the hope had plagued him since he burned his bridges with Montana Skies. Helping her might not get him into her bed, but he needed to know about Makers. And about her. Marcy would be his new project, his interim career. And tomorrow he would see her again, a prospect he savored all the way home.

When he got there, Bobby had arrayed his empties in a circle on the coffee table. Bright figures moved silently on the wall screen, their luminous mouths miming a commercial.

"What time is it?" Bobby groused.

Everett stopped in the laundry room to strip off his leathers, wet from tule fog.

"Sorry," he said. "I stayed to board up the windows, in case there's trouble."

"Every night, you're late."

Everett drew a comb through his matted hair and joined Bobby.

"What are you doing, Dad?" An accusation.

Bobby hoisted a bottle, admired it.

"Celebrating."

Everett diverted to his bedroom.

"You got snail-mail," Bobby said.

Everett returned for the envelope, already open, from the Federal Aviation Administration. *Notice of Suspension* was all he needed to read.

"I thought you got your stolen ID straightened out with them."

Everett tried to look annoyed about the rifled envelope. He took a deep breath before confessing his most recent detention. Regarding Montana Skies, he said nothing.

"Well, if that doesn't beat all." Bobby lowered his bottle to the table with deliberate precision, then chuckled low and mean. He shook his head and slapped his knees.

"I can't get a job, and you can't stay out of trouble for more than three weeks." He threw back his head and laughed as if it were a great joke. He laughed so hard the tears came.

"I put everything I had into your career." He coughed and swallowed. "Everything. And this is how you handle yourself? What is your problem, Son? What do you think you're doing?"

"Helping."

"You can't leave it alone, can you?" Bobby coughed again, reached for his cigarettes. "Always sticking your pecker into some knothole, just to see what's in there."

"I was helping a friend. You'd like her."

Bobby snorted. "You've got the hots—that's what I see. Always hot for more trouble than you can handle. What were you thinking? She's black, for crying out loud."

"She's your best friend's niece, your only best friend." Everett couldn't believe his father had said that, drunk or not.

Bobby stood up, swayed. "You just have to find the most trouble there is and jump right in there, don't you, Son? Can't resist anything that jiggles. When are you going to wise up?"

"Wise like you? Not in my lifetime."

"Going to be a short trip, the way you're headed."

"Go to bed, Dad."

"Don't you want to know what I'm celebrating?" Bobby lit a cigarette. "The bank put our cash in escrow, see, until they prove it's not counterfeit. Nobody knows when that will be, so yesterday they bounced our rent payment. I called the agency to explain, but they don't care. They got lots of tenants with the same excuse." He reached for another beer.

Everett tossed his envelope on the table.

"So copy your guns, Dad. Sell them at the club. Copy your dirt bike and my road bike. Sell them too. Sell everything. The agency knows we're good for the rent. We never miss."

Bobby shook his head.

"Owner wants us out. Before the real estate market chokes and pukes like the stock market. She's booting us whether we pay or not. By the time we appeal, the house will be sold out from under us."

He blew a jet of smoke through his nose. A challenge.

"Out there in the yard," he said, "we have this damn fine machine to make us anything we want, make us rich by copying stuff, but in ten days we are on our asses, evicted for nonpayment. Far as I'm concerned, she can keep her security deposit. I'm not putting any more work into this dump." He took a pull from his bottle.

"In Ireland, they celebrate times like these. They call it a wake."

Fourteen

Livermore, California. Friday, April 24
Day Seven

IN THE MORNING, fog from the bay penetrated Livermore Valley, chilling Everett's commute and stitching ice into his disposition. He arrived at Shoes-for-You chilled and achy. His neck burned from the tension of splitting lanes for an hour. He parked at Maurice's Bar and strode alone across the vacant avenue, wondering if the whole world was up there on the freeway, creeping through the mist.

General's security curtain was up, the plywood covers were put away, and the display windows glowed with warmth. He was late.

Up the avenue, a bag lady shepherded her rusty shopping cart to the burger joint and tried to trade a fifth of whiskey for a burrito. Somebody had egged a brown Nissan parked in front of Maurice's, and Everett figured the car's owner was lucky. The news said rowdies had set fires last night to illuminate their street parties before they looted an electronics store on West Grand Avenue.

General looked up from his screen as Everett plodded through the door.

"Crude oil just fell to five bucks a barrel, and Wall Street is shut down. President Washburn declared a ten-day bank and market holiday. They say he's going to outlaw Makers."

Everett waved and proceeded to the storeroom. Who cared about Wall Street or oil prices? Or whether he would fly again. Earning the rent had been his proof to Bobby of his worth. He was the responsible one, the provider. But now their rent could not be paid even if he earned it, and come payday, what would his check buy? He was only trying to carve out one little place in this corner of the world, but he was failing: failing Bobby, failing himself, failing their future.

Always the world touched him, never could he touch it back. And when it punched him, hard and out of nowhere, he simply had to endure it. Every time.

He emerged from the storeroom to find the bag lady, unsteady on the wet sidewalk, peering at him. She of indeterminate age and dubious hygiene wore a fur coat. She leered and waved a fifth of Jack Daniels. In trade for what? Shoes?

Yesterday, Charlene encouraged her with a tuna sandwich. But not today. Enough was enough. Everett rushed outside to confront the bitch.

"Get the hell out of here. Stop coming by. We don't want you hanging around anymore. Understand? Go take a bath. Sober up. Beat it."

She gyrated her bony hips and leered.

"You wanna see my refrigerator? It's full."

Everett picked up a stone. "Get moving."

Bourbon Lady propelled her treasures clinking and rattling past him. After a short distance she paused to spit.

"You just got to be free," she said.

He threw the stone at her feet. "Don't come back. You hear me?"

"What are you doing?" General appeared at his side, matched his hands-on-hips pose and glared, not at the wraith but at him.

"You smell that?" Everett said. "That's urine and vomit, with a dash of Pine-Sol. The woman reeks. She keeps hanging around, driving off business."

"What business would that be, do you suppose?" General waved in each direction, up and down the empty sidewalk. A lone car hissed by as Charlene joined them.

"What's wrong?" she said.

"Nothing." Everett swept around her and into the store. They followed him to a fitting bench, where he flung himself onto his stomach. They hovered nearby until he rolled over and sat up.

"I got a flying job, up in Montana, but I turned it down. Now Bobby and I are getting evicted." He told them about the rent and the deadline to vacate. "He was drunk when I got home last night, then he got a whole lot drunker when I told him about Monday and the FBI. I didn't mention Montana. He would have punched me. Says if I can't stay clear of trouble, I'm too dumb to be a pilot, too stupid to be his son. Said he's going to stay drunk and shoot it out with anyone who tries to put him out of his house. His house, not ours. There's no *us* anymore."

General retrieved his Cambiar and keyed it.

"Don't bother," Everett said. "He won't answer."

"Bakery up the street is open," Charlene said. "How about a Danish, Everett?"

General put away his phone. "Maybe I should go over there and see him."

"Go where, Uncle?" Marcy bounded down the stairs in a quick rhythm.

"Tracy. To see Everett's daddy."

Marcy detected Everett's funk and kept her distance. Meanwhile, a customer came in, giving him an excuse to slip away. He could feel their eyes on his back, but tending to business was why they were paying him, wasn't it? He rushed up one aisle, forgot why he'd gone that way, and blundered into the customer, Alonso the jeweler. Everett apologized, continued to the counter where he pretended to arrange an important display of socks.

Charlene introduced Alonso to Marcy, and the suave *paisano* seemed to purr. He begged a favor. Would General help him copy a Powerpod? For his sister, up in Kensington? "She doesn't have one," he said.

"Of course, of course. Be happy to."

General and Alonso conspired in pleasant tones until General called, "Everett."

Who shook himself and returned. The women had departed.

"I need you to build a ramp to copy a Powerpod." General smiled benignly. "Can you do that?"

Yeah, I can do that. He sketched a frame and listed the materials he would need. Then, while he copied lumber in the storeroom, General took the van with Alonso to fetch the jeweler's Powerpod from his store.

Everett was measuring for a saw cut when Marcy reappeared, sleek and sexy in tight slacks and a black pull-over. She set a steaming mug and a cinnamon roll before him. Despite his hunger for her and her offering, he drew a pencil along his carpenter's square, unable to meet her eyes. She twisted off a flirty glance before sashaying away, just like Monday. *Damn.* He needed to talk to her, but first, he needed to tamp down his feelings and get his head straight.

ONCE THEY COPIED Alonso's Pod, Everett and General towed the copy north through Berkeley, into the Kensington hills, searching for a beige stucco house with a green roof and a fig tree in the yard. An offshore breeze was clearing the fog, spreading wispy sunlight in its wake.

"Do you have all your clothes on, General? We are getting looks."

General grunted as he braked for a stoplight. "Gawkers," he said.

"Must be the Pod we're towing. Probably wondering where they can get one."

"Beggar's eyes," General said. "Never thought I'd see that up here."

The light changed, and General drove the remaining blocks in silence.

Once they rolled the new Powerpod into the lady's backyard and finished hooking it up, Alonso thanked them by pressing small gifts into their hands. Everett opened his while General drove them back to Oakland. Crystalline teardrops on a bed of cotton. Probably worth a thousand dollars, before last weekend. Until now, he'd never had much use for diamond earrings, though he couldn't spring them on Marcy just any old time. It would have to be an occasion.

Back at Shoes-for-You, a dozen people queued at the showroom door. As General pulled into the driveway, the crowd rushed to surround the van.

"You have Powerpods? We need Powerpods."

"Please, sir, I will buy your Powerpod. How much do you want?"

General opened his door to block them.

Everett got out on the other side, made downward sweeps of his hands. "Okay," he said. "Calm down. We have a couple of Pods, all right?"

"Only two? I will buy one." The man waved his checkbook.

"Two is not enough. What about the rest of us?"

"This is a shoe store," General groused, and he bulled his way through them.

"We seen you haul that Powerpod. You got one of them Makers in there, don't you? The kind that copies theirselves? It don't cost you nothing to make copies, mister."

"We will pay you."

"Okay, okay," Everett said. "Go around front, and we will meet you there, one at a time."

"What's your price?"

General shouted, "Man said go to the front," and the crowd backed. He frosted the glare he gave Everett. As he unlocked the service door, a woman broke clear and rushed him.

"We need to get a Pod, Mister General, so our lights don't go out, like last night."

"Yes, ma'am." General softened. "Just go to the front." Then he pulled Everett inside and bolted the steel door.

"The hell are you doing, Aboud? We can't be selling Powerpods."

"Hey, you saw those people. What could I say? No, we don't have any. Now go away. That's lame, General. They know it, and you know it."

"So what? This is a shoe store."

"Yeah, well." Everett bobbed his head. "It's a shoe store, and maybe it's also a place you can get a Powerpod." He rubbed his sore neck.

"What are you going to do, General? Those people live around here, don't they? That's why they came. 'Cause they live here, and the power went out, and they saw that Pod we copied for Alonso. I don't know about economic terrorism, but it seems to me you can't shun your neighbors if you want them to be there when you need them. You can't eat shoes, you know."

"What are you saying?"

"You're worried we might be helping Philip Machen? Hurting the country, like those faces say on TV? Well, I say screw Philip Machen, and screw those birds that squawk about stuff they can't control.

"This is our country, and this neighborhood has got to be the most important part of it, right? So how does it hurt anyone if you help your neighbors? What good is a person who won't help the folks next door, or up the street?" He licked his lips. "Especially if he can make a few bucks."

General bore into him. "What do you plan to charge them,

smart guy?"

Everett led the way to the sales room and strode to the counter.

"About time you two got back." Charlene squatted nearby, fitting shoes for a little girl and her mother. "I had to lock them out. Been waiting on shoe customers, one at a time. The rest want Powerpods."

General grabbed Everett's arm. "If we copy more Pods, we are doing exactly what that starry-eyed idealist wants us to do."

"You did it for Alonso."

General didn't offer an excuse but said, "From a legal standpoint, we could be slitting our throats."

Everett shrugged. "Maybe the point where the law stands should move a little."

General's eyes widened. "Where did that come from?"

Everett didn't know either, but the words kept coming.

"Don't you get it? They'll just call you stingy and find their Pods someplace else. But they won't forget you refused to help them. All you can offer people now is your goodwill and a pile of shoes they can get elsewhere. So what business are you really in?"

Everett was shouting. He didn't know why except it pissed him off that the whole world had changed and nobody was altering course.

General stared, open-mouthed until someone rapped on the glass door. "All right. All right," he said.

Everett waited for General's nod, then keyed the register to make it ring. He smiled at Charlene and bestowed a flourish on her customers.

"Attention Shoes-For-You shoppers. We are no longer a shoe store. From now on, we are a footwear and Powerpods emporium. No cash, please. Credit subject to approval."

Outside, the crowd was pressing against the windows, peering and grumbling.

"What are we going to charge them?" General whispered.

"Whatever they want," Everett said. "If they set the price, they won't feel cheated. Anything we get is pure profit. What do we care if one of them lays out big bucks and the next one wants to swap for a case of motor oil? Either way, we're ahead, and the customer gets what she paid for."

"Better keep the price down," General warned. "Better keep it even too. Soreheads carry guns in this town."

"Two hundred bucks," Everett declared. "That's way less than Powerpods Company was charging." This came to him so easily, so clearly. Could it also melt some of his cosmic inertia? He tipped his chin toward the crowd outside. "What do you say?"

General palmed his keys and went to the door. He loosed the bolt and stepped back.

"You're right, Everett. I believe you're right. We need their business, and we don't want to start a riot. But I still feel like a dope dealer."

Everett cracked a smile then reeled it back.

"It ain't dope, General."

The first customer rushed in.

"You guys take Visa?"

FIFTEEN

Oakland, California. Still Friday, April 24
Day Seven

AGENT PARKER'S duty phone rattled on the kitchen counter. It displayed the dour face of his boss, Special Agent in Charge, Derek Majers.

"What are you doing, Parker?" Majers wasn't asking. He was clearing the decks. "Did Ms. Lavery give you anything worth a damn?"

Parker massaged his forehead. All week, facts and notes from the case file had wandered aimlessly through his mind, soldiers without a map, while Philip Machen's diary, stuffed with equations and technical jargon, had yielded only confusing glimpses of the man who wrote them. Parker could not deflect the judgment in Derek's voice, so he said nothing.

"Okay, Les. Nice try. Get some lunch, then report to the office. I'm reassigning you."

The connection dropped, confirming the new assignment could only be bad; that it had already been decided; and that no appeals would be considered.

You couldn't tell me over the phone, could you, Derek? You're going to shame me in front of the troops, aren't you? Parker smacked the counter with the butt of the phone. Then he called his erstwhile partner, Nedra Gaffin.

"It's robbery," she said, meaning he was reassigned to that division.

Worse than stupid. Every moron knew cash was trash, that there weren't going to be any more bank heists. And that solving old bank jobs should not be a priority while free drugs and firearms were celebrated nightly in the streets. Capturing Philip Machen was everyone's top priority, yet Derek was pulling him off the case.

"It was Nick Brayley, wasn't it?" He kicked his stool.

"Would that please you?"

"Okay, listen. I'll be taking lunch. First alarm that rings in, you call me."

Nedra told him to stop feeling sorry for himself, so he disconnected her. She wasn't the one being slammed.

If they were taking him off the case, there was only one reasonable response: put himself back on it. Track the bastard, no matter what they said. If he couldn't decrypt this guy, get inside his head, they might never find him. He needed a frequency or a channel to which the suspect attuned himself. Which brought him back to the case file and the suspect's diary.

Philip Machen had not blundered into Powerpods and Makers. He'd planned from the beginning to yoke matter and energy to his personal agenda. And hidden within the mathematics and the personal notes of his diary was a most unscientific term, a religious word. Which impelled Parker, now that he thought about it, to dig into a drawer and retrieve his Cambiar net phone, the one with encryption. He searched its directory for Dr. Harpreet Sugand and called the number. If the priest was also using a Cambiar, it could mean he was a Machen sympathizer. Or it could mean he just liked free phones.

"Sugand comma Harry," said a familiar voice. "Please leave your message."

"Dr. Sugand, please call Les Parker at your earliest convenience. Thank you." He linked his own number.

Ten minutes later, Harry's reply saved him from returning to the office.

They met at the food bank Harry ran in Emeryville, near the bay, off the East Shore Freeway. Wedged like a gym locker between an auto body shop and a tire emporium, the Fellowship Food Bank presented itself as a steel roll-up door, currently shut, and a dented man-door, currently open. Garlands of rusty razor wire had stained the flat roofline and streaked the yellow walls.

Harry came to the door wearing his trademark look of repressed amusement. In a baseball cap and scuffed sneakers, he resembled a convenience store clerk rather than a doctor of divinity. No doubt his vein of natural goofiness was why Harry worked here instead of uptown with the bishop, but he had once proved invaluable on a kidnapping case.

"Lester, good day. How are you?"

"Hello, Harry. It's Leslie, but I'm pleased to see you."

"Leslie. Sorry. So many names." He tapped his head. "But I have kept your face."

Cartons of food piled to the skylights reminded Parker that he had skipped lunch. Between the door and Harry's tiny office stood a small Maker, not a Maker Maker, its garden hose sagging from the upper cone like a limp noodle. So this was what the fuss was all about, the sheet metal Gorgon that held the world in thrall. Parker had never actually touched one.

Harry noted his interest.

"We don't stock-out anymore," he said, "but donations used to come by the truckload. Now we get a box or two from the back seat. No more vans or semis. Mostly, our clients don't have Makers, so we are running extra deliveries until we must stop. After that, I don't know. The Lord will provide."

He ushered Parker into his cluttered office. They sat on folding chairs, faced each other across a wooden, tea-stained desk.

"What brings you, Leslie? Not our Maker, I hope. Not another kidnapping."

"Nothing like that. It's personal this time, Harry, so please keep this confidential." He laid an old USB memory stick on the desk. "I would appreciate your professional opinion."

"Truly?" Harry doffed his cap. "A priest's opinion won't buy you much in a courtroom, I am thinking." He folded his arms. "Sure, why not? I sit all day. Brains and buttocks need exercise."

Parker's chuckle drifted back to the subject before them. "I want to know what sort of man wrote this," he said. "Who does he think he is? What drives him? What does he want?"

"He is your suspect?"

"A fugitive."

"But not the common criminal. Nobody cares what a hooligan thinks. What did he do?"

Parker nodded at the stick. "Better if he tells you."

"Okay then, what did he give us?"

"It's a ten-year diary, beginning fifteen years ago. Thirty-one hundred pages."

"Then you have him." Harry tapped the stick. "He's in here."

Parker nodded and made his plea.

"Our people scanned it. They analyzed it. Decided he's a fish, by golly, and they are fishermen. So they are casting nets. They don't appreciate that a rare species might not feed like a mackerel or swim like a salmon. I tried to warn them, but they are busy, casting nets."

"Fishers of men. You are teasing me, Leslie." Harry dropped the chip into the pocket of his polo shirt. "You have read it?"

Parker nodded. "Most of it."

"Then I'm flattered. Cops don't care what I think, usually."

Parker shrugged. "Taking the measure of someone's character is what we do, isn't it, you and I? If a cop or a priest can't read people, we are useless to our professions."

"Suppose we disagree?" Harry's lip curled toward mischief.

"Then one of us is a baboon-faced fraud."

Harry's guffaw made his day. If this guy couldn't help him, no one could.

"I can't afford to be mistaken about this, Harry. I'm betting the farm on this one."

The convenience store cleric nodded solemnly and donned his ball cap. He reached behind his desk and came up with two bottles of Belgian beer, Hoegaarden, slick and icy. He opened them with a flourish and stood for a toast.

"To fishers of men."

Parker rose and clinked on it.

"To fishers of wayward men."

SIXTEEN

Oakland, California. Still Friday, April 24
Day Seven

WOOZY FROM THE BEER, Parker drove home mechanically, suppressing all but the mundane thoughts and motions he needed to arrive and park safely. He unlocked his ninth-floor condo and carried in the box containing his Gaggia machine. All week he'd endured paper-cup coffee and looked forward to a fresh cappuccino in the morning after a full night's rest. This was the plan, so far, for his one-day weekend, starting tonight. A plan he affirmed by switching on the lights.

He unclipped his service pistol, laid it on the counter, then retrieved a tall, black can from the fridge. Barley-colored suds soon flowed into a glass that he raised to eyelevel. Guinness never tasted quite so cold as the can felt. Did the froth insulate the ale, or was it a trick of the senses? A physicist would know the answer, a wiz like Philip Machen.

The broken doorbell thunked and hummed, as it had for a year, whenever someone pressed the button. He checked his watch.

Friday, 7:56 p.m. *Damn.* He'd forgotten.

He turned on the wall screen and selected his security camera. The expected swathe of white hair appeared over a chalky forehead and a lens-distorted nose. He switched the screen to a news channel before answering the door.

"Mrs. P, I'm so sorry. I just—"

"Leslie, may I come in, please?"

Lucille Petzold, well into her seventies, did not seem angry. She clutched a cardboard box to her bosom and beamed like a proud six-year-old, the sparkle in her eyes overpowering the pallor of her cheeks. He'd never seen his neighbor so excited.

"Of course." He drew open the door.

"You are forgiven," she said, "but not off the hook. I just have to tell you the good news. You remember my sclero-friend, Jimmy? The one with three months to live? He got his Swiss Treatments yesterday, and—" She jostled the carton. "He sent Maker copies to the whole darn group." She put down the carton, raised her gloved hands, and wiggled her blue woolen fingers.

"No more scleroderma. This stuff sells for ten-thousand a bottle, though you can't buy it around here, even if you have the moolah. Not approved. But our group studied the data. It's definitely a cure. Doesn't just treat symptoms. It knocks the disease right into remission. So the scars and the thickening heal up as soon as your immune system stops attacking your tissues."

Parker shut the door and followed her to the yellow chintz sofa his ex-wife had once adored.

"I only have these skin things," Mrs. P said, "which is bad enough. Jimmy's disease went straight to his lungs and kidneys. It was killing him. This stuff is saving his life."

She rattled the box, and her joy made him smile.

"Are you sure it's safe?" he said.

She looked hurt.

"The website tells you the doses, Leslie. Jimmy takes one-hundred milligrams. I'll take ten. Ever since the chemotherapy triggered it, I've had these cold hands and awful skin. I want to stop wearing gloves all the time. I want to wash in cold water without firing up the pains. I want to go swimming. And now I can." She dog-paddled the air but stopped. "You're not going to report me, are you?"

"Where did I put those handcuffs?" He patted his trousers. "No . . ." He grinned and gently took her hands. "Prescriptions are not my jurisdiction." He danced her in a circle until she dimpled up a fresh smile. "Unless you start selling that stuff," he warned.

She broke free, scooped the box, and cradled it. To her left, the wall screen displayed a familiar face, toward which she nodded.

"I should send her some Swiss Treatments, for her little girl."

On screen, Senator Selena Gilmar, in a trim, dark suit, was addressing reporters on the steps of a courthouse. Recent polls had given her a slight lead over the other Democrats running for president. The chyron crawling below her waist said, *Gilmar Opposes Powerpods Ban.* Parker reached for his remote control.

"I didn't know her daughter had scleroderma," he said, and he turned up the sound.

"Who says the American people can't be trusted to produce their own electricity?" Senator Gilmar glowed with well-dressed confidence. "If we trust our citizens with automobiles and handguns, we ought to trust them with electric generators too. I say we can't afford to shut down millions of Powerpods in the middle of a recession. I say we should put covers on them, so they can't be used as Makers, then lock those covers. Confiscation and blackouts are not the American way."

Parker muted her. For good measure, he stepped between the screen and his guest.

"I believe I will," Mrs. Petzold said. Which puzzled him until she added, "Send her the treatments."

"She can probably afford her own, don't you think?"

"Then she can share the surplus with somebody else."

Parker nodded. "About dinner . . . I'm so sorry. I forgot."

"Right," she said. "It's Eggplant Parmesan. You're still coming, aren't you?"

"Well . . . . What wine goes with that?"

"Chianti?" She guessed. "Pinot Grigio? You choose. It's going to be a lovely dinner. No politics."

"I'm looking forward to it, Mrs. P." He grinned. "Can you give me ten minutes?"

"Oh, dear." She leaned around him. "I hope they don't hurt that poor man."

On screen, a passport photo of Orin Machen, Philip's uncle, hovered at the shoulder of a trench-coated reporter on some rain-slick, big-city street. *Shanghai*, said the crawl. Then in bold letters: *Convicted.*

"He was here, you know."

"Excuse me?" Parker stared at the retired school teacher as if she had said penis.

"Him. Not the young one. Orin Machen spoke at the dedication when they opened Prospect Shores. His foundation built this place." She nudged Parker with a wink and an elbow. "But you knew that. You're investigating him, right?"

"Of course."

"I have a picture of him and me. I'll dig it out for you."

"Yes, I'd like to see that," he said, not quite believing her.

"You're such a nice man, Mr. Parker, trading dinners with an old lady." She patted his hand with gloved fingers and moved to the door.

"Well, I cheat," he said, provoking an eyebrow. "When my turn comes—that salmon and dill sauce last month? Catered."

Her giggle buoyed him.

"I love a man who can't lie," she said. "See you in ten."

"I'm glad," he said, as she clutched her drugs, "that you'll be getting better."

He escorted her out, then rushed to the utility closet at the end of his hallway. Each Prospect Shores apartment had its own

Powerpod, tucked out of sight. His was still there, beneath the shelf on which three dusty cartons had perched since he and his wife had moved in, three years ago. He pulled down one box and split its seals. Cone segments, black and shiny, came to hand. He left them there, returned to his Cambiar, and linked it to the wall screen.

A quick search brought up the Leonard Machen Foundation, chaired by Philip's uncle, Orin. Worldwide, their foundation had built or converted 937 residential complexes, 889 within the United States alone. Most were smaller than Prospect Shores, but every single residence had its own Powerpod. They'd planned it from the beginning, sequestering Pods and cones inside gated, ready-made enclaves.

The ale in his glass had gone warm. So far, the Maker crisis had spared him no shopping time. He should ask Mrs. P to copy a few cans for him, along with her medicine, to tide him over. Or he could attach the cones and do it himself. So simple, so easy.

And this, too, was intended—by Philip and his uncle. Could their machines ever be stopped? If Congress banned Powerpods, as President Washburn demanded, would Parker be searching his own building to root out the lawbreakers? Would he be arresting Mrs. P?

He switched off the wall screen and sank into his chair. Every cop's nightmare was enforcing the law upon a friend or a family member. Only the hope of due process would allow him to do that. Just thinking about it depressed him.

But if Orin Machen was the first degree of separation and Mrs. P the second, that put him just two degrees away from his quarry. He reached for his phone. He was thinking Derek Majers should send him to China to beg the authorities to let him interview a convicted American spy.

SEVENTEEN

Prince George's County, Maryland. Saturday, April 25
Day Eight

IN NICK BRAYLEY'S DREAM, a grapefruit buzzed like a hornet. The buzzing grew insistent, and he woke with a start, his Cambiar rattling on the nightstand. He brought it to his ear and said, "What?"

A female voice jabbered about alert and duty, while beside him Yvonne rolled away, taking the covers with her.

"What?"

"Sir," the woman enunciated, "this is a national security alert. I am DOJ Duty Officer Natale Rosales. President Washburn has ordered DEFCON-2. You are required to report, sir."

Defense Condition Two. One level short of going to war, all military assets on full alert.

"What's happened?"

"Your car is on its way, sir. You are required to report to the Situation Room."

"I know what's required. I need to know who is threatening us."

"Sir, I only know—"

"DEFCON-2. Yes. Thank you, Natale. You've done your job."

He hung up and reached for his encrypted STU-5, the ugly black one. He punched in the Pentagon number for the Chairman of the Joint Chiefs. Clint Holmes would know the score.

"General Holmes's office. How may I assist you?"

"Tell Clint that Nick Brayley wants to know what's going on."

"Yes sir, one moment." The bastard put him on hold. A different voice came back.

"Sir, this is Colonel Silva. The People's Republic of China is shooting down satellites. And they executed an American citizen."

"Whose satellites?"

"Commercial Commsats. Cambiar birds. We're not sure why. Five so far, but it looks like they're not done shooting."

"Who did they kill?"

"Orin Machen, Philip's uncle. *People's Daily* claims he was running a CIA operation to destabilize the country, so they stood him up for a ten-minute trial and hanged him an hour later."

"I don't suppose he told them where his nephew might be."

"No word on that, sir, but the PRC has mobilized their military and sealed the borders. Our State Department says they are burning up the diplomatic wires too."

"Burning?"

"Figure of speech, sir. Telling us they're upset. They threatened to break diplomatic relations and expel our ambassador."

"Thank you, Colonel. I'm on my way. Tell Clint to return my call when he has a minute, will you?"

"Yes, sir. Good night, sir."

Nick hung up and rolled out of bed. Good night, my ass. If the Chinese hanged Orin Machen, how are we going to find out what he was doing over there?

He dressed in the dark and did not kiss Yvonne goodbye. Despite her earplugs, she was disturbed already.

When the car arrived, he slouched into the back seat. What if

Philip Machen's team was trying to provoke hostilities? He phoned the FBI office in Oakland, California. That dipstick, Parker, took the call.

"You got anything new on public enemy number one?"

"Sir, we believe he's still in California, and—"

"So, same as yesterday."

"Sir, we have six—"

"Shut up, Parker. Listen to me. China is shooting down Cambiar satellites. Now, what do you suppose those satellites have been doing over China that got those nice folks so riled? Don't answer that. Just find Machen. I don't care how you do it. Tell Majers to blow his people out of bed and don't let 'em go back until they catch that son-of-a-bitch."

He hung up. Incompetence was not worth listening to.

THE WHITE HOUSE Situation Room was in full crisis mode when he arrived. Video projections extended three of the walls into cyberspace. A trio of suits presided at a central table, their backs to the door. President Washburn hunched in one leather chair between his chief of staff and a pudgy, red-haired man whom Nick had not seen for six months—Alec Drexler, the National Security Advisor. Secretaries of Defense and State, plus Central Intelligence and Homeland Security, gazed from wall panels to the left. To the right, military readiness symbols dotted a Mercator projection of the Earth. And dead ahead, a map of Asia glowed green with yellow markers denoting military sites of the People's Republic of China. Three Xs blinked red, two within the PRC and one over the Western Pacific, possibly the intercept points of the downed satellites.

A staffer briefed him. "Six hours ago, all Cambiar satellites simultaneously triggered their ground units—which is to say, every hand-held Cambiar—to activate continuous encryption. Since then, all Cambiar net traffic has gone encrypted. Only the senders and recipients know what's exchanged between them. With digital tunneling, peer-to-peer algorithms, and satellite routing there are no choke points to restrict the flow. We can break the encryption, but it takes hours." Someone called the staffer away, and Nick took a seat in the corner.

No wonder the Chinese are pissed. Makers have flooded them with counterfeit money and free goods, and now this. They've lost control of peer-to-peer communications, including the internet. And so have we.

Two Trojan horses in one week, both pushing the world toward chaos. Philip Machen gave the bad guys unlimited weapons and supplies with his Maker machines. Now his Cambiars are giving them secure communications. Space-X had launched 26 satellites for Orin Machen's Cambiar Company, yet the Air Force was tracking 32 in orbit.

Nick stood up and spoke loudly. "We should tell PRC to keep shooting. Take out all his birds."

Everyone looked to President Washburn, who frowned over his shoulder.

"No missiles," he said. "Not yet, anyway. We are not going to risk starting World War Three over a handful of commercial satellites." He addressed Drexler, his National Security guy. "I want threat assessments on this encryption thing. Specifically, I want to know if we need to shut down the Cambiar satellites ourselves or go after the hand-held units, or both. But we are not going to launch until we are convinced it is the best course. I need intel, analysis, options." He stood and spoke to the wall screens.

"I want State to reassure the Chinese through regular, front-door channels. Tell them Philip Machen is trying to destabilize us too. I want Defense to reset DEFCON to normal. And I want those Cambiar threat assessments on my screen by noon today."

On his way to the door, the president flagged Nick and General Clinton Holmes.

"Walk with me, gentlemen." He set a pace down the hall that

had the older men huffing.

"Nick, I need more than you've given me on Philip Machen. If you can't grab him, at least find out what he wants so we can block it. We are outlawing his machines, and we can kill his satellites, but we are playing catch-up. We need to get out ahead of this guy and stop him cold, whether or not we find him. Before the public starts believing the crap he's telling them.

"If people get used to trading free goods, their own selfishness might turn them against the rule of law. We have to avoid over-reacting, but I want you and Clint to find a way to trump this guy. Bring me a show-stopper, to be employed if moderate measures fail. One way or another, we have to stop Philip Machen before the elections, way before the elections. Do you understand?"

"Yessir."

"Yessir."

The president nodded, then slipped through a door held wide by his chief of staff. Nick and General Holmes continued down a narrow hallway.

"How's your asshole, General?"

Holmes chuckled.

"Better shape than yours, Colonel."

Nick led the way and spoke over his shoulder. "Jack knows I'm the only cabinet member with feet-on-the-ground military experience. The rest are careerist weenies. That's why he's put you and me together on this. I was in Bosnia when the fly-boys took credit for stopping the ethnic cleansing. And you," he indicated the ribbons on Holmes's chest, "you've done it all, haven't you?"

Holmes calculated his response. "I report to SECDEF."

Meaning, "I don't report to you." They both knew Jack Washburn was going under-the-table with his request, and the general's reminder was standard turf defense.

"Clint, you and I don't have to front this thing. We only have to push it up to daylight. Let SECDEF think it was his idea. Philip Machen is a greater threat to this nation than any man alive, and

Jack is finally beginning to appreciate it. We both know the legislative approach is too little, too late. So let's give Jack his trump card." He slowed to eyeball the general. "Before the damned election."

"I don't see a military solution here," Holmes said. "You don't need my people to take this guy down. But if you want help finding him, I'll recommend it to my boss."

Nick stopped.

"It took ten years to get Osama bin Laden," he said. "What if nobody stops Philip Machen? What if half the country hides their Makers and keeps using them, no matter what the law says? How do we prevent that? That's what Jack wants us to do. I don't give a shit who gets the credit."

Holmes laughed.

"You're a piece of work, Nick." He jerked his head toward the Oval Office. "Glad I'm not part of Jack's tap dance. Right now, I need to make sure DEFCON gets wound down, so call me after lunch, all right? We'll talk."

Nick shook the offered hand, but Holmes had not declared his intentions. So their agreement—if it was one—remained provisional. Maybe Clint had something in mind.

Nick was about to leave the building when Alec Drexler bounded over to him, his rust-red hair flouncing. He was waving a blue Cambiar like a Bedouin with a Popsicle.

"Nick, you gotta see this. The pro-Machen bloggers invented a name for themselves, and the anti-Machen crowd is choking on it."

Nick regarded Drexler's Cambiar as if it were a turd.

"Don't you have anything real to do, Alec?"

"They're calling themselves Freemakers."

Nick arched his lip.

"If they are the hippy-dippy Freemakers, who are we, the Establishment?" He laughed at Drexler's frown.

"They're calling us Tories."

EIGHTEEN

Victorville, California. Still Saturday, April 25
Day Eight

THE SUN ROSE plump and yellow over a low rim of the Mojave, promising heat before noon. Beneath the giant purple tail of a retired Federal Express MD-11, Tanner Newe scanned a news report on his Cambiar.

"They killed him," he said.

Philip's wrench rattled off the scaffold and disappeared with a clank.

"They hanged him," Tanner said, "for spying and sedition."

Twenty feet above, Philip grasped a handrail, waited for the hangar walls to melt or his legs to fold. He swallowed hard and shuffled along a wooden plank to the ladder, which he descended one metal rung at a time. At the bottom, he staggered three paces before squatting in his coveralls. He crossed his arms over his head and rocked like a peasant.

With every fiber of his body, he cried, "Spook!"

His knees hit the floor and he fist-slammed the concrete. Once, twice, then harder still.

"Not him. Not him too."

He'd done it again—killed another precious, irreplaceable family member. He rocked and rocked. *Spook. Uncle Orin.* The Bear with a booming voice. The wily, tough, generous second father whom he loved beyond words. *Is dead.*

A gust rattled the hangar doors, spoons in a can.

"I should have stopped him. I should have made him come home."

Tears welled as the fulminations in his chest bore him back to a hospital in Michigan, sixteen years ago, the day after the memorial for his family. Pillow-propped and drooling, he'd shut his eyes against the morning glare, willed himself back to the void. Yet three sharp knocks held him fast. A towering figure in a jet-black overcoat swept into the room. It wore a tweed cap and dragged a steel chair.

"Go away," Philip said, and a lizard of dread wriggled down his spine.

The intruder placed his chair and sat, just breathing, letting his foreboding presence blot out the light. In a voice as dark as his coat, the man said, "You have unfinished business."

Philip jerked his restraints. He called for the nurse.

The stranger shook his great dismal head. "They're not coming."

"Go to hell," Philip said.

The head inclined. "Popular place, now and then."

"Get out. Can't you see I'm dead already? Soon as I quit breathing."

From beneath the cap, gunmetal eyes regarded him—until Philip recognized their Machen family squint.

"Spook."

It popped from him like a bubble, this name his father used. When Dad was young, his older brother got shoes with crepe soles and made a reputation sneaking up, startling people. Now at Philip's bedside, Spook declared loud enough for the nurses to hear him,

"Leonard was a fool who failed to see his effect on people. So they called him an atheist and killed him."

Which was half-right.

"Would have killed you too," Spook said. "But that's not why I came. You and I have business, and I mean to finish it."

From his coat he withdrew a paperback book, creased and broken, and tossed it on Philip's lap: a grief recovery handbook.

Philip shook his head. "No thanks."

Spook heaved to his feet, yanked the chair, and strode out the door.

Next morning, when the big man returned, the nurses removed Philip's restraints. Spook coaxed him upright and got some pancakes into him, which was how they began.

For two days, he and Spook diagrammed their losses on paper. They sketched relationship graphs, drew their connections to Leonard, to Rebecca, and to young Sandra. They wrote declarations of amends and forgiveness, in which they conveyed their unsent messages, their unfinished feelings, for each of the dead. Silently they attended each other, as first one and then the other read his papers aloud, according to the book. Philip wept and beheld his uncle sobbing, but they continued. On the third day, they signed and read their goodbyes-to-the-dead. Saying goodbye out loud hurt worse than the funeral, worse even than the flames he could never forget. Yet it purged him.

In that moment, Philip resolved never to call him Spook again. No matter what lay ahead, so long as he drew a breath, this great, weeping grizzly would be his Uncle Orin. Who soon enough became his second father, the one who believed in him, even before Tanner did, who made Tanner pay attention and get to work.

Orin didn't know physics from flapjacks, but he bet everything he owned on what Philip was doing. Without Orin's strength and nurture, Philip could not have achieved his vows: to remain among the living, to create a quantum duplex, and to jolt the world in a new direction. Without Orin, there would be no Powerpods, no Makers, no advent. And the hole in the universe once occupied by him was also the hole in Philip's heart.

"It wasn't your fault," Tanner said. "Playing Johnny Appleseed with the Cambiars was his idea. You warned him."

Philip quit rocking. He splayed his hands on the floor, pressed the aching cold into his palms. "He was having the time of his life over there, giving away encrypted satellite phones and sneaking the uncensored internet into China, his little joke on official stuffed shirts. He thought the Chinese would be so distracted by their Maker problems he could give away a few more Cambiars, then sneak out through Hong Kong. But he was wrong. We were both wrong. I should not have announced Makers until he was home and safe."

A ray of sunlight projected through the gap between the hangar doors and cast a bright line at his knees. Philip stroked the line as if to draw it closer, as if its brilliance might confer wisdom or sympathy. People in pain did that. They imagined patterns or voices that weren't there to help them survive their terrible moments.

Philip unfolded himself. He picked grit from his damaged knuckles and wiped his face with a solvent rag. Inspecting his hands again, he considered their thirteen-point-seven-billion-year-old protons and electrons, bequeathed to him through his parents' love. Even real consolations came with righteous burdens.

Tanner joined him on the floor. "He was my friend too."

Philip nodded. There was so much left to do.

NINETEEN

Victorville, California. Thursday, April 30
Day Thirteen

"THEY DON'T GET IT," Tanner said to his computer screen. Last night, after working four days with only twelve hours of sleep, they had finally given in to their need for distraction and opened a fifth of Cabo Wabo. This morning, Tanner's black eyebrows arched like hairy caterpillars.

Philip ignored the facial larvae. Cantina chants still echoed in his head. *Anejo, anejo, reposado. Anejo, anejo, reposado. En tequila es verdad. Aguave forever, Amen.* For each age of tequila, imbibe one shot, sing the verse, and repeat. Until you wake up with concrete kissing your ear as you dance quite slowly with the floor.

Philip groaned and rolled over. Tanner had gulped tequila shooters all night, daring him, racing him, while Philip employed tactical sips, nominal tastings that should have transported him to oblivion smoothly, with milder effects. Yet the liquor disappeared apace, one sip at a time.

Now, behind two crispy eyeballs, a squadron of regrets

demanded his response. Unmoved by the tide of alcohol, they stood precisely in the order he'd left them. First came Karen in her shimmering gown, a vision of hope and possibility. Then his parents, his sister, his uncle—four dead faces. Every friend except Tanner, gone or abandoned. Alcohol did not forgive him his long and contemptible record of hurting everyone he loved.

He probed his mouth with a corncob tongue, seeking moisture, a single tear of sympathy.

"They don't get it," he rasped, testing his voice.

Tanner ignored the croak from the floor and focused on the poll results displayed on his screen.

"We are dead in the water," he said. "It will be two weeks tomorrow, and domestic Maker conversions remain fewer than ten percent of all Pods, even in California. Overseas, it's worse. Short Fat Guy reports no new enclaves have formed anywhere. Just loners and a few neighborhoods are experimenting, biding their time, waiting to see what happens, while the Folks-in-Charge-of-Pounding-Us keep pounding us."

Philip raised himself on a tender elbow. Auto-resonant hairs thrummed upon his scalp. "What fat guy?"

"Art Buddha, Short Fat Guy. High-profile internet blogger. Number-one Maker enthusiast."

Philip belched. "Index case."

"Huh?"

"Never mind." Philip thrust himself upward, approached the vertical before falling back. He launched again and managed to sit.

Tanner regarded this milestone with indifference. "The cure is behind you."

"Agua," Philip croaked. He crawled to the office refrigerator. The first swig of water hissed as it lapped his mouth and irrigated his tongue. He drank half a liter without pause. "Gawd, that's good."

"He's running a survey." Tanner leaned back, crossed his hairy arms.

"Who?"

"Art Buddha."

Philip rubbed his eyes. He appraised their hangover cure, the green oxygen tank, twenty paces distant across a granite-hard floor that no longer loved him.

"He's promoting our cause. Wrote a manifesto for you to read. I downloaded it."

"Nuh." Philip coaxed his limbs to ford the expanse, urged them to go, go, go until they delivered him to the shrine of all combustion, where he collapsed.

"You call this oxygen?" He inhaled from a squishy mask. "They got better oh-two in Cleveland." He imbibed the antidote and let the morning curdle.

Tanner rapped his screen. "He's up for a chat. Wants you to read his masterpiece."

Philip scaled an office chair, spun it about and sat, sucking relief by the liter. The cure was working. His headache subsided. Across the desk, Tanner activated a speaker.

"You da boss? I gotta say dis to da boss." A middle-aged Hawaiian, by tone and inflection. "Go get dat Boss Man, hey? We gotta *parlezvous*, Brah."

Philip swiveled toward the Fat Buddha avatar grinning fixedly from Tanner's screen. Its animated lips wrinkled as it spoke. "You dere, Boss Man?"

"He's here, Fat Guy." Tanner released the key, aimed a yes-or-no look at Philip.

What was Tanner doing? Philip laid down the mask and turned off the gas.

"He's on our side," Tanner said. "Pseudo-Zen intellectual. Loves Makers. Loves sharing. Hates gatekeepers."

"Hey, Boss," said the Buddha's smeary lips, "I punked dat name for you. Dat name it went viral. Hoo boy! You da Freemaker now."

Philip suffered a tequila twitch and a sour burp.

Tanner pressed a key. "Speak to us, Fat Guy. He's listening."

"Boss, you makin' a big mistake. You leavin' us out, Brah. You gotta tell da peoples, or you gonna go honohono, stinky-stinky, like da kine roadkill."

Philip looked at Tanner. *Huh?*

"We stickin' our necks out, and our big fat bue-tocks, way out for you, Brah. We swimmin' da bay, but we gettin' nowhere. You gotta tell da peoples why to keep swimmin', an' where dey goin'. Or dey gonna quit, Brah. Go surfin' instead. No more enclaves 'cause nobody likes you."

Philip squinted. "Who are you?"

"You gotta tell 'em, Boss. Tell 'em what dey gonna get when dey swim dat bay. New lives, new customs, new mores. A brand new ethos." The voice tightened, turned flat and mid-western. "Sharing the common bounty is going to change our psyches, Mister Machen, not just our jobs and our stuff. Makers are changing the way we think about the world, the way we feel about each other. I can say it a million times, but it won't mean squat until they hear it from you or feel it themselves. Money empowers elites, but radical sharing empowers everyone who owns a Maker. You have to save us, man." Then he resumed his Island Boy shtick.

"You da Big Kahuna, Mista Freemaker. You gotta tell da peoples. Or dey gonna drown."

"I did tell them . . . ." Philip scoffed. "The Maker Handbook, appendix one, downloaded onto every Cambiar. It's there, waiting for them to—"

"No!" Fat Buddha's jolly smile didn't falter as he shouted. "You da one waiting, Boss. You da one waiting for dem. But dey ain't gonna see nothin', 'les you put it in dey face. All da time, you put it in dey face. Tell dem da story, 'til dey see it too.

"Like dis. Who da owner of you? You da one? Or you alla time sell youself, jes to put lime in da coconut? Maybe you wanna be da owner of you, 'stead a da Man, 'stead a da Company, 'stead a da Kahuna dat owns you. You gotta be free, Brah. No more chump.

You get some Maker Makers an' make whole family free. Not maybe, not someday. Real peoples be making real freedom, right now."

Philip massaged his temples. He had no plan, that was true, but why plan the obvious? *Just do it.*

Tanner reached for the speaker. "We got it, Big Guy. Thanks for the heads up."

"About dat manifesto—"

But Tanner killed the link and swiveled to Philip.

"Everything Art said, that's what I'm trying to tell you."

Philip cast about, rubbed his wrist, gazed at his scar, freshly tattooed to keep it from fading. All his work, years of struggle, his family murdered, Uncle Orin executed—by people who didn't get it.

He stood, fetched another water from the fridge, and sipped. If he started to preach, that's what people would hear—preaching. A few might listen, but most would tune him out.

"Why can't they figure it out, Tanner? Why do we have to spell it out for them?"

"Pattern recognition," Tanner said. "They've never seen it before, so they don't have a reference. People can only build what they can imagine, which is not so much. You gotta tell them what it looks like, Boss, a world of neighbors using Makers to share and live free."

Philip sat and sipped. Everyone still expected scarcity, struggle, domination. Their default assumption was that ancient code of survival, predating law and religion, and baked into every culture. Winners take what they can, as their natural right, as natural as scarcity, and too bad for the losers. Why can't people see how Makers blow the doors off that crap? That a new social order is brewing right in their backyards at the speed of Maker copies?

They are the Freemakers, not me.

Terry Quinn's lawsuit had forced him to reveal Makers too soon. Ryle's Theorem said Makers wouldn't tip over their social acceptance threshold and persist in the culture until there were eighty-million of them worldwide. In his own way, Uncle Orin had worked for that goal too.

"I don't know if Big O truly believed in Makers, or whether he helped us just for fun. With Orin, you couldn't tell sometimes. But he gave his life for us, Tanner. He was spreading the word over there, you know? Getting people to copy and share."

He drew his Cambiar from a pocket and keyed it to display a status update.

"They're killing our satellites," he said. "Let's get this beam engine back in the plane. Then I need to call Tiffany Lavery and find out who was that reporter who interviewed Karen."

TWENTY

Oakland, California. Friday, May 1
Day Fourteen

TODAY, EVERETT WOULD HAVE begun flying for Montana Skies, but instead he and General Johnson sold thirty-six Powerpods. If you owned one before midnight, when possession of Maker paraphernalia—cones—became a federal crime, the authorities could not claim you used illegal means to acquire it. All week, Marcy had lingered upstairs, doing Marcy things, not tracking any Maker stories, and Everett's decision to dump Montana Skies was feeling more and more foolish.

In just two weeks, three hysterias had swept the country: the currency collapse, the commodities implosion, and the financial market wipeouts. People continued to stock up for the emergency, though some stores, fearful that Maker copies would put them out of business, were limiting sales to onesies—one of each item per customer. Meanwhile, bloggers and the news media were showing laid-off truckers, idle factories, and lines of unemployed workers queuing for benefit checks. As usual for a Friday afternoon, the mood on Grand Avenue had lightened, but Everett's confidence was swinging in and out of existence with each passing hour.

Near sunset, General departed with Charlene, leaving Everett to lock up the store. He hadn't seen Marcy all day, but as he finished hanging the plywood window covers, she appeared at the foot of his ladder, a vision in tight slacks and a sequined jacket.

"There's a party," she said. "Last chance to share stuff before they outlaw Makers. It's two blocks. We can walk."

Everett feigned disinterest. He descended the ladder and stood deliberately close, tugged at his Shoes-for-You T-shirt.

"Forgot my party duds."

She leaned into him, eyes full of mischief.

"How about those sexy leather pants you ride around in, and that cute leather jacket that tapers to your butt?"

"The ones with bugs on the front?"

"All work and no play makes Jack a pain in the ass," she said. Her voice went as husky as wood smoke. "Best tamales and red sauce you'll ever eat, Flyboy." Then she fired a flirty smile straight into his lust-addled heart.

"Okay," he said and clamped his jaw against a rush of gratitude. She might be gaming him, but he could game her too.

They secured the store and hiked uphill to Mira Vista Street, to a whitewashed bungalow behind a blue picket fence. A thumping bass rhythm assaulted them from an open door where an ageless Vietnamese in a baseball cap eyed them from the porch. As they opened the gate, the man put down his beer.

Marcy introduced Ray Vu, who smiled broadly as he hugged her. Ray shook Everett's hand.

"Welcome to the wake," he said. "We are saying goodbye." He pointed to a stack of Maker cones bound for collection at the curb. He gestured to his door. "Come in, come in. Terri is in the kitchen."

He ushered them to a display of bottles and glassware.

"Help yourselves, folks." He shouted over the din. "The bar is open. Cold stuff in coolers under the table. Did you bring something to share?"

"Movies." Marcy produced a paper sack.

Everett shrugged, embarrassed. "Swiss Army knife?"

Marcy patted his hand. "I ambushed him, Ray. Didn't give him time to change clothes."

Ray appraised Everett's boots and leathers.

"Swiss Army is cool. Our trading table is in the back room. Park your stuff there and help yourselves to anything you want. Except for Terri and the kids, that is." He laughed at his own joke, then excused himself to the porch.

The living room crowd was lobbing paper balls into a flaming fireplace, some kind of game. A skinny teenager scuttled to the newcomers.

"Hey, mister, have some ammo."

Everett accepted the boy's offering without enthusiasm, discovered a fifty dollar bill.

"We got money to burn." The kid leered. "You didn't bring a thousand dollar bill, did you? I'm going to paper my room with thousand dollar bills, as soon as I can trade for one."

Everett shook his head, handed back the fifty.

"We have gold, too, but that stuff won't burn."

Everett stood mute, so the boy slouched away and rejoined his friends.

At the bar, Marcy poured cold Chardonnay into a tulip glass. Everett tasted an unfamiliar Scotch but abandoned it for a beer. Together they strolled through the crowd.

Ray must have brought his Powerpod through the patio doors because the machine stood in a bedroom to one side, its top cone festooned with a banner: *Sharing Machine (Not a Maker)*. A Sharing Table, designated by another sign, held a profusion of loot: recordings and jewelry, coins and watches, liquor, a tuxedo, a blender, computers, smartphones, and Cambiars. Three sandwich bags of foliage labeled "Portland Oregano." Nothing he regarded as rare or precious. No shoes.

Marcy searched the table while he copied his Swiss Army knife. Was the one he returned to his pocket the original or the copy? Did it even matter?

Three young boys rushed into the room, jostling each other. They copied a candy bar twice, then ran off, giggling and punching each other.

Marcy scanned a tray for titles before adding her movies. At the table's edge, an unmarked baggie of white powder caught Everett's gaze. Soap? Rat poison? Cocaine? He sipped beer and fingered the bag while Marcy delved into the jewelry. He snatched the white stuff. Face powder, maybe, or heroin. Nothing on this table belonged to anyone anymore, so why was he hoping Marcy did not see him tuck it up his sleeve?

He shouted over the noise. "No way I'm going to haul everything from this table for you."

She waved him off. "I'm shopping. I'll carry it."

This was the response he wanted. He made his way to a bathroom, found the light, and locked the door. As white powder flowed cleanly into the toilet, tension eased from his neck. Ordinary problems were bad enough. He didn't want any anonymous powders screwing up the evening.

He soothed his hands under warm water and returned to Marcy. She led him to the kitchen.

"You must be Everett." A black-eyed, black-haired pixie grinned up at him. "I'm Teresa Vu. Call me Terri. Marcy told me *everything* about you." She giggled.

Everett accepted her hug and noticed the flour now transferred to his jacket.

"At last," he said, eyeing the dough on her breadboard, "a real treasure."

"Everett likes to eat," Marcy said, then laughed at the look on his face.

"Me, too, Everett." Terri patted her own ample frame. "Welcome to Tortilla Heaven." She handed him a plate with silverware rolled in a napkin.

"Everything is in trays outside," she said. "Help yourselves, guys. I gotta turn down that damned music."

The patio was cooler, less frenetic, and suffused with pinkish-gray twilight. Everett loaded his plate with steaming rice and beans, fish tacos, pork tamales, and topped them with a fragrant sopapilla. A squeeze of honey made it perfect.

Marcy led him to a picnic table near a lemon tree where General and Charlene were engrossed in their dinners. Had the Johnsons conspired to bring him here to cheer him up? The food and the beer found their marks, and when Marcy sidled against his leg, nothing else mattered. For a moment, he wished he'd brought those diamond earrings Alonso had given him. When the music softened, couples got up to dance, just like a real party.

A girl of twelve or thirteen crossed the patio, lugging a bucket of kitchen waste. In the corner of the yard, she opened a gate and climbed a step ladder. She dropped her bucket into a Maker top-cone. When she shut the lid and pressed the button, there came a rush of water flowing down a drain. Apparently, a hose and a float valve kept the top-cone filled, and her trash turned to water in the opposite side cone. Having finished, the girl took a new bucket from a stack, shut the gate, and returned to the house.

Half a beer later, as Everett sliced his last tamale, a mountainous woman in a flowing blue caftan approached their table.

"You must be General Johnson." Her voice boomed like a man's.

General stood and accepted her ring-encrusted fingers.

"I'm Alicia Maybury, and I need your help, sir."

Marcy stood also. "Hello, Councilwoman."

General gave his niece a look. Ms. Maybury widened her smile.

"Marcy, yes. I believe we chatted during my reelection campaign."

When no one offered her a place at the table, Ms. Maybury

dragged a chair to join them.

"Sit, please, Mr. Johnson." Her tone left no doubt she knew the rank of a shoe salesman and that of a city councilwoman.

"Oakland is dying, sir. Some say it was beyond hope before that idiot and his machines, but now even the better neighborhoods are threatened. We really must reinvent our communities, and we don't have much time. We need to make some hard choices."

Her gaze alighted on Everett, registered a demerit, and flicked back to General.

"You have stature among us, sir. We need you to employ that stature now. Please help us form a self-protecting neighborhood. I support President Washburn's Maker ban, but that won't stop the criminals, will it? We need every able person to help us preserve order and decency. If we fail, the vermin will take over, as they have on the west side. If you and I and a few others don't take the necessary steps, we shall be forced from our homes, driven into the streets by hooligans. Shall we become refugees from our own neighborhood?"

She leaned toward General, who cleared his throat.

"Well, I haven't thought about it."

She leaned further, nose to nose.

"Please, do think, General. We are meeting tomorrow at nine, at St. Joseph's. At noon we will host a community-building rally in the park across the street. Please think about what you can contribute—as a leader—because we don't have time for elections. Those will have to come later."

"I can do media and computers," Marcy offered.

"Excellent, Ms. Johnson. Please bring your man with you."

Everett cringed. He was Marcy's man only when she needed him.

General stood and strained a smile. Ms. Maybury slapped her thighs and stood with him.

"I'll leave you folks alone now," she said. "Thank you for your time. Please join us tomorrow." She offered her hand to General.

"It was a pleasure meeting you, sir." She nodded to the others.

Marcy stopped her. "Are you forming an enclave? Like Prospect Shores?"

Ms. Maybury stiffened. She addressed General, not Marcy.

"We have a few square blocks to defend. A military man should appreciate the concept. When sanity resumes, we can open our streets and rejoin the city. So this is temporary." She drilled Marcy. "No Maker enclaves."

Then smiling again at General, "If there's someone you'd care to recommend, sir, please let me know." She pressed a card into his hand. "Thank you, folks. Have a pleasant evening."

Despite the warm food, a chill swept through Everett. Marcy must have felt it, too, because she snuggled against him, inviting his arm.

"Quite an experience," Charlene said.

"Guess that's what it takes," General said. Then to Marcy, "You didn't set this up, by any chance?"

"Negative, sir." She raised a hand. "Scout's honor."

"Then why is she after me?"

Marcy shrugged. "You going to do it?"

He pursed his lips. "I don't want to be on anyone's list. I'm no politician. Just an old sailor gone to seed."

Marcy batted her eyelids. "You forgot the part about cute and sexy."

Charlene coughed.

General reclaimed his seat and focused self-consciously on his food.

The sopapillas and tamales truly were the best Everett had ever tasted, even after they cooled. He sipped Budweiser until Terri Vu emerged from the house, headed straight for him.

"Come with me, young man. You're gonna love it."

Marcy trailed along while Terri charged through her guests, towing Everett into a well-stuffed garage. Before them stood a white plastic booth, brightly lit, with a dressing mirror facing the open door.

"Did you ever use a laser tailor?" Terri said. "You go in there, and you take off your clothes."

He chuckled until Terri poked him.

"Not everybody," she said, "just you. Take off your clothes and press the button. It tells you how to stand so the lasers can do the measuring. Then, while you get dressed, the computer calculates how to cut any piece of clothing you want—except shoes—and it downloads that to a cutter. Soon as you pick the styles and the fabrics, it cuts perfect panels. You turn those over to somebody who knows what they're doing with a sewing machine and, I swear to God, you will never go back to rack clothes. Ray's company makes the booths and the cutters, and we just love the clothes. You wanna try it?"

"I'm not getting naked for any laser."

"Oh, you scaredy cat. Check this out." Terri passed him a silky chestnut shirt with French cuffs and sparkling amber studs. He fingered the sleeve.

"It comes with matching underwear." She giggled. "Just kidding. Get in there and let me do a shirt for you. I'll sew you a number that will drop Marcy's jaw."

Marcy helped her push him into the booth.

"Okay, okay," he said. "A shirt. I'm not dropping my pants so you can blackmail me."

Marcy's Cambiar chimed, and she turned away to answer it. Everett strained to hear, but Terri shut the door. When he emerged a minute later, Marcy was ending the call with a flat "Okay" and a stunned expression.

Terri handed him a memory chip.

"Your dimensions, big guy. I'll call Marcy when your shirt's ready." She seemed enormously pleased. "You're gonna love it, kiddo. I promise."

Marcy stared at the phone in her hand.

Terri indicated a table stacked with shirts, slacks, and

underwear, all neatly wrapped, as if on sale.

"You guys are not still doing laundry, are you?" She checked back and forth between them, then laughed. "You are." She put her hands on her hips. "You gotta stop that stupid laundry stuff.

"Look, you clean your clothes and fold them in wrappers like we do. When you change in the morning, empty your pockets and toss your old duds into your Maker. Oops, I mean your laundry machine. Then you copy what you want to wear. Just put one copy back on the shelf when you're done, and you can wear brand new clothes every day. Jeez, I thought you single, upscale kids would be way ahead of us married stiffs."

"What about the ban?" Everett said.

Terri shrugged. "We put some cones out by the curb like they said. Now they can mind their own business."

"Terri, we have to go." Marcy slipped her arm around Everett's waist, daring him to resist. They followed Terri back into the house, where they retrieved Marcy's loot sack. Prominent on the Sharing Table lay another baggie of white powder.

General and Charlene were outside, dancing, so Everett and Marcy waved farewell. At the front door, they said goodbye to their hosts. Terri insisted on a big hug for each of them. Ray kissed Marcy and shook Everett's hand. "You guys take care," he said.

When they reached the sidewalk, Marcy whispered, "I just landed the biggest interview of my life, and I need your help, Everett. Please? Tomorrow night."

Precisely what he had hoped for, though he wasn't going to say so.

"Don't worry," she said. She drew his hand beneath her jacket and snugged it to her waist. "I'll protect you."

TWENTY-ONE

WHEN EVERETT GOT HOME that night, a flatbed truck blocked the driveway, and a mob of yawning cardboard mouths filled the living room. Bobby was building boxes with masking tape. "You sleep with her?"

"None of your business."

"But she conned you into that illegal party."

"It was a fiesta, Dad. Just a party. Remember fun? Or was that too long ago?"

"It was a party for making booze and drugs and counterfeit with a one-hundred percent illegal Maker machine."

Everett hung up his riding gear.

"I suppose those extra pistols you copied today are not counterfeit? There's a grace period to surrender the cones, Dad, so don't give me your life-of-crime shit. You know I didn't do anything wrong."

"President Washburn is giving people a chance to set

themselves straight, Son. Makers are illegal right now, tonight. The authorities are going to round them up like diseased cattle. Copying those guns was my bad.

"But you," he said, "you gotta start thinking about the consequences of what you're doing and who you're doing it with. We can't take any more hits. If the cops connect you to this Maker monkey business, they are going to throw your butt in jail and yank your pilot license forever. Did you call about your suspension?"

Everett strode past him, to his bedroom. The license could wait. Day after tomorrow, he was going to video-record an interview with the fabulous Marcy Johnson.

Bobby followed him, leaned on the door jamb.

"While you were over there making another mistake, I called Jesse Cardoza. He says we can stay at his ranch in Livermore until we find another place. There's a toilet and a shower and space for two beds. Unless you're moving in with Ms. Hot Pants."

Everett peeled his shirt and unbuckled his belt. Moving to Livermore would shorten his commute by half.

"Jesse loaned me his bobtail truck. Said we can store our furniture in his barn, now that the weather's dry. I told him we would come first thing in the morning."

Everett threw himself onto the bed, and recalled Marcy's sandalwood scent.

"Night, Dad."

"So tomorrow we move, Maker Boy."

IN THE MORNING, Bobby shambled through the kitchen, sour and puffy-eyed. Across the breakfast table, he sat smoking, not eating, always a bad sign.

They loaded Jesse's truck with their cartons, headed west across the Altamont, and shoveled the load into a corner of the Cardoza's steel barn. Bobby kept a steady pace, only resting when Everett drove them back to Tracy.

"I couldn't look him in the eye," Bobby said, "yesterday."

Everett imagined the conversation. "Hey, Jess, can I borrow your truck? And, by the way, do you have a spare room?"

"We won't stay long," Everett said, hoping it was true.

Bobby kneaded his fingers, cracked his knuckles. Tracy lay twenty minutes east of Livermore, and he didn't dare stink up Jesse's truck with tobacco smoke.

Their second load was furniture and bedroom things, which took two hours to load, haul, and stuff into Jesse's barn. During their return to Tracy, Bobby switched on a radio talk show.

"It depends on whether you think we can stop this thing," the host was saying.

"How are we supposed to know?" a caller demanded. "Makers are hurting the economy, but if we don't keep one in reserve, our families could starve before the government straightens things out. How are we supposed to know?"

"Makers are immoral," said the host. "That's what you need to understand. Think about it, folks. In one week these machines have wiped out all the cash in the world and brought every major corporation to its knees. Trillions of dollars gone. That's our national wealth, gone. Makers are forcing people to cheat each other with counterfeit, and when the last business closes because it can't compete with all that free stuff, then the layoffs will be permanent too. We could be facing the Antichrist, my friends.

"As a legendary actress once said, 'Fasten your seatbelts. It's going to be a bumpy ride.' Our next call, from Marty in Idaho Falls, will continue right after these messages."

Something clicked inside Bobby and he switched it off. He fumbled a cigarette to his lips, letting it dangle like an unlit fuse. Last time he looked this awful was when Mom left for Canada.

"Somebody has got to stop that son-of-a-bitch," he said.

Everett couldn't see how catching Philip Machen or calling him names would make any difference. His machines would still be there, hidden if necessary. But telling people what to think, he wasn't doing that.

"It's just more stuff," Everett said, hoping to deflect the hostility brewing next to him.

By lunchtime, they had loaded Bobby's dirt bike and the last household items. Then they made sandwiches and sat on the back steps drinking copied beers and gazing at the refrigerator strapped to the truck, a bulky white monument to their labors. Only their tools and hardware in the garage remained, plus one more item.

"What about our Maker?"

Bobby lobbed a half-empty beer at the machine. It clunked off a strut and rolled foaming in the grass.

"Leave the cones for the landlady," he growled. "We paid for the Pod, so we'll keep it, but we are not going to cheat anybody with more counterfeit."

Everett shrugged. They might need those cones, later, but right now he had a more urgent concern.

When Bobby went inside to pee, Everett rushed to the truck. He wrestled Bobby's dirt bike aside and unlocked the gun safe. Racing Bobby's bathroom noises, he copied the little Seecamp pistol, a stainless job that looked like a toy. Seven shots, .32 caliber.

Last night was a mistake all right. He should not have told his father. From now on, he wouldn't talk about Marcy or what they were doing. From now on, he would make his own decisions. He slipped one pistol into his back pocket and returned the other to the safe. Bobby didn't need to know.

TWENTY-TWO

Berkeley, California. Sunday, May 3
Day Sixteen

AT 5:00 AM THE NEXT MORNING, Everett hunkered with Marcy in her car near a dark and vacant public playground. Headlights that might be a cop swept over them. Two strangers in a white Mitsubishi would attract suspicion in this upscale neighborhood, but the car turned away. A greater worry was that Marcy had exposed herself by pursuing this interview. He patted the stainless steel assurance in his jacket pocket.

"So, how do you know it was him?" he said. "Somebody could be leading you into a trap."

"Well, it was a Cambiar number and the digital signatures checked out, plus I could see his face, okay? His voice was the same too."

Three sharp knocks on the right-rear window sent Everett's hand to his pocket. He shoved Marcy down and steadied his tiny pistol between the headrests. The intruder crouched beside the car and shined a light under his big white chin. When Everett took aim, the flashlight winked off.

"It's the bodyguard," Marcy said. "Put that thing away."

"Unlock his door," Everett said. He held a spotlight in his left hand, the gun in his right. Nobody was going to take them without a fight. When the door opened, he triggered the light and shouted, "Hands. Show me your hands."

The man covered his face against the brilliance as he ducked into the back seat. He was a big guy with a big head and lots of glistening black hair. Famously hairy arms.

"If you agree to be searched at our destination," the man said, "we will continue. Otherwise, this conversation is over, and we will watch you leave."

"Shut that thing." Marcy swatted Everett. "You're blinding everybody." She extended her hand across the seat.

"How do you do, Mr. Newe. I'm Marcy Johnson. This is my cameraman, Everett Aboud."

The guy shook her hand. Then he gripped her seat and squeezed the cushions flat.

"We accept your conditions, Mr. Newe. I apologize for Everett. He's a little nervous."

"All right," Tanner said. He withdrew his hands and shut the door. "Straight ahead, please."

Everett stuffed the light and the gun. He started Marcy's car and drove up the empty street. He didn't know this part of Berkeley. The highlands were upper-middle-class or downright rich. White and Asian. Not many blacks or browns up here.

Marcy spoke to Tanner, "You knew him in high school?"

"Yeah."

"And worked with him ever since?"

"Yeah."

"Why?" Marcy peered into the gloom behind her.

"'Cause we were doing stuff that was way cooler than working for The Man." His voice smiled for him.

"And?"

"And he brought me along, Ms. Johnson. Maybe that doesn't sound like much, but he saved me from eating my gun, you know, when I was down. I couldn't help him when his family got killed, but he remembered me being there, trying to help him, and he came back to Michigan afterward, just to bring me along. We're not gay. We're not related. But we're family. *Capiche?*"

They rode in silence for three blocks until Tanner told Everett to turn uphill, and they arrived at a driveway concealed by dense shrubbery. The pavement rose steeply for fifty yards, then leveled to a carport beneath the house, where Everett parked. He killed the lights and stopped the engine.

"Leave your keys. Leave your equipment. Keep your hands away from your pockets, and follow me." Tanner led them to a stairway of foot-lighted stones.

Everett had expected an elaborate, circuitous route, a blindfold perhaps, with a switch to a different car. Guards with guns. They were calling on the single most-hunted fugitive in the world, but their escort turned his back and marched up the stairs ahead of them.

The entry was dim, the house dark and cold. Tanner switched on a table lamp as he led them through a spacious living room. At the end of a short corridor, he opened a carved mahogany door and flicked on the light.

"Wait here," he said, and he ushered them into a vacant bedroom, white on white.

"He didn't search us," Everett whispered.

"Did you bring that thing in here? You're going to get us kicked out, Everett. All my work to set this up, and you are going to scare them off. Or get somebody shot."

"If they want you, sweetheart, they gotta take me first. The man knows I have it. He didn't search us because he's got friends with guns. They know exactly where we are. We just have to be careful, that's all. And polite."

"I didn't see anyone else," Marcy said. "But the room's

probably bugged. My guess is Machen's not in the house."

"Maybe the FBI knows this place," Everett said. "Maybe they'll bust the door and come in shooting. They wouldn't care about a couple of freelancers who happen to be in the wrong place at the wrong time." He rubbed his face.

Last night he had dreamed of meeting Philip Machen, of drawing his pistol and raising it to the guy's face. He even imagined pulling the trigger—a reckless, shameful urge. No matter what anyone said about the man, Everett could never do such a thing— murder someone in cold blood. He shivered.

Marcy dropped her purse and put her arms around him, held him like a pillow.

"Cold in here," she said.

He held her for all it was worth. In his twenty-two years, he had made enough huggy-bear, kissy-faces to have rid himself of his virginity, but Marcy was a grown woman, far more potent and intoxicating than any Florida bar girl. And more maddening. Connecting with her would never be just a party favor, it would be—special. He needed to say so, but this was hardly the time or place. So he held her close, imagined they were lovers, and enjoyed their moment.

From the kitchen came footfalls and voices. Drawers pulled, and flatware clinked. A cupboard door slapped, then the furnace came on.

Promptly at five-thirty came the knock. When Everett opened the door, Philip Machen stood before him, close enough to touch. Here was no myth or disembodied image. Here was the World's Most Wanted Man, taller than expected, and thinner, breathing the same cool air. Machen's gray, unblinking eyes widened.

"Good morning, Mr. Aboud."

When the fugitive stepped closer, Everett Aboud, the automatic Arab, shook Philip Machen's hand and grinned like a tourist blundering into a celebrity.

"Morning," he replied.

There were no guards. He could shoot him now. Or stick the gun in his face and tell Marcy to call 911. That would bend the world sideways. But, Jesus, what crazy ideas. The craziest was that in some weird sense, shooting Philip Machen would amount to shooting himself. He finally remembered to breathe and to step aside.

The great man's face came alive with the pleasure of meeting Marcy. Seeing her effect on him spun Everett's feelings in yet another direction. When the fugitive gestured to the living room, Marcy led the way.

Behind her, Machen pressed something into Everett's hand— a brass key on a leather fob.

"You're the pilot, right?"

"Huh?"

"Keep it," Machen said, squeezing his hand. Everett stuffed the key into his pocket and rushed to catch up.

They gathered in the dining room, where a red lacquered table awaited, complete with calligraphed name cards and monogrammed napkins. Machen seated them as Tanner wheeled in a serving cart. He served fruit, glasses of juice, rolls, muffins, and jellies. Machen set cereal bowls beside a pitcher of milk and encouraged them to enjoy whatever they wished. He strode to the kitchen door.

"Draw the curtains, would you please, Tanner."

The house floated it seemed, as the curtains parted, on a lake of misty green foliage. No walls or streets intruded. Across the way, pine boughs partitioned a row of rooftops that glistened wet and slippery while San Francisco glimmered in the distance. The entire wall was glass.

"This early, it's still hazy," Machen said. He set a chair with its back to the view, while Tanner placed rice paper screens to shield him. Then Philip Machen sat and sliced a banana onto his cereal.

"We will be more at ease, Mr. Aboud, if you would remove your jacket and place it on the chair by the kitchen door." Machen waited.

Everett hesitated long enough to draw a scowl from Marcy. He stood to doff his jacket, but instead of the distant chair, he laid it on a sofa, closer to the table. Machen met his eyes then nodded to Tanner, who gave Everett a hard look.

"We should be recording this," Marcy said. "A beautiful breakfast in a beautiful house."

"Wouldn't that be wonderful, Ms. Johnson? No agendas. Just breakfast with friends." Philip beamed. He indicated Marcy's cameras, positioned on tripods. "We took the liberty of setting up for you. But first, let's eat."

His bodyguard seated himself across from Everett, selected three rolls and a helping of fruit. For a moment he returned Everett's stare, then speared a melon slice and placed it deftly in his mouth. The man ate as politely as a diplomat, but there was nothing fragile about him.

"It would be a pity if this house became notorious," Machen was saying. "We warned our friends they might regret loaning it to us, but they insisted. I am so pleased they did." He gestured to the view. "Isn't it grand?"

"Two bridges and two skylines," Marcy noted. "How ironic that your Makers have brought so much darkness where Powerpods promised only light."

Machen stopped chewing.

"If I may say so, Mr. Machen, the world is in chaos, and everyone is blaming you."

TWENTY-THREE

EVERETT LOOKED UP from his plate. "Did we start?"

Machen shifted in his chair. "How shall we proceed, Ms. Johnson?"

Marcy pitched a nod to Everett. He stuffed the remains of a blueberry muffin into his mouth and made his way to the cameras. Tanner stood as he passed the sofa, then the bodyguard scooped up his plate and departed for the chair at the kitchen door, out of the video frames but in clear sight of Everett and his jacket.

Everett switched on his equipment and slowly panned the room. The authorities would welcome these images. Then he focused one lens on Machen, closeted within his screens, and the other on Marcy, who loosened her shoulders and licked her lips.

"This is Marcy Johnson, and we are meeting today with Philip Machen, inventor of Powerpods, and a central figure in our current economic turmoil. My cameraman and I traveled to this hidden location at Mr. Machen's invitation to discuss with him the machines he calls Makers."

Philip Machen, so relaxed before, sipped orange juice and sat up. Everett poised a finger to balance the audio.

"Mr. Machen, yesterday WebNews showed an elderly woman telling President Washburn at his town meeting in Decatur, Illinois, what her life has been like since you announced your Makers. She begged the president to help her. Did you see that broadcast?"

"Good morning, Marcy. No, I missed the show."

"This woman is terrified," Marcy said. "From her home, she's seen fires and looting. Her husband is ill. Their pension and insurance policies have been wiped out by the financial markets collapsing. Her husband needs a medicine produced by a company that may go out of business. Since their neighborhood grocery was looted, she doesn't know where to find food, and she's afraid to go in search of it. She and her husband feel as if they are captives in a war zone, with no means of escape and no one to help them. If you met this woman today, what would you say to her?"

"I would say, Madam, you are not alone." He looked into the camera. "A community of caring and sympathetic people surrounds you. Seek them out and help them establish a mutual-aid community, a Maker enclave that will care for each other, produce what your talents allow, and share or trade for what you lack. I would say all the politicians in the world are of less importance to you right now than one good neighbor willing to share a Maker or two."

Marcy pursed her lips.

"Mr. Machen, you call your Makers a gift. President Washburn has called them a financial Trojan horse meant to destroy our economy. What is the truth? Why did you do this?"

"Marcy, the possibility of Makers has always been inherent in the natural world. Powerpods are one incarnation of matter-energy transmutation. Makers are another."

"But you tricked us."

"There is nothing false about Powerpods or Makers. No one

was defrauded. But let's not quibble. Can you think of another way I could make a simultaneous gift to millions of people in a single day?"

"You could have told us what you were doing. You could have published your research and let the experts decide how to proceed."

"Marcy, it's clear to me that the world's power elites—the ones who employ those experts—would have stolen my gift and used it against ordinary people. They would have appropriated Makers for themselves to continue subjugating their fellow human beings. They would have deprived you of the opportunities that I have freely given. As we speak, most of them are trying to do exactly that."

Marcy frowned.

"But here in the United States, we would have voted about what to do with your machines."

"Really? Would our politicians and their wealthy sponsors allow a direct vote of the people on such an important matter? Cite for me a single precedent. If you are a decent, nonviolent person, why should anyone's vote deprive you of the means to produce what you need to live? You alone must decide what to do with your Makers. That is the difference between symbolic voting and a real choice. No government on Earth dares to trust you with such a genuine, empowering choice. But I have."

"Are you trying to overthrow the government?"

He scoffed. "Makers are force antidotes. They give everyone the personal wherewithal to resist subjugation, and the means to withdraw their sanction from distant, unresponsive elites. Makers emancipate us not just from scarcity, but from the tyranny of unelected, unresponsive overlords. Real freedom for real people."

"Isn't that anarchy?"

"Not at all. We are devolving from vast nation-states to small, cooperative communities, with local people put in charge and held accountable by their neighbors. People with Makers don't need guns or violence to improve their lives. They just do it." He licked his lips.

Marcy read from her notes.

"Mr. Machen, the Depression of the 1930s did not bring the number of business closures we are seeing today. Markets everywhere have collapsed. U.S. unemployment may soon reach 50 percent. Did you foresee this? And if so, are you not therefore responsible?"

"Marcy, I destroyed nothing. Traditional businesses simply can't compete. The cost of capital just went to zero—for everyone, not just the wealthy." He leaned toward her.

"If I had not given away millions of Makers, the mere fact of their existence would have brought the same effects. Take Philip Machen out of the picture, while leaving free Makers, and you would still have plummeting prices and mass-market collapses. When everyone owns a personal means to produce, it's not the end of capitalism. It's the beginning of personal, universal capitalism."

"So what do you want?" She bore in on him. "What's your goal?"

"I want free Makers in every household. I want people to stop fighting over scraps so they can share the pie. I want them to gather all of human providence into their communities, then share it. Above all, I want them to share their Makers."

She leaned forward.

"I mean, what's in it for you, Philip Machen?"

His eyes flashed.

"I believe Makers are going to spark a moral awakening that our religions have failed to achieve, a worldwide moral renaissance. I want to be part of that."

Marcy rocked back.

"We have not had Makers long enough," he said, "to experience it yet, but using them every day is going to generate a new sharing sensibility, a mutual, sustainable benevolence, that will replace the bitter calculus of scarcity and hoarding."

He rubbed his wrist.

"Maker owners are forming neighborhood communities

because they need one another's support. Within these enclaves, sharing will create a new expectation that most goods and all consumables should be shared. And why not? If it costs you nothing to share, why hoard?

"Likewise, every community will need to trade for desired goods and services, so networks of artisans and traders will arise, spontaneously. Every enclave will lack certain skills, so they will compete to attract new members, first by ensuring their communities are desirable places to live and work and to raise families. The new reality will be shared prosperity within healthy, secure neighborhoods. And through all these communities will run a vigorous new ethos of cooperation and fair treatment, fostered by daily routines of sharing.

"This sensibility will spread wherever Makers remain free. It will transcend older traditions because it is free and beneficial, practical and humane. Not political or religious or exclusive. It is simply the proper thing to do. In time, it will become the new normal, as common as saying hello.

"Under scarcity, love-thy-neighbor was a test of character. In a Maker community, the test is over. Excuses will not be tolerated. If you fail to share, you will no longer look strong or sophisticated. You will appear twisted and stingy, utterly pathological. If you won't share your Maker and your goods, you are a hoarder and a parasite."

Marcy fumbled her cards.

"President Washburn says—" She cleared her throat. "— that he banned Makers to defend the country."

Machen scowled.

"Jack Washburn is protecting the power holders, the hoarders, and the special interests. For ordinary people, complying with his ban amounts to social and economic suicide. Sooner or later, if you surrender your Makers, you will become serfs to those who are keeping theirs. Once they have Makers, nobody's going back to poverty or scorn or symbolic democracy. Nobody's going to work for the glory of kings or billionaires."

"But the world is in chaos," Marcy said. "Everything is—"

"Ms. Johnson, the sun still rises, and human compassion remains True North on every sane person's moral compass. Only our possibilities have expanded."

"Mr. Machen." Marcy cocked her jaw. "A friend would never pull a rug from under our feet and claim that our crash to the floor was not his fault. He would not pretend his arrogance was anything less than naked aggression. Aren't you just another rich know-it-all trying to impose your worldview on us?"

Machen jerked as if she had slapped him. He aimed his reply at Everett.

"Every other alternative," he said, "will enslave you to the hoarders. I made the only choice that gives everyone on Earth a genuine, personal chance for liberty, prosperity, and a moral awakening. I did what's right. Now it's your turn." He stared into the lens, straight through Everett.

"You must choose your path and defend it," Philip said. "If you will not share your Makers, you do not deserve them. If you surrender your Makers, you may never get them back."

He kissed the scar on his wrist, stood abruptly, and marched from the room. Marcy popped to her feet, only to sit again for the camera.

"Thank you, Philip Machen. It is Sunday, May third, and this is Marcy Johnson in Berkeley, California." She stared into the lens until Everett drew a finger across his throat.

At the kitchen door, Tanner Newe was on his feet, pistol in hand. Everett spun the camera toward him and held his breath. Philip Machen's bodyguard backed into the kitchen and shut the door. When footfalls and door closings gave way to the measured ticks of a grandfather clock, Everett released the breath he was holding.

"Still recording," he whispered.

"Did they leave?"

"Would you stick around? You got 'em, girl. They're pissed.

We had better load this onto the internet before anyone can stop us."

He headed for the stairs, to fetch the uplink.

"Be careful," she said.

He looked back, suddenly hopeful. If they shot him, she might care.

TWENTY-FOUR

Oakland, California. Sunday, May 3
Still Day Sixteen

AFTER MARCY DROPPED HIM back at Shoes-for-You, Everett had no idea where she might go, and he didn't ask. The interview was safely embedded in the folds of the internet. They had broken no laws and owed no favors, so why notify anyone, especially the cops? Besides, how could most people learn these things if journalists didn't reveal them? He crossed the boulevard, straddled his motorcycle, and sat in the warm sunlight. For once, he might have touched the world.

First concern: Machen's key. Too small for a door, it might fit a padlock. Penned on its fob was 5749 South Tracy Boulevard, #3. How could Machen have known he would recognize this address, and that he would go there?

He pocketed the key and started his motorcycle. Instead of returning to Jesse Cardoza's ranch, he continued east, past Livermore and up the Altamont Pass. From the summit, the flat midriff of the world's largest valley sprawled before him, its air so uncommonly clear the Sierra snowpack glistened across it from eighty miles away.

Tracy Municipal Airport comprised a few dozen hangars rusting behind the wire fences at 5749 Tracy Boulevard. Weeds were slowly digesting the asphalt where he parked. No services here anymore, just an old strip for touch-and-go landings, and a row of metal hutches rattling softly in the breeze. He peeked into hangar number three, where sun-damaged skylights cast a malarial pallor over a lithe and female form. In better light, she would be the exact color of lust. He slipped inside and traced the curve of her wing, fondling her with awe.

When he opened her canopy, the scent of leather invited him to slip into her interior and be absorbed. Controls came perfectly to hand. A twist of the mystery key in her master switch produced the sigh of tiny fans, then the glow of flight instruments on her screen. *Hello, Handsome.* The lady could flirt. She was sleek and primed with fuel, bejeweled with the latest avionics. Everything about her cried out to be touched and to be flown.

What was he supposed to do? Had Machen entrusted him with his personal mistress-of-the-air to escort her to some future rendezvous? Or had he given her outright, to have and to hold? But that's crazy. Nobody gives away an airplane. What did The Fugitive want? From a pouch at his knee came the Owner's Manual, with two words scrawled on its cover: *Share Me.*

Everett licked his lips. He recalled Tiffany Lavery's comment at the mall three weeks ago when she abandoned her bicycle. "I have another one—identical actually." That's how you give away an airplane, you copy it and share the copy. Identical, actually.

Yet this *Share Me* idea seemed to run deeper and less gracious than a plain invitation. Once you accepted a free copy, shouldn't you share it? Make another copy to give away because that's only fair? People would expect that. So sharing would snowball, if it was free, into a social obligation. People would expect it. Then they would demand it.

Still, it broke tons of cosmic inertia. How could he refuse?

Though Bobby would kill him. He had crossed a line this morning, helping Marcy, and here was another boundary, flashing red. Could an airplane be just a copy-table bauble, belonging to whoever used it? What harm could there be in flying her, keeping her, copying her? What did it matter if her previous owner was a notorious fugitive? She could be his now, if that's what he wanted. Until he made his own decisions, he would just be somebody's pull-toy, Bobby's marionette.

He climbed from the cockpit and shoved open the hangar doors, flooding the bay with daylight. A steady pull on a tow hook rolled Philip Machen's crimson mistress into the open air, her thin arms outstretched to receive the warm sun.

Everett sat in the cockpit, reading her specifications, memorizing numbers. Then he fastened his harness and drew down the canopy. When he spooled up the fan-jet, she glided forward, eager and confident. A pair of crows lifted away as he aligned her with the runway. Levering ten degrees of flaps, he scanned the pattern for traffic. Then he fed the throttle into its stops and released the brakes. Slender Lady surged a hundred feet before leaping into the air. Arcing vertical, still accelerating, he fed in a roll.

"Yeeeeehaaaaa!"

At ten thousand feet, he pushed her nose over, and the airspeed zoomed, setting up a vicious rattle. He was overpowering her skinny wings. He throttled back, cleaned up her appendages, and the vibration stopped. At 60 percent, she held 200 knots, straight and level. A quick calculation of fuel-flow versus pounds-remaining revealed they could reach Denver without refueling. Or Mexico. Or Canada.

He slipped her into a languid figure eight, scanned for traffic, then hauled the stick into his lap. G-forces made him gasp. The lady did screaming-tight loops. He caught his breath and did another, and another. She could loop faster and harder than he cared to endure. She could loop his brains out or pull off her wings, whichever came first.

"All right!"

He tried an Immelmann, then a floppy Hammerhead. He drew back the throttle, lowered the flaps, and hovered kite-like, barely doing thirty knots. He could land her in a parking lot if he wanted to.

To his right, the snowy Sierras gleamed. To his left, beyond the East Bay hills, San Francisco wedged itself between the dim bay and a shimmering sea. How could anyone traipse around day-after-day in earth-bound ruts, having once flown through a wide-open sky? Up here, out of reach, every minute could be a celebration, affirming his right to breathe. He was right to fly her, right to take her. They belonged together, up here, doing this.

He didn't need to obey Philip Machen or pretend that he cared enough to oppose him. Protecting Makers or destroying them weren't his fights. There had to be a middle way, a path between the extremes. No doubt he should copy this fabulous machine, to share her with others, but nobody was going to push him into doing stuff he didn't want to do.

Just now he needed a name, something historical, to honor his lady of the skies. Glamorous Glennis had been a great beauty in her time, so that would be it.

He powered up and raised the flaps. There might be answers he would never know, but there was no question what he would do. He had found his place in the world, his path forward, and he couldn't wait to show Bobby.

Soaring west on idle thrust, he descended from 6,000 feet. The Altamont Pass, so daunting from the ground, slid beneath him like crumpled green paper, a procession of ant-cars and bug-trucks traversing its folds. He descended rapidly, skimmed the warehouses east of Livermore, stayed low to hide his profile, and angled toward Poppy Ridge Golf Course. When the vineyards appeared, he banked west to skirt Livermore's southern flanks.

Between the wineries and the gravel pits, Jesse Cardoza had

windrowed his hay in a north-south direction. Everett could land between rows, so long as the crosswind stayed light. He skimmed Jesse's house and barns, picked his row, and muscled a sharp right turn. Dumping power as he raised the nose, he kicked the rudder and plunged, hawk-like. He could balloon again by hauling down the flaps, but he feared overshooting, so he lowered the landing gear and popped the spoilers to shed lift. Then he drew back the stick and settled rapidly.

All was peachy until Jesse's hay bailer appeared, dead ahead. He hadn't noticed its rusted hulk, lurking in the center of his chosen aisle. He jabbed left rudder, then right, in a wild yaw, barely aligning again as the wheels struck in the adjacent row. On his second bounce, the right wingtip snagged some mounded hay and spun him thirty degrees to a jarring halt. Glamorous Glennis had arrived none too elegantly. With a thumping heart and an empty head, he killed the engine and released the canopy. *So this is love.*

Jesse Cardoza's one-ton truck careered onto the field and bounced toward him. When it juddered to a stop nearby, two men got out, and the driver raised a rifle. When Everett removed his headset and sunglasses, its barrel swung aside.

"Jesus Christ. What are you doing, Everett?"

Bobby said this, but Jesse's eyes were saying it too. The rancher scowled and laid his .223 on the hood of the truck.

"Hi, Dad. Hi, Jesse."

In scuffed Wellington boots and a Rural Supply ball cap, Jesse Cardoza was one of those men Bobby called wiry. Despite his button-straining belly, there was no doubt Jesse could draw a barbed wire fence as taut as a banjo string with his bare hands, which was Everett's first memory of him. He still walked pigeon-toed too.

Everett stepped from the cockpit and couldn't help smiling.

"Where have you been?" Bobby demanded. "And what's this?"

"My airplane."

Two sets of eyebrows shot up.

"Good to see you again, Jesse." Everett tried a casual tone. "Sorry I couldn't make it this morning. Got sidetracked." He offered his hand, knowing what was coming. Jesse always squeezed an order of magnitude too hard. Everett endured the ritual and returned Jesse's grin, which was fierce and friendly.

"Good to see you, Everett. I think."

Bobby seemed unsure, as well. "What's this all about, Son?"

"We need to copy this plane."

"Where'd you get it?"

"Tracy."

"Why's it here?"

"I'm . . . taking care of it."

"Take it back."

"Nobody's there."

"Are you nuts? Nobody saw you take it, so it's yours?"

"I didn't steal it, and I'm pretty sure it's a copy."

"Copy, schmoppy. Take it back."

"It's mine, and I want to make more of them if you guys will lend a hand." Jesse was enjoying this, but the twinkle in his eye could turn to cast iron the instant Everett gave a weak response. "We can fly to Canada, Dad. To find Mom and Melinda."

Bobby staggered. His shock turned to disgust.

"Where's your Honda?"

Everett jerked his head eastward.

"So how are you getting to work tomorrow?"

Everett shrugged.

"Did General fire you?"

"No. I just have this airplane now. We can fly, Dad. We can go anywhere we want and start our own service."

"Who? Who gives away airplanes?"

"She's our ticket, Dad."

"Somebody is searching for this thing, and you brought it here? So now Jesse's in trouble too? Is that how you repay a friend? Get it out of here, or so help me I'll call the cops myself."

Jesse's twinkle disappeared. Without a word, he returned to the truck and stashed his gun behind the seat. Bobby paced the length of a wing, waving his hands.

"Why couldn't you steal something small?" He grabbed a wingtip. "C'mon, help me turn it around."

Everett shook his head, kicked at the oat stubble.

"Soil's too soft here for takeoff. She needs a hundred feet of hardpan."

"What were you thinking?" Bobby threw up his hands. "What are we supposed to do with a damned airplane?"

"Cover it up."

Bobby snorted. "Before the cops find it."

"Or the satellites."

"Damn, Everett, whose plane did you take?"

Now Jesse strode over and planted himself under Everett's chin, bumped him belly-to-belly. "Tell us straight, kid."

Everett squirmed. "This morning I helped Marcy Johnson interview Philip Machen. He gave me the plane."

Bobby flung his ball cap to the ground and stomped it. Even Jesse backed away. "Jesus," he said, and his hands clutched at the empty air.

"You stupid shit." Bobby twisted. "Now you're playing footsie with a maniac, and he's bribed you. What the hell's wrong with you?"

"You're just jealous 'cause I did something without you. Something important."

Bobby charged, knocked him down, and pummeled him with open-handed slaps. Everett put up his hands but deflected only half the blows. Jesse took approximately forever to get a bear hug around Bobby and to pull him off. When the thrashing and the cursing subsided, he rolled Bobby across his hip like a bale of hay.

Bobby lay on his side, gasping. After a while he got up, brushed himself, and trod away, plucking straw and dirt from his ball cap.

Everett spit blood and mucus. *Keep going, you bastard, just like*

Mom did. I should have gone with her, but you wouldn't say it. So I stayed. For you.

Jesse fetched a white pouch from the truck, which he twisted and laid on Everett's face. The cold pack turned colder as Everett pressed it to his mouth. Without a word, Jesse returned to the truck and backed it away, churning through the field in reverse.

Everett lay on the oat stubble and surveyed the sky, found it bluer than it had been all spring. Not a bird or a cloud or a plane.

Whenever he took matters into his own hands, Bobby criticized. That was the pattern. But he didn't have to take it anymore. He had flown to the ranch to take his father with him—didn't the jackass know that? No matter what the world did about Makers, this plane was his future, his and Bobby's.

The roar of Jesse's one-ton returned, and Everett sat up. Bad idea. The spins twirled him somewhere between the earth and the sky, so he laid back down. Knowing Jesse, it would be chainsaws and hay hooks to chop up Glamorous Glennis, to haul her off in pieces. But instead, the gruff old Portuguese parked nearby and looped a tow cable through his hitch bracket, playing it over to Everett.

"Get up kid. You're milking it. Help me get this pile of parts over to the barn. I got some tarps to cover it up if you'll get off your ass."

Everett blotted his mouth on his sleeve, inspected the spot for blood.

"People still need pilots, don't they, Jess? I mean besides the airlines? That's what I'm going to do. Take people where they want to go, in this plane."

"Your dad is right. You're dumb as a fish fart, but maybe not a criminal. So get up."

TWENTY-FIVE

EVERETT AND JESSE had just covered Glamorous Glennis when a dark gray sedan crunched up the driveway and stopped at the barn, not the house. Only Bobby and the Cardoza's knew Everett was here. How could anyone have found him so soon? Were they watching when he landed? Or had Bobby really called the cops? This was not the best moment to have a .32 pistol in his back pocket.

The lone driver parked and got out. It was Hollywood, the FBI crewcut from Ms. Lavery's place, the one with all the questions. Same blue suit and leather shoes. He removed his sunglasses and grimaced as if pained to ask for directions. He nodded to Everett but approached Jesse.

"Mr. Cardoza? My name is Leslie Parker, Federal Agent. Mr. Aboud and I have already met." He flipped open his badge wallet and grinned like a model from a toothpaste ad.

The king of Portuguese staredowns ignored the badge and

locked onto Parker's eyes. Agent Parker stared back, more amused than surprised.

"Mr. Aboud, may I have a few words with you, in private, please?"

Jesse puffed his considerable chest and answered for him. "What do you want, Officer?"

"Philip Machen, actually."

"Not here, actually."

"But you know where he was this morning, don't you, Mr. Aboud?" Parker still hadn't taken his eyes off Jesse. "Unless Mr. Aboud wants another ride to our facilities, I hope you will excuse us, Mr. Cardoza. Thank you for your cooperation, sir." He cut the chit chat by turning to Everett.

Jesse shrugged and ambled to his truck, grinning all the way. He had won the staredown. He hopped onto the flatbed and sat with his Wellington boots dangling.

"Whatever happened to your face, Mr. Aboud?" Parker approached him.

"I was wrestling an aardvark."

Parker nodded, tucked away his badge.

"And what do we have here?" He peeled a tarpaulin, exposing a cherry-red wingtip.

"My airplane."

"Registered to you, is it?"

Everett looked away. For all he knew, it wasn't registered to anyone. *And where the hell is Bobby? Doesn't he want to see this?*

Parker scanned the yard, too, then flipped more canvas until he reached the cockpit. He stood there, listening perhaps to the gob of plastic in his ear. He glanced again at Everett and Jesse. Then he produced a notebook and scribbled numbers from the cockpit. When he finished, he left the canopy open and the tarpaulins scattered.

"Tell me," he said, "how does a shoe clerk afford his own private jet?" Parker drew closer, removed his sunglasses. "Payment for services?"

"You wish." Blood had clotted in Everett's nostrils, and he sounded stupid, even to himself. "I only met him this morning, Mr. Parker. We didn't talk. He gave me the key to the plane and told me to keep it, that's all. He didn't say why."

"Nice man. Generous."

Everett showed him the key fob and explained how he didn't know it was for an airplane until he went to Tracy. "It's not a bribe," he said.

"Yet you flew it here and told no one. Not even Ms. Johnson."

Sweat trickled between Everett's shoulders. *Do they have Marcy too?*

Parker squinted. "Did he recruit you?"

"He fed us breakfast, and we did the interview. There was no time for anything else."

"Before the interview, did he say or do anything unusual? Any kind of ritual or gesture? Did he use the word *secular* or *humanist?*"

Everett shook his head. "He wanted breakfast without agendas."

"So what's your impression, Mr. Aboud? What is Philip Machen all about?"

Everett shrugged. "He believes his own shit."

"And?"

"And I don't know. Doing good? He thinks he's doing good?"

"Saving the world."

"I wouldn't know."

"But he does." Parker drew within cologne range. "Behind all that posturing this morning, what do you suppose he really wants?"

"Forgiveness?"

"Hardly."

Another shrug. "He wants it to happen," Everett said. "He knows what's going to happen, and that's what he wants."

"Ah, yes, the plan. Chaos and anarchy. Destroy America so he can thump his chest, take our scalps, and count his coup. But where does that kind of thinking come from, Mr. Aboud? That book he published on the internet, its title is *Maker Advent*. Now, that's a religious word, advent. It means a progression toward something that's coming or a person who's coming. A prophet, maybe. People say he's a nonbeliever, because of his father, but that's not true, is it? You said it yourself. Philip Machen believes his own shit."

Everett crossed his arms, looked at Jesse, who looked back just as dumb.

Parker donned his sunglasses, concealing the gleam in his eyes. James Bond had fleeced the casino, but what had he snatched?

"Thank you for your efforts this morning, Mr. Aboud. Your video will be of help to us. And thank you for this little chat. I will say in your file that you cooperated." He offered his hand.

Everett shook the FBI's hand, certain he'd been gulled.

"You and your father live here now, is that right?" Again Parker surveyed the yard. "You will call me then, if Mr. Machen shows up, wanting his airplane?"

Everett nodded his throbbing head.

Parker grinned like a lottery winner.

"If I were you, Mr. Aboud, I'd stay here on the ranch, where it's quiet. I wouldn't go traveling. I wouldn't do more interviews." He strode to his car and opened the door. Before him, Glamorous Glennis lay exposed and vulnerable. "Try not to kill yourself in that thing. They're not safe, you know."

He started his car and drove slowly toward Vineyard Road.

As he passed the tool shed, Bobby emerged into the sun, empty-handed. Bobby's gaze followed Parker's dust until it disappeared. Then he returned to the shed.

Thanks, Dad. Thanks for your support.

Jesse hopped down and trotted to Everett.

"What did he want?"

Everett moved into the shade of the barn, to pull off his sweaty leather jacket.

"Jesse, if you ever see that guy again, and he looks pleased with himself, you'll know you're in trouble."

"Because of the plane?"

Everett shook his head. "He wanted me to say something, and I guess I did."

"Like what?"

"I don't know, but it made his day." Everett leaned against the barn, to doff his leather pants.

Jesse hitched his thumbs in his belt. "Good thing he didn't give you any grief." He nodded toward the tool shed. "Your daddy had his rifle trained on him the whole time."

Everett stopped and peered across the yard. He couldn't see through the glare from the tin roof, but with sunglasses maybe Parker had. Maybe he was calling for reinforcements right now. The ground beneath Everett's feet threatened to crack open and swallow him.

Jesse strode for the house. "C'mon, kid. Lunch is ready."

Everett glanced again at the tool shed. Then he collected his leathers and followed Jesse. He called out to Bobby as much as to Jesse, "I'm going to start a flying service."

PARKER PHONED DISPATCH as soon as he reached the pavement.

"Philip Machen's airplane is at the Cardoza ranch, between Pleasanton and Livermore." He gave the address. "Get a bird in the air and a tactical squad out here as soon as you can. I'm staging at Rock Springs Road."

He stopped on the shoulder of the road and hoped he hadn't ruined everything by dawdling with the kid. He hadn't drawn his pistol against a human being in seven years but checked it now. No way was he going to miss the party he had just called. The buzz in his earpiece would be the SAC, Derek Majers.

"This is not your case, Parker."

"I found Philip Machen's airplane. I called for air support and a tactical team."

"Yeah, well, I just canceled them. I'm sending someone over there to babysit the ranch, just in case, but I want you to stop meddling and get back to the office

"Beg pardon?"

"We have a dozen little red airplanes scattered around the country, each of them identical, including Hizzoner's fingerprints and DNA. Yours is lucky thirteen."

"You could have told me."

"It's not your case. And the Bureau doesn't want this leaked."

"Philip Machen gave this particular airplane to the Aboud kid, personally, this morning."

"He gave away the other ones too. He'd be pretty stupid to fly one now, or even go near one since we know what to look for."

"What if he takes off from the ranch this afternoon?"

"Then we track him on radar. Every damn raid we launch winds up in the news, Parker, and Machen is counting on it. He loves federal agents charging around, assaulting farms and empty hangars. Makes us look dumb. No sir, we are going to corner this guy before we snatch him. He's not killing people. We can afford to be sure. Did the Arab kid give you anything?"

As a matter of fact, he had, but sitting as he was at the top of Parker's shit list, Derek Majers would not be hearing it.

"Last warning, Parker, stay the hell out of the Machen case, or I will suspend you for insubordination. If Brayley finds out, he'll screw both of us out of our pensions. You got that? No more freelancing."

"Right." Parker switched off the phone, switched off his boss, who didn't understand how close he was to this fugitive's psyche. While others scouted the Berkeley hills for after-the-fact clues, he was perfecting his theory of Philip Machen. If the core of every sociopath was the lie he never stopped telling himself, Parker only needed to uncover that lie.

TWENTY-SIX

Oakland, California. Thursday, May 14
Day Twenty-seven

ELEVEN DAYS HAD PASSED without a single bank robbery when Parker's Cambiar vibrated and Harpreet Sugand's face appeared on its screen. He rushed to the men's room, dove into a vacant stall, and latched the door.

"Parker."

"Leslie, we must talk."

"Shoot. I mean, go ahead." He descended to the throne.

"I finished his diary." The connection clinked and rustled as if Harry were making tea. "Do you know the greatest spiritual hazard we novitiates faced, entering divinity school?"

Parker straightened, almost said runaway hormones, but remembered a fancy word. "Theodicy?"

"Hey, very good. Theodicy fails sometimes, yes. It's when you examine your own faith, Leslie, and compare it to the teachings, to their history and origins. There's always the chance you will encounter a doubt you cannot reconcile—and conclude that something about your faith is mistaken. In my class, two fell apostate. One tried to hang himself. Your fugitive reminds me of the other one, my roommate before he withdrew."

"Does that mean Machen is not lying?"

"Well, they are mistaken, of course, these secular humanists, but their idol is integrity. If they cannot reconcile some teaching with what they determine to be true, they throw out the teaching, sometimes the whole book. The way they see it, they are refusing to lie to themselves. My roommate came to feel he was worshiping the words and not the reality, so he quit seminary. Nobody could talk him out of it. Since fourth grade, he wants to be a priest, yet he refuses to continue, even to save his soul, because professing a doubtful truth would make him a dishonest priest. We can say he is mistaken or delusional, but that is the sort of fellow you are facing. Philip Machen knows exactly what he's doing and precisely why. He has taken his vows, and he pursues his mission."

"For revenge."

Harry snorted. "I thought you read it, Leslie. It's atonement, to redeem his guilt for not dying with his family. A guilt so vast, he needs to prove his Makers, and the mind that created them, merit the attention of the ages. When Makers achieve what his father's books and lectures could not, the son will be redeemed."

Parker squirmed. *So Machen's lie is, only he knows how to right a cosmic wrong?*

"You can thank me with a case of Hoegaarden. Also, I want to meet him."

"Wait." Parker's voice echoed.

"Are you in the toilet, Leslie?"

"Yeah."

"Where you've gone to hide your baboon-face?"

"I thought you'd say he's a fraud, or evil, or something."

"Because he deceives us," Harry said.

"Sure."

"You do not forgive him?"

"That's your job, Harry. He needs to answer for what he's done. That's my job."

"Don't tell my bishop, but if some of this guy's writings were in God-speak instead of humanist-speak, he might have earned a few points as a spiritual thinker. You and I know it's ego, that he is spreading his machines for selfish reasons, but in the end, it's the result that is counting. Even for saints."

"Jesus. I mean . . . Harry, we need to talk. I'll bring the Hoegaarden."

NEXT DAY, Derek was giving him the eye while the world continued to fall apart. Parker's sister in Des Moines, a single mother of two, had lost her eight-year job at a maternity shop when it closed. Protest demonstrations were expanding in number and vehemence. Every nation except the U.S. had outlawed both Powerpods and Makers. And still having a job to complain about consoled him not at all.

No ordinary Maker could copy thirteen red airplanes. Somewhere there had to be a Super Maker with cones big enough to disgorge forty-foot wings. So behind Derek's back, Parker was canvassing warehouse operators and airport managers, asking about vacant or disused buildings within or near every airport in California. Plus, he was reading Leonard Machen's old books to gauge Philip's dedication to his father's ideology.

After lunch, Derek assigned Parker an urgent chore. Everyone expected Ms. Lavery's attorney to petition a federal court to release her, which wouldn't do at all. Transferring her to a less-liberal jurisdiction would force Terry Quinn to file his writs there, thus slowing the process. So the Bureau was flying her to Maryland, to a fancy lock-up disguised as a boarding school, thirty miles from Washington, D.C. Then if, as rumor had it, a grand jury would charge her with sedition, no court would grant bail—not with the entire country demanding her head and every pompous twit in a tizzy to do something.

Parker's task this afternoon was to drive to the San Leandro Best Western Hotel where Ms. Lavery was held and tell her the long knives were taking over.

Instead of barging in like the others, he gave notice, a simple call to the desk phone in her room. While other agents drew nothing from her, Parker had collected two verbal portraits, one of herself and one of Philip Machen, before he was taken off the case.

He knocked.

The door opened to a scene out of an old movie: auburn hair brushed to a sheen, silky blue pajamas with padded shoulders, and red, open-toed sandals. She was everything the custody room was not. It seemed the hairdresser he arranged last week had improved more than her appearance. She greeted him with a slinky pose and the first genuine smile of her captivity.

Behind her, the television was saying, "A friend would never pull a rug from under our feet and claim that our crash to the floor was not his fault." She switched it off.

When her gaze alighted on the white carnation in his hand, he entered and laid it on the table between them. He shut the door, waited for her to sit, then took the other chair.

Whether Derek realized it or not, serving notice on Ms. Lavery this afternoon was giving him an unauthorized chance to question her one last time. She no longer held the key to Philip Machen, if she had ever had it, but his latest ideas might provoke a telling response.

"He wants to be a secular messiah."

She took up the flower. "What?"

"Beginning with the ontological inversion," he said. "My friend the priest says that's the proposition that humans have created their gods for human purposes, not vice versa. If God did not exist, we would have to invent Him, and so we did. Philip's father was spreading this parable before he was killed."

"A priest said this?"

"Quoting Philip's father."

She shook her head. "Philip didn't talk about his father. He never mentioned religion. I doubt he cares very much, one way or another."

"Leonard Machen *is* Philip's religion. Not hero worship, idea worship. Leonard was making waves, calling for a secular millennium, promoting rational secular morality. He wanted people to admit the ontological inversion, then move beyond it. He claimed morality is human and natural, not divine or supernatural. His views got him fired from four different school districts, and the family had to move each time. Philip called it the Family Curse, one that eventually gave the arsonist an excuse to kill his family. I think Philip wants to atone for those murders by completing his father's agenda."

"By giving away Makers?" She sniffed the flower.

"By standing civilization on its head. By shaking every authority to its foundations. Divine authority, especially. If heaven fails, Makers will provide. No need to pray, just add water. Do-it-yourself salvation."

He waited for her to look up.

"He's avenging his family's murder by continuing his father's crusade. If we construct our gods to suit our needs, and those needs change, then we must update the old gods to suit our new conditions. Two thousand years ago, when things changed abruptly, monotheism wiped out polytheism. Philip thinks when Makers change everything again, humanism will prevail over theism. His father's legacy will be confirmed."

"Preposterous."

"You said Philip is not a philanthropist, that he's not giving away Makers to help the poor. He claims no ambition and seeks no power, but that's an artifice, isn't it? He lied to you about Powerpods. He betrayed you to advance his agenda. What makes you think you are the biggest patsy in his campaign? Or that Powerpods are his boldest deception?"

She shook her head.

"He's maneuvering us toward stage two. This time, he's playing the whole world, advancing his father's agenda to deconstruct theism. If human needs created God, then relieving most of those needs should free us to un-create Him. By deliberately throwing the world into chaos, by challenging our deepest fears and assumptions, and by offering a powerful, secular remedy, Philip Machen entices us to kill our gods."

"That's insane."

"Did you read his diary?" He took out a notebook and flipped to a marked page.

"Here's what he said about the arsonist who killed his family. 'If you kill the killer, you only remove one man. His victory stands. To nullify that victory, you must invalidate the killer's sanction. You must dethrone his myth. Then, when his gods are gone, there can be no divine mandate, no supernatural blessings, for murder. A nonexistent divinity cannot command or forgive the evil done in its name, and the killer's moral sanction disappears. This will be my perfect revenge.'"

"He wrote that when?"

"A year after the fire."

She tipped the flower to her lips. "If my family was incinerated in front of me, I might think that way for a while. Just the sort of thing an angry young man would say, even if he were not a genius. Your secular messiah is nothing but a victim's rant, Parker. Philip never said anything like that to me, or to anyone else. It's rubbish."

"He used that phrase twice, and he never took back his vow of revenge."

"Listen to yourself," she said. "It's been what? A decade and a half? You can't seriously believe a teenager's anguish amounts to anything after so many years."

"It doesn't matter what you or I believe, Ms. Lavery. As soon as those words hit the Washington leak factory, his enemies will spread them from blog to blog, and pulpit to pulpit. I imagine their effect will be quite spectacular."

She nuzzled the tender white florets. "Well, don't expect me to feel sorry for him."

Parker dropped his gaze.

"I worry that someone might aim a similar cannon at you, Ms. Lavery. During your testimony before Congress."

She stiffened.

He laid an envelope between them. "Congressional subpoena. You are served."

She pursed her exquisite red lips. "Bail?"

He shook his head.

She faced the pastel green walls of her confinement, shut her eyes, and inhaled comfort from the flower.

"Goodbye, Parker."

TWENTY-SEVEN

Victorville, California. Sunday, May 17
Day Thirty

SHE GAVE UP THE DIARY, or they took it from her.

Philip needed Karen to understand and to forgive him, but it seemed she hadn't even read it. He pedaled his stationary bicycle faster, straining toward a cobweb guarding the hangar wall. If she'd understood, if she'd read any of it, she would've protected that memory chip or burned it. He spun free of his toe clips, furious that his most personal outreach had not moved her.

Now the red news talk shows couldn't stop flogging their atheist messiah mantras, to whip up more outrage. His youthful speculations about religion should interest no one. He'd forgotten he wrote them.

From a folding table they used as a desk, Tanner redirected the internet conversation they were having with Art Buddha, Short Fat Guy. Unlike his jolly website avatar, Art's human face appeared pinched and pasty on the screen between Philip's handlebars. The blogger's dark, avian eyes glanced off-screen intermittently as if he were about to say, "Nevermore."

"I wanted her to know who I am," Philip said.

Art adjusted his rectangular eyeglasses and brushed a dark lock off his forehead. "Well," he said, "a drug-addicted child-pornographer would have gone down better than an atheist messiah. The Tories couldn't have picked a more offensive slander. We just lost most the country south of Nashville. Even the Lutherans up north don't abide no uppity infidels."

Tanner stepped onto a treadmill and took up a stride. "So tell us the bad news."

Art clicked an icon. "Here's the latest—"

The YouTube clip began with an old Leonard Machen speech, probably recorded on a cell phone fifteen years ago. Seeing his father alive and standing at a hotel lectern sent pangs of longing through Philip, but the video played without sound. Leonard's lips moved in silence until a single line rang clear: "Religion is poison."

That outtake, just three words, looped four times—religion is poison—then it froze on one grainy frame. Between the curtains near the lectern stood a callow, pimply-faced youth, barely a teen, yet recognizable. A circle highlighted the boy's face, brightening his blond hair and pale skin, while a name in gold letters hovered conveniently: Philip Machen. The clip had been viewed 236,844 times in three days and ended with a neon rendering of its title "Like Father, Like Son."

Philip swayed. He'd heard that speech a dozen times. The full quotation was "Religion is poison if it makes you hate." If it makes you hate, any idea is poison. Even believers believed that, most of them.

Art grimaced. "The really bad news is Noemi Ryles is working on a time factor for her social tipping point theorem. So far she hasn't proved any limits exist, but she thinks social memes may expire deterministically. The slower they approach their tipping points without achieving them, the more likely they will fail. Bottom line—we might have fifty days to lock in the Freemaker paradigm before it starts to die."

Philip stopped pedaling. "Fifty days since we announced Makers a month ago?"

"Right."

Philip resumed pedaling. Twenty days to share twenty-five million more machines. *Damn.*

Tanner adjusted the video screen on his treadmill. "So what's the good news, Art?"

"Mavens. People who connect with lots of folks. Mavens can spread a meme by sheer enthusiasm, like those viral clips on YouTube."

"Marcy Johnson's interview has been out there for two weeks," Philip complained.

Art switched to pidgin. "Dat interview gonna kill you, Brah. You say more machines, more machines, but da lady say whatta bout da peoples? You gonna lose dat one, Brah. You gotta take it to da peoples." Then back to English. "So far, we have less than a dozen new enclaves."

"What about mavens?"

"Well, I'm trying," Art said. "But our guy Philip Machen would be a perfect maven. He could show up anywhere, and people would gather to listen."

"Before they lynched him," Philip added.

"Depends," Art said. "You gotta fire up the friendlies, Boss. Identify your base and get 'em moving. Give 'em reasons to join the cause. You could be the maven for a whole lot of folks, but you gotta put some skin in the game. 'Cause it's their game now, isn't it? They're the ones risking the consequences if they follow you. You're just a trickster who messed with their heads and upset their routines. They don't care if you play peek-a-boo with the *federales*. Lots of them think you deserve some jail time. But you gotta get out there and press the flesh, man. Touch some folks. Kiss dem babies. 'Cause right now they could use one good messiah."

"What?"

"Do it for real," Art said. "Save their asses."

Philip swung off the bike and paced away. He returned to glare at Art. "What sort of moral chameleon do you think I am? I can't do that. Everybody'd know it's a lie. It would only confirm the propaganda."

"So don't lie," Art said. "Don't claim to be any sort of savior. Just *be* one. A real messiah would save us now, *before* we're dead."

Philip clenched and turned away. "I'm not a fraud, dammit."

If he started playing messiah, he wouldn't be himself anymore. He'd be living a lie, the sort of malarkey he and his parents despised. *The truth at any price, Son, including the price of your life.* It was a bedrock tenet of his family. The Powerpods maneuver had gained him a foothold for Makers, but it had cost him Karen Lavery and thousands like her. The damage from more sleight-of-hand could ruin everything if it boomeranged. Yet if he waited for people to develop Freemaker sensibilities and share their way to new communities, the bullies and fear-mongers might grab all the Makers and co-opt the advent by force.

Maker copies aged and degraded at the same rates as their originals, so shelf life would eventually drive people to share fresh comestibles. But that could take months.

He sought the purple V on his wrist, which tipped into an A as he raised it. His secret A-for-atheist: a permanent reminder of the sectarian hatred that killed his family. And of his younger self squatting in the snow before a burning house, unable to stop the evil. But he was no longer a kid, captive and impotent. He had friends now, allies, and the latent testimony of 55 million Makers.

Art Buddha was right about showing himself, about taking a risk. Leonard Machen had never given up on the American public, never feared their potential for sectarian violence as Philip had. The only way forward was to find people who wanted to move in that direction. And to help those people. No more waiting. And no pretending. He had to let go of his expectations and accept the obvious. Only one person could save the Maker advent.

"Download Art's manifesto," he said to Tanner. "Then find the most active enclave. We need to go there."

TWENTY-EIGHT

Sao Paulo, Brazil. Wednesday, May 20
Day Thirty-three

THEY LANDED AT DUSK, in a drizzle that blurred the great city around them yet barely lubricated the windscreen wipers. Tanner taxied their retired Federal Express cargo jet toward the customs apron at a deserted freight terminal. He followed the yellow line to a numbered space facing a rusty chain link fence, where he shut down the engines and opened the cockpit door. Winter huffed into the cabin, uninvited.

Outside, a single sodium-vapor lamp generated more glare than illumination. Two vehicles rounded the left wing: an official white sedan flashing an amber beacon, and a somber black van, an Airporter Special. Tanner lowered the aluminum extension ladder they used for a stair, and Philip descended to foreign concrete, acutely aware he was betting the future of the advent, and possibly his life, on the goodwill of people he'd never met.

Tanner joined him, dressed alike in navy blue FedEx uniforms, complete with captain's gold sleeve markings, matching epaulets, and a winged medallion over the breast pocket. If the customs agent emerging from that amber-blinking car didn't accept their documents, there was no way they could turn the plane around quickly enough to escape. Philip calmed himself and let his worries congeal where they would.

The customs inspector approached them in a reflective vest, limping a bit, and clutching a wooden clipboard.

"*Bem vinda*," he said without enthusiasm. "Welcome." He did not smile but nodded as Philip offered their passports and a fake transit order.

"We are dead-heading," Philip said. "No cargo."

The inspector nodded. He fingered their passports but did not open them. He looked up to the cockpit where Chuck Zarbaugh, their bald-headed flying partner, was hauling up the ladder and shutting the door.

"He stays with the plane," Philip said, "for security."

Customs scanned their FedEx form with a flashlight. "Tomorrow departing?"

"Yes, sir."

"No cargo?"

Philip nodded. "That's right."

The inspector indicated their overnight bags. "No drugs or weapons?"

Tanner held forth the bags, but the man ignored them and glanced over his shoulder.

From the black van, a stout figure emerged and stood a few paces away, his back to the glare and the fence, his face in the shadows. He clasped his hands before him like an usher.

Customs said nothing. He produced a pocket stamp, which he rolled onto each passport. He dated the marks and returned the documents. Then, without a second glance to the attending stranger, he limped to his car and drove away, bestowing amber flashes on the mists and drizzle.

"Mr. Machen." The mystery man approached, dark and tanned,

about fifty years old. He could be a peasant or a boss: strong-like-tractor, smart-like-bull. Despite his plain cotton jacket, an impeccable white shirt and tailored slacks bespoke a man of means. "Otavio Frias," he said.

Philip released the breath he was holding. Otavio Frias was the Powerpods franchisee for Northern Brazil. During an email exchange on Monday, *Senhor* Frias had offered to assist them. Philip shook the man's hand and hoped his sense of connection was mutual.

The drizzle gathered into rain, and the men hurried to the passenger compartment of the black van. Otavio shut the door and spoke in Portuguese to the driver. As the van circled away, Otavio rubbed his hands. He produced a thin, glossy book from his jacket, and offered it to Philip.

"Please, senhor. Will you sign for my wife? She is a fan."

Astonished, then pleased, Philip accepted the book and relaxed into his seat. Someone had published his online *Maker Advent* and bound it in warm Brazilian hues. The cover featured a hand-drawn Maker at the pinnacle of a familiar Rio de Janeiro landmark, its dark cones spreading arm-like over the city. In place of the Corcovado statue of Christ.

Oh, shit.

He showed it to Tanner, whose eyebrows spoke faster than his mouth. "Whoa."

"I can't sign this," Philip implored. "This is not why we came." He returned the book. "Whoever printed this is trying to get somebody killed."

Otavio nodded and brushed invisible crumbs of doubt from its cover. He tucked the book away and leaned closer.

"You should know what you are up against, senhor." He searched Philip's eyes. "What we are up against."

Otavio must have influenced the customs inspector on their behalf because their bogus transit order could not have withstood scrutiny.

"Thank you, Senhor Frias. Your assistance is most—"

Otavio raised a finger to his lips, then indicated the driver.

"We will discuss your vacation plans at the *condomínio*, senhor." He winked and turned away.

Philip folded his arms, tried to absorb Brazil through rain-dappled windows. Their van hurtled passed an idle checkpoint onto an unlighted frontage that conveyed it up a ramp. Heading west on the freeway, they accelerated into the spray thrown off by heavy traffic. Low buildings near the airport gave way to apartment clusters, fifteen or twenty stories high. In the distance, taller spires marked the bright, downtown hub of the city. But Philip had not come for lights or skyscrapers.

He was here for the slums, the *favelas*, and one in particular. On a hillside northwest of Guarulhos International Airport, five thousand impoverished and heretofore powerless residents of *favela Xavier* were holding off the Brazilian Army. Whatever the issues behind that confrontation, Tanner and Philip had discerned a brave and spontaneous Freemaker enclave defending its right to exist. These *favelados*, who had so little to lose and so much to gain, might show the rest of the world what a Maker enclave could become.

The van left the freeway and arced onto a tree-lined boulevard clotted with cars and darting scooters. Gradually, the pavement narrowed and roughened. Where it turned lumpy, there were no streetlights, just a dull glow cast by surrounding apartments, dozens of them. The road ended at a concrete wall and an open gate that admitted them to a turning apron. They disembarked under the gaze of three security cameras. Otavio waved to the guard inside as he led them through a vacant lobby.

"In Brazil," he said as they entered an elevator, "we have five social classes. This condomínio is class C, mostly salaried workers, what you in America call middle class." He pressed a button marked 12. "The wealthy elites are class A. Professionals and business owners are class B. The working poor are class D. The remaining thirty percent of Sao Paulo live in favelas which have no legal status and are controlled by gangsters or militias. Right now, the militias are winning."

At floor twelve the doors opened, and he led them to an apartment at the end of a baren hallway.

"Please, come in."

Off the common room with its chairs and sofas were a tiny kitchen, two bedrooms, and a bath, all painted white and floored with uneven parquet. A single bulb in the stove hood provided weak illumination. Otavio drew back a wall of curtains, revealing two windows and a glass door.

"Behold our neighbors." He unlocked the door and led them onto a narrow balcony. Twelve stories below, an invisible stream of water swished and gurgled, bisecting a swath of inky black soil and debris. Across the divide, heaps of dark and tangled shapes arose, a crust of packing crates and boxes deposited on the hillside by successive tides of human backs and shoulders. Between them flowed meanders of greater and lesser darkness, punctuated by eerie blue flickers from video screens. Voices thrummed and music tinkled. A chilling breeze carried the scent of mud, of sewage, and of over-cooked food. "Favela Xavier, gentlemen."

"Don't they have Pods?" The place was darker than Philip expected.

"Hundreds of them, but only two Makers." Otavio led them back to the common room, shut the patio door, and switched on the lights. "You have to understand, senhor Machen. They are prisoners."

Philip traded glances with Tanner.

Otavio hauled a Cambiar from his pocket and tapped it. He spoke to it briefly in Portuguese. Satisfied with the response, he folded it away and motioned for his guests to be seated.

"When you live in a favela," he said, "there are no services, no police, no courts, no rights. To the government and the other classes you are not legitimate, you are not *gente*. So the gangsters and the militias control everyone who lives there. No one leaves or enters without their permission.

"These militias," he said, "are mostly cops, retired or off-duty. Regular cops don't go there, but the militias invade with machine guns. They kill the gangsters, then impose their own rules. They extort money, demand information and favors. Makers threaten their authority and their profits, so they don't allow them.

"Also with the *traficantes,* they still have their drugs and their guns, but cash is worthless and former clients stay home now, to make free cocaine. So the gangsters hide in their favelas and fight the militias just to survive. For themselves, they keep a few Makers. But both sides control who owns the Powerpods, and both sides forbid Maker cones."

Philip sat heavily on the sofa, his plans for tomorrow deflated. "So, what is the Army doing here?"

"Ah." Otavio inhaled his disgust. He sat opposite Philip, elbows on his knees. "That is our complication, senhor. To keep the militias out, our resident traficante, a thug named Kojo, has kidnapped the daughter of an Air Force colonel. Her name is Mariela Santos, and she is eight years old. Presidente da Silva herself has declared that if this little girl is not returned by Friday at noon, unharmed, the Army will crush favela Xavier."

A long moment passed while Philip digested this. Even Tanner slouched in his chair. What could they hope to accomplish, now? Favella Xavier wasn't the active enclave they were seeking. It wasn't an enclave at all. How could they lead these people away from conflict and toward a sharing sensibility, during a siege? Philip rubbed his face.

Three knocks, light but firm, brought Tanner and Otavio to their feet. Otavio strode ahead and gestured for calm.

"It is not the police, *senhores.* I have invited a friend." He peered through the peephole and unlocked the door. "You will like her, I think."

A trim European woman in a blue medical jumpsuit entered and waited for Otavio to secure the door. Hawk-nosed and alert, she wore her dark hair in a bob and her face in a tight mask of done-everything competence. Otavio introduced Dr. Jacqueline de Beir, a Belgian physician who worked for the charity, Doctors Without Borders.

"Dr. de Beir would like to join us," Otavio said, "if we go into favela Xavier tomorrow."

Her keen eyes swept the room and registered their pilot uniforms. She moved past Tanner to confront Philip.

"I know who you are," she accused. "I will not betray your presence in Sao Paulo." She ignored Otavio's gesture to be seated. "There is a fever, Brazilian dengue, endemic to favelas, often fatal. Tomorrow I will bring a vaccine to inoculate the children, who are most susceptible. And you, if you have not received it."

Philip nodded.

"But what I want," she said, "is Mariela Galena Santos." She looked at Otavio. "You have told them about her?"

"*Sim, sim,*" Otavio said. Yes, yes.

"Then you will take me with you." Her expression dared Philip to deny her. Noting the wrinkle of concern that creased his brow, she said, "I will be safer than you will be, senhor."

Philip believed this, agreed to include her if they proceeded tomorrow, but warned her it might not happen. "Complications," he said. She declared herself to be a realist, thanked him, and turned to leave. She lectured Otavio in curt Portuguese as he escorted her to the door.

He chuckled as he bolted it behind her. "She said I must make you do it."

Philip scoffed, too tired to appreciate the levity. The problem of bolstering an existing enclave had become the impossibility of creating a new one within a prison camp. They should not waste their precious time. Yet, who but these favelados had a greater need for Makers? What good was the advent if it only helped prosperous North Americans?

"Okay," he said. "This is going to require some coffee."

Otavio described his contacts within the favela and outlined his preparations for tomorrow's giveaway. He still thought they could pull it off. After mentioning the food they would copy, he ventured a wry smile. "My wife calls it our loaves-and-fishes party."

Philip stared. Had Otavio read Art Buddha's manifesto, too? Philip shrugged and took a Cambiar from his valise, attached a screen and a keyboard, and began making lists. If they were going to do this, they needed a plan. They worked until midnight: brainstorming, debating and, finally, deciding.

TWENTY-NINE

Otavio's Apartment. Thursday, May 21
Day Thirty-four

OTAVIO WOKE THEM AT DAWN—middle-of-the-night, California time—and had his cook serve them a black bean stew with rice and melon slices. No time for coffee or chit-chat before he led them downstairs and out through a security gate. Otavio wore the same cloth jacket as yesterday, but against a cold and lidded sky, he added rubber boots and a tarp hat. Philip and Tanner followed in gray pants, hiking boots, and hooded white sweatshirts.

They crossed the creek, single-file, over a downed utility pole, scrambled into grass and brush still dripping from the night rain. Downstream, atop the security wall of the next building, an armed soldier saw them. He turned his back. They continued up a footpath beaten through the foliage. It led into a canyon that widened before rising to steep rock cliffs on either side. From the heights, a mist swirled and dispersed, part liquid, part slum breath.

Otavio's route forked at irregular intervals, branched up weedy paths between rotted brick walls or wood or cardboard. Like a child's enormous Lego fantasy, two thousand rectangular boxes clung to the canyon walls. Painted brightly or not at all, the shacks seemed truncated, as if a mad barber had scissored their flat tops. Rivulets that gathered beneath the shanties became ropy veins that carved islands out of dense mud and rocks, before tumbling into the creek. Philip leaped from stone to plank to brick, until there were no more.

They turned a corner and arrived at an open plaza on which three lanes converged, muddy spokes that dumped congestion from the slum onto this hub of raw concrete. Tiny businesses, obscured by flapping canvas, rimmed two sides of the plaza. One establishment had customers. The square also bridged the creek, thus joining favela Xavier to an asphalt road on the opposite side. This highway, as Otavio called it, looped past the plaza before bending south into the non-muddy city. At pavement's edge squatted a two-story colonial-era hotel, the *Baluarte*, long abandoned, its ponderous walls blistered with handbills and tattooed with graffiti.

On the nearest corner of the square stood a plywood stage complete with microphone, amplifier, and speakers. A small Maker and a quad motorcycle were parked beside it. The quad was hitched to a trailer containing a Powerpod and a rack of cone segments—a portable Maker kit. Opposite the stage, in the far corner, three women in Health Department caps and smocks were administering free vaccinations from a folding table. One of them was Dr. Jacqueline de Bier.

Odd that the Belgian doctor would wear a Brazilian nurse's uniform, but two men in Powerpods Company blazers rushed to Otavio. They reported in anxious tones, gestured to the road, to the stage, and to the muddy favela. Apparently, the large cones they needed to copy the quad and its Maker Kit had been impounded at an Army roadblock. Food and other gifts were stuck in traffic. Also missing were the DJ and his music, which they needed to draw a crowd, plus the camera crew to broadcast everything to the rest of

Brazil.

Otavio apologized. "It will be all right," he said to Philip. "You will see." He instructed the men to hang a banner over the stage, and then he stepped away to make phone calls.

Free food, music, and jewelry were supposed to entice the people emerging from favela Xavier in search of work. The party atmosphere would relax them, and Otavio would give away as many free quad-and-Maker-kits as he could. The idea was to send dozens of kits up into the favela before police or the local bullies could react. But circumstances had diverted half of Otavio's preparations. Last night Philip spent an hour writing a speech he hoped would inspire the favelados, but now . . .

Endless gray clouds offered only sour suggestions. The cowl of his Brazilia hoodie seemed to block every choice except those directly before him: this place, these people, and his own bare hands. Art Buddha's manifesto had pounded a single, loud drum—radical sharing—but how would that fare in this foreign land? He gave Tanner his satchel and told him to copy it. "Then do some cone segments," he said. Meanwhile, he searched the people's faces for clues that might help him.

Above the stage, Otavio's men unfurled a banner. *Maquina que cria = Somos gente.* The machine that creates means we are gente, we are people. Crude as it was, Otavio assured them the slogan would appeal more deeply than gifts. What the favelados want, he said, is to be somebody rather than nobody. To be recognized, not shunned. "That's what it means to be gente," he said. "And respect flows between equals, therefore *we* are gente."

Philip approached a gaggle of preteen boys, street thieves most likely, illiterate probably, as they drifted across the plaza to inspect the stage equipment. He nodded to them and made eye contact.

"Somos gente," he said, which could also mean we are family. He indicated the banner.

They circled him warily. One wagged his bottom in Philip's direction. "Somos gente," he squeaked. They whooped and scattered, regrouping a few yards away, still chattering but also on guard.

Tanner returned with a bulging satchel and held it open. From it, Philip scooped a handful of jewelry. He draped five necklaces over his left sleeve and tugged six bangles onto his hand. He approached the vaccination table, stood patiently at a young mother's side until she noticed him. He offered her a diamond-studded torus of gold. The woman backed into the table, but not before the infant in her arms snared the ornament and tried to ingest it.

Philip peeled back his hood. He did not smile, which could only look false to her. He nodded solemnly and offered a necklace. "Somos gente."

She slapped it away, plucked the bangle from her baby's mouth and shook it at him, accusing and scolding. Until she stopped. Across the street, a television camera appeared at an open, second-floor window of Hotel Baluarte, and the banter at the vaccination table fell silent.

Women whispered right and left. Philip tugged his hood back over his head, but this only intensified their interest. They pointed and nodded. The infant shrieked for her lost treasure, while her mother stared at Philip and returned the bangle to her baby's mouth. Hoping she might accept another, Philip angled another bracelet to reveal its inscription.

"Somos gente," she read aloud, and a rush of intrigue passed through the others.

Philip proceeded slowly, so as not to alarm the in-welling inspectors, each one seeking a glimpse of his face. He offered his hands, one bare and one bejeweled. The mother touched him but recoiled. Others touched his fingers, his wrist, his scar. But not the swag. He shrugged the worthless gold onto the table, left it there, and waded into the crowd, their curiosity giving him permission to continue. He nodded to each person he encountered and touched their hands. Their warmth flowed into him. Never before had he felt such a connection outside his family. His hood forced them to step intimately close, to confirm his face, to seek the favor of his famous gray eyes. Children quit playing to follow the hooded man.

The people were not afraid. Their interest and excitement displaced all suspicion. They pressed closer. One man removed his hat; a woman curtseyed. Their conspicuous deference attracted more passersby and more interest. The crowd seemed to marvel that he was here, among them, bestowing nods and touches, and saying this odd thing, somos gente.

Their delight seemed less due to his notoriety or his motives than the mere fact of his presence. They must feel this way about every curious happenstance. Someone or something drops unannounced into their lives, and Philip Machen must be no more to them than this week's casual miracle, appearing briefly before passing away, leaving no lasting effect. They hungered not for him or his cause, but for the transcendence they gleaned from him. Transient flickers of something magical beyond their daily struggles. With no expectation of personal gain, they gladly settled for a glimpse of his fabled life, so rich, so foreign, so impossible to them.

Music erupted, loud and pulsing. The DJ had arrived along with three taxis filled with food, clothing, and tools, to be copied and dispensed. Tanner waded into the crowd, bestowing a fresh baguette on every taker, and grinning at their responses. In his wake, Otavio's men distributed tins of salt pork and mackerel.

Otavio bounded to the stage. His amplified voice beckoned everyone and welcomed them to the dance, to the free food, and to the Maker giveaways. But the commotion around Philip sapped their attention.

"Celebridade," Otavio called. "Our celebrity." He motioned for Philip to join him.

On his way to the stage, Philip acknowledged by touch each person he encountered. They blessed him with stares and tears. They chanted, "Celebridade." He had come to empower these people, yet it was their strength that flowed toward him. Never before had he experienced such mutual, reflective gratitude.

When he took his place beside Otavio, the music stopped. The chanting died. And absorbed in the burden of so many expectations, Philip knew what he must do. Otavio introduced him effusively without saying his name. Then he handed over the microphone.

"*Ola*," Philip said and doffed his hood.

The whispers flashed into applause. "Filipe Machen," someone cried. Others shouted words he couldn't understand. Across the square, from the safety of a second-floor window, an unblinking lens fixed on his face. Last year, a TV Globo crew was beheaded for daring to record videos inside this favela.

Philip addressed the people in halting phrases translated by Otavio.

"Last month," he said, "two kinds of *criminosos* infected Sao Paulo. Those with guns to make demands, and those with money to make demands. Today, the money men can no longer force us to yield. Soon, the gun thugs will learn that they, too, are out of business. The way to rid ourselves of gun thugs and money thugs is to share our Makers and create a new community, *Cidade Xavier*. No longer a slum but a shining new city. With Makers, you will build Cidade Xavier. With Makers you will earn respect. Makers will make everyone gente."

Bang!

A gunshot jerked everyone's attention to three young men who swaggered onto the square, their bare arms oozing blue tattoos. One brandished a pistol, the other two, assault rifles. The oldest couldn't be more than twenty. People cringed or scurried. Mothers rushed their children across the vacant highway or up into the favela. Dr. de Beir cowered at her table but calmed the nurses.

"Traficantes," Otavio muttered. He greeted the intruders over the loudspeakers as if they were friends. Playing the gregarious host, he invited them, explained to them, cajoled them. The *pistolero* strolled to the stage, took the microphone from his hand, and shot him. Otavio twisted and clutched his hip as he fell.

The pistol swung toward Philip and Tanner while Otavio squirmed at their feet. They raised their hands.

"*Dispersar*," demanded the gunman. Disperse. Then he commanded the favelados, his amplified words ricocheting up the canyon. "*Ir para casa.*" Go home. He threw the microphone at their retreating backs.

On stage, Otavio crawled with one leg, grunted into a gap between the equipment. His helpers, shielded only by the speakers, seized his wrists and dragged him out of sight.

The pistolero ignored them. He watched his riflemen encourage stragglers to depart, then turned to the Americans.

Philip's fingers went numb. He couldn't let these goons erase everything. He had to stop them or find a way around them.

"Otavio made a deal," he said, "with Kojo." He licked his lips to lubricate the lie.

The keen-eyed pistolero squinted. His weapon segued to Philip's stomach.

"*Como?*"

"I can help." Jacqueline de Beir hailed them from the table, where one of the riflemen restrained her. She called again in Portuguese, offered her empty hands and a look of stricken availability. "I can translate."

The pistolero hesitated. Dr. de Beir addressed him, no longer shouting.

Opposite her, the street kids were stealing the quad motorcycle and its Maker kit. They got it running, blasted across the square, and roared between the two riflemen, into favela Xavier.

As those weapons veered, Tanner jumped the pistolero, toppled him away from the stage and skidded on the punk's acne-marred face. By the time the riflemen noticed the scuffle, Tanner had rolled his captive into a headlock and shoved the punk's .40 caliber bravery hard against his right ear.

The riflemen took aim. They shouted but did not fire. The

pistolero squawked, and they shut up, widened the space between them.

Philip stepped carefully from the stage, fingers splayed to show he was not threatening or trying to escape. He took one deliberate step after another toward Dr. de Beir. She approached him as well, and they met at the center of the square. Rifle barrels flicked back and forth between them and Tanner.

"Take us to Kojo," Philip said. It was the only way.

Dr. de Beir gripped his arm and searched his eyes, ignoring the banana peel of mistrust between them.

"Take us to Kojo," she said in Portuguese. She said it three times.

Tanner propped up his wriggling hostage, hugged him by the neck.

"Not a great idea, Boss."

The riflemen protested also.

"Take us to Kojo," Philip said. He drew Dr. de Beir by the hand toward Tanner. She freed herself but joined them.

"What makes you think they won't kill us?" Tanner said.

Philip indicated the hotel where TV Globo continued to stare.

"Whatever they do," he said, "there's going to be a million witnesses."

Dr. de Beir conveyed as much to the riflemen, who glanced over their shoulders and switched to whispers.

While the gunmen conferred, Tanner grunted his pet thug upward to a standing position. Tightening his hold, he danced the little monster onto his lizard leather toes, making him gag. Then he extended the pistol in a neutral direction and released its ammunition clip. When the magazine skidded clear, he tossed the pistol over his head into the creek. His newly unconscious amigo, he released.

"This had better work," he said.

THIRTY

THEY MARCHED SINGLE FILE between the two riflemen, up into favela Xavier. The mists turned to drizzle, and Philip's blond hair gradually soaked to transparency over his scalp. The fleece hoodie clung to him like a poultice. At least Dr. de Beir had her nurse's cap and a cheap poncho.

They turned a corner and came beneath an extended canopy of corrugated plastic, shiny new and translucent green, supported on sapwood sticks. They entered an arcade of steps and corners—dry but dim—until people appeared as if the coffee-brown walls were percolating them from the soil. People clotted their path, curious or suspicious, though not hostile.

Mothers watched them from open doorways as the parade route steepened. Dogs and children darted through the procession, oblivious to the guns, to the Health Service uniform, even to the pale *Americanos*. Behind them, the city lay smeared in the misty gaps between shanties.

They negotiated an alley and discovered a courtyard where a lone acacia tree jutted skyward. Across the hump of the yard, they came to a whitewashed building taller and wider than the others. A low, shadowy entrance blemished it like a birthmark. The lead gunman approached this cavity and knocked. The dogs and children disappeared.

Through a door of rough planks, a man spoke. The gunman returned, approached Dr. de Beir, and mumbled to her.

"Kojo is not here," she translated.

Philip shook his head. "Tell him, take us to Kojo."

Dr. de Beir jabbered until the gunman grunted.

"He curses me," she said.

"Tell him I will slit his throat unless he takes us to Kojo."

Her eyes widened.

"Tell him."

She glanced from thug-to-thug, then crossed herself, apologized in Portuguese, and translated his threat.

The leader lunged at Philip, raised his rifle, and fired. Three punishing rounds boomed past Philip's scalp and down the alley. Shell casings tinkled off the man's shoulders, rattled on the stone pavers. The other gunman aimed at Philip's chest.

Philip dismissed them with a sweep of his hand. To Dr. de Beir, who was cringing and plugging her ears, he said, "Tell him again."

From the shadows of the doorway, a man shouted in English, "He is not here." Then he gave orders in Portuguese.

The gunmen shoved the captives to their knees, prostrated them, and searched their wet clothing. They turned out pockets and dumped the doctor's rucksack. One hundred single-dose syringes fell in a tangle of wrappers. When this was done, the unseen man stepped out from his lair, a man Philip had never seen the likes of before. The solemn brown dermis of his face was tattooed or painted with scores of oily black leeches. His neck below the jawline glared rooster red, while coarse dreadlocks drooped to a prizefighter's shoulders.

"*Amadors! Turistas!* If Kojo were here, he would kill you." The painted man turned and disappeared inside.

Silently, the riflemen trussed the visitors by their wrists and hoisted them to their feet. Their wallets, watches, and Cambiars were left behind. Gun muzzles prodded them through the door and down a wooden chute from which they stumbled onto a dusty oval of hard-packed earth. Tiered on corroded scaffolds around them, bare wooden planks marched upward. Dry rot or vandals had claimed a third of the seats, leaving random gaps. The arena stank of sawdust and poultry. The opposite wall—either damaged or unfinished—stood open to a panorama of flat roofs decorated with bright blue cisterns. Through this hole, and from an equal one in the roof, a grim light suffused upon a wooden crate and the painted man.

"Kojo," Philip called to him.

A rifle butt doubled him.

"Kojo is not here."

Rough hands shoved Philip to a chair and forced him to sit facing the crate. No sooner was a heavy wooden table dragged before him than a whistling steel blade struck it. Its ringing crash panicked a roost of pigeons, who escaped through the roof. The leech-painted man grinned, bent to his machete with both hands, and jerked it free. Behind him, Philip's companions were shoved onto benches and made to sit.

The crate made a thump.

"What do you want, Turista?"

Philip swallowed. "We bring the vaccine, and we came for Mariela."

Again, the machete crashed to the table, splintering it.

"Kojo would take your head, but I am merciful." He strolled behind Philip and sawed the yoke of his shirt with the flat of his blade. "Kojo does not have Mariela," he said.

"Is that why he covered the streets with plastic? So the Army can't see him take little girls?"

Quivering steel stroked Philip's neck.

"You are the hunted one, Yankee. Kojo should take your head for the price it will bring."

Philip cleared his throat.

"Kojo's old ways are dead, senhor. His drugs and his money are worthless. He can't hide in his mansion or leave the favela because the police and the Army are hunting him. He can't enjoy his Mercedes because favela Xavier has no streets. Today, every treasure he owns is worth no more than a loaf of bread. If Kojo refuses our vaccine, dengue fever will kill him in a few days. Or the Army will."

The machete levitated.

"Unless he releases Mariela." Philip wriggled against the strap binding his wrists.

"The Yankee messiah offers salvation. We have heard about you, *ateu*—atheist."

"These vaccines will save you and your people."

The machete whistled from above and cleaved a corner of the table. "Liar!"

It whistled again but did not strike. The impenetrable stare circled him.

"You bring the fever to poison Kojo."

Again the crate thumped.

"Choose any syringe," Philip said. "Vaccinate me. Then the nurse will vaccinate you."

To his left, a furtive movement. A glint stabbed into his arm, its plunger rammed home, and his tormentor laughed.

"We will see who dies."

"Come to the plaza," Philip said. "I will shake your hand on world-wide TV. For releasing Mariela, you will become the Mayor of Cidade Xavier. The world will see us together and they will know you are sincere."

Philip worked his wrists while Kojo circled him, feral and grinning.

"I took a policeman's nose last week when he came sniffing. Now he sniffs through two great holes." He made circles with his fingers, held them to his eyes, and laughed.

Philip swallowed and tried again. "If Kojo commands it, his men will bring Mariela. Then I will reward Kojo with a treasure no one can take from him."

"Go to hell, Turista. You cannot possess Kojo by putting him in your debt."

"Mariela is our debt, mine and Kojo's. We will be judged by her fate. If Kojo wants to survive, he must do two things."

The blade levitated, hovered beneath Philip's chin.

"You do not command Kojo. Kojo commands you."

Philip licked his lips. "Kojo's empire is gone. His new life begins today. A life based on trust and respect, not violence and fear. A man who shares with his neighbors earns their loyalty. Kojo's future is to build Cidade Xavier, the new city, at no risk and no cost. Grateful favelados will call Kojo their hero when he gives every household its own Maker."

A cruel laugh. "We have heard your sermon, holy one." He spat on Philip's head.

Philip wiped the spittle. As he did so the machete flicked under his arm, incising a wound that made him gasp.

"People see only the old Kojo," Philip cried. "Let us show them a new one. I will go with him."

"This turista cannot save his own worthless carcass. How can he save Kojo?"

Philip held one arm tight against his wound while the machete circled.

"Behold Kojo's savior." The blade wiped itself on Philip's shoulder, trailing a crimson smear. "Kojo takes what he wants, Yankee. Respect comes from power, not gifts. Kojo will teach you."

Philip shook his head.

"If Kojo does not release Mariela, the Army will hunt him and kill him. It does not have to be that way."

The crate thumped.

"Show this silly man."

Philip was seized by the arms, shoved forcefully onto the table. They cut his bindings, pinned him in hardwood stocks that clamped his wrists to the table. Then they backed away.

"The lesson begins with fingers."

Philip tugged at the stocks, rocked the heavy table.

"If Kojo does not help the favelados, they will betray him. If he refuses to share his Makers, they will kill him. It does not have to be that way."

"In this favela, all Makers are Kojo's. Those who challenge him know they will die."

Raising his voice, Philip said, "Tell Kojo his people will not be denied. Tell Kojo he can survive only by helping his people. In return, they will honor him and protect him. Somos gente."

"Hold the fool."

Rough hands seized his arms and shoulders. Philip strained to escape, but the machete flashed.

And Philip screamed.

His terror merged with the thunder booming from his left hand. He raged at the indecent gap between his smallest finger and its quaking, bleeding source. The digit lay askew, curled like a French fry, and Philip raged at the painted man, bellowed like an ox.

Across the table, dust and agitation could not disguise the pleasure gleaming back at him.

"Do we play the game, Turista? Do you like my souvenir?" He plucked his trophy and inspected it. "This one is Kojo's." He tapped his blade near Philip's other hand. "The next one is mine."

Philip bucked against the stocks. Mucus dripped from his nose and saliva from his mouth. Then four distant *crumps* heralded a clatter of rotor blades, overhead.

"*Exercito! Excercito!*" the man called Kojo shouted to his men. The Army, the Army.

With a mighty grunt, Philip heaved the table upward. Kojo's machete rose to intercept it. The blade chopped and chopped, but Philip hauled the table over himself, hunkered beneath it, and crawled toward the crate.

Across the room, Tanner disappeared backward through a gap in the bleachers, taking two guards with him and smashing their heads. Before the machete could rise again, Tanner bounded from the shadows, wielding a metal rod. He parried Kojo's blade and boxed his ear. A second blow shattered Kojo's wrist. A third flung his knife to the dirt. The riflemen fled through the damaged wall, and Kojo scurried rat-like up the chute.

Tanner hurled his rod at Kojo's back but missed. Then he righted the table and freed Philip from the stocks.

"Sorry I took so long."

He tore his shirt to wrap Philip's hand. As he worked, artillery shells whistled overhead and exploded on the ridge above the arena. "How did they know?"

Dazed and trembling, Philip said, "Open the box."

Tanner pulled him by his uninjured arm. "This way," he said.

"No." Philip refused. "Open the crate."

Tanner released a strap and lifted the top. Inside, on a bed of filthy sawdust lay a dark-eyed young girl, bound and gagged, still in her party dress. Tanner freed her and lifted her out, but she shrieked and struggled.

Philip knelt to make himself small. Tanner placed the girl before him and released her. Philip bowed his head and waited for the helicopters to pass. When the racket subsided, he looked up into a snot-smeared face, smiled, and said her name.

Mariela blinked, wiped her nose, then shuffled tentatively into his open arms. He swept her up and followed Tanner through the hole in the wall.

They emerged into fluttering daylight where three mantis-ugly helicopters hovered, giant leaf-blowers in the sky. On either side of the swaying acacia tree, helmeted teams descended on dangling black ropes.

Tanner chose a downhill path between two shanties away from the noise. They zigzagged from shack to shack, crashed through barriers of rotting trash. Their retreat became a blur of walls and mud, unpainted doors and droopy clotheslines. They rounded a corner where three wooden posts stood out to bark their shins.

Philip squeezed his precious cargo, wondering where Dr. de Beir had gone. He paused for breath, and three dogs appeared, yapping and scattering the chickens. When he looked back, flames were climbing a wall high on the ridge.

"Kojo's mansion," Tanner surmised. The shelling had stopped, and there were no gunshots, only the din of helicopters.

They ran until a mesh of rusted wire blocked them. Beyond it lay paved streets with cars and trucks and immaculate buildings. Except for this gap, the fence ran tight against shanty walls in both directions. Tanner attacked it, levered himself from a post, kicked the mesh flat, and jumped onto its springy back.

"This way," he called.

Philip tripped, staggered until he found his footing. Tanner tried to take Mariela, but she kicked at him and clung fiercely to Philip. The men dropped to the street and crossed it, stamping mud from their boots as they went. A car was coming, a block away, so they hid beneath a stucco balcony. Mariela understood hiding.

They rested while sirens echoed from many directions. After a Volkswagen Beetle rattled by, they headed up a cross street and over a rise where they encountered a clean, well-lighted shop, and ducked inside. Into a hot and stuffy beauty salon, with four stations busy and one customer waiting. Philip slumped against the wall and pressed Mariela's face to his shoulder, shielding her from the stares and commotion.

Tanner charged through the tiny establishment, searched the back, and returned.

"No way out," he said.

Astonishment doused the ladies' chatter as nine mouths gaped.

Both Americanos dropped to the floor, away from the door.

"Pardon us. Pardon us," Philip said.

Instead of panicking, the women spoke all at once. Between bouts of alarm and concern and disbelief, they gabbled in Portuguese, arriving finally at a nervous fascination. One of them shut the outer door, which was thick and painted sky blue. Another peered out the front window and drew a gauzy curtain across it. The others whispered, "Senhor Machen." And, "Mariela."

Wonder settled onto their faces. The shortest one waved her comb at a television high on the wall while the rest stared openly at the fugitives. One brave woman clasped her hands and approached Philip, masking her trepidation with a crooked smile. Behind her, a henna-rinse customer whipped out her Cambiar and thumbed it earnestly.

To which the Americans called out, "No, no. *Por favor.*"

The caller hesitated, turned aside, and spoke to the phone.

The brave woman took Mariela, passed her to the others, and offered Philip her hand. He struggled to stand as she took his arm and nodded encouragement. She shooed Henna-rinse out of her chair and seated Philip in it. Tanner joined them while the brave one held Philip's injured hand. Delicately, she scissored its bloody wrappings.

Whimpers and gasps attended the unveiling, though Philip felt nothing. He gazed up at the video screen, which had split between a yammering announcer and a growling helicopter. He let the beautician work, with Tanner observing, and focused on the screen. For there now appeared the dark head of a painted man, next to a skinny white one, yoked to a table. A blur swept the screen, and Philip yelped. Fresh terror seized him and startled the women.

The guy up on the video screen, seated at a table, screamed. A sharp sting brought Philip back to the beauty parlor. He blinked at the blood-soaked towel, but up there on the wall—how was that done? Had Dr. de Beir sneaked a camera? And how was it not discovered? All along, the authorities must have watched them and known their location.

Half the women tended to Mariela. The others crowded to Philip and whispered. He marveled at their faces, alive with wonder and compassion, and his ears burned with shame. He didn't deserve their beauty or their kindness. He had failed them as much as he had failed the favelados.

The walls tilted and slowly turned. He panted, blinked to clear his vision. The brave woman tied a snug bandage, and when she was done, he loved her with all his heart. He loved every woman who had ever done him a kindness. To his left and his right, anxious beauties fanned him with movie magazines.

The spinning subsided, replaced by a reek of alcohol. His shirt had vanished, while under his right arm a row of adhesive butterflies arrayed themselves along a thin, red line.

Tanner hove into view speaking on a Cambiar, though they had lost theirs at the arena.

"He's okay," Tanner said, "but we gotta get him out of here. I'll text you when we reach the airport. Yeah, you too. Bye."

He peered into Philip's watering eyes.

"Chuck says Otavio is okay, and Dr. de Beir made it out too."

Philip shook uncontrollably, and the women fretted like mothers at a bicycle crash.

"What about—" He looked around. "Mariela?"

"The ladies are taking care of her."

But a rap-rap-rap on the sky blue door silenced everyone.

Henna-rinse challenged the knock. A gruff response led her to open the door and pull a worried man inside.

"Taxi," she said to Philip, gesturing to this off-kilter fellow in a pink shirt. She introduced him as her husband, Carlos, and added with pride, "*Motorista taxi.*" Then in a flurry of Portuguese, she made Carlos understand he must take the *Americanos* to the airport.

Carlos eyed the bloody towel, the bandages, and the foreign faces. He shook his head.

Henna-rinse glared. She pointed to the TV and made chopping

motions down the length of her arm.

Carlos winced. "*Sim,*" he said. Yes.

Much jabber accompanied their procession to Carlos's Chevrolet. Tanner held the door open while the women jostled each other to touch senhor Machen. Philip wanted to see Mariela, to say goodbye, but he kissed the brave woman's hand, doubling her excitement, then slipped into the back seat, followed by Tanner.

When Carlos drove off, the women waved and called, "*Adeus despedida.*" Farewell.

Tanner shook his head. "Some guys will do anything for applause."

Philip closed his eyes and lay back in the seat. Behind his throbbing hand, he let the tears take over.

THIRTY-ONE

AT OTAVIO'S APARTMENT BUILDING, Tanner went upstairs to retrieve their uniforms. He returned with the overnight bags and a look of relief.

"No cops," he said. "The cook is still here, watching a soap opera. She didn't know about the shooting."

Carlos drove through the side streets, avoided the avenues and the freeway. His slow progress allowed them to change into their Federal Express uniforms before they reached the airport. Clear for all to see, two American pilots were heading to work.

Tanner urged Carlos away from the passenger venue, toward the cargo ramps, where a lone civilian guard, armed with a portable radio, stopped them. In the shack behind him, a disinterested customs officer poured coffee from a thermos.

"*Identificacao,*" said the guard.

Tanner pointed to the big, three-engine jet with the purple tail, alone on the ramp. "Federal Express," he said, and held out their passports.

The guard bent to inspect them.

Philip looked toward the plane. From here, they could run for it, if necessary.

"*Rapido*," Tanner said. "*Por favor.*"

The guard withdrew and waved them through. When they arrived at the ladder Chuck had lowered from the flight deck, Tanner said, "We need to thank our friend."

Philip agreed. "I have an idea."

By gestures, they urged Carlos to wait, then climbed the ladder. In two minutes, Tanner returned to him with a surplus NASA space suit, complete with gloves, boots and a silver-visored helmet.

"*Obrigado*, Carlos." Tanner heaped the garments in the back seat of the Chevrolet and shook the man's hand. Carlos scratched his head. Tanner scurried up the ladder and hauled it aboard.

As each fanjet whined toward ignition, Philip stood in the open door and waved. Carlos waved back. The port-side engine added a growl to its whine, and Philip watched the cabbie hurry away. How much kindness could the world devour in one day? Or did compassion float in the air, as immune to cruelty as a Brazilian breeze? He wrestled the door shut and latched it.

Chuck and Tanner guided the cargo jet to a clear runway while Philip retired to a jump seat behind the flight deck. One-handed, he searched his Cambiar for a list Uncle Orin had sent him before going to China. Since the first gold ingots emerged from their Maker prototype seven years ago, they had quietly funded the Machen Foundation. Without fanfare, Orin had built schools, clinics, and hospitals in Leonard Machen's name in communities around the world. They hoped these seeds of healing and education would prepare those places for Maker communities to come. But until today, Philip had not imagined a need to visit them.

Only three of the foundation's projects adjoined an airport in countries too weak to hunt him and far enough from his enemies. Only one had a resident surgeon. He copied the foreign name from his list along with its latitude and longitude and texted them to Tanner's Cambiar.

As the big plane lumbered into a thick gray sky and banked away, Philip looked down upon Sao Paulo. He wished for his Brazilian friends a better outcome than he alone could provide. *Obrigado, Carlos and ladies, Otavio, Dr. de Beir. Adeus despedida.* Then he wrapped himself in a blanket and tried to rest.

SWEAT POOLED IN THE CORNERS of Philip's eyes. It trickled to his temples and curled toward his ears, which woke him, stiff and achy. Noise and altitude had stuffed his hearing. His left hand throbbed with every beat of his heart. To quell the pain, he raised it over his head, then looked out the window.

They were descending over dirt roads and a sunlit quilt of green fields. Puddles and ponds gleamed ahead, drawing Philip's attention to the impending runway. The big plane hung nose-down and wobbled through unstable air. Chuck was using all his tricks to plant the tri-jet on the threshold of a very short runway. At the last moment, he hauled up the nose, and the main gear screeched onto the pavement. Beside him, Tanner levered thrust reversers and shoved full throttles. When the nose slammed down, it pitched everyone into their harnesses. Chuck stood on the brakes. At the final exit, he turned and taxied back to a service ramp, just like always.

"Good work, Chuck." Tanner unclipped his harness and stretched. "Here comes the welcome wagon."

Across the tarmac, a topless Jeep and a boxy white ambulance approached, each flying the same flag, a pale blue globe on a field of white. Within the globe, a golden cross and a golden crescent, the merged symbols of Chrislam.

The vehicles disappeared beneath the wing, and Philip rubbed sweat from his neck. The conditioned air flowing from a vent overrode his fever and chilled him. He tried to stand but fell back.

Behind him, Tanner opened the outer door and a gush of hothouse moisture condensed into a miniature cloud.

Chuck deployed the ladder, and an African man in a lime-green polo shirt climbed to greet them.

"Welcome, my good friends. Welcome to Ibadan. I am Administrator Joseph. Where is our injured brother? How shall we proceed?"

Tanner lifted Philip from the chair, tucked his shoulder between Philip's legs, and gripped the opposite wrist. He straightened with a grunt. "Make a hole."

Administrator Joseph's thin face swept by as Tanner swiveled and descended the jiggly ladder. At the bottom, he ignored a waiting gurney and dumped Philip instead into the open rear seat of the Jeep.

"There might be a reporter with them," Tanner whispered. "Sit up, or the bastard will claim you're dying."

"Getting there," Philip said. The heat and the glare made him woozy.

Tanner joined him in the back seat and called to the ambulance crew. "Can you spare a bed sheet? Something to cover him."

Instead, they brought trauma kits and oxygen, as ordered by a perspiring white man in a green surgical smock.

Administrator Joseph waved off the doctor and the medics. He ousted the Jeep's driver and took his place behind the steering wheel. An older African was seated beside him. This man wore a square, black cap and a white surplice. Over shower shoes. A dozen granular moles stood proud on his cheeks. He smiled at the visitors and recited, "Welcome honored guests." He pumped their hands and made an odd gesture, a sort of benediction, and his smile expanded.

Which was more than Philip could manage.

Administrator Joseph passed Tanner a white cotton towel, from the medics, then started the Jeep. While Joseph drove, Tanner wrapped Philip in the cloth, forming a cowl to shade his head and eyes.

"How far to the hospital, Joseph?"

"Two kilometers, sir. Only two." But he slowed as they approached a dirt road. What the rains had long ago softened was now set in endless camelbacks, scarred by deep ruts. Behind them, the ambulance fired up its siren, sweeping their backs with a pointless wail.

The Jeep lurched forward, and Philip clutched the back of the priest's seat. He curled his injured hand away from the fluttering towel and focused on the pink rubber dice dancing on a string from the Jeep's mirror. Fifty humps into their journey, he took up Tanner's old drinking mantra. "I hope I don't, I hope I don't, I hope I don't puke."

Tanner nudged him. "Try 'I think I can, I think I can.'"

Philip let his head roll.

"Don't do that, man. Keep your eyes on the horizon."

Philip straightened. "Okay. But get ready for slightly-used black beans and melon slices."

The road curved through a settlement of packing crate shanties, their tin roofs eaten by rust and their odor far worse than the sewers of favela Xavier. Stagnant puddles festered along one side of the road while pedestrians held to the other, indifferent to the motorcade and its wailing siren.

"We gave them Powerpods and cones," Joseph shouted as he indicated the pedestrians. "But they trust no one. The stronger ones pushed the weak aside and refused to share. Especially with tribes not their own. We will bring Makers to the outcasts again until everyone understands."

The motorcade emerged from the stench and approached a metal grillwork embedded in a low wall. Just inside a cast iron arch hung the green-white-green Nigerian flag, limp on one pole, with the banner of Chrislam on another. They entered and—mercifully—the siren stopped.

To the left, scores of half-finished bungalows straddled hand-dug ditches in which lay black pipes, white pipes, and blue ones. Building materials lay scattered among the weeds. Beyond the houses, an equal number of tents gathered around a thatched barn, their canvas flaps pinned to catch breezes.

To the right, row crops abutted a rice paddy, which gave way to an orchard of saplings. Then zinc-roofed pens containing cows, goats, and chickens. The convoy passed an ancient tractor hitched to a sway-back wagon, plus five derelict trucks. The lane angled around a crypt-like monument, a tile-roofed residence, and approached a beige, institutional building.

Immediately, scores of men, women, and children, all dressed in fresh, new clothes, converged on the visitors. Someone shouted, "Machen," and they swarmed forward, smiling and waving their Cambiars. Administrator Joseph slowed as people meandered on the road like cattle. His warning honks only brought them closer. The Jeep crawled forward as women in wrap-around dresses laid palm fronds on the pavement ahead.

"They saw you on the internet," Joseph said to Philip. "The whole world saw your sacrifice for the little one." Palm fronds snapped and crunched beneath the tires.

But I failed. Philip tried to wave them off until Tanner pulled down his arm.

"Use the other one," he said.

Philip hoisted his bandaged left hand, and the crowd burst into shouts and cheers. Wide-eyed children paced the Jeep, chanting, "Mock-en, Mock-en," until it stopped at the beige building and its gleaming glass doors.

Men in lavender *dashiki* shirts encircled the Jeep and pushed back the crowd. Cambiars bobbed and winked to photograph the hero. It seemed an acre of smiles had blossomed, with adults lifting children to see.

Philip gazed at their faces, absorbed their joy, and fought his panic. He stood from his seat, clutched the roll bar, and hoped not to faint. Then, raising his authenticating hand, he dared to bow.

Someone tugged the towel from his head, and he stood revealed.

The crowd cheered and leaped and applauded. Some of them wore T-shirts emblazoned with tri-cone Maker silhouettes. They bestowed congratulatory pats and hugs on each other and continued to chant, "Mock-en, Mock-en, Mock-en."

The priest in the front seat gripped the top of the windshield and labored to stand. He balanced and stretched his arms before the crowd. He quieted them with waggling fingers, then made a benediction.

"Amen, *Inshallah*," he said.

A scorching hot breeze stole parts of their response. "Amen, Inshallah."

The dashiki brigade helped Philip dismount. They cleared a path to the hospital, the Leonard Machen Memorial Clinic. When the glass doors shut behind him in the cool, bright interior, the crowd pressed fingers and noses to the glass.

He waved with the hand that ached and tingled, its flesh and sinews throbbing with ancient stardust. The clock showed 4:46 p.m., as illness seized him and his knees buckled.

PHILIP AWOKE DRY-MOUTHED and dumbfounded, no longer in pain. He did not recall collapsing, as they said he had, before the surgery. Now in the morning after, only a fever persisted from that slaughterhouse table and Kojo's chicken-chopper. Treatable sepsis, the staff said, not Brazilian dengue. The gruff European doctor assured him he would survive, but Philip knew it already. His mind was clear, and his strength was returning.

He breakfasted on porridge and toast, downed a pint of sweet milk, and asked the nurse to part the curtains. She curtseyed before drawing the linen from a six-pane window. She curtseyed again and departed. Philip hoped her gestures were just a local custom.

Tanner arrived freshly shaved, almost human. He knuckled Philip's shoulder.

"Good morning, Bwana. How do you like the safari, so far?"

In another time and circumstance, they both would have laughed.

Tanner forced a smile that sagged away. "Mariela has the dengue."

Philip caught his breath. He choked and turned away. "Tell me."

"She's with her family and getting the best care."

Philip met his friend's eyes.

"Alive is good. What about Otavio?"

Tanner tapped the Cambiar in his pocket. "From his hospital bed, he says you owe him lunch. Sometime."

Philip nodded. He turned to the window. Across an empty courtyard, the Chrislam chapel gleamed smooth and white, as oblivious to suffering as the stone from which it was built. Then onto a footpath flowed a dozen men in lavender *dashikis*. They trotted the court perimeter, clockwise, hands clasped to their chests. Once, twice, three times they circled, before pad-padding away, barefoot.

"Running deliverance," Administrator Joseph announced. He strode into the room also wearing a dashiki but over blue jeans and cowboy boots. "They prayed for you," he said.

Then he noticed their faces. "What has happened?"

Tanner shook his head. "Our friends, back in Sao Paulo." He laid a bundle of clothes on the bed, and told Philip, "Admin Joe and the old guy want us to stick around, but Chuck and I think we better get going. Before certain people spoil everyone's day."

"How long?"

Tanner shrugged. "Troops or cops, take your pick." He pointed to the ceiling. "They know we are here."

Joseph wrung his hands. "Gentlemen, I am very sorry about the little girl, but stay with us, please. We owe you so much." He spread his hands. "Here on our land, the corruption no longer touches us. Thanks be to God—and to you—we serve the Lord with new hope. Even the belligerent imams of the north have proclaimed your machines to be a gift from Allah. They scorn your ways, but secretly they would kiss your hand. I have heard them say this."

Philip glanced away. "Joseph, your people deserve everything they are building here. Your enclave is an inspiration for more to come. Which is why we must go."

"Stay, I beg you, sir. We are strong. We have shelters and weapons. Let us defend you. The Army won't leave the capital, and our neighbors fear us. You are safe here."

Philip pushed himself up.

"No, Joseph, not one life. Neither yours nor theirs. Tell your people they are beautiful and gracious, and we thank them." He slipped the covers, swung his pale white landing gear over the edge. "We must not endanger you." He loosened Tanner's bundle, unfurled the pants and the shirt.

Joseph squirmed in his boots.

"Sir, before you go, The Prophet requests the honor of an audience."

Tanner tapped his watch, shook his head.

Philip nodded, continued dressing. "Five minutes, Joseph."

Relief flashed over the administrator.

"One moment," he said. He drew a Cambiar from his tunic and spoke in an African tongue. He gestured as if the person he spoke to could see him. Abruptly he nodded and tucked the phone away. "Five minutes," he said. "Follow me, please."

He led them out from the hospital, across a wooden breezeway, to a screened sitting room of the adjoining residence, furnished with wicker chairs and overstuffed sofas. Grime-encrusted fans stirred the heavy air over the priest, who awaited them in full regalia. His brilliant green vestments seemed to float on layers of white satin. For him to sit would ruin an hour of his valet's meticulous work. Behind the priest, a video camera stood on a tripod, directed at an altar where a golden crucifix merged with a golden crescent. To the right, a second camera focused on the stage curtains behind the priest.

"Gentlemen, may I present The Prophet, Third Patriarch of Chrislam, His Holy Royal Highness, Libor Tella." Joseph bowed to the priest.

Philip put his hands to his chest as he had seen the courtyard joggers do, but he did not bow.

Tella's moles bobbled happily on his cheeks.

Joseph pronounced the visitors' names then translated Tella's words.

"You are the Mock-en? The one who gives us land and a hospital?"

Philip nodded.

"The one who blesses the poor with abundance from a three-headed machine?"

"I am."

"You are not a god?"

Philip shook his head. "No."

"What is your faith, my brother? What guides you?"

Into the priest's stern gaze, Philip said, "I believe justice, morality, and freedom cannot be enacted without sufficient and universal means. I intend to bestow those means on all who will take up the responsibility of caring for each other. That is my faith." He offered his left hand in testament, while his mind filled with faces—Nigerian, Brazilian, and those of his family.

Tella noted the bandages but focused on Philip's scar. "Our visions foretell the coming of a divine messenger," he said. "An emissary in white raiment, a bearer of glad tidings. The apocalypse is rescinded. There will be no rapture. And Allah who is God shall reign on Earth during our lifetimes. All peoples shall be saved. All peoples, not just Muslims and Christians. The emissary will prepare us for His return. We shall know this messenger by his bountiful gifts, and by a mark." Tella pushed back his sleeve and raised his hand. "During holy benediction," he said, revealing his tattoo, "the

V becomes an A. The mark of Antiochus."

He pointed to Philip's wrist, clapped his hands, and spread his arms. Joy radiated from his face. He hugged Philip and began jumping up and down, urging him to hop, as well. "You are the one. You are the one."

Philip refused to pogo, so the priest released him and turned to the curtain. He drew it open, revealing two golden thrones, each with the Chrislam logo embroidered in gold on blue cushions.

Philip stared in silence until Tella's gaze hardened. "You deny the prophets, yet you wish to move our hearts. Whom do you serve?"

Philip stiffened. "We serve each other, we who build the new ways."

Tella pointed upward. "You are a mortal son of Yahweh, servant to Allah upon His Earth." He pointed down. "This I know. Why do you not know it also?"

Joseph stopped translating, said something that made Tella scowl. The priest raised his palm, imperious. He ordered Joseph to continue.

"You are the instrument of God," he said, "sent to deliver us from the evils of scarcity, the sins of hoarding. Open your eyes, Lord Mock-en. Accept who you are. Like me, you are His prophet. A greater prophet than I, for bringing gifts from heaven. Let us proclaim your prophecy." Tella indicated the thrones and the cameras. "Together we shall spread Allah's gifts, and honor His revelations."

He raised his green-silk wings and spread them wide. His entire face smiled.

Philip accepted the old theist's warmth and humanity and longed to express the gratitude swelling in his throat, but he could not wrap himself in make-believe. Though it would be so much easier than birthing a new moral vision without shortcuts. The temptations had briefly occurred to him in Brazil, and now again here—the adoration, the glory, and the immunity on offer. He could be a saint, a god, a deity. If only he would play that game.

"My brother," he said, "I honor your compassion and your good will. Your community is an inspiration for all the world. Tell your people I love them. However, our mission lies elsewhere, and we must go. Thank you for your kind hospitality. I hope we shall meet again." He offered his good hand.

The priest dropped his arms, dismayed. But he gripped Philip's hand in both of his and bowed to him. Then he clasped his palms to his chest, lifted his gaze to Philip, and pronounced, "Welcome honored guests. Amen, Inshallah."

Joseph backed from the Patriarch. He turned and led his guests outside, into the oppressive Nigerian heat. As they rushed to the Jeep, he said, "His Holiness meant no offense, sir."

"None was taken," Philip said. He touched the man's sleeve. "Thank you, Joseph. You are a good man."

They shook hands.

Across the dusty street came a jittery fellow in a sweat-stained frock.

"Administrator," he called.

Joseph stopped, one foot in the car.

"There is a coup, Joseph. The Army has sealed the capital. Muslims and Christians are barricading their neighborhoods. They say it is civil war."

Joseph digested this. "Are they shooting? Do you know?"

The man shook his head. "My sister left the city. She did not say about shooting. May I bring her here, sir?"

"Yes." Joseph nodded. "I will return in twenty minutes. Alert His Highness. Tell the others."

Philip surveyed the hospital, the crops, the men building houses. Two sentinel Makers stood nearby, surrounded by bricks and pipe and lumber. He wanted a peaceful future for these people. He wished he could help them deflect the angry winds blowing down from the North.

Now in the back seat, Tanner squinted at the clear blue sky and spoke to his Cambiar.

"Warm up the engines, Chuck. We are rolling."

THIRTY-TWO

Washington, D.C. Friday, May 22
Day Thirty-five

ATTORNEY GENERAL NICK BRAYLEY paced the red carpet between the work table and his burled walnut desk.

"Nigeria is having a *coup d'etat*, and Machen can't escape? You're certain?"

His intel flunky, a baby-faced Ensign on loan from the Pentagon, pointed to her screen.

"Not in that old MD-11, sir. Even stripped down, with minimum fuel, that runway is a thousand feet too short."

Nick wanted to pop her.

"So how did they get that clunker from Brazil to Nigeria in 83 minutes?"

Intel did not respond.

Nick continued to pace. Central Intelligence said they had no operational assets within a thousand miles of Ibadan. For the FBI or the military to enter Nigeria through the front door would require Nigerian permission. And neither the National Security

Adviser nor the President would authorize a covert mission, much less an armed invasion. He doubted the Nigerians, in their present chaos, would offer much help.

"Are they still on the ground?"

Intel tapped a key. "Yes, sir. Haven't moved."

Nick returned to the screen of his STU-5.

"What's your take on this, Majers? What are they doing over there?" For once the California twit was prepared.

"There's a religious compound near the Ibadan airport, sir. Agent Parker has confirmed the Machen Foundation donated the land and built a hospital for them."

Nick sat down, drew the bulky STU-5 closer. He had been wondering how Orin Machen's non-profit foundation figured in Philip Machen's scheme. Nearly four billion dollars spent on real estate and infrastructure, then sold at cost or given away. But why? The goal was never profit, of this he was certain. During the past six years, according to Agent Parker's report, the Machen Foundation bought sixty-one parcels of land overseas on which they constructed schools, houses, and hospitals. In the U.S. they built 889 private, gated communities. Acres of condominiums, laid out in towers, duplexes, or stand-alone units, in twenty-four states. 70,000 dwelling units in all. Each with its own Powerpod.

"He's built 900 Freemaker enclaves right under our noses."

"Yeah," Majers said, "but if he expects those people to go Freemaker, he never told them about it. So far, we haven't uncovered any *quid pro quos*—no closet ideology, no secret agreements. He hasn't asked them to do anything except share their Makers and help each other."

Nick shifted in his chair. "But they *are* helping him. That's why he went to Nigeria, right? Folks are more disposed to help a benefactor than to turn him away, yes?"

"Well, if there's activism in his American projects, we haven't seen it."

"Maybe so," Nick said, "but his foundation is just another

social-activist stunt—who builds free schools and hospitals in foreign countries, not-for-profit condos here at home? And that's who Philip Machen is. He is social. He is active. And he is subversive as hell.

"He gave those people everything they need to secede from the . Union. Free Makers tucked away inside gated communities. Those places are his sleeper cells. Starting overseas in those countries like Nigeria, ripe for social upheaval. The weakest fall first, encouraging their neighbors to follow them, down a line of nation-state dominoes that tip straight back toward us. All they need is a nudge, and over they go. Let's not forget, every one of Philip Machen's gifts has come with a hidden agenda."

Intel interrupted him. "Sir, they are moving."

Nick shoved the STU-5 onto his desk and got up. "You done good, Majers," he said over his shoulder. "Don't go away."

He rushed to the worktable where Intel swiveled her screen for him to see. Her satellite feed was fast-scan, not real-time, and the MD-11 twitched from point-to-point like a bug on a skillet until it aligned with the end of the narrow runway. Then it hopped half-way down the strip and disappeared. A brilliant streak of white light flashed where the plane had been, igniting a needle-thin line of orange flames that extended off-screen to the right.

"Ho!" Nick jerked. "What was that? Play that again."

Intel cut the feed, replayed the segments and aligned the frames side-by-side, in stop-action sequence. Nick jabbed the screen.

"What is that? What's happening there?"

"Dunno, sir. Bright light burns a stripe. Catches fire. Length of the runway, plus . . ." She called up a scale ". . . three kilometers past the fence. Could be a rocket burn."

He shook his head. "Too skinny. That's not an exhaust plume. It's a focused beam. He's got a weapon there." He leaned over her shoulder. "Go live again. Show me the runway. Highest resolution."

She clicked four times. On-screen, the pavement no longer burned, but a knife-cut ran midline down the runway and into the fields. Tendrils of smoke curled from its dark crease.

"Is that concrete or asphalt?"

"Checking." Intel looped her cursor, but Nick changed his mind.

"Later," he said. "Pull back, pull back. See if they crashed."

She widened the view and scanned the area. No plane, no wreckage. Just a vacant strip of pavement, a sprinkle of rust-red roofs, and thousands of empty green acres. Nick cuffed her shoulder.

"Track him, damn it, track him."

"Yes, sir. This feed is optical, sir. We can see him with high-res, but the magnification cuts our field-of-view. We need radar to pick him out of the ground clutter. Without it, I can only guess where to look."

"So your bosses can track him, but I can't?" He meant the Pentagon with their satellites.

She averted her eyes.

"All right," he said through gritted teeth. He turned away, clutched his bald scalp with both hands, and reviewed the situation.

"Eighty-three minutes from Sao Paulo to Ibadan. Beam weapon. Makes our lasers look like flashlights. Doubles as a propulsion unit. Matter-to-energy. E=mc2. That son of a bitch has done it again. He's disappeared and left us with another problem."

Nick returned to his desk, gathered the STU-5, and shook it.

"Wake up, Majers. Machen has flown the coop. We don't know which direction, but he's flying an MD-11. Where did he get that plane? And where did he get that beam engine?"

"Beam engine?"

"Never mind. Tell me where he keeps the plane, I'll show you the engine. Same hidey-hole."

"Agent Parker may have a lead on that, sir, down in Victorville."

"Where the hell is Victorville? Never mind. Call me as soon as you get something on that plane." He lowered the STU-5, broke the connection, and keyed a different number.

Guardhouse eyes gazed back at him from the screen.

"Get me the Secretary of Defense," Nick said.

The young Army officer came alert. "Yes, sir."

Nick sat heavily, oppressed by his belly and by his many years. A lieutenant colonel returned to the screen.

"Sir, Secretary Reynolds asked me to tell you he has the situation under control. He will call you within the hour."

"Right."

Nick jabbed the disconnect and swore. He swiveled to his intel kid. She was Navy, he remembered. No wonder she couldn't do shit.

"That will be all," he said and turned his back.

As soon as her boney butt was gone, Nick pounded the desk. He eyed the Cambiar, lurking at his elbow. Another Trojan horse? He swept the contraption to the floor. Then he punched a familiar code on his STU-5. The fourth buzz yielded a doe-eyed floozy who cleared her throat.

"Federal Bureau of Investigation, Director Vinckel's office."

"Tell Hambone his paycheck is calling." At least the FBI couldn't put him on hold.

"Mr. Attorney General." Doe-eyes blinked. "Yes, sir. I'm sure Director Vinckel is available."

Momentarily, Harold Vinckel, whose face always reminded Nick of a water-damaged cello, hove into view and tried unconvincingly to smile.

"Nicholas. Good morning. How are you?"

"Update me on Our Lady of Powerpods."

Vinckel coughed. "Ms. Lavery arrived last night at our Maryland facility."

"You put her in a safe house? Get her out of there. No pampering. I want her in a hard cell before sunset. Take that skank out to the brig at Quantico. Tell those Marines I want her loosened up."

"Uh, yes, sir. I understand. In that case, I'll need to call—"

"Just tell SECDEF he owes me one. And if he hasn't heard yet, tell him Philip Machen has a thousand Freemaker enclaves right here in the U. S. of A. Sleeper cells. Then tell him the ones in Africa and South America are already moving into stage four of Machen's social degeneration plan. That's the part where they tell their governments to go fly a kite."

Vinckel recoiled. Nick reeled him back.

"Hambone, I want this Lavery bitch motivated. I want to know everything she knows. And I want to know it before she goes up to The Hill next week to lie to our Congress-critters."

"Yessir. I'll get right on—"

Nick disconnected him. At least that secular messiah diary had opened a few eyes. Half the country was outraged, and the other half could only doubt Machen's sanity. What a great day that was. When you toss a skunk into the jury box, its odor cannot be dismissed. No matter what they believed before, everyone got a strong whiff that day of Philip Machen, the lurking atheist. That should have been enough, but too many were saying, "So what?" And half the anti-Machen protesters were quietly squirreling away a few Makers, just in case.

Nick pounded his desk and reached for his phone. *No.* He put it down and strode to the door. Flung it open, to the surprise of his office manager.

"Get me ten minutes with the President this afternoon," he told her.

To his legal-beagle staffers, he said, "Prepare a brief to shut down every Maker enclave in the country, and make it quick."

They stared, uncertain.

"Now," he shouted, which made them jump.

Next year, when I'm President, you'd better not act so dumb.

THIRTY-THREE

Quantico, Virginia. Monday, May 25
Day Thirty-eight

TIFFANY WHERE ARE YOU?

Karen Lavery paced her narrow cell and stretched to relieve her stiff back. A row of glass bricks near the ceiling randomly warped the afternoon sun into bright shards of light. She wore starchy orange coveralls and green prison sandals. The waxed concrete floor seemed to flow away beneath the bars and drift down the corridor toward freedom. *Touch those bars and die* was her sense of them, though the guards banged them often enough. Metal sink, metal toilet, a steel bench on which to sleep. Every night, the bench installed new agonies that her morning stretches could not relieve. Apart from cold-water splashes, she had neither bathed nor left this cell for three days.

Didn't her keepers believe her? She was cooperating, telling them the ten thousand things she knew about Philip and Powerpods. About Makers, she knew less than they did. She was a witness and a victim, not an accomplice. Yet here she was, imprisoned like a criminal. And her gentleman friend, the attorney, had not yet persuaded anyone to release her. *Hurry, Terry. Hurry.*

In three days she would appear before a Congressional committee to explain herself. She needed to organize, to plan her testimony with Terry, but the Marines allowed her no phone, no visitors, no records, not even a pencil and paper. She didn't know what was happening outside these walls. She hadn't seen a scrap of news since they took her into custody, over a month ago. How could she prepare? Seven more nights on this bench would render her stinky, arthritic, and incoherent.

Which must be their plan. She was beginning not to care. While the hours seeped through the walls, a deeper worry engaged her. *Tiffany, where are you? What are you doing?*

At mealtimes, the guards brought food on a steel tray, collected it afterward, and answered no questions. Except for the sergeant who had booked her, they were all scrub-faced privates and corporals, young Marine hard-bodies, doing their tight-lipped duty. If her notoriety counted for anything among them, they betrayed no hints.

A shadow swept the wall and interrupted her ruminations. Agent Parker, wearing a pristine white raincoat, posed at her door, stiff as a mannequin.

"Excuse me, Ms. Lavery."

The novelty of his voice perked her. Someone had come at last, even if he was a crocodile offering sympathy-eyes.

"You could have knocked," she said.

Parker waved to the overhead camera, and the gate between them clattered aside.

"May I come in?"

"No." She turned her back, defending the sovereignty of her bench. She inspected the farthest corner for spiders. "What do you want?"

"I need your help, Ms. Lavery."

"Helping you is what put me here."

"I can get you out."

"Before or after Congress blames me for everything?" She glanced to the left, trying to toss her helplessness into the toilet.

"Tiffany has run away from your mother's."

Karen caught her breath as an image flashed before her, of Tiffany running alone and frightened down a dark suburban street.

"She's in danger," he added.

"Of not meeting you? Good for her." Anger forced her to breathe.

"She's trying to reach Philip."

Karen shook her head and faced him. "She has no idea where he is."

"Yes, but he knows where *she* is."

Karen snorted. "Philip doesn't care about—"

"You're wrong." Lines of exhaustion marred his perfect face as if he wasn't sleeping well either. "May I come in?"

She resumed her spider search. She needed to talk, yearned to know about Tiffany, just not with him. When no spiders materialized to save her, she nodded. The crocodile and his cologne entered and sat beside her.

"What do you want, Parker?"

He unbuttoned his suit coat.

"Before somebody gets hurt, I want Philip bloody Machen."

"Humph."

"I realize you view this differently, Ms. Lavery, but hear me out. You and your daughter are the loves of his life. He adores you."

Ridiculous.

"Especially Tiffany." His voice softened. "That diary of his? The one you gave me? That chip could have held a hundred diaries, yet the one he gave us stopped precisely on the day you came into his life. Why? Two reasons. He didn't want to reveal his Trojan horse Makers prematurely. But he also didn't want to expose his feelings for you or Tiffany. That's what's missing, Ms. Lavery, what should have been there but isn't. He's boasted he's giving away his life's treasures—Pods and Makers. He even gave away the diary. But he's keeping you and Tiffany. You are his secret treasures, to be shared with no one.

"But—"

"He taught her to fly, didn't he? In his little red airplane? Gave her pride and confidence when she needed it. Helped her grow up. Helped her for six years, Ms. Lavery."

"He could be very sweet," Karen conceded, "but—"

"Where did he take her during those flying lessons? Two, three hours at a time. Did she tell you they sometimes landed on the fire roads out in the hills? They made picnics in the grass. How many hours were they out there? Do you know?"

Karen glared. "She would have told me, right away, if he had tried . . . anything."

"Okay, but what about him? Let's say he's done nothing improper. Have you noticed how close they are? She calls him almost daily. They've talked for years. Father-to-daughter doesn't begin to—"

"She loves him. So what? It's not physical."

"He loves *her*, too, Ms. Lavery. He watches her. He put a sleeper program in her Cambiar, to monitor her movements and forward her connections, all relayed to him."

"How do you know?"

He shrugged. "We found his bug when we installed ours."

"Humph."

"He's been flying over Pleasanton, over your mother's house, and probably over Tiffany's newest hideout. He's watching her."

"Philip's not a pervert, and Tiff is not having an affair with him."

"Okay." Parker sniffed.

"What are you saying?"

"That his interest, his proximity—his love for her, if you will— still puts her in great danger. She begs to join him, did you know that? We fear they could meet before we intercept them. That would be very dangerous."

"So go get her, Parker, since you know where she is."

"That's why I'm here. She's staying on a ranch between Pleasanton and Livermore with people who may be Freemakers."

"What's a—"

"Freemakers want to keep their Makers. Often as not, they have guns too. If we rush the ranch, they might resist, take your daughter hostage. She could be hurt or killed. But if you and I approach them together . . ."

Karen shook her head. The bastard had her. She yearned to denounce him, to tell him to go to hell, but how could she?

"So it's a trap for Philip," she said. "With Tiffany as bait."

"We want her safe. We want Philip in custody to answer for what he's done. That's our job." He rubbed his nose. "You need to understand that a great many people want him dead, Ms. Lavery. They've lost their jobs, their businesses, their ways of life. They're frightened, they're mad as hell, and they're making guns as fast as they can. We are closing in on him, but if Tory vigilantes find Tiffany with Philip before we get there?" He clenched a fist where she could see it. "Help us, Ms. Lavery."

She slumped. He might be lying. Or mistaken. It didn't matter. She hated him for using her, as Philip had used her. She hated them both, although Parker's treachery offered to repay Philip in his own currency. But that didn't matter either. She could not abandon Tiffany to strangers, no matter who they were. Nothing mattered except getting her daughter back.

"You were supposed to protect her."

"We did. We are. We need your help."

Karen shut her eyes, opened them. "Go to hell, Parker."

He stood and buttoned his jacket.

"I don't know how long it will take to put you back in my custody. A few hours, I hope." He reached into his London Fog raincoat, withdrew a Cambiar. "Call her," he said.

He left it on the bench and stepped to the door. "You can

speed dial her but no others."

She picked it up. "It's bugged, isn't it?"

He inhaled deeply and released the jailhouse air. "Thank you, Karen."

It was the first time he had used her given name, a warm, personal touch. How sweet of him. She aimed a finger-pistol at his face.

"If anything happens to her, Parker, I'll make it my life's work to destroy you. Your career, your pension, your smarmy sanity."

"I know," he said.

He buttoned his spotless raincoat, waved four fingers at the camera, and steel bars shuddered home between them.

"I'll be in touch," he said.

Then he strode down the hall and out of range of her loathing.

THIRTY-FOUR

Oakland, California. Thursday, May 28
Day Forty

AGENT PARKER SWUNG HIS OVERNIGHT BAG into the hired car and slipped into the front seat with the driver. When he stated his destination, she cocked her head in recognition.

"Short ride," she said.

Prospect Shores' twelve blue-and-white stories rose directly across San Leandro Bay from Oakland International Airport. From Terminal Two he could see his own balcony, though he didn't dwell on it. Instead, he sat back, shut his eyes, and massaged the bridge of his nose. Let his driver steer the universe for a while.

Tuesday, he had taken his proposal to FBI Headquarters in Washington, D.C., to an assistant director who surprised him by liking the idea. Before lunch, the two of them presented his plan to Director Vinckel, who informed them that until further notice Ms. Lavery's availability was controlled by Senator Gilmar and her subcommittee. But Vinckel liked the plan, too, and promised to plead for interim custody. The three of them shook on it.

At lunch, however, the assistant director took a call midway through his chicken salad. By the third uh-huh, the A.D. was no longer smiling, and by the sixth, he seemed to have acquired an ulcer.

"No can do," he told Parker when he hung up. "The A.G. stomped on Vinckel for suggesting it. Said he's already taken you off the case, personally. That you are freelancing, and if Gilmar's committee finds out about your Quantico foray, they will come down on the Bureau for witness tampering."

Parker excused himself and left the building. He had flown to Washington, taken a room, rented a car, and would soon fly home again, at his own expense. But Nick Brayley had personally vetoed his plan.

Early that morning when he told Ms. Lavery he'd failed, she demanded he stop trying to use people and to get Tiffany out of there, meaning the Cardoza ranch. He said he would try to persuade her, but unless Tiffany was being held against her will, there was little he could do. He didn't elaborate his troubles with Brayley but said goodbye to Ms. Lavery and took the only flight back to Oakland. Thirty-thousand feet over Tennessee, he poured a warm scotch down his gullet hoping to dissolve a clot of self-pity.

Now, as his taxi turned north from the Hegenberger industrial corridor, Prospect Shores appeared ahead. Its sweeping curves and shaded balconies reclined at the bay's edge, a dark beauty lounging in sun glasses. Whether or not the Machen Foundation built it to subvert its residents, Prospect Shores was the best thing to happen in south Oakland in recent years. After his divorce, keeping his apartment there had been a singular and welcome consolation.

"Check it out," the driver said. Onto Oakport Street from the Prospect Shores parking garage emerged a trio of canary-yellow Ferraris, little-bird coupes, revving ostentatiously before zooming away. Parker noted their identical license plates and shook his head.

"Glad I'm not a street cop."

The driver agreed. "Too much fun, heh? I should get me one

of those. Some kind of hot Yellow Cab, yeh? Just one passenger, but reeeeeal fast." She laughed as she circled to the PS drop-off curb.

Parker paid with his Cambiar and tipped her fifty percent. "Short ride," he said.

Then he drew the tow handle from his case and headed for the lobby, his white London Fog draped over one arm. He'd never seen the place so busy.

Half the visitor's parking lot was cordoned off for vendors and traders. Foot traffic came and went through a narrow gate on Oakport Street. Prospect Shores security guards were wanding each visitor and inspecting their sacks and boxes while residents marched to and from the building hauling similar bundles.

Had someone set up a Maker over there? Bored vendors were peddling food, clothing, and small stuff from canopied tables, with little success, while the principle activity seemed to be the furtive sharing along a shadowy wall. Those people were animated, excited as kids sharing forbidden things under the school bleachers. In one corner, a chubby white guy in a bright red Aloha shirt was extolling the virtues of a silver Aston Martin to a young Indian couple. Behind him, a navy blue Rolls Royce and a creamy white Bentley stood in reserve. It was some crazy swap meet, but no Makers were in sight.

Across the driveway, that WebNews correspondent, Marcy Johnson, was posing for her Arab cameraman. Before Parker could turn away, they spotted him.

"If you're here," she shouted, "he must still be free."

Parker shrugged.

"Did you come to bust the Freemakers?"

"Turn it off," he said.

The camera sloughed from Aboud's shoulder. "Let's go," the kid said, but Ms. Johnson was admiring Parker's London Fog.

"Not much weather today," she said.

Parker didn't like this woman, didn't want to speak with her, yet couldn't resist.

"What are you doing here?" she demanded. Then she noticed the key card in his hand. "You live here? How does that work?"

"Bit of a comedown for both of us," he said, indicating the swap meet. "From fugitives to zucchinis."

She nodded. "Our story is the biggest Freemaker enclave in California."

He looked again for Makers, while another Ferrari growled onto Oakport Street.

She saw it too. "How about an interview?"

"You know I can't."

She crossed the driveway and approached him while Aboud waited.

"We can blank-out your face, disguise your voice. Nobody will know it's you."

"No can do." He jiggled the handle of his case.

"What's it like these days," she said, "being an officer of the law? Sworn to serve and to protect, but not so sure who or why?"

He turned for the lobby.

She called after him, "Nobody gives you guys enough credit."

He stopped, knowing he shouldn't.

"For having a brain," she said. "Or a heart."

Damn. When he looked, she rocked her hips. Backfield in motion, penalty on the play. He abandoned his valise, took out his Cambiar, and laid it in her hand.

"Give me your number."

She keyed ten digits into his directory.

"Can you get us into the meeting tonight?" Her smile turned Playmate-of-the-Month.

He snatched the phone and quirked an eyebrow. "What meeting?"

"The big enchilada—a Maker referendum."

He missed the intended pocket in his jacket, and his Cambiar slid toward the pavement. "I've been away," he said, as he doubled over to capture the phone.

She smirked. "Seven o'clock tonight," she said. "Can you get us inside?"

"You're not members." He only meant that the media were barred from homeowner's meetings, but her nostrils flared.

"I see."

He needed to leave, to not be seen with her. "Have a nice day, Ms. Johnson."

He pocketed the phone, recovered his suitcase, and towed it into the building. At the far end of the lobby, he swiped his card, passed through a turnstile, and crossed the airy promenade. Sure enough, a middle-aged duo in red-white-and-blue election bibs were manning a table and offering clipboards.

"Sign the petition, sir?"

Their poster said *Don't Ask, Don't Tell*, and they wore buttons touting the Prospect Shores Barter Club. Signs at the next table urged, *Just Say NO to Makers* and *Recall the Board*. A third table— manned by a flock of white balloons—said *Freemakers for Peace* and *Repeal the Ban*.

He stopped to phone his neighbor, Mrs. Petzold.

"We need to talk," he said.

"Are you home, Leslie?"

"Crossing the lobby."

"Stay there, please." She used her political voice, the one she wielded at Board meetings.

Two minutes later she strode from an elevator with Prospect Shores' Security Chief, Sergio Mangabay, in his official blue uniform. The chief's Filipino tan and spiky crew cut belied the fifty-plus years on his odometer. The men nodded to each other as Mrs. Petzold drew Parker into her wake.

"Follow us, please."

For a seventy-year-old retired school teacher, Lucille Petzold was a white-haired torpedo in a green pantsuit. They dodged a potted ficus where Parker dumped his belongings, then proceeded outside, across the driveway. Through a gap in the privets, they entered the visitor's lot. Lucille zoomed straight for the pudgy car salesman, accosting him without mercy.

"Mister Gastelle."

The man responded amiably until he recognized her.

"Lucille." His smile turned toward Los Angeles. "Always a pleasure."

His pleasure vanished entirely when Mrs. Petzold planted her feet and crossed her arms.

"I want that Barter Club Maker of yours out of here today. *Muy pronto. Comprende?*"

Gastelle affected amusement, glanced at Chief Mangabay, then at Parker.

"You're calling in The Heat?"

"Shawn Gastelle, meet Special Agent Parker, Federal Bureau of Investigation."

Gastelle grimaced.

"Agent Parker does not know the location of your Maker, but if you and Shawn Junior do not shut it down and remove it from the premises by sunset today, I am going to tell him where to find it—and what to do with you."

"You got me, ma'am." Gastelle raised a hand. "We are just a little slow to comply, that's all." To his left, Marcy Johnson and the Aboud kid had arrived.

"No need for the strong arm," Gastelle said, "or the press. We're loyal, paid-up residents here, just helping folks acquire a fine automobile on a lovely spring day."

"And don't leave any messes up there," Mrs. Petzold said. "I want that area spotless." She turned and strode away.

Gastelle approached Parker.

"No offense, friend, but are you really a Special Agent?"

Parker checked his watch, glanced at the sun. "One way to find out, friend."

Gastelle bobbed his head. "Yes, sir. Have a nice day, sir."

He seemed disappointed that the news team was not filming his cars. He adjusted his collar and retreated to the Bentley while Mrs. Petzold confronted the journalists.

"What are you doing here?"

Marcy introduced herself. "We're from WebNews. Are you Mrs. Petzold?"

Lucille looked her up and down, then Aboud.

"I got your message," she said. "You can't film inside, and you can't come to the meeting." She glanced at Parker. "As a board member, I should not be seen with any of you." She turned to leave.

Marcy called after her, "Would you give us a few minutes, please? Just a short interview?"

Lucille motioned to Parker, drew him toward a winking display of electronic gizmos.

"She's that same girl, isn't she? The one who interviewed you-know-who? I can't be seen with her, Leslie. People will say I'm taking sides. But I need her to set things straight about Prospect Shores. Would you be a dear? Take them up to your place while I skedaddle?"

"I just got home."

"Please." She touched his arm.

"What's this about a referendum?"

"Maybe more than one," she said. "But we need this. Steam is building up." Her knuckles looked pink and healthy today. No gloves. "I'll join you in a few minutes. I promise."

"I can't . . . I just got . . . all right."

"Thank you, Leslie." And she was off at full speed, Chief Mangabay in tow.

Parker approached the journalists.

"This is not my idea," he said. "You're to come with me, if you wish."

At the visitor's desk, the attendant took their photos and thumbprints and issued one-day badges. Their video equipment went into a locker, for which they were given a key. Parker led them through the turnstile, past the petitioners, and gathered his belongings from the stalwart ficus. In the elevator, Marcy broke the silence.

"So, Agent Parker. Are you a Buy-in, or a Move-in?"

He was surprised she knew the difference. Half of Prospect Shores' 550 units had been donated, via lottery, to Fruitvale District residents who paid only the Homeowner's Association dues when they moved in, plus taxes. This was popular with Fruitvale but detested by the other members who paid full price.

"Buy-in," Parker said. "My ex had money."

"Oh. Sorry. About there being an ex, I mean."

At floor nine, he led them to his apartment. Lights on, door shut, he dumped his case and strode through the living room to part the drapes. Someone in the estuary below was sailing in zero wind, enjoying the calm. Or cursing it. To the west, a weary sun was casting lines and shadows from the Alameda shore. To his left, a silver airliner ascended from Oakland International and banked away toward the outer bay, the one called San Francisco. He had always loved this view, and it refreshed him now.

Marcy strolled behind him, appraising the silk wallpaper, the damask armchairs, the floral sofa. She stopped at his Tuscan oils.

"Nice digs. Are you gay?"

Aboud staggered behind her.

"My ex had taste," Parker said, not adding that he had chosen every piece himself. "As for me, I prefer Guinness. Would you care for one?"

"No, thanks."

Aboud was fingering the granite counter that separated the kitchen from the dining nook. "I'd like one, please."

Parker repaired to the kitchen and Marcy followed.

"So this is it," she said. "A Freemaker enclave. Every apartment has its own private view and its own private Maker. Where's yours, by the way?"

He pointed without looking. "Utility closet, end of the hall. It's a Pod, not a Maker."

"I hear your neighbors are using their cones, most of the Move-ins, anyway. What about the Buy-ins?"

Parker handed Aboud a pilsner glass and sipped from another. The cool, thick ale nearly made up for Ms. Johnson's prying. Before he could respond, however, someone double-tapped the front door. He didn't need the entry camera to know it was Mrs. P. When he opened the door and she swept inside, one of Chief Mangabay's huskier constables assumed a vigilant pose in the corridor. Parker nodded to him and locked the door.

"They're all yours, Madam President."

"Get a grip, Leslie. They're just kids." She joined them at the counter and perched on a stool.

"Here's the deal," she said to the reporters. "I talk, you listen. No recordings, no quotations. I don't have time to argue."

They nodded.

"Eighteen hundred people live here, and I'm responsible, along with the rest of the Board. That doofus with the Bentley downstairs—"

"Mr. Gastelle?"

"—is one of our more active members. He and his son sell exotic cars through the internet, and they swap them with members of our Barter Club. Before the ban, they took a Maker up to the roof of the parking garage and quadrupled its cone sizes. Anyway, they've been copying cars up there even though we told them to stop. Oakland cops won't touch them because the ban is Federal, and because Oakland has bigger problems. I don't know if Leslie is supposed to arrest anybody, and I don't care, so long as Gastelle dismantles that oversize Maker. It's provocative, and he knows it."

Behind her, Parker was loading his coffee maker. Marcy took the stool beside Mrs. P.

"Is Gastelle a Freemaker?"

Mrs. P lowered her voice.

"We don't use that word around here, dear. There's enough

trouble already."

"Like what?"

Lucille sighed. "Don't tell Mister FBI over there, but the board has received warnings slipped under our doors."

"Threats?"

Mrs. P nodded.

"Sergio—our security chief—he thinks it's just one person, some nutcase. The notes said if we hold a referendum on Makers, we will be shot. The goofy part is, this could be coming from either side, pro or con. It's that crazy."

"I checked your Codes, Covenants, and Restrictions," Marcy said. "The Board can't stop a plebiscite if the members collect enough signatures."

Mrs. P nodded, impressed. "Takes a hundred valid signatures to bring a petition up for a vote," she said. "But we need to do this. So far, it's been gossip and dirty looks, and the rumors keep escalating on both sides." She shook her head. "People are letting their imaginations run wild. We have to get them talking sensibly, face-to-face. That's why we need this meeting, and why I need you to get your story straight." She eyeballed Marcy. "We also need as many voting members present as possible, just in case." She glanced over her shoulder at Parker.

He set a steaming mug of coffee before her.

"Thank you, Leslie."

He took the fourth stool and sipped his ale.

"So what's the plan?" Marcy said.

"We are going to fight the polarization. Get them talking instead of whispering terrible things about each other."

Aboud tipped his glass toward her. "When they vote, which side will win?"

"Hard to say." Mrs. Petzold sipped her coffee. "It depends on which petitions get enough signatures. If none qualify, I'll push for comments and discussion, sense of the membership, that sort of thing. No matter what happens, we have to get people talking. And listening."

"How many petitions are circulating?"

"Four, at last count." In her hip pocket, a Cambiar sputtered like a cicada.

Parker leaped up, grabbed the edge of the counter, and said, "Rattlesnake!"

Marcy drew back.

Mrs. Petzold shoved him and giggled. Her cheeks dimpled as she took up the phone.

"Yes?" She looked surprised and gave it to Parker. "For you."

He said his name, and a voice responded. "Transferring your call, ma'am." Then Nedra Gaffin, his long-lost partner, commenced pounding.

"Turn on your phone, jackass. Majers is passing peach pits over here trying to reach you."

Parker turned away from his guests. "I'm available tomorrow, as per my leave chit, the one approved by His Majesty."

"All leave is canceled. Headquarters wants every office to enforce the Maker ban, top priority. Majers is putting together a joint task force with the local PD and the U.S. Marshal's Service. He wants you down here, post haste."

"I just returned from Washington."

"The first raid's tonight. At your place."

He gasped. *Here?* He mashed the phone hard onto his ear, so the pressure would quell his urge to argue.

"I'll be there as soon as I can," he said and pressed End. *So we're going to enforce the law and make an example of my neighbors.* Not what he wanted to do tonight, or any other time.

He doubted Majers would send anyone to fetch him. Nedra would not reveal his return unless she was asked directly, so he had a few minutes. Mrs. P was more important than missing the raid briefing, a thought which surprised him, yet there it was.

"We are not Freemakers. Is that clear?" Lucille was urging Marcy. "Prospect Shores has the same issues as everybody else.

Except if Congress bans Powerpods, too. Then Prospect goes dark and cold, water pressure falls to zero, and our homes become uninhabitable. The anti-Maker crowd wants us to connect to the PG&E power grid, but that would take months and cost a fortune. Meanwhile, we're trying to do the best thing here."

Parker gazed at Aboud. *What might he know about Tiffany Lavery?* "Any new faces at the ranch?"

Aboud returned a steady gaze. "Should there be?"

Marcy ignored them. "Can you get us into the meeting, Mrs. Petzold?"

Lucille shook her head.

"No, but Sergio can put you on his staff, as ushers. No recordings or transmissions. You can report everything later when we're done. You got that?"

"Thank you, ma'am." Marcy beamed while Aboud nodded.

Parker swilled the last of his ale and downed it.

"Well, if you'll pardon me, I need a shower." He leaned toward Mrs. P. "Make sure they don't steal the china."

Then he collected his suitcase and retired to the bedroom. He undressed behind the closed door while Mrs. P gave the reporters directions to the security office downstairs. By the time he drew the shower curtain, she called to him, "Thank you, Leslie. See you at the meeting."

He was glad Mangabay had assigned her an escort, even if the guy was a resident and potentially a partisan. If someone nasty wanted to make an example of Mrs. P, they would want to do it before the largest possible audience.

THIRTY-FIVE

AS SEVEN O'CLOCK APPROACHED, the five-member board gathered on the bare stage and seated themselves at a folding table. Prospect Shores' auditorium was a true theater, with sloping floors, high ceilings, and abundant spotlights, even an orchestra pit. Parker counted this to the good, as it kept folks from directly approaching the stage. An assailant would have to mount the stairs at either side, both visibly guarded, or pounce from backstage—also guarded—or spring up from among the audience. He took an aisle seat on the right side, half-way down.

Sergio Mangabay supervised a technician at the lighting and sound console, high in the middle of the back row. From there, the security chief could oversee everything. Outside in the lobby, his minions were shepherding residents through metal detectors and validating the voter-participation apps on their Cambiars.

The software required an encrypted ID card for casting votes. As expected, everyone slotted their IDs as soon as they took their seats. Parker slipped his card and his Cambiar into a pocket with no intention of using them.

What had been a cool and silent hall grew snug and boisterous. On stage, Mrs. P and her cohorts could easily pass for a school board. At 7:05, she stood and keyed her Cambiar.

"Good evening and thank you for coming, ladies and gentlemen. Please take your seats."

Parker scanned the audience. Shiny Cambiars, emblems of democracy, waved at the end of three hundred wrists like casual handguns. A bodyguard's nightmare.

Across the room, a conga line danced down the left aisle, chanting rhythmically to a drum beat. "Free Makers now. Free Makers now. Free Makers now." The dancers wore flowers in their hair and wooden-bead necklaces over Day-Glo shirts.

People laughed, and Mrs. P's amplified voice boomed. "Be seated, please. Be seated or leave the auditorium."

Ushers approached the group, and they quit chanting and took their seats. From the back, someone shouted, "Power to the people." This brought hoots and a raised-fist salute. "Right on, right on." More laughter.

Mrs. P tapped her Cambiar. *Tump-tump.*

"Whether you agree with them or not, you have to admit some people know how to party." Her dimples rode a wave of groans.

"Tonight, we are here to develop a common understanding of what our members want the board to do about Makers. Three petitions have qualified for presentation." She glanced over her shoulder. On the jumbo video screen behind her appeared a tabulation of the members present-and-logged-in: 389, with a note that 367 were required to make a binding plebiscite.

"One petition has been withdrawn by its sponsors, leaving two measures for consideration." The screen displayed a page of text.

"Measure A requires the board to permanently evict all persons residing in any Prospect Shores dwelling unit found to contain a functioning Maker or Maker paraphernalia." She paused for people to absorb this. The screen switched to the second proposal.

"Measure B requires the board and the staff to refrain from investigating, notifying or discussing with any person, any alleged violation of law pertaining to Powerpods or Makers." Again she waited.

"Fortunately, there's no overlap between these measures. We seem to have a clear choice—'Hang 'em high' versus 'Don't ask, don't tell.'" She smiled hopefully but no one laughed. Behind her, the screen displayed both measures, side-by-side.

"Before I open the floor for comments, I would like to point out that, if enacted, each of these proposals would require the board to perform actions that may lie beyond our scope of legal authority, as per the Homeowner's Articles of Incorporation. Clearly, the board must obey the laws of the land, or be held accountable. That said, the board needs and wants to understand everyone's concerns, so that we may properly serve the will of the majority while respecting the rights of those who are not in the majority. "The floor is now open for discussion of proposed measures A and B."

She seated herself at the end of the table. One-by-one, speakers stood to be recognized by Mangabay's technician, who activated the microphones in their Cambiars, in turn.

A fifty-something fellow cited drug overdoses and said we must be a nation of laws, not wishful thinking. He supported President Washburn and Measure A. Then a self-described patriot and veteran said he was no friend of Philip Machen, but derided anyone who would snitch on their neighbors. "This is our community, not President Washburn's, and if he wants my Maker, he will have to pry it out of my cold, dead hands. I support Measure B and so should you."

"What I want to know," said a petite Malaysian woman, "is what does this mean? If we vote Measure A, do we go too far? If we vote Measure B, do we go too far? I just want to know." She shrugged and sat down.

A younger man tipped up his baseball cap and bellowed.

"Has everyone gone fucking crazy?" He swept his arm from side to side. "I thought we had some smart people here. Some of you run businesses and schools, parts of big companies. You raise your kids to be loyal, God-fearing Americans, and all you can do is come down here and nod your heads like sheep, and let these atheist anarchists take control of our country? You say you're no friend of Philip Machen, but you're doing everything that bastard says. The President has banned Makers, and you want us to defy him. So what if Philip Machen doesn't have any weapons or armies? He doesn't need armies when people get all goofy and full of his freedom-and-self-empowerment crap. Haven't we lost enough already?

"Think about it. If you keep using Makers, you will have to do everything for yourselves. Who's going to protect you? Rent-a-cops? Volunteers? Are we going to play at being our own government? Set up our own little farms and groceries? Our own fire station, our own courts-of-law? Is that where you people are headed? Well, it's not freedom if you gotta do it all yourselves. You are going to be working your butts off—not to make a living—just to keep yourselves safe and fed. You can't take over the work the government does. It's too much. If you vote us into this Freemaker malarkey, it isn't going to be prosperity-and-freedom-for-all, it's going to be long-term shortages, the destruction of our nation, and hard work for everyone, just to scrounge enough to get by.

"You Freemakers think you're getting something for nothing, but you're throwing away America. You might as well vote for the Devil himself if you vote for Measure B." He pitched his Cambiar into the orchestra pit and shoved his way to an aisle.

Parker braced to intercept him, but the guy turned away from the stage, headed for an exit. Mrs. P took up her phone.

"Mr. Givens, come back. There's no need to leave. We need your vote."

Someone shouted, "Keep going, Tory bastard."

Mrs. Petzold rapped her Cambiar. *Tump, tump, tump.*

"Stop that. No name-calling. If you can't keep a civil tongue, you don't deserve to inflict yourself on the rest of us." The board nodded agreement.

"Next speaker, please."

A sharp-eyed woman in a silky blouse stood up.

"I'm Karen Lorenzo. I teach third grade at Whittier Elementary, and I'm afraid of what's happening, just like Mr. Givens. But we shouldn't be threatening each other. Mr. Givens is wrong about Prospect Shores. We are just neighbors doing our best. If the government can't help us, then we have to help ourselves. It strikes me as plain silly to say that voting for self-determination threatens America. Self-determination *is* America. It doesn't have anything to do with labels like Freemaker or Tory. I think these Makers are only as good or as bad as the people who use them, so we had better get to work doing some good things, instead of calling each other names, or crying about what's been lost. Whatever we lost, it isn't our homes or our families. And I don't think we are losing our country either. America doesn't exist out there someplace." She pointed. "It lives right here." She laid a hand on her bodice. "And right here." She touched her head.

The audience applauded with enthusiasm, though some abstained, and she sat down.

Someone shouted, "What if both measures pass?"

Another replied, "Why don't we just vote and get it over with?"

Voices bubbled and feet shifted. Mrs. Petzold rose and strolled to the foot of the stage.

"Are there any further comments? We have plenty of time." She seemed disappointed.

A flickering glow distracted Parker. The woman beside him was watching a live feed of the proceedings on her Cambiar. He dug out his own device and nudged her.

"Where's that coming from?"

She linked the web address to his phone.

"If you have not yet logged in to vote," said Mrs. P—her voice and image radiating from his hand—"please do so now." She glanced at the board members, who fingered their Cambiars. None indicated an urge to speak.

Parker got up and strode up the aisle toward Mangabay and his technician. Marcy Johnson and the Aboud kid were with them, near the control console.

"Will the technician please lock-in all active and registered voter apps?"

Onstage, the screen behind Mrs. P assembled a list of names, their corresponding device numbers, and scrolled to completion. Total authorized votes available: 388. Mrs. P cleared her throat.

Parker showed Mangabay the image on his Cambiar screen. "You've got a leak," he said.

Mangabay nodded, unconcerned. Johnson and Aboud loitered behind them, watching the video feeds on the console. One screen showed figures moving rapidly in the outer hall.

"Measure A," Mrs. P read from a scrap of paper, "requires the board to permanently evict—"

Shouts and scuffles erupted as the lobby doors swept open.

"—all persons residing in any Prospect Shores dwelling unit found to contain—"

A burly figure in bone-white slacks and a blue windbreaker jogged down the center aisle, toward the stage, a bullhorn in one hand.

". . . to contain a functioning . . ." Mrs. P squinted at the commotion.

Footfalls descended. Uniformed officers, led by more blue windbreakers, flowed down the aisles and into the corners. The jogging man reached the orchestra pit, where the letters on his raid bib announced FBI.

"May I have your attention, please." The bullhorn screeched with feedback.

He mounted the stairs and strode across the stage to Mrs. P.

"May I have your attention, please. Please remain seated. You are not in danger. I am Derek Majers, Special Agent in Charge,

Oakland office of the Federal Bureau of Investigation."

Mrs. P countered, "This is a lawful assembly. We are voting here."

But Derek beckoned sternly until she laid her Cambiar in his hand. No longer amplified, her voice still penetrated. "Am I under arrest?"

The room quieted.

Majers shook his head, made calming gestures. "Nobody is under arrest. Please remain seated." From his pocket, he took a folded page.

"By authority of this warrant—"

Below the stage, a man waved his Cambiar and shouted, "Hurry, everyone. Vote now."

Vote now swept through the crowd as a flurry of thumbs tapped keypads.

"Shut that down." Majers pointed at Mangabay's control console. "Shut it off."

Parker gripped the technician's shoulder. "Pull the plug," he said.

The guy looked at his boss, who shrugged. Parker grabbed the younger man's copious hair, yanked him off his chair, and shoved him into Mangabay's ample belly. Parker knelt to the electronic racks and the nest of cables beneath the console. He pressed anything that looked like a power button until he noticed wires from a multiplexer, feeding into three Cambiars. Each phone's screen showed a different perspective of the hall and the stage.

Marcy Johnson and her cameraman grabbed Parker's shoulders and pulled him off-balance. "You have no right to do that," she said. "The world needs to know what's going on here."

Parker pushed them away, stood up, and drew his badge wallet. "Interfering with a federal officer is a crime." He waved the badge in their faces until they retreated.

Mangabay and his technician stood aside also, but two conga dancers dashed from their seats and shouted, "Free Makers now."

Black-helmeted marshals met them in the aisle, batons at the ready. Closer to the stage, shouts and shoves escalated into a fistfight. Officers swarmed the melee, but the punching, wrestling, and cursing continued until a shot rang out.

Derek Majers stood at center stage with his pistol pointed at the ceiling.

"Sit down!" he demanded. "Sit or be taken into custody."

The crowd stood up, en masse, and pushed for the exits. Officers beat them back with batons and pepper spray.

Beneath the control console, Parker raced the shouts and the scuffles to yank the cords from three Cambiars. Their screens went blank, as did his own, but not in time. Not before the raid, the gunshot, and the riot escaped the building onto the internet.

He recovered to his feet, ready to rock and roll, but Ms. Johnson and the Aboud kid assaulted him only with grim stares. Gradually, residents were pushed and shoved back to their seats. Two combatants were handcuffed and frog-marched out of the auditorium. Three others were on the floor, handcuffed and being treated by tactical medics from the Marshal's office.

Majers holstered his weapon and started over.

"By authority of this warrant, peace officers shall search every room of these premises for illegal contraband. Specifically for Maker cones. Persons found to be in possession of said contraband shall be cited under provisions of Presidential Security Directive Seventeen and said contraband shall be seized."

The house lights came up to full brilliance. Murmurs swept the room.

"You will be escorted to your apartment by a uniformed officer. That officer will assist you in complying with the warrant. Nobody is going to jail." He let this soak in. "I repeat, nobody is going to jail. If we find Maker cones in your possession, we will confiscate the cones and cite you for violating the directive. That is all. If at a later time, you violate the directive again, you will be subject to arrest."

He asked Mrs. P to take her seat.

"On your Powerpod," he urged the audience, "if you have not already installed the mandated copy prevention appliance—commonly called a chastity belt—we will install one for you. Once the cover plates are sealed and registered to you, a missing or broken seal will constitute evidence of intent to commit counterfeiting or fraud. So don't fiddle with the seals or remove them."

Mrs. P did not sit. She lunged to regain her Cambiar, prompting Majers to raise it over his head, out of her reach.

"Please, ma'am. Take your seat."

"You can't do this," she shouted.

The crowd squirmed and grumbled but kept their seats.

Mrs. P threw up her hands. She returned to her chair, unharmed but defeated.

Parker waited for the crowd to settle. Then he yawned. *Mission accomplished.* Now he could go home, to be searched and certified with his neighbors.

Someone from the audience pitched a gelatinous lump that plopped at Majers' feet—a prodigious oatmeal-colored spit wad.

Parker nodded. *Touché, Dennis.*

"YOU GOT 'EM, BRAH." Art Buddha sounded like a baseball fan whose team had just won the pennant. "Ms. Johnson came tru for us."

Art was somewhere on the internet, preserving and editing the Prospect Shores uploads, while Philip and Tanner viewed a single stream taken from the rear of the auditorium. As fighting broke out near the stage, Philip shook his head. At least nobody was shooting. Then he heard the pop.

"Was that . . . ?"

Tanner fingered the FBI guy on his screen. "Seems like that would scare 'em more," he said, as indeed it did. The crowd panicked, and the clip ended.

"Okay," said Art Buddha. "We ready to send dis to alla enclaves and den to YouTube."

Philip nodded to Tanner, who relayed his permission. "Go for it, Big Guy."

Art grunted and there was some rustling. "Hey, check it out, Brah. I did you a solid."

Tanner clicked on the new transmission, which was a clip of someone in a white cowl seated among the Prospect Shores crowd and waving a bandaged left hand. When the figure turned to the camera, its face was overlaid by Philip's delirious countenance from Nigeria.

THIRTY-SIX

Cleveland, Ohio. Saturday, May 30
Day Forty-two

NICK BRAYLEY STUBBED A TOE on the shower sill and hopped out onto a Turkish bath mat. He cursed and rubbed the toe as he toweled himself. You would think Ritz-Carlton tiles would be more guest-friendly. It was his second shock of the evening.

His campaign speech at the arena had earned him a standing ovation tonight. He was returning to his suite, tired but encouraged, when he encountered a maid pushing a cart of linens. Something about him made her smile, and he smiled, too, enjoying the moment. Until she turned the corner and called softly over her shoulder, "Somos gente."

Which stopped him in three paces. That chipper little phrase didn't exist two weeks ago, yet it pinned him there on a Berber carpet, like a run-over bug. Already, the lower classes had spun the Brazilian slogan into a trendy greeting. He shrugged it off, but the feeling lingered through his shower. A sense that whatever he accomplished tonight wasn't enough, with a smashed toe for an exclamation point. He wrapped himself in a thick robe, poured two fingers of twelve-year-old bourbon, and limped to his wife in the TV room. Its walls, carpets, and furnishings were green-on-green with Navy accents. Genuine old-world crap.

Last night, the news had featured two Indonesian policemen beating a man with long-handled canes, while a third dragged the guy's wife from their plywood hovel and machine-gunned their Powerpod. Worse scenes followed, from Russia, China, and the Middle East. Tonight, American mayhem was on display. Thirteen killed in Chicago food riots. A Powerpod dealer lynched by West Virginia vigilantes. A civilian and a Federal Agent shot dead during a Maker enforcement operation in Arizona.

"My God," Nick said. "Turn it off." He angled toward the bedroom.

Not in my country, dammit. Not here.

He'd seen killings, nasty ones in Bosnia, but never American-on-American, never rank sectarian murder on U.S. soil. These he could not abide. Jack Washburn could have prevented this if he'd acted sooner.

Yvonne was knitting, not watching.

He returned and switched channels to a political site where multiple "speedometers" clocked the winds of opinion blowing through the Internet. America's political wings, left, right, and weird, were lobbing invectives at each other. Conservatives blamed liberals, and vice versa, while a pair of commentators traded fatuous remarks about the chirons crawling beneath each meter. A new one in the corner, weak at seven percent, challenged the others, denouncing all of them as incumbents and proclaiming an ancient motto: "Live free or die." Its label said *Freemaker.*

Nick grunted. He muted the TV and paced the room, swirling his snifter of Maker's Mark. The way things were going, he would have to switch brands. A ridiculous concern compared to riots and killings, though rooted in the same source, Philip goddamn Machen.

As he drew near her, Yvonne frowned at the liquor. She patted a silky jade cushion.

"Sit with me, Nicholas?"

"People just don't grasp the enormity of the man's treachery," he said. "The greatest democratic nation on Earth is crumbling around them, and they don't get it. He is destroying America while the world wrings their hands and cries, Oh my. Nobody is stopping him."

He swirled the whiskey and sipped.

"Jack Washburn wasted a whole week getting Makers banned, two more to begin enforcing the ban, and Congress still hasn't outlawed Powerpods. Selena Gilmar has the Democrats believing they can ride Powerpods all the way to the White House if they can just delay banning them for a few more weeks. California's even got a referendum to legalize private Makers. I ask you, who is winning?"

Yvonne offered a shrug and patted the cushion. Again he ignored her and shuffled away.

"That secular messiah business, that opened a few eyes, but the media still treat him like Robin Hood riding a Jeep through Africa, like some kind of prophet.

"He told the world what was going to happen and, by God, it's happening. Makers are giving everybody the means to drop out, and mass unemployment forces them to do it. Commerce Department is going to report 58% unemployment on Monday. So his economic independence isn't a path to utopia. It's a damned lie. If we don't stop that man, America is going to collapse into a shell of its former self—a union of no states, a nation of micro-communities, isolated islands of barely-organized yokels, surrounded by zones of chaos. When governments fail, the gangs and warlords take over, and my campaign donors are screaming about losing their fortunes. Philip Machen says he's enabled freedom and self-reliance, but what approaches is not a passing swoon of the economy but a permanent retreat of civilization."

He was lecturing and couldn't help it. He sucked his amber solace, inhaled its vapors deeply into his lungs.

"The ministers and the rabbis, they saw right away what was at stake, but Jack . . . he's a good man, Yvonne. I warned him this isn't just a terrorist stunt, a shock from which we can recover and retaliate. No. Makers sprout tumors—drugs and guns and unemployment. They ignore property rights, undermine law and order. They're not salvation machines, they're anarchy pods. And those hand-wringers in the media haven't figured it out, yet. Philip Machen is evil, Yvonne, as evil as that bastard from Afghanistan."

"If you mean Osama bin Laden, he was Saudi."

Heat flared on his scalp. Only Yvonne's deep and abiding dignity prevented him from shouting, *Who cares where they come from?*

"One of them crashes airplanes into our buildings. The other destroys our money, our industries, our markets. When Makers bring down the government, which of these guys will have done more damage? Killing three thousand innocent people is heinous, but toppling every advanced nation will destroy much more, probably kill more. America is under attack, I tell you, and so far we have no traction against it."

Yvonne patted her cushion to no avail.

"Vice President Fletcher—that jerk. He's daft as Gilmar, trying to have it both ways with his stupid chastity belts. If he spoils my nomination next month, our party deserves to lose the election.

"I told Jack we need an unequivocal public demonstration that Pods and Makers are deadly. We need to shock the people into abandoning them. I told him Machen's power and influence hang by one slender thread. We need only to cut that thread, and everything he has done will collapse." He paced closer, let her capture his hand.

"I know you will do the right thing, Nicholas. You always do."

He stopped to marvel at the adoration beaming up at him, as it had thirty-two years ago. *Do you, Yvonne Slavinskaya, take this man?* To this day he could not fathom his incredible luck, that this delicate flower, his prima ballerina, had ever desired Captain Nicholas T. Brayley, U.S. Army. He shook his head.

"Don't they realize, these foot-draggers, what they are forcing us to do? If we don't assert full authority—and soon—the anarchy and the violence will spread." He gestured to the screen. "We have six weeks before the nominating convention, and they are forcing us to make powerful decisions, Yvonne. Dreadful decisions."

"Not a war?"

"To prevent one." He swallowed and stared at the clouds of destruction overhead. "There are moments in battle when a commander must strike at once. Debate the wisdom of it later. In order to prevail. The more I think about it, the more I feel that such a moment is here."

Yvonne stood and tugged him into her orbit, pressed her thighs against his. Her silken touch, the floral scent of her hair, flooded him with yearnings and inflamed his outrage.

"The Lord will provide," she whispered.

He set down his empty glass. "The Lord expects us to show some spine."

She nuzzled him. "You will do the right thing, Nicholas. You always do."

He kissed her head and reveled in it. Then he cast his anguish into the warm currents of her dark Slovakian eyes.

"We must," he said. "We will."

THIRTY-SEVEN

Livermore, California. Sunday, June 7
Day Fifty

A WEEK LATER, Everett Aboud was mixing gray powder in a wooden trough the size of a mattress. Twenty-seven shovelfuls of fine Olympia sand, nine of Portland cement, three of fireclay. Chop the mix with a hoe, wet it with water, and blend the paste. Between mixing and delivering this mortar, he stacked cinder blocks to either side of Bobby's and Jesse's boots, up on the scaffold, as they laid the walls for Jesse's new slaughterhouse. They planned to stop around three o'clock before the heat grew oppressive.

"It's called shelf life," Jesse was saying. "Everything wears out, rusts or rots at the same rate as before. You can't live on copied stuff indefinitely because things still spoil. So any day now, fresh food is going to be a serious form of wealth, and guess who's got plenty of that?" He nudged Bobby.

Helping Jesse had smoothed things with Bobby, who grumbled about the charters Everett was flying around Northern California

—three so far—and deflected some of Bobby's wild anxieties. Working long hours side-by-side had drawn them together again, so quitting General Johnson's shoe store had been a good choice. It pleased Bobby that Everett wouldn't be selling any more Powerpods. Now, if he could land a few more charters, the world might once again feel round.

At one-thirty-five, as he rinsed the mixing box for their next batch, his Cambiar rattled.

"Everett, I need you." Marcy only called him when she needed something. "We gotta beat the helicopters."

He turned aside, lowered his voice. "What helicopters?"

"Massive explosion, down by Coalinga. Traffic reporters saw it from Fresno, forty miles away. They say there's a mushroom cloud. We gotta get down there before we get locked out."

Everett glanced to the mound of tarpaulins baking nearby, then to the mortar-encrusted scaffold behind him. If he left now, Bobby would be pissed.

"This is gonna cost you," he said.

"I'll pay, I'll pay. I'm on the Dublin Grade. I'll be there in five."

He broke the connection and pocketed his phone. To Jesse and Bobby, he said, "I have to go," then strode away without explaining. Bobby whined but didn't follow him. Jesse said nothing.

Twenty minutes later, from the front seat of Glamorous Glennis, Marcy complained, "Can't we go faster?"

"Two-hundred-twenty knots," he said. "The wings come off at two-fifty." This was not true, but he didn't want to explain speed buffets. Or discuss radioactivity. If she didn't bring it up, neither would he. Because the risk would bond them, he hoped.

The haze filling the Great Valley grew thicker as they raced south, and soon it obscured the grasslands below them. He reduced speed and descended while Marcy readied her video camera.

At the edge of his navigation screen, a red icon blinked. An emergency NOTAM, a notice to airmen, from the Fresno Flight Service Station. When he touched it, a window appeared.

"Emergency: All civil aircraft aloft between Stockton and Bakersfield are directed to land ASAP and remain grounded. Civil departures from Emergency Area forbidden until further notice. All aircraft must observe Exclusion Zone thirty miles radius around Coalinga, California, to flight level 40, until further notice."

"Read your display," he said. "We are six miles from that exclusion zone."

"We didn't get the message," she said, "Broken radio or something."

"Watch for strobe lights," he said. "We are not the only ones out here."

They passed low over a molasses-colored tank nested near an oil well. A dirt road ran from the tank and disappeared into thick knuckles of yellow grass. Abruptly, the grass turned black, and Everett slowed even more. Before he could shut the vents, an ash-bucket stink blew into the cockpit. Marcy was recording, narrating softly to her camera as they sailed over three blackened lumps and a thousand smoldering doughnuts.

"Cows?" she guessed.

"And pies." His Nav display showed Interstate 5 ahead, and there it was—a thin silver line bisecting the soup. No mushroom cloud, just smoke in every direction. Everett banked, followed the vacant freeway southward, and descended. They crossed a lone pickup truck, charred and collapsed on its axles, tires burned off. Then a car and a van, dead in their lanes, incinerated.

"There it is," Marcy said. "The rest stop."

From a flat zone on the right, black snags poked upward like sharpened fingers. Carbonized vehicles, eight or ten of them, rested on smoldering rims in the parking lot. Between them, a collapsed and roofless ruin that must have been the toilets. Where a lawn should be, there lay bodies, charred and twisted. The grim tableau swept by and disappeared in their wake.

"Go back," Marcy said. She tapped a red dot on her Cambiar. "Center of the blast," she said, holding up the image. "They cut off the satellite views, but somebody snapped this first. Those ruins are ground zero."

"Hang on," he said, and he banked sharply. He idled the engine and dropped full flaps. Which pitched them forward, slowed them to a crawl, and hunched the nose like a sniffing hound.

"We're crashing," Marcy shrieked.

Everett held 35 knots at 200 feet, dragging Glamorous through hot, stinky smoke. When the rest area reappeared, he circled on a whisper of thrust. They tiptoed like aerial burglars for two rotations, while Marcy recorded the devastation. This time the bodies had limbs. And hairless, skeletal heads.

Everett swallowed. Those were people down there, seven at least. Men and women—please, no children—and their demise did not look accidental. Somebody did this to them. Ashes filled his mouth and demanded he spit. Instead, he swallowed his anger and leveled off.

"You want another pass?"

Marcy's elegant head wobbled *no.* "Let's go home."

He powered up, raised the flaps, and turned for Livermore, 130 miles north. They hadn't gone two miles when Marcy twisted in her seat.

"Go back. We have to land." She waved her Cambiar. "They are calling it a bomb, a weapon of mass destruction. But there's no crater, Everett. Why is ground zero not vaporized? Why is everything burned but not exploded? We need to prove what happened."

"Maybe it's not ground zero."

"We need to prove this thing was nuclear, Everett. Or not."

"Okay, but that rest area is a crime scene. We can't mess with it. I'll put us down on the freeway. That should be close enough." *And maybe not so radioactive.*

He descended in a turn. As the soot-streaked pavement rushed to meet them, he teased Glamorous level, and she settled gently. They touched with grit swirling from her wingtips. Everett killed the engine and braked with care to minimize the junk her fanjet was ingesting. When GG rumbled to a stop, he released her canopy and got out.

"Careful," he said.

Marcy stepped to the ground clutching an empty sandwich bag.

"Here," she said. She gave him a painter's mask, a gauzy paper shell with rubber band straps. She slipped a second one over her nose and mouth. "Better than nothing."

"Thanks."

She passed her camera to him, and he steadied himself, recorded her strolling to the edge of the pavement. Roadblocks were probably stopping any traffic, but someone might slip through, crazy-scared or just crazy, and run them down.

Marcy composed herself.

"I'm Marcy Johnson. Today is Sunday, June seventh, and I am standing on Interstate 5, just one hundred yards from ground zero, a few miles from Coalinga, California." She indicated the rise behind her, saying it was the rest stop where the explosion occurred. Everett widened the view, then narrowed it again as she stooped to whisk debris into her sandwich bag. She motioned for him to focus on her Cambiar, which displayed the date, time, latitude, and longitude. She wrote these on the bag and sealed it.

"While it is too soon to say what caused this devastation, a laboratory analysis of our sample should determine what happened here today. I am Marcy Johnson for WebNews." She waited three seconds for Everett to close the shot, then bounded to the plane.

A glint at the edge of the road caught his eye, a squashed soda can, which he plucked for a souvenir.

Marcy dropped her sample into her backpack and was peeling a foil pouch when a rhythmic patter-patter came from the sky. Everett snatched her towelette.

"Get in," he said.

Her annoyance switched to alarm as the patter-patter became a wop-wop.

"Get in," he ordered. He pressed her down, hopped into his seat and started the engine. With one hand he shut the canopy, with the other, he opened the throttle.

If that helicopter caught them on the ground, it could squat ahead and trap them. A shadow passed overhead, left-to-right, and he craned to follow it. GG's turbofan roared mightily, but the big white chopper was turning.

"They see us," he said. Without her headset, Marcy could not hear him.

A blunt-nosed Huey arced toward them until, at 150 knots, Everett hauled the stick into his lap and launched Glamorous Glennis. The chopper closed the gap but passed beneath them. It was a CalFire Helitack machine, not the police or the military, and it would never catch them now. Everett rode the jetwash straight up, whooshing to 18,000 feet in just three minutes. Any other day, this would have been a *yeehaw* moment.

Marcy fumbled her headset into place but said nothing. When Everett leveled off and angled north, he told her to put on her oxygen. He peeled off his paper mask and exchanged it for a real one.

"Are they gone?" she asked.

"No, but we are."

He squinted in the high-altitude glare, alone with his thoughts. Above the smoke now, he contemplated those blackened figures on the knoll. The more he swallowed, the more he needed to swallow. Nausea, thick and yeasty, churned in his stomach like a clot of grief. Which was nothing compared to flames-on-skin, hair igniting, throats seared shut, eyeballs bursting in their sockets. How they must have screamed, those poor, poor people.

Who could do such a thing? What are their names? We need to tell the world those people were murdered.

Marcy was working, not crying. She removed her headset, took up her Cambiar, and placed a series of calls. In twenty minutes, she had reached a chemistry professor and made arrangements.

They passed over Livermore and skirted Mt. Diablo, continued north to a reservoir hidden in the hills behind Orinda. They couldn't land where they might be arrested, so the chemist had suggested a meadow in Briones Regional Park, at the foot of the dam. They could land there, the man said, and Everett did. In dry, knee-high grass that whipped GG's wings as she settled into it.

He left the engine running while a lanky, sunburned, white guy jounced toward them on a mountain bike. The cyclist wore a two-cartridge filter mask and dismounted with a military-style Geiger counter in one hand. Any clicking it made was masked by engine noise, but he read the meter and shouted, "You are contaminated. Throw away your clothes and take a shower right away." He seemed concerned, but not afraid.

Marcy gave him her sample, which he deposited with gloved hands in a parcel box strapped to the bike. He removed his gloves and dropped them in too. Then with a nod, he mounted the bike and stroked humpty-bumpty through the yellow grass. After fifty yards, he stopped, pulled off his mask, and waved.

Marcy waved back. She gave Everett a thumbs-up. He couldn't see her face but imagined she was as relieved as he was. They flew back to Jesse Cardoza's ranch, landed without incident, and jostled to the barn. At the last moment, he opened the canopy, scooping hot, dry air onto their faces.

"Kiss me," he said.

THIRTY-EIGHT

MARCY STEPPED OUT OF THE PLANE, somber and unsteady. She waved her Cambiar at Everett.

"They quarantined three counties," she said. "Closed the roads and the airports. They're calling it nuclear."

He nodded, looked for Jesse or Bobby, but saw no one. He didn't really want a kiss. He wanted distraction from the mental radioactivity clicking in his head. If Coalinga was possible, any evil was possible.

"This way," he said.

He led her to the tin-roofed shed he shared with his father. At the door, he called Bobby's name and got the reply he wanted—silence. He drew Marcy into the dim interior, to the counter with the two-burner cooktop and a scratched metal sink. Plastic shower curtains, strung on a wire, divided the room. He yanked spare trash bags from a bin under the sink and gave her one.

"Clothes," he said.

She nodded, began unbuttoning. They shed their garments, stuffed them in the bags, and stood facing each other, naked. Her humidity, her body heat, glistened at her throat, beaded along her shoulders, and trickled down her chest. A thousand tensions hovered between them until their feelings magnetically aligned. She gazed at nothing, but he knew what she was seeing. If she weren't so very close, he'd be seeing it too. Death. Destruction. Murder. For a long moment, she was Lady Paradise, staring into Perdition and not comprehending. He fought the urge to touch her.

"It wasn't terrorists," he said.

She stared, vacant and still.

"Those bastards wouldn't waste a nuke on a four-seat crapper out in the boondocks. They'd go for a big fat city, full of victims. What kind of psychopath wants to terrorize us, but not too much?"

Marcy looked at him, still uncomprehending. Her scent crossed the electric gap between them. It zoomed to his loins and charged him, before rebounding with a crucial concern.

"What are we doing, Marcy?"

She came alert, whispered, "Wash up."

"Shower's here." He stepped aside from a much-painted door.

She sidled past him, eyes averted, guarding her thoughts but not her modesty. When she shut herself in the bath, a milliwatt of fear blinked in his head, that he might never see her again. Naked and alone, he longed for her: to hold her, to please her. But the slightest touch, uninvited, would shatter the trust between them— if that's what it was. If she came out of the bath flaunting the same old teases, he would throw her sweet brown rotunda into the driveway and be rid of her.

Aroused, annoyed, and agitated, he fired up the video screen where a panorama of blackened earth swept down to a vacant Interstate. Eight or ten versions of this, plus a thin, gray column rising distinctively, swelled at the top before dispersing. The voice-over mentioned Coalinga twice before he muted it. He flopped onto the bed that doubled as a sofa. A cold beer would hit the mark just now, but he needed to keep a clear mind. For what, exactly, he wasn't sure. There was nothing he could do now but gawk and wait, like everyone else.

When the shower stopped, he remembered she needed clothes. He rousted a carton from behind the bed, dumped trousers, shirts, and socks, found some old sandals that might fit her. He thought to copy them but couldn't muster the drive to do it. His legs had gone hollow, drained of substance, just like his head.

Bumps and rustles made him look. Marcy leaned from the door, towel at her throat. No smile, no attitude.

"Is there something to wear?"

He went to her, tugged the towel away and spread it across her shoulders, covering her. When she crossed her arms to hold it in place, he kissed her cheek.

"No freebies," she said, but the warning carried no spunk.

He returned to the counter and the clothes.

"Take what you want."

She padded over, touched his naked back. In silence, she chose a chambray shirt and a pair of gray chinos, his old flying school togs. When she retreated with them to the bath, he followed. She stopped and let go the towel.

"Are you going to let me dress?"

"I'm contaminated," he said. "So is the bed where I sat." He shuffled around her, careful not to touch, and entered the bath. "Don't go away," he said.

When he emerged three minutes later, the video screen was still playing death and destruction, and the bed covers lay heaped on the floor. Beneath a fresh percale sheet, Marcy lay watching him, Sphinx-like.

He approached her, his towel precarious on his hips. He found the remote and switched off the screen. He wanted to say something, but words would not condense. He wanted her; he didn't want her. This was not a good time; there would be no better time. The world was going to hell, and they were circling the drain.

"No games," she said.

He searched her face, seeking sincerity, but discovered a gaze so indrawn it shocked him. He stroked the pulse at her temple. She leaned into his caress and rose to him. The sheet fell away. She pressed her cheek, warm and urgent, to his neck, and he felt her swallow.

"Marcy, I want to know." She pressed closer. "About you and me. Because you are more woman than I ever hoped to find. You have more guts, more smarts, and all those sassy-classy ways. I can't keep up. I don't want to keep up if I'm just going to be your errand boy." Her touch infused him, thickened the air, aroused him.

"Hold me," she said.

He slipped his arms under hers and tipped her face up to his.

"No," he said.

She shut her eyes and trembled. "I need you to hold me, Everett. Please. Just hold me."

He shook her, made her look. "I'll take you down to the floor. I'll take you down and use you and throw you away."

"All right."

"No," he cried, "it's not all right. Soon as I do that, we are finished, and you know it. Is that what you want?"

"No."

"So, what *do* you want, Marcy?"

She gripped his arms.

"I just need you to hold me. I'll do whatever you want."

He shook his head, nearly lost the towel. She didn't understand. He couldn't believe he was not going grab her and take what he wanted, just for spite. *Didn't she know what she had in him? Didn't she see that every molecule of him wanted every molecule of her?*

"Tell me one true thing," he said. "And it better not be what a nice guy I am."

"I'm not doing so well, Everett. I'm not coping. You can't ask me to—"

He shoved her onto her back and dropped across her beautiful, bare chest, hauled her wrists to her startled throat.

"I'm not asking," he said. "This is a shitty time, and you're upset. So am I. But we can't go on like this, Marcy. I'm not coping either. We come together, right now, or we split for good. That's what I want from you. No more screwing around."

She closed her eyes. "I'm sorry."

He released her and pushed himself up, hoping not to embed the sight of her breasts into his memory, though infinitely aware he already had. Her lips tightened. She made a face and opened her eyes.

"God, you're stubborn." She pulled him down. He resisted. "See?"

He cantilevered, inches from her, his loins tingling in revolt.

"I was nineteen," she said, biting off the *teen*, making it ring. "My sweetness, my baby daughter. Aborted herself. Eclampsia, they said." She sucked a breath and held it. "I swore . . . I swore I would never let another man mess up my life." She glared and exhaled, bleak and furious. "So it's against my principles to screw a guy who might truly want me. Do you understand?" She sniffed. "And you're looking for some kind of guarantee?" She shook her head. "You don't even know me."

He drew a knuckle down her cheek, past her ear to the mattress, where he made a fist and leaned on it.

"So what are you doing in my bed?"

"Waiting," she said. She tugged away the towel.

He checked her eyes, for the Marcy he wanted to find, the truth-seeking Marcy, the one who reflected the hopes and the vast uncertainty within him. Then he laid himself down the length of her smooth, brown body. He drew her head onto his shoulder and kissed her, long and easy. Then strong and deep.

She arced in his hands, pressed her mouth hard against his. Her scent, her taste, her heat inflamed him. Caresses spawned strokes that brought graspings. They keened to merge, to melt into each other until the room itself overheated. They found each other and moved as one, breathed as one, stroked as one. Until wild, undifferentiated pleasure sealed them in a heaving, protracted rhythm. They tumbled from their Everest, still entwined, gasping and clutching. Kissing. For a long time, nothing moved but the languorous rise and fall of their sweat-slick bellies. For a long time, the tin shed and all the world's tin sheds did not exist.

"Thirsty," she said.

He stumbled to the sink, which triggered three unlikely events. On the floor, Marcy's Cambiar rattled. The front door banged wide open. And the water glass slipped from his fingers.

Bobby stomped into the room, his gray mane a torment, searching until he saw them.

"Jeeezuss." He backed out, pulled the door shut, and swore again.

Marcy ignored him, as she did the crash in the sink, and took up her phone.

"Shit," she said, recognizing the face on its screen. "It's whats-his-name, the FBI."

Everett froze, as he always did when things were falling. He listened—for Bobby, for Marcy, for the damned FBI.

Marcy said hello and absorbed what the man told her. When she put it down without replying, Everett brought her a fresh glass of water.

"They seized our sample," she said. "Agent Parker says he will keep us out of jail, but only if we help him with the girl."

"Screw that. I'm not helping him. What girl?"

"Tiffany Lavery."

"She's here?"

"At this ranch, hiding like we are."

Everett blinked. "I'm not hiding."

Marcy accepted the water and acknowledged his nether parts. "I'll say."

On that note, they dressed and stuffed the bed covers into a poly bag. When they finished and washed their hands, Marcy sat on the mattress and fretted.

"I was going to get a Pulitzer. You were going to get kissed."

Everett switched on the screen.

"Everybody's gotta get kissed," he said, and he made a dive for her neck.

She feinted aside and punched his leg.

"I have a brother," she said. "I know how to defend myself."

On the opposite wall, the screen synced to a brightly lighted room, probably at the White House, where five men, two in uniform, stood behind a familiar, grim-faced bureaucrat. The crawl at the bottom of the screen said, *N. Brayley, US Attorney General.* Everett un-muted it.

". . . was caused by a faulty Powerpod, apparently being transported when it failed catastrophically. We do not know what caused it to explode, but when we speak of Powerpods, we are talking about the power of the stars, harnessed inside two microscopic entities, each dependent for its stability on a process that no one fully understands. At this time we have no reason to believe the Coalinga event was deliberate. Every indication points to a tragic, accidental release of nuclear energy from a single, faulty Powerpod. Three other Pods on the same truck did not explode. We are examining their remains for clues to the nature and causes of what happened."

The screen switched to a grainy view of Interstate 5, shot from high over the rest stop, before the blast. At one end of the parking lot sat a truck with four white lumps on its open bed. The next view went dark and murky. The curbs disappeared, and the charred vehicles had scattered at odd angles. To the right, encircled by a white cursor, lay a crumpled mass that could be the truck, and beside it lay three lumps the size of basketballs.

"That's wrong," Marcy said. "Those weren't there." She stood and grabbed her gear bag from the table. Everett muted the broadcast and moved to help her. The data she had posted to WebNews, and to three other sites, was still in her camera, unedited.

She found the fly-over and played the sequence on her preview screen.

"There," she pointed. Everett followed her finger. "That's the truck, but I don't see any Pods." Their angle was lower than the official shots, which presumably came from a satellite, so it was hard to tell, but no lumps appeared anywhere near that truck. Marcy fast-forwarded to their second pass, which was both closer and taken from a steeper angle. No lumps on the truck or near it. She squirmed and shut off the camera.

"Omigod," she said. She hugged her camera as if to console it, then accused the wall screen. "*They* did it."

THIRTY-NINE

EVERETT WAS ABOUT TO SAY, *No, they couldn't.* But . . . the reality of it pressurized the room, stuffed his ears. He wiggled his jaw to clear them.

"Dirty bomb," he said. Monstrous big, salted with radioactivity, but not a nuke.

"They're going to quash our videos," Marcy said, "but they won't dare arrest us."

"Because that would draw attention," he said.

"They control the images and the forensics," she said. "They control the story. We are just crackpots, and this"—she raised her camera—"is fabricated evidence. They're going to screw us, Everett."

"I have another sample," he realized out loud. "A soda can from the highway. In the plane."

"Way to go, Everett." Marcy jumped to her feet.

He stood and grasped her elbows. "They don't know we have it."

"Yeah, but the ranch is under surveillance," she said. "That's how they found the Lavery girl."

"I haven't seen her," he said, dropping his hands. "Where should we hide the can?"

"Anywhere but here." She stuffed the camera into her pack. "C'mon. We have evidence to preserve."

They jogged to the plane, passing Bobby, who glowered in the shade of the barn, sucking on a cigarette. He said nothing but watched them intently. At the plane, Marcy slipped the crushed can into her remaining plastic baggie. Then she pecked his cheek.

"You're the greatest, Everett."

She strode for her car, pant cuffs scraping. He followed, intent on riding along, but when they reached the door, she stopped. "I need you to stay."

"No." Her logic escaped him. "I'm going with you."

She pressed herself against him, a whole-body kiss.

"Please," she said. "This isn't over, Everett. We need to find Tiffany Lavery. We need to know what Parker wants from her."

Everett swayed, checked his shoelaces, glanced to the barn from which Bobby had disappeared. He shook his head three different ways.

"No," he said. "Just get in the plane, and I'll fly us out of here."

She tossed the backpack into her car.

"I know somebody else who can analyze it," she said. "I need you to stay." She gripped his shoulders, kissed him firmly, then searched his eyes for acceptance. "I'll be back, I promise."

She drove away, crunching gravel and raising dust. When she was gone, he festered in the yard for a while, then scanned the shed for indications. It was Bobby's turn to make dinner, which is what he hoped his father was doing, though he also needed to avoid him. What he really needed was a pine board to plane into shavings.

He left Glamorous Glennis exposed to the voyeurs of the sky and entered the barn. Where Jesse had once parked a backhoe, a full-sized Maker now stood. Its cones crowded the walls and threatened the rafters. He kicked one of its struts. *Wake up.* From the mess of aircraft parts he had been copying, he liberated a bulgy red jug labeled *Jet fuel.*

He opened a Maker side-cone but encountered a jig made of black pipe, a custom-made frame to hold a particular large object that was, at present, not there. He removed the jig and replaced it with a shelf, onto which he heaved his fuel jug.

Maybe he should fly to Nevada or Oregon or up to Canada. He could search Calgary for his mother and sister, with or without Bobby.

He pressed the remote control Jesse had rigged, and worried, as the Maker thumped a new fuel can into existence. *What if this thing went kaboom instead of thump?*

His finger rose clear of the button. Only Philip Machen really knew what happened inside these things. Who could argue that Coalinga was *not* caused by a defective Powerpod? That millions of Pods would operate flawlessly, forever? Suppose Machen had missed a decimal point. We only have his word and our personal experiences to vouch for them.

Everett removed the new jug and placed it beside its parent in the opposite cone. The message of Coalinga was clear: Pods and Makers were either inherently safe or randomly deadly. But there had been no Pods down there. Whatever their shortcomings, Pods and Makers had not killed anyone. And Marcy was doing the right thing. They were doing the right thing.

No longer angry, he lugged two new jugs out to the plane and released the fill cap on GG's left wing. He inserted a funnel and tipped the first jug to its lip.

Even if Marcy's videos proved there had been no Pods at the rest stop, would anyone believe them? Would anyone care? How could the world *un-see* that hideous cloud and those poor, incinerated people? It seemed fears of Hiroshima were going to destroy Pods and Makers, even if a thousand tests proved them safe, and the blast today was an evil fraud. Even if the killers confessed, the world would remember Coalinga, and it would tremble.

A taste of grit invaded his mouth. How could they thwart a lie so overwhelming? He didn't care about Makers or Philip Machen. He cared about murder and stopping monsters who kill people. Out of the east, a williwaw twirled through the yard and scoured him with dust.

By the time he finished refueling, the sun had sunk through a cleft in the hills and taken the breeze with it. Sweating in the barn, he shuttled up and down the ladder, disposing the empty fuel jugs into the Maker's top cone. Yesterday, Jesse had dumped garden waste in there and, dilution notwithstanding, the slurry stank. Everett topped it off with a hose, submerged the buoyant jugs, then escaped the barn. A fresh and airy twilight soothed him.

Across the yard, Bobby's shadow passed to-and-fro behind the window shrouds. Everett couldn't put him off forever, so he returned to the shed and went inside. Bobby was shoving clothes and ammunition into an old Navy duffel. There was no evidence of the dinner Everett hoped for. He shut the door and tried to sound upbeat.

"Where you headed, Dad?"

Bobby punched a shirt into the bag. "Pack your stuff. We're leaving."

"What for?"

"You took her down there, to see that thing. You tell me what for."

"We had to report what happened."

"And came back here to celebrate." Bobby kicked the bed. "You lovebirds made another propaganda flick, didn't you? To get your guy off the hook."

"It wasn't a Powerpod, Dad. There were no Pods down there. We recorded everything. We have proof."

Bobby spat. "You went down there and saw that, and you don't even have the decency to be upset."

"We saw the bodies . . ." Their black husks rose again in his mind. ". . . so close we could smell them. So stay out of my head, Dad."

Bobby shoved past him, through the shower-curtain drapes. He returned with a handful of boot socks.

"Get your gear. I signed us up for the Concord Militia." He crammed the socks into his bag. "I'm mustering-in as a sergeant, on account of my prior service. You'll be a private. We start in the morning."

Everett moved to the counter. From its pint-size refrigerator, he extracted a Budweiser and popped it open, taking a long swig before sliding a tin of franks and beans off the shelf.

"Militias," he sniffed. "Tory know-it-all's itching to shoot people they don't like."

"Those *volunteers* may be the only hope we have for preventing the next explosion. Being as the cops and the Army can't handle the situation, it's up to we-the-people. So pack your gear."

Everett spooned brown glop into a pan and switched on the hotplate. Bobby straightened.

"You moving in with her? Is that the plan?"

"I'm not joining your militia, that's for sure." Everett poked the food with a spatula.

Bobby watched and tamped his duffel. He cinched it with a padlock. "I'm trying to save you from making another dumb mistake."

Everett jabbed his beans.

Bobby drew closer. "We can't stay here, Son. Jesse thinks he can keep his damn Makers. They're his property, he says, nobody else's. Figures he and Marie can hold off the government and the vigilantes. If he doesn't come to his senses, there's going to be a shoot-out. We can't be part of that."

Everett said nothing, which seemed to inflame Bobby's conjunctiva. His father blinked and blinked until he whirled and switched on the wall screen. It resolved to a moss-green parka inhabited by a disheveled Latina newswoman. She wore a cartridge-filter face mask.

"Live from California. Behind me is the apartment building where military police have taken a man into custody. The local news service, here in Coalinga, posted an interview with that man, Jungo Ilgunas, in which Mr. Ilgunas claims he saw an aerial bomb drop to the freeway east of here this afternoon. A military spokeswoman said she has no information about Mr. Ilgunas or his claims. She acknowledged only that the authorities are questioning him."

Bobby switched it off.

"Hey, I was watching that."

Bobby tossed the control into the wastebasket. "Freemaker propaganda, trading on other people's troubles."

Everett frowned, worked his beans. "Dad, let's get out of here. Let's take the plane to Canada. Find Mom and Melinda. Find a place to stay and let the chips fall without us."

"And live on what? Makers have killed just about every job there is, and Coalinga just killed the Makers. From now on people are going to have to *earn* their livings, like they used to. No more freeloading."

"Me and Marcy," Everett said, "are not partisans. We just want to know what's going on, show people what's happening—without getting slammed for it."

"You're so close to them now, you don't even see it," Bobby said. "But I do. Every time you use a Maker, you boost your addiction. You're a Maker junkie. You're going the wrong way, Son. We are going to stop this guy, but you've turned into his accomplice. The Vatican put out a papal bull today. Do you know what that is?"

"You haven't been to church since you married Mom."

"The Pope knows what he's talking about." Bobby jabbed the air. "Did you see that bastard, parading through Nigeria? In white robes? Women laying palm fronds at his feet? He was mocking Jesus, don't you see? People say Philip Machen is the Antichrist. As far as I'm concerned, Coalinga proves it."

Everett rolled his eyes. "Jesus doesn't need a militia."

"Don't you smart-mouth me, boy." Bobby punched the air. "Don't you—I've had just about—" He worked his rant down to an accusing finger. "Is that our last can of franks and beans?"

Everett stifled a laugh. "I'll get some more tomorrow."

"Beg Jesse for another handout," Bobby said, "to copy in his Maker."

"We earned our beans today, building his walls. That ought to make you happy."

"You ingrate. I sacrificed everything to get you into an airline cockpit, and you give me lip. I sold my business and my house. Took out a loan to keep your sorry ass out of jail. Everything I've done for you, you're throwing away—your career, your future, everything. For what? You'll never fly for the airlines. You're too damned lazy. You just want to hang out and copy stuff. Party hardy and play hide-the-salami with your girlfriend. At least Jesse grows food. You're just a parasite."

Everett sucked more beer.

"There's not going to be a world without Makers, Dad. Just people who have them and people who don't. You know the fat cats are never going to give up theirs. Not in a million years. Once they strip us of our Makers, they won't be letting guys like you or me near one. Once the Maker Lords take over, they are going to own our asses and we will be their slaves."

"Beats anarchy."

"It's not about them, Bobby. It's not even about him. It's about us."

"That's what I been trying to tell you," Bobby shouted. "It's up to you and me. We have to do the right thing, Son. Right now. You gotta stop messing with Makers and the people who want them and come with me."

"Or what?"

"Or there's gonna be another Coalinga."

"Coalinga was rigged."

"I don't care if those damn things are safe as beach sand. I don't want 'em. I don't need 'em. And I'm not gonna live like a hippie mooching off people, pretending what's theirs is mine, living in a commune like bugs on a log. Makers are wrong, that's all you need to know. They're immoral. We have to stop 'em before they suck our souls."

"I'm not going with you, Dad. I don't know what these Freemaker people are all about, but I'm no vigilante." The feeling washed over him again, the frisson of resisting a false either-or. Choose your mom or choose your dad. Choose Tory or choose Freemaker. Nobody could make him do that. "You can't make me."

Bobby fell into a protracted wobble, glared until Everett lost patience. "I thought you were leaving."

Bobby stopped, no longer seeing. His voice went cold.

"Yeah, I'm leaving." He parted the curtain and returned with his rifle, the bolt-action Winchester with a bull barrel and a sniper scope. He strode to the door, opened it, and heaved his duffel into the dark. Then he stomped out after it.

Everett rubbed his face. It was always him who had to make amends. He went to the door and flung it open. Why did Bobby have to be so—

Boom!

By the glare of a muzzle flash, Everett saw his father shoot their Powerpod. Behind him, the shed went dark.

"What'd you do that for?"

"One less Pod."

"You can't shoot all of them." Instantly, he regretted saying it. "Dad?"

"If Jesse won't get rid of those damned machines, somebody will have to do it for him." Bobby's voice trailed toward the barn.

"Dad?"

A figure stirred on Jesse's porch, and the yard lights winked on. Beneath a flickering orange lamp, Bobby rushed into the barn.

"Stop!" Everett chased him. He powered through the door and shouted the one thing his father might respect. "It doesn't belong to you. It belongs to Jesse."

Bobby froze in mid-aim.

"It's not your property," Everett said.

Bobby lowered the gun. He glanced at Everett, then headed for the side door, where he aimed again.

"Dad, stop!"

But it was too late. From ten feet back, Bobby fired into Glamorous Glennis.

Everett sprinted.

"The hell is going on out here?" Rural Supply boots came running from the house.

Bobby chambered another round as Everett pounced on him. They spun in a sloppy jig until the gun discharged between them. *Boom!*

"Stop shooting!"

They careered through the door and fell—arms, elbows, and knees digging for purchase. Everett grabbed the rifle. Bobby thrust it high, then released it. In the slack, Everett got hold of the barrel and held on, but Bobby swung a meaty fist. Everett's ear banged sharply, though now he hugged the rifle. He twisted it away and kicked at Bobby, who grunted, kicked back, and swung another fist. Which missed.

Then a torrent of Portuguese curses laid hands on Everett's shoulders, flipped him like a turtle onto his back. A boot slammed his stomach, knocking the wind out of him and releasing the gun, which levitated into Jesse's hands. Another boot thudded but brought no pain. Bobby went *oof* and curled like a leaf in a campfire.

"Gimme that piece," Jesse growled. "Nobody shoots up my place, goddamn it. Get up, you jackasses."

Spittle rained on Everett as he crawled for the airplane.

"Don't shoot," he rasped. He reached GG's nose and gathered his legs. One shaky thrust heaved him onto her canopy, where he spread himself. "Don't shoot my plane."

Behind him, the rifle snicked and slapped, snicked and slapped, flipping its remaining shells away.

"The hell is going on out here?" Jesse demanded.

"Stay out of this, Jess." Bobby grunted to his knees. "This is between me and him."

Jesse slung the rifle over his shoulder and kicked the dirt.

"We go back a ways, Bobby, but this is too much. This time you screwed up. I'll just keep the gun while you cool down. Go collect your things. I want you out of here. Tonight." Jesse strode for the house. "My supper's getting cold, damn it."

When he reached the porch, he stomped twice before looking back. A shake of his round head propelled him inside.

"Damned fool," Bobby muttered. He steadied himself then loped away to the darkened shed.

Everett clung to his airplane, lungs heaving, ear ringing, protecting his possibilities. Bobby was right. He would never fly for the airlines now. Having his own plane had spoiled him for fixed routes and rigid timetables. He fingered GG's canopy, sighted anxiously down her wings, and surveyed her delicate skin. He found the hole, a single puncture aft of the rear seat, directly over her engine. He folded himself, smeared his forehead across the wound.

"You might as well have shot me."

A lidded moon hung low in the eastern sky. Everett straightened, brushed dust from his back and his elbows. *Suck it up, jackass.* He could repair the engine. He had found a worthy woman. And this wasn't over. By his reckoning, the future was still half-full.

Across the yard, under a buzzing light, Bobby strapped his duffel to the old Yamaha dirt bike. He kick-started it and charged with a ragged *blaaat* to Jesse's front walk. He sat there, revving the engine until Jesse came out with the Winchester. If they spoke, Everett didn't hear it. When Jesse turned away, Bobby slalomed the hundred yards to Vineyard Avenue, rifle over his shoulder, ripping gravel and spewing dirt. The racket receded until it was gone.

Everett waited alone in the yard. After years of gathering the threads of their two-man family, struggling to keep them knitted together, the split had finally come. And it was Bobby leaving *him*. He'd always thought it would be the other way 'round, that the time and the place would be his to choose. The reversal burned hot on his neck. Losing his family had always been his worst nightmare.

He hadn't trembled like this since his mother left. He swallowed and returned to the shed.

Inside, he lit a candle and sat down to a cold pot of beans. The plane he could fix, but not his old man. They could have handled the situation, with or without Powerpods, with or without Makers. They could have lived off his charter business and kept their family together. The problem wasn't Marcy or Makers, it was Bobby, running hard from his demons. The real terror, that he might have to change and adjust his self-concept, was simply too dangerous for him to contemplate. Rather than think a new thought, he had abandoned the only person who still loved him.

Everett ate in the flickering gloom. The burden of ancient taunts and expectations lifted slowly from his shoulders, but it was a sour deliverance. The human rock against which he had always pushed and pulled, to balance and measure himself, was gone. First, Coalinga, now this. Even his fearful buzzes had departed.

He finished the beer and called Marcy, just to hear her voice. She was crying too.

"They arrested Uncle General," she said.

FORTY

Washington, D.C. Monday, June 8
Day Fifty-one

MAIN JUSTICE, they called this building, and despite his rush, Nick Brayley stole a moment while crossing its foyer to absorb a celebratory dose of gravitas. Thirty minutes ago, in the White House oval office, he had conveyed a ceremonial pen into Jack Washburn's hand, and the President had signed the document Nick had written, his executive order outlawing Powerpods.

Exiting the elevator on the fifth floor, Nick clutched that special pen and looked down on a sun-dappled Pennsylvania Avenue, his attention catching on the sharp northwest corner of the J. Edgar Hoover FBI Building.

Finally in his chambers, Attorney General Nicholas T. Brayley stood in the full light of summer, absorbing divine approval. He turned from the window to extract from his desk a crystal decanter and its matching glass, into which he poured two fingers of Maker's Mark scotch whiskey. Drawing the amber liquid into his mouth, he received its salute—a warm jolt of victory.

As usual, the Russians, the Europeans, and the Chinese had swung their enforcement hammers first, seizing Pods, blocking the internet, and jailing Freemakers. But Jack Washburn had finally addressed the nation and signed the American order. And this one had teeth. To restore the national security, to ensure the public safety, all non-federal Powerpods must be destroyed forthwith, without notice, without compensation, and without appeal. As Abraham Lincoln had once done to quell Civil War draft riots, Jack also suspended habeas corpus, up to ninety days, for scofflaws and resisters. The order did not include the additional sanctions Nick had wanted, but Justice had finally gained the upper hand against Philip Machen and his anarchy pods.

Nick toasted their achievement—his achievement—with another sip and stuffed the ceremonial pen into his pocket.

"Now who's going to save that sonofabitch," he said out loud.

Coalinga was smashing those starry-eyed Freemakers and clearing the political decks. Jubilant campaign donors were bound to reward their most effective champion.

By nominating Selena Gilmar back in February, and adopting her pro-Powerpods agenda, the Democratic Party had sealed its fate. Though Gilmar had yet to withdraw from the race, it pleased Nick to imagine the panic flooding her sanctums this afternoon. Come November, Republicans would sweep the elections, and a grateful nation would elect the architect of their salvation, Nicholas T. Brayley, President of the United States. A prospect that warmed him more than the whiskey.

Very little stood in his way: a few holdouts; a few enclaves; a journalist here and there. Nut jobs and head cases linked by their fuzzy ideas and dwindling Cambiar connections. Knock out a few more satellites, and the whole insurgency will suffocate. Then everyone returns to nice, clean cell phone communications and safe, non-nuclear power. Back to honest labor and political sanity.

Nick keyed his Cabinet Officer's Notebook and checked the status of General Holmes's anti-satellite operations. From a peak of thirty-two when Makers were announced, the joint efforts of three nations had whittled the Cambiar fleet down to nineteen. As he watched, the screen updated itself to eighteen, and he toasted the ceiling.

"Thank you, Clint." He drained his glass and sat down to contemplate the beautiful, backlit photograph of his wife.

Yvonne didn't like Philip Machen—especially his arrogance—and she didn't care for Freemakers, who were the usual left-wing scum, but she refused to believe Powerpods could explode. Hadn't the one in their basement worked for years? Last spring when that tree crushed Mr. Toomey's Pod, it didn't blow up the neighborhood. Pods died all the time, she said, without hurting anyone. Coalinga could not have been a Powerpod.

Nick broke his own judicious rule and poured a second whiskey.

"No," Yvonne had said, "Coalinga could only be the work of terrorists, Islamist thugs or their ilk, still intent on destroying America." She wanted Nick to catch them and punish them. Bring them to justice. Ambitious though he was, Philip Machen would never shoot off his own foot with exploding technology. Her eyes had shone brightly when she said this, as they now did from the silver frame on his desk.

He could save the whole country yet lose the only voter who mattered to him. Coalinga might not be enough. It might succeed in all the obvious ways, but he could still lose Yvonne and the other Yvonnes to simple, insidious doubt. To Philip goddamn Machen, traitorous Sower of Doubts.

We must link that bastard to another blast, so there will be no doubt. There must be a way to do that. But first we need to find the sonofabitch.

There was no other choice. He picked up his encrypted STU-5 and punched a number he was loathe to call, the Oakland office of the FBI. He would have to swallow his pride, reverse his earlier decision, and hope a useful idiot would once more prove himself useful.

FORTY-ONE

Western Nevada. Tuesday, June 9
Day Fifty-two

GODDAMN BRAYLEY.

Parker seldom thought of anyone that way, not even his errant boss, Derek Majers. He squinted through the scratched, dollhouse window as it channeled daylight onto his arm. The steady rush from the 737's engines relaxed to a sigh as the jetliner descended into California. There were no attendants, no other passengers, just him and his prisoner, installed on first class thrones. Across the aisle, Karen Lavery lay restless and pale in her recliner. Her auburn locks spilled lustrous and incongruous across her faded orange prison coveralls.

Goddamn Brayley.

Overnight, the AG's office had summoned him to an audience with Brayley, who apparently had changed his mind about Philip Machen. Who abruptly thought Parker's plan to ensnare the Great Fugitive would work, after all. Who wouldn't stop talking about it. Who asked no questions but pronounced a litany of orders. Pick her up. Take her home. Collect the daughter. Make them call Machen. Get him to come for them. Tell us where and when, but do not approach him. Do not pass Go. Do not collect $200. Even sober, the AG was a caricature of himself.

Parker, on the other hand, had liberated four Scotch miniatures from a convenient locker up forward. Poor substitutes for a creamy Guinness, especially without ice, but subtlety was not on the bill of fare today. The choice before him was a hard-liquor decision if ever there was one. So he ripped off the caps, slugged the firewater, and shook himself like a wet dog.

Goddamn Brayley, ensconced in his stodgy old office, redolent of power, reeking with anxiety. Parker could smell the man's fear, sour as a flophouse mattress. But if Coalinga is Machen's Waterloo, what more does Brayley want?

Not Machen in court, defending himself before citizens who could see and hear and judge for themselves. This lawless fugitive, this social nightmare who should answer for what he's done. Was there ever a crime so vast as destroying whole nations? Brayley must think Machen's gifts-to-the-world exceed mere criminality, that his offenses transcend a court's power to contain them or to mitigate them. Despite Coalinga, Nick Brayley was flat-out afraid. He'd even said as much.

"He's not just some criminal, Parker. He's destroying Western civilization. He's out there destroying us, and we have to stop him. So find him, then call me."

Maybe.

Ms. Lavery wasn't the only one on the plane who chafed at doing another's bidding. This was no longer about his job or reputation. His career, it seemed, was whatever Brayley demanded. His fate, as much as Ms. Lavery's, had been usurped. Now he could do anything—anything at all—and the result would be channeled, interpreted, and defined by a sixty-year-old lard-ass, desperately trying to steer Western Civilization from the helm of a quarter-ton of polished walnut.

Parker could do the company thing, what Brayley expected, or he could do what he would have done in any case. By ordaining a particular outcome, Brayley had unwittingly given him license. And clarity. No more distractions. Whatever hopes or threats were converging on him and his prisoner, Special Agent Leslie D. Parker was abundantly free to follow his conscience.

"Wake up." He touched her arm. "We're almost there."

Ms. Lavery blinked and swept a lock of hair from her eyes. She scowled and looked away. The cabin shuddered, prompting an exchange of glances. Parker leaned across her to check their progress beyond the window. From a base of smooth, yellow slopes grew a prominence, its ridges coursing off sharply to the north and the west, hollowing toward the south. In that valley sprawled Livermore, California, which gave him the name of the peak, Mt. Diablo, the Devil's Mountain.

They were five minutes from Oakland, which reminded him. He sat back and keyed his Cambiar. He'd tried to call her over Colorado but got a busy circuit announcement, which had never happened before. He tried again now.

"Mrs. Petzold? It's Les Parker."

"Oh, thank God, Leslie. Are you home?"

"I'll be there shortly. What's going on?"

"Well, it's bedlam." Her voice quavered. "Tory vigilantes killed six people on the first floor this morning. Shot them dead. Security and a few residents drove them off, but the bodies are still lying there, and the police haven't come. I think they've been told to let the vigilantes do whatever they like. Some of our residents have skedaddled. The ones who stayed are copying guns and setting up barricades. They've abandoned the first floor because of all the windows, but I think that's a mistake. Vigilantes could block our exits and lay siege until we surrender. Please help us, Leslie."

"Are they still shooting?"

Across the aisle, Ms. Lavery turned, alert and attentive.

"No, not now. But you should take the garage entrance anyway, not the front."

His mind raced. "Lucille, listen to me."

"I don't want to shoot anyone, Leslie." There were tears in her voice.

"Draw your curtains and stay away from the windows. I'll be there in twenty—" The connection dropped.

Ms. Lavery shifted in her seat. "What's happened?"

He pocketed his phone.

"The curse of interesting times," he said.

FORTY-TWO

Victorville, California. Wednesday, June 10
Day Fifty-three

PHILIP ADJUSTED HIS HEADSET and requested clearance for takeoff. A voice as dry as an heirloom bagel granted permission. Philip guided the lumbering MD-11 tri-jet to the center of the runway, steering with his feet, and advanced the throttles. Beneath each wing, a fan-jet the size of a concrete truck spooled to a crescendo, in a roar that used to excite him. As they accelerated down the tarmac, Tanner called out airspeed from the co-pilot's chair. At 200 knots, Philip drew back his control wheel and lifted off from the sleepy desert strip a hundred miles north of Los Angeles.

"Gear up," he ordered.

Tanner flipped the lever, and they each gave Victorville a parting look. Whenever the airlines could no longer fill enough seats, they parked their idle assets in safe, dry deserts to await better times. Rows of plastic-shrouded Boeings and Airbuses crowded the field below, making Victorville a perfect base of operations for a large commercial aircraft flying irregular missions. But since

Coalinga, the intrigue of hiding among these bulging white husks had morphed into restless dreams, pregnant silences, and an unresolved conundrum: *What are we going to do?*

"Gear is up," Tanner confirmed.

For most of a month, they had departed twice weekly in their chubby MD-11, with its faded Federal Express markings, taking off at dawn and returning a day or two later, to land after dark. No one noticed that while every MD-11 has three engines, this one used only the two beneath its wings and never the one in its tail.

Fifty-two-year-old Chuck Zarbaugh, their bald perpetual instructor, sat in the jump seat behind them.

"Flaps," he scolded. Chuck owned this MD-11 and two others he'd converted to wildfire bombers, but only through Philip's generosity.

Philip nudged a lever, noted the indicators, and twisted to check the wing. *How many more flights does the old girl have in her?* They'd been working her pretty hard.

"Flaps are up," he confirmed.

He banked eastward and continued climbing into a wispy sunrise. Both he and Tanner squinted ahead, though they expected no traffic. In minutes, they crossed the southern tip of Nevada and passed over Arizona, headed for an even more sparsely populated region, near New Mexico, where few groundlings would notice thunder booms or bright lights, high in the summer sky.

At thirty thousand feet, Philip throttled back and leveled off. Behind him, Chuck retrieved a lap panel and passed it forward. Philip slid the panel into clips on his armrests and switched on the screen that displayed instruments and controls for their third engine. Ten minutes later, each man donned thick gloves, which they sealed to their sleeves, then bulky white helmets, which they snugged to the neck rings of their government-surplus space suits. Once everyone was sealed and pressurized, Chuck switched on auxiliary heaters to protect vital systems from the deeper cold to come.

Philip selected the prestart program on his panel and patted Tanner's arm. "Go," he said.

Tanner drew back the throttles then pushed the nose down into a dive. Chuck and Philip braced while Tanner hauled the nose up sharply. The MD-11 shuddered in self-generated turbulence, struggling toward the vertical. Just as stall warnings squawked and a recorded female voice warned, "Attitude. Drop your nose," Philip double-stroked the red icon on his screen.

From the third engine nacelle at the base of the tail, a thin beam of intense, blue-white light winked into existence with a gunshot *bang*. Its brilliant rapier extended straight aft for three miles. Only at its furthest extent did the beam widen into a corkscrew of billowing steam.

In the right seat, Tanner worked swiftly to shut off fuel to the fan-jets, then to silence a cacophony of engine alarms. Philip touched a control icon, moved it slightly, and the plane tilted southeast.

The MD-11 rode its column of plasma and steam, accelerating steadily, less a thrill ride than a steady shove in the back. It did not exceed the speed of sound until they passed 150,000 feet, where the air was too thin to rip off the wings. Because Philip's matter-energy converter—a modified Powerpod—produced a steady, hypersonic thrust, their ascension into orbit felt slow, downright casual. More important than a smooth ride, this modest push kept stresses on the MD-11's aging airframe within design limits. Even so, thermal contraction in the vacuum of space made her hull creak and groan like an old wooden schooner.

Twenty minutes later, Gloria, their makeshift space plane named for Chuck's wife, pitched forward, and Earth's brightness came into view over the nose. Their south-easterly trajectory was hurtling them past Mexico, over the Caribbean, away from North American radars. Philip switched his ground-oriented navigation screen to a new display showing position, speed, acceleration, and trajectory. He opened an orbital Nav window to guide them to their first rendezvous. Or rather, to the position a satellite should have occupied in that orbit. Cambiar 21 had disappeared yesterday, having met the same fate as the other Cambiar birds the authorities were destroying.

Philip stirred a tiny joystick with his gloved hand, manually testing thrusters for pitch, yaw, and roll. Gloria wobbled as the autopilot corrected for the test. On his screen, he called up an estimated time of intersection when Gloria would match the speed and trajectory of the ghost satellite. His display indicated this would occur over the Indian Ocean, on the night-side of Earth, in thirty-eight minutes. Now in microgravity, the men loosened their seat belts and harnesses.

Chuck unbuckled completely. "Cabin pressure is steady," he said. "Taking off my beanie." The rule was, one of them must remain fully suited at all times, in case of sudden depressurization. They had to caulk new leaks almost every flight. Chuck tethered his helmet to his seat.

"After this is all over," he said, "I'd sure like to bring the real Gloria out here, just to float around and see this." He craned to the window over Tanner's shoulder. "You bring your woman out here, and she'll fall in love with you all over again."

Philip's woman was down there and captive. He unclipped the lap board and passed it to his right. "Tanner has the aircraft," he said. Then he removed his helmet.

Gloria's cargo hold was stuffed with six replacement satellites, so this would be a long trip to release each of them into separate orbits. Gloria's flights were not keeping up with the losses.

As he drifted aft, Philip's Cambiar vibrated.

"Tiffany," he said. "What's up?" He put her on speaker.

"Philip, we need you."

He grabbed a hand-hold.

"Mom called. She's out of jail and she wants to meet with you right away."

"I'd like that."

"It's a trap. She's helping the FBI."

Philip glanced at Tanner. "Tiff, are you okay?"

She groaned. "Philip, what are we going to do?"

"About your mom?"

"No, dammit, about Coalinga, the jihad against Powerpods."

"You're upset," he said.

"Because nobody is stopping them. We need you to lead us. To make people understand."

"As long as enough Makers remain free, we can prevail."

"Philip, they're killing us! We are dying for you. Don't you get it? The country has turned against us. Vigilantes are going door-to-door, destroying Pods and Makers. People are ripping out their Pods, not converting them. Gangs and looters are running amok, and Congress is calling for martial law. If you don't do something real soon, it's going to be the end of everything. If you don't help us, I hope they hang you, because you'll deserve it."

Whoa. Fifty hornets in the face.

"Where are you?" she pleaded.

"I'm keeping Cambiars and the internet free and available so people can help each other. So they can see me on the video clips we've been posting."

"Words won't stop bullets," she said. "We need soldiers."

Philip shook his head. "Listen, Tiff. They can't win. Makers will subvert them too. Makers will subvert everyone. We are all Freemakers now. Some of us just don't know it yet."

"Have faith that heaven will provide?" She leaned on the sarcasm.

"No," he said. "Don't join the insanity. Don't fight. Don't kill. Let the Tories think they're winning. Keep a Maker or two in a safe place. Share them with your friends. Do you understand? Don't wait for me. Don't wait for heaven. The universe does not care. Only we care. Be your own messiah."

He cringed. She didn't deserve that.

"Sorry," he said. "I thought they'd come after me, arrest a few people. I didn't expect them to go berserk."

"You're just like Mom," she said. "Fussing over details while the Tories steamroll us." A moment dangled between them. "When will I see you?"

Philip held the Cambiar before his face, activated its camera, and winked. From its speaker came the fizz of a broken connection. Because the satellite which should be forwarding its signal was gone.

Have I lost Tiffany as well? After Sao Paulo, Art Buddha reported dozens of new enclaves had formed, plus thousands of individual households had joined the Three Cone Club. Until, that is, Art's site was hacked, and Coalinga blew out all the candles. For the first time, their Ryles numbers were declining. *What could anyone do against a tsunami of fear? Stop pretending Cambiars are sufficient to keep Makers and their owners free? Make a stand someplace, beat my chest and dare the haters?*

"Back to work," he said. He tucked the phone away and reached for his helmet. "I'll do the first launch."

Tanner floated near and made eye contact. Because he had built the cargo handlers and could fix any problems, he had always released the first birds.

"You really believe what you told her?"

"We need to do this," Philip said. "I need to do this." He put on his helmet and sealed it. "Whether she believes me or not."

Tanner stuffed his apprehensions into his voice. "Be careful out there," he said.

Philip entered the airlock and checked his suit. He shut the door and tested his radio.

"Ready," he said, and he cycled the chamber. By handholds, he drew himself to the dim bulk of the first satellite, then by straps and frames he reached the cargo door and its latching lever. He loved this stuff, floating around, doing astronaut things.

He tethered himself to a pad eye and recited each step as he performed it: open the cargo bay door (Hal); extend the release rails; remove four restraining pins; then launch the bird by shoving its two-thousand pounds along the rails until it floated free. In the minute it took to drift clear of Gloria's left wingtip, its majestic progression no longer inspired him. It was just slow.

"While you're at it," Tanner said, "how about sweeping the porch?"

Philip braced in the open door, contemplating their new Cambiar 21. Its dark limbs unfolded to receive a vast solitude. Twenty-one was a replacement bird, not a supplement or a counter-punch. But six satellites, twenty satellites, a thousand wouldn't save the advent if people didn't share more Makers. Tiffany was right. He was hiding in his work again, hoping the world would come to its senses.

His father once said that any messiah who actually arrives is no good to anybody. A hope fulfilled is already half a disappointment. So what could a fake messiah expect ? Top billing for a few media cycles? One media cycle?

A brilliant light shot across Gloria, reflecting off Twenty-one and streaking into the distance.

"The hell was that?" he said. "An attention-getter?"

"Close everything up," Tanner replied. "And get in here, quick."

Philip secured the cargo bay door and reentered the airlock. *A newbie messiah could use some fireworks.*

Chuck joined them on the radio. "Fellas, I think we have company."

FORTY-THREE

IN THE MINUTES IT TOOK Philip to return through the airlock, Tanner maneuvered Gloria away from Cambiar 21 and slewed her to face the direction from which the missile had come. When Philip emerged from the lock, Chuck was hunched in the left chair, reaching for something under the panel, his helmeted head thumping against a windshield coaming.

Philip removed his own helmet. "What do we have?"

"We have weather radar," Chuck groused, "not the North American Aerospace Defense Command." He jabbed at the controls with gloved hands. "Trying to tune this thing."

"Twenty-one is clear and active," Tanner announced. He held the lap panel loosely and clicked through several displays. "Checking the other birds."

Philip floated past Tanner's shoulder, to the copilot's chair, and switched off the interior lights. He pointed. "One o'clock, drifting right, ten degrees up."

"Got it," Chuck said.

"Cambiar 14 passed while you were on the porch," Tanner said. "It's still responding, but our radar is full of clutter—could be countermeasures."

Philip glanced to Chuck. "What do you think, Pops?"

"I think somebody doesn't like us."

Philip activated a sensor they seldom used. "There's a hotspot on infrared," he said. "Weak definition, but we are closing with it. Match us up, Tanner. Use Fourteen's orbit for a baseline."

Tanner fed a two-kilometer offset into the orbit-matching software, which would have to be corrected, and the beam engine began firing in a feathery hum. He clutched Philip's backrest against the acceleration.

Philip collected a pair of binoculars. "Closing," he said, "dead ahead."

Seconds later, the propulsion computer switched the beam engine from aft projection to forward projection, and Gloria's acceleration reversed. Her attitude thrusters fired corrective bursts, and a loose mission binder sailed with Philip's helmet into the windshield. When the deceleration beam winked out, Philip spied a white-tailed delta-wing, similar to the first space shuttles, only smaller.

"Give me the controls," he said.

Tanner exchanged his board for Philip's binoculars.

"Holy cow," Tanner said as he peered. "It's one of those mini-shuttles the Pentagon says they don't have."

Philip guided them closer, and the damage became apparent. Multicolored scorch marks radiated from an external rail aft of the cockpit. The pilot's canopy was crazed and deformed, but a white helmet remained visible inside.

"Weapons malfunction," Tanner guessed. "Probably hung on the rail before it broke free."

"Well, he missed Cambiar 14," Philip said, "if that was his target."

"He was shooting at us," Chuck said.

Tanner squinted through the binoculars. "He's not moving, Boss. Could be dead."

Philip nodded. *Dead would be all right. This guy for Uncle Orin.*

"Okay," he said. "Only one way to find out. Chuck, you stay here. Tanner and I will investigate." *And maybe leave him for the space buzzards.*

He sealed his helmet and joined Tanner in the airlock, where they finished suiting-up and cycled out. In the bay, they tethered themselves to Gloria's frame and reopened the cargo door. Philip retrieved a length of polypropylene rope from a gear locker and handed it to Tanner. Without jetpacks, they could reach the damaged shuttle only by ballistic leaps, good old-fashioned long-jumps.

"I'll go get him," Philip said. "You haul us back." *Dead or alive.*

Tanner unclipped his tether and secured the rope to Philip's belt. He tied the other end to a pad eye on the cargo deck.

Philip braced himself in the doorway and crouched. "Stand by," he said. He pushed steadily against his grip on the door. "Release on one."

He counted down from three, then leaped. He flew with arms extended, a slow-motion Superman, across the gap. He sailed over the cracked canopy, inches from the lone pilot, who remained slumped and unmoving. The overshoot continued in silence until the rope jerked him to a halt. While Tanner retrieved him, he scanned the shuttle for hand-holds. Whatever made those scorch marks had also burned a man-sized hole in the fuselage. If the pilot wasn't dead, his ride certainly was.

On the second try, Philip snared the exposed weapons launch rail, and his momentum swung him into the canopy with surprising force. He held fast through the impact and located an emergency release, which he levered. The canopy flung itself away and knocked him adrift again. On his third attempt, he got a leg into the open cockpit and wedged his boot. The stranger's helmet and shoulders were charred but intact. Grasping the man's arm produced no response, so Philip cut his restraints and pried him free. He wrapped his arms around the pilot and wriggled him clear of the cockpit. Like that time his sister Sandra caught her ankle in a drainage grate, he just did it. Not a matter of concern, really. When people needed help, you helped, that's all.

"Okay," he said, "haul away."

Two minutes later, Chuck helped Philip extract their unconscious guest from Gloria's airlock. When they removed his helmet, a stench of charred flesh huffed into their faces. Fabric and metal had fused to the man's neck, just above the name tag, *Captain J. Melzer, USAF*. Viscous blobs drifted outward from the wound, staining Chuck's gloves with red splotches.

"Jesus," he said. "The guys drowned in his own blood."

Philip braced himself, and with a booted foot compressed Melzer's chest against the deck. This produced a spray of pink droplets, along with a sputter and a gasp. The captain stirred and gurgled. Philip compressed the chest again. Melzer heaved one great breath and continued breathing.

Philip waved a path through the expanding pink cloud and wedged the captain's helmet under the jump seat. He yanked their medical pouch from its locker. While Chuck pressed thick dressings to Melzer's neck, Philip inserted a curved plastic airway to keep the captain's tongue out of his throat.

Tanner emerged from the airlock and removed his helmet. "What a mess."

"Oxygen," Philip said.

Tanner propelled himself to retrieve the tank and mask. Chuck cradled Captain Melzer's head and neck while Tanner set the regulator and fitted the mask. Still unconscious, their patient groaned.

"That's better," Philip said, half-pleased and half-annoyed.

They wrapped him in an electric blanket and strapped him into the jump seat, careful to avoid the ghastly fusion on his neck.

Tanner began snatch-blotting airborne debris with soft, white dressings. Chuck joined him.

"Lucky duck," Chuck said as he hovered over the patient and plucked away.

Philip floated to a corner where he flexed his right hand, observed its patterns of flesh and sinew, born of protons and guilt. Saving Melzer would require a full stop landing at a major airport. Even if they got airborne again, the authorities would track them, maybe cancel their tickets in midair. At best they might be forced down somewhere, arrested and locked up, unable to replace satellites or to help anyone.

"He's dying, you know." Tanner stuffed bloody bandages into the medical pouch and took up a fresh set. "He's gonna croak before we get him downstairs."

Philip nodded.

"If we take him to a hospital," Tanner said, "the boogeyman will get us. We could be wasting ourselves on a corpse."

Philip drew a breath and let it go. "This isn't war, Tanner, even if Captain Melzer thinks it is." *If war has not already been declared.*

Tanner drilled him. "What about all those folks counting on us?"

Philip envisioned their faces: Karen and Tiff; Otavio and Dr. de Bier; Admin Joe and the priest; the beauty shop ladies; nurses at the clinic. Thousands more in Maker enclaves around the world.

"What about them, Tanner? You know the deal."

Tanner bunched his eyebrows. "Yeah, but—"

"Letting someone die because we don't like him—that's murder." He reminded himself as much as his partners. *Though Melzer's no better than the bastard who killed my family.*

"Yeah, but—"

"We are not giving up," Philip reasoned. "We can do this."

"But he's doomed, Boss, killed by his own ordinance. If we put him back in the saddle over there, nobody needs to know we ever found him. His orbit will decay, and he'll burn up when Mother

Gravity collects him."

But we would know. And ground radars might detect our presence.

Chuck tried to split the difference. "You don't suppose we could lay him down beside a runway someplace, and then skedaddle?" He looked at Philip. "Gloria can out-climb anything but a missile. Outrun those, too, if she gets a head start."

"Maybe they'll get us," Philip said, "but I'm not going to abandon this guy while he's still breathing. Unless we hand him over as gently as possible to qualified people, Captain Melzer is going to die." *And if I don't really believe that, I should.*

Tanner shook his head, but the discussion was over.

"Ain't that a bitch," Chuck said. "If that's what you want, Philip, I'll do 'er. But ain't that a bitch."

"Best burn center I know is in Santa Clara, near the university." Philip said it quickly before he could change his mind. He reached for his lap panel, began tapping and clicking. "Chuck, you've flown into San Jose Mineta before. You do the landing. Soon as Tanner puts us on the down escalator, would you please call up the approach plates? Any better ideas, I need to hear 'em now."

Tanner made a show of securing the medical pouch, then wormed his way into the co-pilot's chair and strapped in.

"Hold Mach point seven down to flight level 60," Philip said, "then light the windmills. Fly the profile to the waypoint, and head for San Francisco. They'll think we're inbound from Hawaii."

Tanner nodded. "Okay, but—"

"Well, it had to be something, didn't it?" Philip allowed. "We always said it was going to be something. Turns out, this guy was killing our birds. Hunting us, too, maybe. But who would we be if we didn't help him?"

Tanner turned to the instrument panel and nudged his joystick. He pitched Gloria end-for-end and steadied her. Behind him, Philip transferred his calculations to Tanner's screen.

"Counting down for de-orbit burn," Tanner called. "Three, two, one."

The mass-energy engine fired and built up thrust as if they were not decelerating from 18,000 miles per hour but starting from zero.

On the hard deck behind the pilots, Philip jammed himself at Melzer's feet, leaned against a locker that held their parachutes, and considered the illusions he'd been entertaining lately. Control and superiority. Things to do when nobody's watching. His stomach churned, not from the effluvium alighting on his forehead, but from the welter of bad endings glaring at him from Gloria's nooks and crannies. Saving Melzer could destroy it all. Ten years of struggle; everything they'd worked for; his father's legacy; humanity's moral tipping point. The Maker advent might die and extinguish a billion shining possibilities.

For which he would have to destroy himself. That was the deal: a new world for everybody, or no more sunrises for Watashi-san. From the beginning, that was the bargain he'd made with himself, and he still liked it, still wanted it, that perfect self-administered clarity. The truth at any price.

So, don't fail, Dumbass. Make a stand. He texted Art Buddha and asked him to announce a Freemaker rally in the East Bay.

"Chuck," he called, "you're going to have to land this thing by yourself. Give our regards to the folks in San Jose. Tanner, where did we stash your cutting torch?"

FORTY-FOUR

THAT SAME AFTERNOON, Special Agent Parker wasn't sure what his plan should be, but until he brought Tiffany Lavery and her mother together, he would not ask Ms. Lavery to contact Philip Machen. He would figure out what to do once they got to the Cardoza ranch. Which was taking decades.

They had left San Leandro and Castro Valley behind and were climbing the eastbound I-580 toward Dublin when all five lanes ground to a halt. Parker plonked a flashing red beacon atop his Ford and charged along the shoulder to exit at Palomares Road. After a few minutes, he switched off the flasher. Both lanes of Palomares were jammed, as were the shoulders, and progress came in lurches.

Three cows stared through a barbed-wire fence, and the word *mosey* floated through his head. He drummed his fingers, inspected the dusty oaks and stiff yellow grass, switched on the air conditioner. When he looked again, the cows had lost interest.

Beside him, Ms. Lavery scrolled her Cambiar to a local news

site. Somebody was shooting into the traffic near the 580/680 Interchange, between Dublin and Pleasanton, quickly jamming those freeways, as well as every arterial within ten miles. Police and the Highway Patrol were responding, but the gunfire continued.

Palomares Road finally dumped them into Niles Canyon, and they turned east. A hundred yards later, a thundering dark shadow passed low overhead, raised swirls of dust, and rattled their bones. A military helicopter with two main rotors and a huge, half-open loading ramp at the rear. Parker glanced at Ms. Lavery, who checked the news again.

Her screen showed National Guard bulldozers shoving civilian vehicles from the outer lane of Freeway 680. They were clearing a path for a convoy headed north from San Jose. By one o'clock, Parker was easing his Ford into that same lane, and three more helicopters had zoomed by. Now the news showed the Guard convoy rolling through the 580/680 Interchange and continuing, without engaging any snipers. Ms. Lavery put down her phone and looked away.

Except for the incessant glare and rising heat, nothing about this day was making sense. He should have called the office to report in but resisting that impulse had become a matter of pride. Both Derek and Nedra knew he was home from Washington, but they hadn't seen fit to contact him since the raid.

Another hour crawled away. Finally, he edged through Pleasanton and out onto Vineyard Road, achieving a giddy 35 miles per hour. He braked hard, almost overshooting the ranch, and swerved onto its gravel driveway. As they neared the charred remnants of a barn, a gunman in full battle regalia emerged from a thicket of pampas grass and leveled an assault rifle at them. Parker slewed to a stop, then released the breath he had impounded. The gunman wore an FBI raid bib. Parker kept his hands in view and made Ms. Lavery place hers on the dashboard as well.

The sentry approached, and Parker lowered his window. A wave of heat pushed into the car.

"Top of the mornin', McGee."

The sentry squinted. "You're not supposed to be here, asshole."

"It's pronounced ah-sole-ee," Parker corrected. "So what's going on?" Visions of Tiffany Lavery, injured or worse, ticked through his mind.

McGee safed his weapon, keyed his radio, and reported. "I have Les Parker down here at the gate, along with one female prisoner. Where do you want 'em?"

While they waited for a reply, Ms. Lavery squirmed across Parker's legs to shout through the open window.

"Is my daughter here?"

Parker pushed her back. "Sit down."

She punched his shoulder, swatted his hands. "Tiffany Lavery," she shouted to Agent McGee. "Is she here?"

Parker shoved her, grabbed her arms.

"Maybe you want the handcuffs."

McGee bent and peered at their *tête-à-tête*. "That's her, huh?"

His radio dished a familiar female voice. "Send them to the house."

Nedra. Why didn't she warn me? Parker looked at McGee. "What's going on?"

McGee ignored him, acknowledged his orders, stepped back, and waved them through.

"Watch out for bodies," he said.

He wasn't kidding. Two inert figures—one curled fetal, the other belly-flopped—had fallen near the smoldering barn. Another lay supine but twisted on the walkway to the house. In the yard, a body lay under a trellis, and another hugged a sycamore. No vehicles remained, but the ranch house was peppered with holes. Every window was shattered, and the entry was a Roman arch of splinters coated in powdery gypsum.

"Tiffany?" Ms. Lavery seized Parker's arm as they left the car. "Tiffany?" Her voice rose toward panic.

Nedra met them at the bombed-out entry, nervous and tentative, wearing tactical coveralls and her gunslinger's holster. She had stuffed her flaming orange hair tightly into an FBI ball cap. She nodded at Parker's drawn pistol.

"All clear," she said, and to Ms. Lavery, "Your daughter's not here, ma'am."

An odor of scorched hair lingered, but no smoke or flames appeared, just a wash of heat wafting in from the fields.

Parker holstered his weapon and followed Nedra inside. Wary of her tension, of her suspicion, and of what her silence might conceal, he said nothing. The dread ticking down his spine must be dancing along hers as well.

"I need your car," she said, as they entered a dim, debris-strewn kitchen.

A bald white man was duct-taped to a chair, his face and head a mass of bruises and open gashes. One eye had swollen shut, while the other blinked desperately at Parker. When Ms. Lavery joined them, the rancher managed a broken-tooth smile.

"Sorry I'm not so pretty, ma'am." He snorted to clear his nose. "Don't worry, though. We gave them way more than they gave us." He nodded in Nedra's direction. "Her and her buddies invited the Tories to leave, so I guess I owe my life to the FBI, but I'll be thanking them when they let me go."

Ms. Lavery swallowed. "Release him," she said.

"No, ma'am. Mr. Cardoza's going to jail, as soon as I borrow Agent Parker's car." Nedra apprised Parker, "Felony possession of automatic weapons, felony construction of a man trap, felony possession of counterfeiting tools, and the county sheriff will probably want to discuss those bodies in the yard because we didn't shoot 'em."

"Don't tread on me," Cardoza frothed.

Parker confronted him. "Where's Tiffany Lavery?"

Cardoza worked a lump out of his cheek and spat it aside. "Called herself Gina Borden. We knew who she was, though. Marie and me took her in so she wouldn't get hurt." He twisted to Ms. Lavery. "She got the call this morning, ma'am, and wanted to go right away. But I made her wait. Sent her up with my Marie, with some food and stuff, before the Tories came shooting. Your daughter's a fine, hard-working gal, ma'am."

Surprise raced relief through Ms. Lavery. "Where?"

Cardoza jolted, incredulous.

Parker bent closer."Where'd they go, Mr. Cardoza?"

His good eye shifted, perverse and amused.

Ms. Lavery lunged at the prisoner, but Nedra restrained her. Noticing the prison coveralls and lack of handcuffs, Nedra frowned. But Parker was kneeling before the rancher.

"She's just a kid, Mr. Cardoza." Parker touched his arm. "She has her whole life ahead of her. Philip Machen is the single most-hunted man on the planet. The vigilantes know Tiffany is close with him. They will hunt her like a rabid dog. We can protect her and your wife, but only if we reach them before the vigilantes do." He produced a switch knife and slit the tape binding Cardoza's arms. "Help us protect them before it's too late."

"Like you're protecting Ms. Lavery, here?" Cardoza's eye flickered, no longer amused. He huffed more spittle and swallowed it, then leaned toward Ms. Lavery. "Jail or death? Prisoner or victim? Those ain't choices, ma'am. Those are sentences."

Karen Lavery dodged Nedra, seized the man's chair, and toppled him.

"I want her back, damn you! All this blood—don't you see? There's no freedom here, no safety. I want my daughter alive."

Nedra dragged her back. Parker helped Cardoza from the floor. Behind them, the window curtains riffled on a breeze that flipped bits of glass into the steel sink. Cardoza sat again and rocked back and forth, gathering himself.

"Get me to my truck," he said. "I'll take you where your FBI buddies can't go, Ms. Lavery. They're on Mt. Diablo, helping Philip Machen."

From one blank face to another he glared in disgust. "Why do you suppose this valley is crawling with troops and helicopters? They're not here to stop the Tories, or to protect us poor, dumb taxpayers. They've come to get *him*."

This and Nedra's stare struck Parker like a blast. The heat, the dust, the stench of battle hit him full force, just as a window-rattling commotion passed over the house.

Nedra swept the curtains clear in time for everyone to glimpse a helicopter landing near the charcoal barn. The chopper was an older model, silvery blue, with civilian markings.

Parker squinted at Nedra. "You going to the mountain?"

She shook her head. "Oakland PD wants my team for a hostage situation at City Hall. Believe it or not, we've been ordered to stay away from the mountain. It's all military over there. You and I are taking this guy to a hospital."

After Nedra's SWAT team departed in the helicopter, Parker drove her and her prisoner to Stanford/ValleyCare Hospital in Pleasanton. Nedra glared, steamed to the color of her hair, when he left her there without a car. But he was pissed too. She had shut him out and gone along with Derek Majers' battering-ram tactics. What did she think she was doing? What did she think *he* was doing?

No one seemed in control of anything today. Everyone seemed scattered and disorganized, including himself. Driving north to Mt. Diablo, however, he had larger concerns—to find Philip Machen and protect Tiffany Lavery.

He kept Ms. Lavery occupied with navigation while he drove. Though Mt. Diablo State Park covered thirty square miles, only two narrow roads led into it. Without the GPS in her Cambiar, they would never have found the south entrance nestled in the fringes of rural Danville.

Mature cottonwoods cast wavering shadows over the Athenian School where a California National Guard roadblock stopped them. A grim private, manning the turret of his Humvee, swiveled a machine gun their way. To the right, in a parched soccer field, more troops loitered among their bulky, sand-colored vehicles.

Parker displayed his badge and ID for the young sergeant who approached.

"Sorry, sir, this road is closed. No exceptions."

"Sergeant, your boss is the state governor. Mine is the president of the United States. I am here on federal business involving the national security. I would appreciate your cooperation."

"I believe you, sir, and I'm sorry, but President Washburn nationalized us at fourteen hundred hours today to enforce martial law. My orders are to have that gentleman over there blow your heads off if you do not immediately depart this area. Do you understand me, sir?"

"Let me speak to your officer in charge."

The sergeant said something into his radio and backed away.

Behind him, the machine gun pivoted and loosed five rounds into a weedy patch. Everyone winced, including the sergeant, who trotted for cover. Up the road, a dozen troops aimed their weapons as the machine gun swiveled back toward Parker.

He dipped his head, displayed all ten fingers on the steering wheel.

"Don't say anything. Don't do anything," he told Ms. Lavery. He put the shifter in reverse and turned the Ford around.

"But we have to get her out of there," she said.

FORTY-FIVE

EVERETT AND MARCY SPENT the morning bailing General Johnson out of Alameda County jail in Dublin. After lunch they were circling San Leandro at 500 feet, recording a street skirmish, when Philip Machen surprised Marcy with an angry Cambiar call. Coalinga was not a faulty Powerpod, he said. It was government terrorism. But then he mentioned an injured astronaut was landing right now at San Jose Mineta, which didn't make sense. Marcy told him they couldn't get there in time to scoop the story, so she would alert some media friends.

"He sounds terrible," she said after hanging up. "Drunk or something." She called a friend about the astronaut, then checked her text messages.

"Head for Pleasanton, Everett. Snipers are blocking the 580/680 Interchange. Governor Alvarez is sending troops."

Everett turned eastward and climbed into a new Temporary Flight Restriction zone that covered most of the East Bay. But so what? His licenses no longer mattered. Just as fuel and spare parts no longer worried him, rules and red tape had lost their urgency. Along with narrow job descriptions, not enough money, and pleasing the Friggin' Man. Flying Marcy around to report stuff made way more sense than any of that.

Up front, she was checking her messages. "Parachutes," she said.

"Where?"

"Somebody landed on Mt. Diablo. We'll check it out after the freeway."

As the 580/680 Interchange hove into view, Marcy raised her camera and began narrating. After one sweep she said, "I don't get it. Nobody's clearing the snipers."

Everett continued east, where they discovered troops, helicopters, and armored vehicles assembled at Camp Parks, the defunct training base east of Dublin.

"What are they waiting for?" she said. "What about the freeways?"

She aimed her camera at Mt. Diablo, and Everett banked left, away from the troops and toward the mountain. Buzzards, dozens of them, circled its summit.

"Something's very dead over there," he said.

"Look out!" Marcy ducked.

Three black shapes flashed by in a perfect chevron formation. Drones, UAVs, Unmanned Aerial Vehicles, not buzzards. They returned and zoomed alongside like great, metallic ravens, each one as big as a man. The ravens slowed to match speed, while their unblinking eyes took the measure of GG. Everett jinked upward, and the ravens followed, never breaking formation. In fact, they drew closer. Marcy saw it, too, the decals.

"Cambiar," she said.

Everett banked right, then hard left, trying to shake them. The narrow gap between the ravens and his right wingtip never varied by more than a meter. On impulse, he broke sharply and accelerated for the mountain. Immediately, the lead raven raced ahead and nudged him back to his previous course.

"They're guarding the mountain," he said. "I do believe they will ram us if we try that again."

Having made its point, the enforcer rejoined its formation. Marcy scanned them again, then focused on the mountain.

"More of them over there," she said. "Nothing on the ground, though. Antenna towers, a couple of buildings, an empty parking lot. The rest is rocks and bushes."

The ravens peeled away, back toward the mountain, and out of sight. Marcy scanned the suburban streets ahead.

"There," she said. "Army tank." She adjusted her camera while Everett maneuvered for a better angle. He idled the engine, added flaps, and hung suspended over Bishop Ranch Business Park. Marcy's tank proved to be a Bradley troop carrier, not a battle tank, but its chain gun could obliterate almost anything. Another Bradley rolled east among the Mercedes and BMWs headed into the upscale neighborhoods that spread toward the mountain.

"Whoa," he said. A military helicopter, a serious-looking Apache, caught him by surprise. It popped from defilade behind a slope and came straight toward them. Everett dumped his flaps and shoved full throttle.

"Hang on," he called. Then he yanked the nose up sharply. The big Sikorski tried to match his climb but could not.

"Time for speed," he announced. He leveled off and rolled south, away from San Ramon and the mountain, toward Jesse Cardoza's ranch. His fuel gauge was hovering near empty, and he didn't bother to look back. GG could easily outrun this guy.

"Nobody likes us today," he said.

"The Army's not here to open the freeway," Marcy decided. "They're here for the mountain, for whatever those bird-things are protecting." She twisted in her seat. "Philip Machen, do you think?"

"Yeah," he said. "I saw one of those UAVs before, on the Biography Channel. It looked like a big model airplane 'cause it was hanging on the wall at his ranch."

He spotted another helicopter, distant in the east, heading toward them. He descended and banked away, raising a complaint from the front seat.

"More company," he explained, "and we're out of gas."

The ranch was only four miles farther. At one hundred feet above the ground, they buzzed I-580, several yeehaws queuing in his throat. Whatever violations he might be committing, screaming along on the deck was major fun.

Their newest pursuer was angling to intercept, so he had to choose. If he popped high, they might anticipate his landing spot and squat in Jesse's field, forcing him away. Already the chopper had swung between them and the Livermore airport. Staying low, he could land before it intervened, though recalling Jesse's bailer, he preferred to eyeball the ground first. Once more he idled the engine, set flaps, and was reaching for the landing gear switch when a column of smoke caused him to pull up and overfly the ranch. Upwind of a smoldering barn, three men with rifles were torching Jesse's house.

Everett added power and turned east. There was nothing he could do to stop them. Marcy twisted in her seat, alarmed. But with the military dogging them, there would be no fuel here or in Livermore, not without questions, confiscations, maybe arrests. They'd be grounded, for sure. Their only options lay inland, in the big valley, where they might find a Maker to use. The one-gallon fuel canister he carried for emergencies might be their only hope of staying free. As if it had read his mind, GG's low-fuel alarm squawked and blinked red: twenty pounds left.

Everett established a gradual, fuel-efficient climb, and angled east, crossing the Altamont ridge away from the airports at Livermore and Tracy. At 4,000 feet, GG's fan-jet flamed out and coasted to silence.

"Congratulations," he announced, "you are now soaring in a sailplane: Engineless flight for the discerning traveler. Please remain seated, and thank you for choosing Air Aboud."

He trimmed for maximum lift, gained some altitude as their airspeed dropped to fifty knots. Behind them, the helicopter was closing fast, an older Blackhawk. Ahead, a clear summer sky offered no thermals or updrafts to keep them aloft. Their best hope was to stretch their descent another twenty miles.

GG jostled over the Altamont wind farms and soared across undulating yellow grasses, headed for the orchards and hay fields of the Sacramento River delta. They needed to land away from the cops and the crazies, and especially away from the soldiers.

As they whistled past two perfectly good runways at Byron, Marcy said, "Hello. The engine is dead. Please tell me you're not trying to prove something."

"We are still in their damn Flight Restriction zone," he said. "Even if folks are friendly down there, they won't let us take off again. Not with these guys around."

A dove-gray Sikorski drew alongside, fifty feet away. Through its open side door, someone was video recording them. Marcy responded in kind, aiming her little Sony.

"They have a machine gun," she said.

"Tell me if they shoot."

He switched his Nav display from the sectional chart to a satellite photo, which he enlarged and scanned. What he needed would not be on the charts. It had to be—there, beside that road. "Hold on," he warned, and he careened downward in a spiral. "Do you see it?"

"Everything's spinning," she said, but she sighted down the left wing toward the bare patch of earth he was circling. "That little thing?"

"It's a duster strip," he said. "Aggies use them all the time." He lowered his landing gear and tightened the spiral.

"Getting dizzy," she shrieked.

He straightened, and GG plummeted like a hawk. He popped the flaps at one hundred feet. Buoyancy resumed, and the wheels struck with a bump and a shimmy. They jostled to a stop in a swirl of dust.

"Welcome to nowhere." He opened the canopy, jazzed as a caffeinated canary. "First class passengers may now deplane."

The big Sikorsky orbited twice, an angry hornet deciding whether to sting or to bite. It whined and whopped and stirred billows of dust, then clattered away, westbound.

Marcy got out and began swatting him.

"Thank you for not killing us, oh Brilliant One."

He corralled her hands. The fun was over. "We need to call Jesse."

She met his eyes, now full of trouble. He remained seated and keyed his Cambiar. The number rang six times before switching to voicemail.

"We saw the fire," he said. "Hope you're okay. Call me when you can." He put the phone away and rubbed his face. "Not good."

Marcy squeezed his shoulder.

"Thank you," she said. "For not killing us." She kissed his forehead. "I hope your friends are okay."

None too stable, he stepped from the cockpit and regarded the Cambiar in her hand. "We can't help Jesse, but if you-know-who is over there—" He cocked his head toward the mountain.

She scrolled through her index, pressed the name, and nodded when it connected.

"Hello, sir. Marcy Johnson from WebNews. Thanks for the tip about the astronaut. I thought you might be nearby."

She bit her lip, nodded, and pointed to the mountain. "If you would, sir, we would like—Yes, sir. I understand." She shook her head. "I'd surely like to be there when—" She stiffened, frowned, lowered the phone. "Damn."

"He's surrendering tomorrow," she said. "Thinks the local sheriff will protect him. Doesn't want us there."

Everett snatched her phone, pressed Redial, and waited for it to ring through.

"Ms. Johnson," the familiar voice answered, "It's too dangerous here—"

"The Army will block your sheriff," Everett said. "Guaranteed. They know you're on Mt. Diablo, and they are going to take you when and where they want. Local law won't have a say in it. We have your airplane. Let us help you."

"Mr. Aboud." His voice came sketchy, breathless. "Good to hear from you."

"There won't be a trial," Everett said. "They won't dare let you speak."

"Then don't come. They'll arrest you too. I need you to help the others."

Everett squinted and shook his head.

"We're not Freemakers," he said. "Not Tories either. We're journalists."

"I need you to show everyone how to—"

"Don't make it easy for them. We have a camera and an uplink. We can feed your situation live to the internet, give you millions of eyewitnesses."

Machen fell silent, or else the connection dropped. "Hello?"

"Write this down."

Everett patted his pockets, appealed to Marcy.

Marcy produced a pen, and Everett said, "Go."

"Six a.m. tomorrow. Transponder code four-one-seven-seven. Furies will escort you to the summit parking lot. Tanner will meet you there. Good luck on your landing."

Everett wrote the numbers on his hand as the connection clicked off. He returned Marcy's pen and phone.

"They're called Furies," he said. "His drones." Then he explained the arrangement.

"I thought you didn't want to get involved."

He shrugged, a bit off-balance.

"The guy's not perfect," he said, "but he's not killing people. We need to stop the ones who are."

She considered this for a moment, then said, "Fuel." She nodded to the only civilization in sight, a three-chimney McMansion, secure on its pad of bare earth, fenced by rabbit wire.

"Yeah," he said.

He jerked his seat cushion loose, and from under it, retrieved a squat red canister. Marcy tugged it out of his hands, suddenly skeptical of his jeans and T-shirt.

"You, they won't trust. Better to send a famous internet reporter."

Everett fingered the replacement Seacamp pistol, snug in his hip pocket.

"Okay," he said, "I'll wait until I see smoke."

"Text only," she said, waving her Cambiar, and she strode off with the jug. It was good, tactical thinking, very stealthy. In case the folks who lived there didn't notice a screaming helicopter chase a bright-red sailplane into their yard. But Marcy was right; she could charm anyone.

He watched her go, then checked the area. Twenty miles to the west, Mt. Diablo gathered her skirts into purple shadows. The mountain's dark gravity seemed to draw the sun down and make it squat. In the opposite direction, across the road, stirred a crop he didn't recognize, dry and rangy, waist-high. The rest was orchards, dry grass, and worn-out fences. *Cotton.* He looked back at the droopy stalks, their brains blown out, fluffy and white.

By then Marcy had disappeared around the house. *Pardon me, ma'am, could we copy a little jet fuel?* He scrutinized the corners and the windows, alert for movement. He held his Cambiar at arm's length, as a talisman, willing it to keep her safe. During his fourth check, *Smoke* scrolled mischievously across its screen, followed by *Nobody home.*

He trotted to the fence, wobbled over, and quickly joined Marcy in a shed appended to a three-car garage. She was lifting red canisters from a small Maker, two new jugs at her feet.

"We need bigger bottles," she said.

Everett checked the garage, which was locked and had an alarm box tucked under its gable. He scouted the yard and returned with a wheelbarrow, crusted in concrete residue. Twelve bottles equaled a hundred pounds, more or less, and that was all they could wrangle in a single load. With each trip they recycled the empties into the Maker's top cone, expecting its owners to show up and assail them for cutting the rabbit fence, but no one came. As twilight seeped into a listless night, they finished refueling and drank cool water from a spigot.

Marcy wiped her mouth on her sleeve. She gazed west toward the loom from unseen cities that silhouetted the mountain. Everett looked the other way, at cotton dots drifting on a sea of darkness.

Bobby was right about one thing. Neither of them could stand aside and watch things go to hell without getting involved. But since Coalinga, all of the decent possibilities had come to depend on Makers. No matter what you called yourself, or which side prevailed, everyone's future now depended on keeping a personal Maker. The middle path, if there ever was one, had vanished in a mushroom cloud. So he wasn't making any big, hefty decisions here, just taking one step at a time.

"You sure we can land on that parking lot tomorrow?"

He gathered her into his arms. "Define *land.*"

FORTY-SIX

Summit of Mt. Diablo. Wednesday, June 10
Still Day Fifty-three

NEAR MIDNIGHT, Philip lay on a horse blanket folded between two display cases in the tiny museum of the Mt. Diablo State Park Visitor Center. Which was dark and closed for repairs but had been forced open earlier today by fugitives.

How do you get from an airborne MD-11 to a mountaintop in three minutes? Have Chuck make a pass, low and slow. Then follow Tanner through that screeching cesarean hole he burned in Gloria's belly. Plummet three seconds before pulling the ripcord and steer a whooshing slab of nylon toward the one and only clearing on the summit. But instead of that nice, vacant parking lot, you careen into a gnarly manzanita bush, where a branch spears your kneecap and lodges deep in the ligature of your right knee. *Oh-My-Goodness-Gracious-Sakes-Alive-and-Double-That.*

Morphine does that—converts agonies into grade-school expletives, though not entirely and not quickly enough. Just thinking about his landing triggered another spasm.

First came the impact, then the agony. Tanner stomped

through the manzanita, helped him cut his lines and free his leg. More agony. Once they grunted their way out of the thicket, Philip lay on the ground, gasping. He phoned Marcy Johnson to get some independent videos of Chuck when he landed at San Jose Mineta. So there'd be proof against Tory lies.

The contractor who excavated the visitor center's open utility trench was nowhere to be seen, but he'd left behind a full-size Maker and a backhoe. Tanner hot-wired the tractor and used its bucket to pop the door. Philip hobbled into the snug, pile-of-rocks building, where he and Tanner splinted his stinking-rotten knee. Then he called Art Buddha to alert any Freemakers near the mountain and beg them for help. If he could just lie perfectly still, the pain might release its pit bull clench.

An hour later, Tiffany Lavery and Marie Cardoza showed up in a pickup truck loaded with gear, including one of Philip's Furies, and—thank you, Ms. Cardoza—veterinary morphine. Tiffany's smile and energy gave the drug an extra kick that made him fall in love with Karen's daughter all over again. Likewise with Marie, who was kind and lovely. But the women couldn't haul him down the mountain because, according to Marie's husband, the National Guard had sealed the roads behind them. Jesse wanted to bring horses up the back way, over a steep and rugged trail. "Maybe in the morning," Philip said.

Then Art Buddha called back to say every charter helicopter not already engaged was grounded by the Feds. "Forget that," Philip said, "and forget the rally we talked about. There's no time, even if we muster a thousand Freemakers."

"I'll get you a lawyer," Art said, and hung up.

After that, Philip held down as much floor as he could and sampled another shot of Marie's Vet Juice. Tanner helped the women copy the Fury they'd brought, and together they began launching its duplicates. With his one good hand, Philip could barely drive the laptop to assign their flight patterns.

So now, after dark, Tanner commenced snorkeling on a thin

mattress in the gift shop, while the women took their sleeping bags up to the meridian rotunda, the watchtower that supported an old aircraft beacon, to escape Tanner's rhonchus recital. Outside, the wind rattled doors and windows while inside an invisible anvil pinned Philip's outstretched leg. The only thing higher than the morphine merry-go-round chiming in his head was a full moon gliding silently through the clouds.

That's when a lizard dashed from the gloom. Skitter, skitter.

"I met your cousin," Philip said, "the cranky one in Nevada."

Lizard stopped and stared, grim as a one-eyed judge, while Philip unpacked a few regrets.

"I wish we could have held that rally," he confessed. 'Pushed back on Coalinga."

Lizard yawned without sympathy.

Pretty much what a tin messiah deserved for skirting his own moral code. The truth at any price, etcetera, etcetera. Sucker deceived everyone. Betrayed the woman he wanted. Used that little girl, Mariela, to embellish a happenstance into fake heroism. Pretended to be the spooky dude some folks wanted him to be. Even indulged a bit of magical thinking, hoping things would work out just because they should. Secular sins to match the shortcomings of any religionist.

He wanted people to think he was doing this for them, for humanity. Wanted to believe it himself. But people do noble things for selfish reasons, Old Shoe, to ward off their private nightmares. 'Cause they can't live with themselves if they don't do that one true thing that proclaims who they are.

All he wanted was to be the guy he was before the fire, who never pissed off that capital-B believer and never cost his family their lives. By now, Ordinary Philip would have published his equations and married a good woman, had three kids and mowed the lawn. He'd be complete, not half-finished, wedged between the fossils and the feathers on Mt. Diablo, hoping no one would discover his midnight name. Talks-to-Geckos.

A touch more morphine and he wouldn't be himself anymore. He'd be . . . Self 2.0. Though not so afraid as the Tories were. They *did* get it, didn't they. They could see what was coming as well as anyone, but if they accepted the new ways, they wouldn't be themselves anymore. If in the morning they couldn't find the pilgrim they used to be, they'd go insane.

No wonder Art Buddha squandered so many pages on stories instead of extolling the facts. Nobody cared for facts, not even juicy ones. They cared about their feelings. Of joy or fear or belonging. Art's manifesto made radical sharing feel warm and good, personal and empowering. Sharing is love or words to that effect. Too utopian for cynics, but catnip to seekers and strivers. So the conclusion must be intuitively obvious to the most casual observer.

It's the feelings, Stupid. Freemaker feelings. Real. Hope. Now.

The anvil on Philip's knee shifted, shooting him back to deepest, darkest Michigan, years ago. He couldn't save anyone that night, but Makers might channel his family's secular kindness and decency into Art's radical sharing. No fictions, just feelings and choices about better ways to live.

Maybe some Freemakers were already winning, and nobody could see it. Building enclaves under Tory noses. If Maker goodwill grew stronger than middle-class fears, the advent could succeed without him. His mission would complete itself. He could take his longings down from their shelf and open a box of Karen Lavery. Accept the risk of loving her. Instead of this pointless, enervating pain. It hurt so much to look at his leg, at his hand, and to consider his faults.

So push another dose, Old Shoe.

He implored the one-eyed judge on the wall, why should consciousness fade to dark, instead of to light? Where does it go, the light? Chatter, chatter, monkey mind—until the monkeys drank tequila and finally shut up.

Thank you, Morphine.

FORTY-SEVEN

San Joaquin County, California. Thursday, June 11
Day Fifty-four

THE SUN ROSE LISTLESS and squinty. Everett rolled from beneath
GG's wing and washed the crusts from his eyelids at a hose bib. He
stroked Marcy's cheek to wake her, then gathered the cushions they
slept on. They stretched, peed behind a bush, drank some water,
and slipped into the cockpit. Warm already, the day would soon be
a scorcher.

As they jetted west to Mt. Diablo, its grassy slopes and ridges
resembled a lion skin pulled taut over the rocks. Impenetrable
aprons of scrub oak, greasewood, and manzanita choked the
summit, blocking all but a few twisty footpaths. Three miles out,
five Furies intercepted Glamorous Glennis, cavorting like
porpoises, escorting her; one in front, two on each side. Dozens
more orbited the mountain.

"We'll cross over and land from the southwest," Everett said,
and the summit was quickly upon them.

They shot past a tower studded with antennas and an empty

parking lot of mottled asphalt. The pavement angled from the southwest with a narrow road leading to a sandstone building in the east. As he banked and swung about, Everett fixed his goal for the landing. *Do not hit the stone tower.* Squinting into the glaring sun, he aligned on a diagonal. He idled the engine, set full flaps, and lowered his landing gear. GG lurched through invisible currents, forcing him to crab sideways toward the parking lot. Up front, Marcy wedged her elbows and hunched behind her camera, bracing herself. He didn't tell her he had never done this before. Basically a carrier landing without arresting cables.

More in reaction than in control, he selected a threshold, dropped toward it, and deployed his thrust reversers. He rammed full throttle just before the wheels struck. GG hit hard and caromed, turbojet screaming. Everett stood on the brakes, fought to influence their bone-jarring progression toward a wall of purple-bark manzanita. The deceleration shoved them against their harnesses. Shuddering, stuttering, GG pitched to a halt—one car length from disaster.

To confirm their breath-defying survival, Everett killed the engine and said, "Okay." But he sat transfixed, not okay, mentally reeling. Marcy shucked her headset, fingered the canopy latch, and vomited over the side. To her credit, she had not made a sound.

At their left stood a full-sized Maker, where two women in blue jeans and white, long-sleeved shirts had stopped their work to stare at the intruders. The older one peered from beneath a straw hat, frayed and tied with blue ribbon. The younger one's blonde ponytail sprouted like a handle from a red baseball cap.

Everett blinked. *Marie Cardoza? Tiffany Lavery?*

A Fury's sharp passage broke his trance, and the women resumed unloading another one from their Maker. A jig mounted within its side cone tipped a newly copied drone down to their hands. Everett watched them lower it, then got out to help Marcy, who was still recovering.

A gas-driven quad motorcycle sputtered over to them, towing

a cartload of plastic jugs. Its driver was Philip Machen's bodyguard, Tanner Newe. His wild black hair and unshaven jaw contrasted sharply with his white NASA coveralls. He stopped at a wingtip and shouted, "Turn it around." Then he dismounted to help.

Everett took the opposite wing as they reversed Glamorous, pointing her downhill, back toward the cracked asphalt. If her landing gear had not entirely collapsed, a return trip over that stuff might finish the job.

"Do you need fuel?" The muscleman indicated his cart.

Still clutching GG's wing, Everett shook his head.

"Well, get ready to leave. I don't know how long we can hold them off."

Everett glanced south, anticipating helicopters, drones, or troops, though none appeared. Between the men, Marcy staggered from GG and hefted her camera, bazooka-style.

"Where is he?" she said.

Tanner glowered, pointed up the path behind them. His coveralls were torn and dirt-smudged.

"If they hit us," he said, "jump in a trench."

Where, exactly, he didn't say, but a dirt pile was mounded behind the Maker. Then, at the parking lot's northwest corner, a Fury whistled low and plunged into a mesh backstop. Upon arresting, it slid tail-first to the ground, a ridiculous transition. Tanner drove to it, corrected its drunken seagull posture, and commenced refueling it.

Everett wanted to see it take off again, or watch the women launch the new one, but Marcy was hiking toward the rock tower. She stopped at an oleander and motioned for him to follow. He scanned the lot once more and estimated their chances of safely taking off again. Less than satisfied, he rushed to join her. She gave him the Sony, and he checked the sky.

"Density altitude goes up when it gets hot," he said.

Which meant nothing to her. "Let's go," she said.

They found Philip Machen, gaunt and supine, on the steps

leading up the south wall of the stone building to the tower. His right pant leg was cut away, and cotton swathes bound his thigh, calf, and ankle to a narrow plank of tongue-and-groove flooring. Blood-caked bandages girded his knee, which looked as if he'd stepped through a volleyball and pulled it up his leg. How could they get him into GG?"

"As you can see," he said, "I'm not much of a parachutist." Through parched lips, he added, "Soon as possible . . . we'll get you back in the air. You need to know . . . what's happening."

With one hand, he dragged a laptop computer down the rough steps and pried it open. On its screen, tiny green dots swarmed a contour map of the mountain. Magenta dots flowed along two sinuous yellow roads.

"The military is probing. We are defending. When they come . . . you need to circle with the Furies. Be our witnesses."

Everett framed him in the viewfinder and adjusted his stance, which released a dirt clod into a cavity he hadn't noticed. The trench cut downhill, away from the steps, and ended at a yellow tractor tipped precariously. Its backhoe clung arm-like to the open slot.

"Not safe here," Machen said. "Everything's targeted."

Behind them, a Fury launched with a distinctive whooping shriek. Everett kept his focus on the fugitive.

"When they come . . . you must be—" Machen pointed upward. "Furies will shield you." He keyed his computer and angled it to show a slowly rotating view of the steps on which he lay. Everett extended his arm and saw it move on the screen. He looked up.

"Do you think the Army will attack?" Marcy thrust her microphone forward.

Behind her, Tanner rumbled up on his quad and shut it off.

"They don't realize . . ." Machen flinched. ". . . they are contingent. No longer in charge."

He looked at his bandaged hand, then at his wrist, the one with the scar, as if he hadn't seen them for a while. He leaned toward

Tanner. "Clear the summit," he said.

Tanner checked across his shoulder. "I sent the women down already."

Marcy squatted beside Philip.

"What will you do now, Mr. Machen? What if we can't get you out of here?"

He wormed his good hand into a pocket and withdrew a medical syrette. He broke the seal with his teeth and stabbed the needle into his thigh. "Morphine," he said as he squeezed the tube and plucked it away.

"We infected the world, Marcy, with an idea that will not die."

"Your machines?"

He shook his head. "Real freedom. Real progress. Don't wait. Do it yourself."

His eyes glazed and the computer skidded from his hands, down the steps, where it bleated until Tanner scooped it up. Everett focused on its screen and recognized a tactical threat display. A throbbing yellow circle drifted toward the center. Tanner clicked the circle to bring up data, which he showed to Machen. The bleating continued.

"Big and high," Tanner said. "Out of range, but not for long."

"Reconnaissance?"

Tanner shook his head. "Transport or bomber."

Machen snared Marcy's sleeve, pulled her to him. Everett knelt to frame them.

"This woman . . . great integrity. Helps everyone . . . see what's happening." He kissed her hand and thrust it back to her. "Now go."

The computer bleated faster as the yellow circle turned crimson.

"Incoming." Tanner cursed and yelled into his Cambiar. "Incoming. Everyone find a hole."

He tapped a computer icon and looked to the sky. "Go get 'em, Furies."

Then he thrust the computer into Philip's hands and struggled to lift him. He staggered upright, glared at the others, and shouted, "Get in the hole."

Marcy dog-crawled to the trench and rolled in. Tanner approached its crumbling edge, sank to his knees, and dumped Philip like a bundle of sticks. Machen's howl seemed to raise the dust into which he fell. Then Tanner yanked Everett—still recording—into the trench behind Marcy. Finally, he spidered himself over his boss and covered him with his body.

Lying on her side, Marcy gathered Philip's computer from the dirt and onto her belly. She opened it for Everett and his camera. A magenta blip departed the red circle, pulsing toward the center of the screen. Overhead, scores of Furies shrieked to a frenzy, tightened their spiral, and jetted upward—an upended tornado. Higher and higher they snaked until the vanguard sparkled in a cluster of flashes.

"Cover," Tanner shouted.

The magenta blip winked out, and the sky flashed, its radiance searing every sliver of exposed skin. A fist of air struck them, and its impact reverberated. Dirt spattered Everett's back and huffed into his face. Then flaming debris rained from the sky. Incandescent metal match heads alighted in his hair, stung his neck, hands, and ears. They sizzled into his clothing and burned his back.

He stood, swatted embers from Marcy's hair and shoulders, brushed them from his own.

"Furies saved us," Tanner said.

Philip unfurled himself and shouted, "Get them off the mountain."

With smoke wafting from his filthy hair, Tanner sprang from the trench, scrambled in a crouch, and rolled in behind Everett. He gripped Everett's collar and belt and heaved him up and out. Then he bent to Marcy.

"Hurry, Ms. Johnson." He swatted his scalp. "Get to your plane."

She hugged Philip's computer to her chest and shut her eyes. Tanner boosted her onto her feet and set her beside Everett. Philip lay in the trench, fumbling with his Cambiar.

"Get them out," he said. "I'm good." Then to the ringing phone, "Philip here."

Everett aimed his camera at the fireball, hotter than the sun, that was devouring the eastern sky. Gouts of flame twisted through its vortex. Against the radiance, he braced himself. First, his forehead, then his ears, then his knuckles, could no longer endure. He tripped over a step and blundered to a sheltering wall.

Tanner vaulted from the trench and seized Marcy's arm.

"Run to your plane," he shouted. "Get out of here."

But a withering blast, as foul and furious as dragon's breath, drove them to the wall with Everett.

"We are not leaving," Marcy cried.

KAREN LAVERY RODE BEHIND the men, in her jail coveralls, sprawled on her stomach atop a plastic tank that reeked of weed killer. She hugged a brace behind the pilot and crowded his ball cap to see ahead. Beside him rode Agent Parker, who had threatened the man earlier this morning to get him to haul them to Mt. Diablo in his crop-spraying helicopter.

Karen was phoning Philip when half the sky flashed to arc-light brilliance. She clamped her eyes and raised a shielding arm, but as the heat dissipated, a concussion punched the helicopter. Behind her, as if it had been switched off, their turbine engine wound down toward silence. The pilot yanked the controls and did something she couldn't see. They fluttered toward the streets below, their main rotor windmilling. They weren't very high to begin with, so the question became how hard would they strike.

Her Cambiar rang feebly as suburban rooftops swirled up to meet them. She squeezed her phone and willed it to connect, to inflate a cushion beneath them, anything to save them. Chemicals in the tank sloshed left then right. A fastener snapped, sending the spray boom on Parker's side whipping fore and aft. The pilot wrestled his machine, restarted the engine, and forced it to lift them once again into the sky. Karen's stomach hit bottom while her phone continued to ring.

"Philip here." He coughed and cleared his throat.

"We are coming," she shouted. A monstrous fireball was sweeping half the mountain. "By helicopter."

"Don't come. Tiffany is . . . Wait one."

Parker glanced back at Karen, noticed her Cambiar. "Are they alive?"

She nodded, covered one ear, heard only muffled shouting from the phone.

"We are coming," she said. "Call off your drones."

"Go back," Philip warned.

"I'm with the FBI. We are coming for you and Tiffany. Is she there?"

"She went . . . . not sure . . . I'll send Tanner. Don't come. They're trying to kill us."

"Call off your drones so we can land." More commotion. "Philip? I want Tiffany out of there. No matter what you say, we are coming. Do you understand?"

"Karen, tell your pilot . . . approach from the southwest . . . altitude three-eight-eight-zero. I marked you . . . friendly. Furies will ignore you."

She repeated his instructions, then relayed them to the pilot. The man nodded and adjusted course. Her Cambiar clicked off.

"Philip?"

FORTY-EIGHT

THE TRACKING CAMERA ON the C-130's belly swung through its arc as it passed over Mt. Diablo. Nick Brayley's screen in Washington showed the flash and the shock wave striking the summit, while the fireball, too high and off-target, did not reach it. Nick swept the STU-5 from his desk and shouted into its handset.

"Dammit, Clint. How can you miss a whole damn mountain?"

General Holmes replied, "Payload was intercepted by drones."

Nick scoffed. "This was supposed to be another faulty Powerpod, not target practice. Never mind. We gotta hit 'em with something drone-proof, whatever you got, and make it fast. He's still there."

"Wait one."

"No. Don't wait." Nick slammed the glass top of his desk, smashed it with the handset, and shouted, "Kill him, Clint. Kill the bastard."

ON THE MOUNTAIN, Everett hammered Marcy's instrument panel,

kicked it to clear more space, ripped the video screen from its frame, and cast them aside. The inferno had scorched GG's paint and warped her canopy, but she could still fly.

"Try again," he said.

He gathered Philip to the cockpit sill, helped him over it while Marcy steered his injured leg. The angle remained too acute, his wooden splint caught again, and Philip howled. His free arm lashed at the canopy, at the sky, at Everett, who heaved him free of GG's confines and laid him, panting, on the pavement. Everett's back spasmed. For the second time, he had failed to get the man into his plane. They should have skipped the damned interview. They should have evacuated him when they first arrived. *So ditch the splint and try again.*

Instead, a helicopter was approaching. Everett shielded his eyes from its whirlwind. The bug-like silhouette settled toward him flailing a broken appendage, barely under control. As it bore down, Furies swooped past it but did not attack.

"Leave me," Philip called. "Save yourselves."

JUST BELOW THE SUMMIT, on a steep north slope, Sergeant Bobby Aboud of the Concord Militia lay on his stomach, catching his breath. A sandstone boulder had shielded him from the blast, yet the concussion had knocked him down the trail headfirst into a thicket of rosemary. The sling of his Winchester had snagged on a branch, and his helmet lay nearby. Now he scrambled to put his size tens back on the ground.

One side of his face prickled from flash burns. Thank God he was watching his feet and not the sky when that thing went off, another damned Powerpod going kaboom. He should have brought his gas mask to filter the fallout. All around him, junk was fizzing out of the sky, igniting shrubs and grasses, while behind the eastern ridge, a firestorm raged.

He stood to brush himself—surprised to be alive—and

grinned.

When the Militia moved onto the mountain at dawn this morning, Major Barrett had sent him on his dirt bike to scout a trail to the summit. Two hundred yards from the top, he encountered a maze of boulders and abandoned the motorcycle. His orders were to reconnoiter and report, but he knew what had to be done. Everybody knew Philip Machen was up there.

"We dodged a nuke," he bragged. "But we gotta beat those fires to the top."

With that, he collected his rifle and doubled his pace, scrambled up the trail, and did not look back. Over the roar of the flames and the crunch of his boots, a distant flutter grew distinct. A helicopter was coming his way. He stopped but could not see it, even as the racket echoed from the rim above. He threw off his rucksack and charged for the top.

Sonofabitch is trying to get away.

FLAMES SCOURED THE MOUNTAIN on Agent Parker's right, baking outrage into his bones. This was no accident. This was a planned attack, punishment without trial, attempted assassination. It was Coalinga redone, and those murders confirmed. The whole bilious spectacle shimmered with madness.

As the helicopter closed with the summit, a defiant thumb of rock appeared at its pinnacle, seeming to hold off the holocaust, unaided. In its lee waited a Maker and a slender red airplane, undamaged. Somewhere in that penumbra, Philip Machen had also survived, the instigator, the fugitive. Though not a terrorist like the maniacs who did this. Parker swallowed his revulsion. Justice should protect the innocent, he believed, though sometimes it must also protect the guilty. From righteousness run amok.

The helicopter surged, its spray boom flailing, while three figures beside the airplane squinted up at him. If only today, he must be the hard justice on this mountain, the unyielding bulwark of due process standing against murder. At the first shudder of contact, he peeled off his headset, released his seat belt, and leaped into the downwash.

NOT THERE, YOU IDIOTS.

Everett couldn't believe they were landing smack in front of him. At least they weren't military. Then he recognized the suit hopping down and knew GG was blocked for as long as it would take.

"Camera, Everett." Marcy crouched under the whistling rotor blades and hustled to the cop.

Everett shouldered her Sony but did not follow. He recorded the FBI shouting at her. Then a woman in faded orange coveralls clambered from the chopper. Everett focused on her flamboyant auburn hair, wild in the turbulence, and recognized Ms. Powerpods herself, Karen Lavery.

Agent Parker led the women toward him, and Everett rubbed his arm. Even his follicles knew James Bond was about to capture Philip Machen. Marcy would scoop the world, and they would witness another slice of history. Maybe the FBI could save the Great Man.

"Go back," Machen rasped. He waved the newcomers away.

Agent Parker let go of Ms. Lavery's wrist, and Everett framed them together.

"Where's Tiffany?" Ms. Lavery demanded.

Parker displayed his badge and drew his pistol.

"Philip Machen, you are under arrest."

PHILIP IGNORED THE COP for the irresistible sight of Karen Lavery. Who shouldn't be here. Who was as lost to him as a missing finger, yet none of his parts or particles would ever stop wanting her. Whose green eyes frowned and then winced.

"Karen," he groaned. He struggled upward, and she helped him stand.

Ms. Johnson thrust a microphone toward them, but a two-legged commotion stormed across the asphalt.

"Stop!" A helmeted soldier, breathing hard, waived his sniper's rifle. "Hold it right there. Nobody move."

The FBI canted his pistol for the soldier to see and held up his badge.

"Special Agent Parker, FBI. Stand down, Sergeant. This man is under arrest."

The soldier's hesitation allowed Philip to hobble between Karen and the rifle.

"Nobody's going anywhere," said the gunman. When he raised his head, Marcy's assistant cried out.

"Dad? What are you doing here?" The kid edged to Agent Parker's side and faced the soldier. "He's the cop from the ranch, Dad. He's the FBI."

"Jesus H. Christ." The elder Aboud recognized them both but jutted his chin at the cop. "Wrong jurisdiction, officer. Martial Law says these prisoners are mine, not yours. Holster your weapon and stand aside." He flicked his barrel for emphasis.

Agent Parker raised his SIG Sauer, cupped it in both hands, and aimed.

"Stand down, Sergeant. You are interfering with a federal officer."

Sergeant Aboud snugged his aim at the cop. "Write me a ticket."

"Dad." The kid thrust his camera into Ms. Johnson's startled hands. 'Don't be an idiot. Put down the gun."

"Stay out of this, Freemaker."

The kid scoffed. "I don't own a Maker."

His father sneered.

"You eat Maker food, burn Maker gasoline, and fly a goddamn Maker airplane. Honest people are losing everything while you help yourself to counterfeit. Now you're defending the bitch and the bastard who started this shit. Get out of the way. I'm running the show now."

"Dad—" The son's hand slipped to a pocket. "Dad, let the man do his job. He's a cop. He's got handcuffs. Everything's under control."

Sergeant Aboud snorted. "Get out of the way, jackass."

In one smooth arc, the son drew a tiny silver pistol and fixed it on his father, a sightless little belly gun staring down a big-bore Winchester. The long barrel tracked right, to align with the boy's eyes.

"Mr. Aboud." Agent Parker spoke firmly, deliberately. "Put down your weapon. I will commend you to your commanding officer. You assisted in the capture. You were instrumental in making the arrest. No hard feelings, no harm done, Mr. Aboud— Sergeant Aboud. Just put it down, and nobody gets hurt."

Philip nudged Karen to back away.

"You." The sergeant ripped off his helmet and assailed her. "You got rich selling treason and counterfeit."

"Everybody stop," Philip shouted. He goaded his leg forward and raised his notorious hand. "Just stop."

Sergeant Aboud shifted his aim.

"I'm the one you want," Philip said. *The unarmed geek who terrifies you.*

He stared down the formidable barrel, taking responsibility along the way for its owner's hatred, for the unholy fires past and present, and for endangering so many innocents. He nodded solemnly and squared his shoulders. "I'm the one."

From behind her camera, Ms. Johnson implored, "Put it down, Mr. Aboud. Please put it down."

EVERETT NODDED, too, and held his breath. *Put down the gun, Dad. Say okay and put it down. Don't make me choose.*

Bobby's visible eye flicked to Parker, then back to Philip. His rifle jerked left and fired. Its thunderous report smacked everyone rigid.

At Everett's side, Agent Parker fired too. *Pop, pop.* And within his body armor, Bobby staggered, but it was Parker who crumpled.

"Dad, stop!"

Bobby's glare lashed him, fierce and flinty. Within his tactical vest, Bobby shrugged off the pistol shots, racked another round, and aimed at Philip

Three voices screamed, "Stop!"

PHILIP WRENCHED HIS LEG forward, one pace then two, drawing the smoking muzzle away from Karen. He spread his arms to shield her. *This is how we prevail, Old Shoe. We do the one true thing, even at the price—*

Boom!

A FLASH LEAPT from Everett's hand. *Bang!*

He hadn't meant to fire, but the blast from his father's gun made him flinch.

Bobby stood confused, immobile, as Philip Machen staggered.

"Dad?" Everett trembled from head to toe. *I didn't mean it, Dad. It was reflex.* He threw the little Seecamp hard away but could not rescind its bullet. Stiff and silent, his father lapsed toward him and then to the pavement, as did Philip Machen.

"Dad?" Every nerve in Everett's body jolted. Beside him, Parker curled fetal and moaned. Ms. Lavery stepped forward and steered Philip to the ground.

"No," she cried. The Great Man gurgled as she laid him down. His arms fell limp, and he tipped onto her lap. She captured the pink effusion huffing from a hole in his chest and tried to press it back.

"No!" she called. Then to Everett, "Help us."

But Everett was departing the vertical, too, drawn irresistibly to Bobby.

"Dad," he called. A mewling kitten. "Dad." A croak.

He fingered Bobby's stomach, tore open the vest, and fought three buttons to bare a torso without blemish. Below Bobby's left eye, a dainty red meniscus quivered, .32 caliber.

Everett took his father's face into his hands.

One agonal breath escaped as Bobby's eyes went vacant.

"Dad, stay here."

He shook his father, straddled him, layered hands over his sternum and straight-armed thirty fast compressions. Two quick breaths huffed back into his face, moist and stale. Thirty more compressions and two more breaths produced no response, no pulse, no life.

"Dad."

His mother's voice shrilled in his head: *What did you do? What did you do?*

PHILIP SPRAWLED over Karen's legs, oddly alert. As long as those pesky fluids drained from his mouth, he could breathe. Balanced precisely, he could inhale her ministrations and exhale his gratitude. More than blood or precious air, he needed her to see him, just this once, for real. Heaven could never be a place, a box filled with eternity. It could only be a feeling. This feeling. At last, she was holding him, caring for him, at a moment he could not speak. Tears and stardust gleamed at the corners of her eyes.

He strained to smile, to comfort her. *Here is your seeker of truth, the one who loves you.*

She stroked his glistening brow and calmed his wayward hair.

He gasped and let go.

She hugged him, kissed him, willed him to breathe. "Stay," she whispered.

But he was gone.

FORTY-NINE

BEHIND EVERETT, someone approached, a misshapen shadow he could barely see.

Tanner Newe shuffled up the footpath and stopped. He surveyed the carnage before him but said nothing. In his arms, he bore a ragged young woman with no red ball cap and no blonde ponytail, no hair at all. Membranous flesh sagged from the curve of her shoulder.

"Momma," she whispered.

"Tiffany!" The mother's screech of joy twisted into terror. Ms. Lavery reached for her daughter. "I'm here, baby."

Tanner plodded past Everett and laid the girl beside her mother. He towered over them, casting another shadow. Then he knelt to Philip, probed his friend's neck, and rocked back. He sucked a great, wheezing breath and huffed it away. He gathered himself slowly, then shut the lids over Philip's ghost-gray eyes.

A gesture that jolted Everett alert. *What did we do?* He searched for Marcy.

There she is. She laid down her camera and helped Ms. Lavery free herself from Philip's body. The mother's elegant fingers fretted the air an inch from her daughter's ruined skin. Shaking her head and trembling, she looked to the sky and quelled a desperate urge to touch. She folded her useless hands and sobbed.

"Tiffany."

Marcy tugged at the bodyguard's pant cuff.

"Put them on the helicopter," she said. "Get them out of here."

Tanner knelt and hugged his knees, rocking and rocking until a gush of embers swept over the group. He sniffed his feelings back into his head and wiped his eyes. He squeezed Philip's shoulder and rose on shaky legs.

"We always knew it would be something," he said to his friend. "Turns out it's this."

He stepped across the body. Gently, paternally, he collected Tiffany and carried her to the helicopter. Ms. Lavery followed, flapping her useless hands, still sobbing. Marcy recorded their trek while Everett stared bleary-eyed at his father.

Dad.

Bobby's hair reversed from another scorching gust as the helicopter spooled up for takeoff. It could only carry three.

Tanner returned and stood over Philip. Nearby, the computer bleated. Tanner scraped it into his hands, checked the screen, and told Marcy, "They are attacking again. You have to go."

"Everett." Her touch drained him. "We have to leave."

"No." *I can't.*

In a crescendo of stinging grit, the helicopter departed slowly to the west.

Again the computer bleated, and Tanner threw it into the oleanders.

"Everett," Marcy shouted. "We have to go."

Not without Dad. He touched Bobby's face, closed the vacant eyes.

Tanner loomed. "Get up." He jerked Everett to his feet and

counter-drilled the rage in his eyes. "Please," he said.

Everett shrugged free, ready to fight.

"Mr. Aboud, you have to tell the people. You have to be our witness. Don't let them lie about what happened here." From the bushes, the computer bleated. "There aren't enough Furies left to protect us. You have to go."

Marcy grabbed Everett's arm but commanded Tanner. "Carry him, dammit."

As the bodyguard reached for him, Everett stepped aside. "I'll go," he said. "I'll go, but you have to promise." He could barely see. "To take care of my father."

"He's your dad?" Tanner glanced at Marcy, who nodded. "Okay," he said. "I promise."

The computer bleated louder and faster.

Marcy towed Everett to the plane, where he broke her grip and got in. He lit the fires, and they plunged at full throttle, humpty-bumpty across the asphalt and into a wicked, roiling sky. A westerly gust buoyed them, swept them clear of the rocks, but the thrill of escape shriveled instantly.

"Circle," Marcy demanded. "We have to stay close. I put a mike on his collar."

Everett banked sharply, pulled some respectable gees, but he couldn't see. Just his hands on the controls, fumbling. Beneath a vast, gray dome of crud, the summit gyrated, sloppy and off-center. The lump in his throat threatened to choke him.

Dad.

Up front, Marcy recorded and narrated. Below them, Tanner hustled.

Everett blinked, smeared snot, and blinked again. There, his father, carried by Tanner to the Maker. Up the ladder to the open hatch and . . . slipped into the top cone. The slosh of water came to his earphones, along with a persistent, demented bleat. Tanner huffed back to the tower steps, hauled Philip to the Maker, and slid him into the top cone too.

"We need to go higher," Everett warned. He widened their turn and climbed, orbiting the Maker below.

The bleating stopped as water thrummed. Tanner grunted up to the raw-material hatch and lowered himself through it, into the cavernous pool within. He peered to the sky, found them circling, and waved.

"We can go their way," he said, "or we can go our way."

He descended into the chamber with the bodies and shut the hatch over his head. For one extended moment, the mountain lay still and silent. Until a gout of bright, clean water burst from a side cone and spread shimmering across the earth.

Discussion Questions for Book Groups

1) After reading *Maker Messiah*, are you more optimistic or less optimistic about the future?
2) Do you wish Philip's Makers were real, or are you glad they're not?
3) What would you do if someone gave you a Maker?
4) Share a favorite quote or scene from the book. Why do these stand out for you?
5) Which character would you most like to meet, and what would you talk about?
6) If you were making a movie of this book, who would you cast in the principle roles?

If you enjoyed *Maker Messiah*, please review it on Amazon.com. because word of mouth is the best advertising. Your review will help others discover Philip Machen, Everett Aboud, and their searches for meaning in *Maker Messiah*.

ABOUT THE AUTHOR

Ed Miracle lives with his wife in an adobe house they built together in Northern California. He is a university graduate who served six years in the U.S. Navy Submarine Service. Now retired from his computer systems career at Lawrence Livermore National Laboratory, Ed continues to support his community as a volunteer firefighter and emergency medical responder.

Ed's award-winning personal narrative, "Submarine Dreams" is available as a free download at www.edmiracle.com.

If you enjoyed *Maker Messiah*, please review it on Amazon.com. Because word of mouth is the best advertising, your review will help others discover Philip Machen, Everett Aboud, and their searches for meaning in *Maker Messiah*.

CPSIA information can be obtained
at www.ICGtesting.com
Printed in the USA
FSHW011750121219
64791FS